OTHER BOOKS

Presented by Claudia Helt

Love Thy Neighbor
2021

Seeking Our Humanity, Part III
2020

Seeking Our Humanity, Part II
2020

Seeking Our Humanity
2020

The Answer in Action
2020

The Answer Illuminated
2019

The Answer
2018

The Time When Time No Longer Matters
…Continues…
2018

The Time When Time No Longer Matters
2016

The Book of Ages
2016

Messages From Within:
A Time for Hope
2011

Messages From The Light:
Inspirational Guidance for Light Workers,
Healers, and Spiritual Seekers
2008

What Awaits Us...

Claudia Helt

BALBOA.PRESS

A DIVISION OF HAY HOUSE

Balboa Press books may be ordered through booksellers or by contacting:

Balboa Press
A Division of Hay House
1663 Liberty Drive
Bloomington, IN 47403
www.balboapress.com
844-682-1282

Because of the dynamic nature of the Internet, any web addresses or links contained in this book may have changed since publication and may no longer be valid. The views expressed in this work are solely those of the author and do not necessarily reflect the views of the publisher, and the publisher hereby disclaims any responsibility for them.

Print information available on the last page.

ISBN: 978-1-9822-7863-2 (sc)
ISBN: 978-1-9822-7864-9 (e)

Library of Congress Control Number: 2022900161

Balboa Press rev. date: 01/14/2022

Foreword

To All who were,
to All who are present,
to All who are yet to come,
We stand in unity with you.

Since you came into being,
this has been our way,
and forevermore,
it shall always be.

Old Friends of long-standing,
our hearts are with you,
and your well being is
our deepest concern.

We urge you to live in peace.
We pray you will live in peace.
We beseech you to live in peace.
For the sake of this day and all days to come,
please live in peace.

Introduction

Dear Readers, thank you for participating in this reading experience. We ask that you prepare yourself for an adventure. While this tale may introduce you to ideas that stretch your imagination, rest assured that this story, presented in fictional format, is founded in truth.

Your history, which is much longer than you imagine, is one that is worthy of review. Some of you, perhaps most of you, will be surprised by what you discover. Hopefully, what you learn will inspire you to evaluate your present course of direction. Obviously, change is inevitable; however, change is most beneficial when it unfolds in the company of reliable, trustworthy knowledge of past events, accurate understanding of one's current situation, and realistic awareness of what is coming based upon the information gathered and carefully reviewed.

The time has come, Dear Readers, for each of us to demand this type of evaluation for the sake of our species' future. Naturally, there will be a tendency to look to others for this type of evaluation to be done. Many of us will expect others who are more learned to carry out such a task, and hopefully, those with specific areas of expertise will participate in this massive project. However, everyone will need to be involved in this discovery process. Each of us will need to review our own circumstances. How have we participated in the evolution of our species? How have we affected our fellow members of the human race and all the other species with whom we coexist on this planet and beyond?

Each of us must carefully review our participation in this life experience. Have we, you and I, been assets to this life experience? Have we helped one another? Have we embraced all others into our circle of life? Have we interacted with all others as brothers and sisters? Have we engaged with all others as equals? Have we noticed that the planet that we live upon is actually a Life Being? Have we treated her with the respect and kindness that she deserves? Have we thanked her for all that she has provided?

Dear Readers, there is much for us to review. The questions about our participation in life are many, many more than the few just listed. We must all open our hearts to the questions of our role in this life that we are presently living. We are here for a reason. This experience called life is not a coincidence. Over seven billion humans are experiencing a life on this planet at the same time, and each one is here for a reason. Isn't it time for us to think about that? Isn't it time for us to wonder why? Why are we here? Surely, there must be more than we are currently witnessing?

Please continue to ponder your present participation in life. You deserve this time and consideration...we all do. And please continue to pursue the information brought forward through the following pages. Perhaps together we can discover why we are here and how we are to proceed. What awaits us is ours to create.

One

Once upon a time, long, long ago, a new beginning began. The beginning, not unlike other beginnings that preceded this one's debut, created great curiosity among all the existing members of the Great Existence. It was a time of many whispers. Various speculations about this new beginning populated the endless regions of existence. Whispers musing over possible locations for the new beginning were abundant, while other whispers focused on the unfolding event itself, guesstimating the precise time when the moment of the new beginning might actualize. It was a time of hopeful anticipation.

Meanwhile faraway in a distant galaxy, negotiations were underway with a Life Being of exceptional character. This One graciously considered the opportunity that was presented to her. Recognizing the significance of this proposal, she deliberated at length. Welcoming a new species into her present ecological system required careful consideration. The request required a relationship of long standing, which would greatly impact those species already residing upon and within her. Many concerns needed to be explored. This gracious Being wanted what was best for her present residents, and at the same time, she desired to assist the new species, as she had done with all those who had come before. It was an extraordinary matter to discern. Comprehending the complexity of the new species, the remarkable Life Being recognized that she had much to offer. Their true potential could definitely be manifested upon her fertile landscapes; however, she would not make such an important decision without consultation with her current residents. These wonderful life beings, living harmoniously together for ages, would be profoundly impacted by the introduction of a new species. They deserved to be informed of the request. Their preferences mattered to the exceptional Life Being and she would honor their wishes.

Upon hearing the circumstances of the travelers who had traveled far, the current inhabitants of the hospitable Life Being agreed without hesitation that they would happily welcome the new addition to their home. The travelers' needs were compelling. Their own planet had reached a precarious state of diminishment, which could no longer provide a viable lifestyle for its residents. Devastated by the rapid decline of their planet's health, the distant dwellers embarked upon an exploratory mission in hopes of finding a suitable alternative that would allow their species to continue. The quest had been long. The travelers, weary from the journey, acknowledged that their expectations had been naïve. They foolishly assumed that the expedition would quickly reveal numerous options from which they could choose, but that wishful thought had not come to fruition. Exhausted and hopeless, they continued their search for the sake of their species' survival. So far away were they from their point of debarkation that the travelers grieved the loss of those who were left behind. Even though they had known from the beginning that this was a possibility, none had allowed themselves to believe that their loved ones would never be seen again. Those who stayed understood the consequences of remaining, and those who departed also understand the consequences of their decision. Their species was facing extinction. The determination to seek another viable setting for their descendants was paramount in the decision-making process. Although the thought of separation from those most loved was unbearable, the possibility that their species might have an opportunity of surviving elsewhere guided their actions. As the quest drew the travelers further and further away from their families and friends, what was once seen as a solution began to be viewed as a folly. Hope waned and unwelcomed doubts grew.

And then, as if an unspoken wish had come true, a beautiful blue planet captured their attention! They immediately altered their course and grew increasingly optimistic as they neared the planet. Their spirits rose as preliminary assessments validated their observations. The atmospheric conditions were perfect as were the landscapes and water resources.

The travelers from afar were ecstatic. The planet appeared to meet all the criteria necessary for their species to thrive. So eager were they to engage with the new setting that they momentarily forgot their good manners. Universal protocol demands permission before approaching a new location. The travelers were well aware of this courtesy; however, in their exuberance, orders were prematurely given to descend into the planet's atmosphere. Other planetary Life Beings may have taken exception to this presumptuous behavior, but fortunately for the distant travelers, they had approached a Life Being of extreme benevolence. Assuming the best of these new visitors, she welcomed their presence and invited the weary travelers to a suitable landing area where introductions were made and truths were shared. At the end of their initial conversation, an agreement between the newcomers and the remarkable planetary Life Being had been established. Speaking on behalf of all her inhabitants, she welcomed the new species to their new home. Her terms were simple and included the same courtesies that all other species had agreed to upon their arrival. From the very beginning, all who came and requested residence upon the beautiful blue planet vowed to treat all other species with the same care and utmost respect as each desired for their own species. All were One. All were equal. And all were family.

On that fateful day, a new beginning began and the travelers who had traveled far were deeply grateful that a new home had been secured for their descendants.

Two

As the two old friends walked together in silence, each was happily lost in the respective chambers of their individual minds. It was a comforting experience to enjoy the sense of alone time while in the company of one's dearest friend. There was no pressure to make idle conversation. The silence graciously satisfied the needs of each, and the panoramic seascape added to the moment of perfection. The view, which never failed to please, softened hearts and heightened the viewers' perceptions to the reality in which they existed. This was true for many who visited this magnificent setting and it was particularly the case for the couple who came daily. Although they lived in an area abundant with beautiful vistas, this was the trail that captured their hearts. Of all the remarkable places they had visited over the years and the many stunning trails that they had enjoyed on their excursions, this trail was the one that had most profoundly changed their lives. And it continued to do so.

As they turned the bend heading eastward, they were stopped in their tracks. There in the center of the trail, back lit by the rising sun, was a resident white tail buck. His antlers, glimmering in a halo from the sunlight, accentuated the grandeur of this beautiful creature. Amazed by their good fortune, the Madisons stood in awe. Aware that the occasion demanded proper etiquette, Anne and David remained perfectly still even though they both instinctively wanted to grab the other's hand. It was a habit of long standing. The two old friends cherished serendipitous moments such as this and believed each one was a gift from beyond. Because of their high regard for these encounters, they preferred to experience them hand in hand, but as is often the case, common courtesy called for honoring the needs of the other rather than their own preferences. With this in mind, the couple remained perfectly still so as not to startle the large deer in the middle of the pathway.

The Madisons, standing in awe, were stunned by their good fortune. *"Why are we so blessed?"* The thought racing through David's mind did not expect an answer to its inquiry; nonetheless, one was quickly forthcoming.

"David, we must never allow ourselves to take these precious incidents for granted. Let us presume that this is happening for a reason. Perhaps, our friend

5

is wishing to communicate with us." Anne's unspoken response did not go unnoticed. While her husband remained perfectly still, the large buck took two steps forward. He was a sight to behold! Anne desperately struggled with her desire to reach out to the magnificent creature. Being of a tactile nature, she delighted in touching animals of all kinds. Managing what seemed like an innate instinct was not easy for her. The buck, sensing her inner conflict, moved closer again. Along with this gesture of connection came a vision of both David and Anne stroking the buck's long muscular neck. Anne mistrusted the vision, suspecting it was a figment of her own magical thinking, but David knew better. He too had received the vision, but unlike Anne, he was not engulfed by doubts. He accepted the vision as an invitation and graciously raised his hands over his heart. With a deep breath and a slight, but noticeable bowing of his head, he took a step forward. The buck braced himself, but remained in place. Anne followed David's lead. Slowly, carefully, they took several more quiet steps until they were literally face-to-face with the large deer. It was a magical moment, and it was real!

"Thank you for allowing us to approach you," whispered Anne. The vision appeared again. At this point, the couple definitely recognized and accepted the vision as an invitation. With respectful reverence, they both gently stroked the buck's neck. Later, they would speak of the strength that emanated from this animal. While he was cautious in their presence, he demonstrated no fear. He was a Being who was confident and in charge of his circumstances. He had extended an invitation, which was graciously accepted, and he was patiently waiting for the appropriate moment to engage in matters of importance.

Meanwhile, the couple, lost in the rapture of the moment, repeatedly praised his beautiful features. He was not surprised by their reactions. Having observed these two from afar on numerous occasions, he was aware of their appreciation for the resident wildlife. While their words were kind and appreciated, the buck did not require the compliments they bestowed upon him. His interest lay elsewhere. Recent observations of this couple had revealed their potential for telepathic communication. This was of keen interest to the buck, and the fact that the one called Anne was accurate about his intentions gave him great hope. As she suggested, their encounter was not a coincidence; it happened for a reason. He had planned for the occasion, situating himself in the right place at the right time. She was also correct about his desire to communicate with them. He did indeed wish to have a conversation from the heart with these two. His desire growing exponentially was instantaneously expressed by another image of connection. David and Anne both received the image at the same time and immediately took action. They gently stepped away from the large buck and repositioned themselves directly in front of him as was seen in the vision. Comfortably standing side by side with hands clasped, they waited in anticipation. The wait was brief. The buck could not contain himself. He adjusted his position so that he could easily stare deeply into the eyes of Anne, and then he readjusted and did the same with David. The moments of connection were electric.

"You are people of goodness," he announced telepathically. *"I am most grateful to have this time with you. Thank you for responding to my invitation."* The Madisons were beside themselves. The excitement of communicating with this remarkable animal interrupted their good sense and old habits rushed forward as questions flowed from Anne's mouth.

"What is best for you?" she rapidly asked. "Do you prefer that we speak aloud or should we speak from within?" Typically, Anne would have been embarrassed by her befuddled behavior, but her excitement was far too great to succumb to the awkwardness of the moment. "I apologize for my clumsiness, but this is a dream come true. I cannot believe we are actually connecting like this." The threesome all seemed equally enamored with the situation. The buck took the lead once again.

"I share your enthusiasm. This is also a dream come true for me as well. Often, I have imagined participating in a conversation with members of your species, and at last the opportunity has arisen. It is most gratifying that you are amenable to this unusual encounter.

In regards to your question, I am adept in understanding both the inner voice and the spoken voice. Please choose what is most comfortable for you. Hopefully, you are able to hear my inner voice clearly." The couple responded positively. David, using his inner voice, urged the buck to continue, while Anne offered her reassurances orally.

"We've always believed in interspecies communication," stated Anne, "but never knew how to facilitate it. Thank you for reaching out to us."

"Your attempts to connect with us were noticed and appreciated; however, we initially were uncertain of your intentions, so we have been observing you. Forgive me for speaking so bluntly, but not all humans have our best interest in mind; therefore, we take a protective stance when we encounter your kind. However, after a lengthy

period of observation and eavesdropping upon your conversations, we discerned that you were humans who could be trusted.

Initially, Anne was delighted by the buck's acknowledgement of their trustworthiness. Her face was beaming with joy, before the full meaning of his comment struck her. "Oh, my goodness," she sighed, "your species lives in fear of us. I am so sorry. I cannot imagine what that must be like."

"Me either," added David telepathically. There was much more he wanted to say, but his heart was deeply burdened. There was absolutely no way to understand the cruelty of the human species, and apologies did not solve the problem. His mind raced about trying to find some way of expressing his sorrow for what his species had perpetrated against the deer's species, but there were no words to be found. Eventually David just shook his head, cleared his throat, and whispered the only four words that he could capture. "I am so sorry," he said aloud. Anne and David stood still while tears streamed down their respective faces. The encounter that they had long dreamed about had not unfolded as hoped.

The buck's perspective of the encounter was very different from the Madisons'. Deeply moved by these two humans, he was inspired by the interaction. His long awaited dream was unfolding much better than he had anticipated. *"The sorrow you feel within you is palpable. I am deeply touched by your remorse for my kind, and because of our encounter, I am hopeful for the future."* His response surprised Anne and David, and in turn, ignited their hopefulness.

"The empathy you show for my species encourages me to pursue more conversation with you. Would you be amenable to that possibility?"

"Yes!" declared the couple in unison. Their reaction was so quick and spirited that the buck instinctively retreated from their presence.

"Oh, please don't leave. We didn't mean to frighten you." Anne's appeal immediately quieted the buck. The large, graceful animal seemed to be embarrassed by his behavior and quickly turned around to demonstrate his prowess. As he moved towards them, his strength and confidence were once again visibly noticeable.

"Your enthusiasm is most gratifying. I too am very excited about this long-awaited opportunity. As you so wisely intuited, our meeting is not a coincidence. I approach you because the time for action is upon us. The Mother is in great distress, and assistance from your species is desperately needed." David and Anne stood motionless, as if they were paralyzed by the topic, but that was not the

case. They were both acutely aware of Earth's declining health and were eager to hear the buck's perspective.

"Thank you," whispered Anne, "for facilitating this encounter. We understand and appreciate the risk you have taken in approaching us this morning, and we are grateful. Please tell us more. How can we be of assistance?" The buck snorted, flicked his large white tail, and moved several steps closer. Once again, the image of the three huddled together in discussion was impressed upon the respective minds of the Madisons.

"Signs of the Mother's struggles are evident. She is out of balance because of the pressures placed upon her, and as a result, major changes are occurring throughout her entire ecological system. These changes are causing great destruction across the planet, leading to more instability. She needs our help. Those of us in the animal kingdom are doing everything we can do to enable her health, but the truth is we are not the problem. Forgive me for speaking so bluntly, but long ago, our kind learned to live in harmony with the Mother. She has not suffered from our presence. Unfortunately, when the human species was introduced to this beautiful haven, they were not properly informed about the necessity for mutual co-existence with all other life beings already inhabiting the planet, including the Earth herself. This lack of understanding caused many problems, which progressively worsened to the point that the Mother is now in a very precarious situation.

Your species can no longer ignore what is transpiring on the planet. What is happening is real and it must be addressed now. Your participation is essential because your species is the pivotal factor in this environmental crisis. Truthfully speaking, you are the problem! I regret that our first encounter requires me to speak so forthrightly, but the situation is of such importance that it demands our attention.

The human species does not seem to understand the powerful, destructive impact it has upon the Mother and all the other inhabitants that reside upon her. You live your lives as if you are the only species that matters. Many of you are so preoccupied with your own preferences that you are truly oblivious to the rights and needs of others, including many members of your own species. Worse yet, there are those among you who are acutely aware of their irresponsible behavior towards others, and they simply do not care. They do what is in their best interest and do not care about their impact upon others with whom they co-exist.

Such callous behaviors cannot continue. Mother Earth cherishes all her inhabitants and she cares deeply for the human species even though they are causing her great pain. She still cares. At her own expense, she continues for the sake of all of us who call her home. She has given too much of herself. She has made too many sacrifices for us. This cannot continue. We must come to her aid.

A call to action is necessary. We must all come together on her behalf. This means that each of us who has the privilege of existing upon this planet must review our behaviors and discern how we are assisting her and how we are harming her. Will you participate in this self-discovery process? Are you willing to review your actions and discern what changes you must make to bring yourself into alignment with the Mother? Will you help her?" Anne and David stood silently taking in every word that the buck telepathically communicated. They were both in awe. The experience confirmed their concerns about the Earth's circumstances, as well as their belief in interspecies communication. It was amazing to be called to task by this incredible life being. Anne responded first.

"Yes, I am willing to ask myself the difficult questions and I promise you that corrections will be made. Thank you for approaching us and for challenging us to do the right thing. Your actions today have changed my life; I am so grateful for this experience." Questions raced through Anne's mind, but knowing that her husband needed time to respond to the call to task, she managed to squelch them. David squeezed her hand tightly in response to her consideration of his needs. Before taking his turn, he took a long deep breath, and then, reached out and gently stroked the long, firm neck of their Messenger. The buck graciously received the act of kindness by leaning into David's strong hand.

"You do good work, Friend!" His words, spoken softly, seemed to be comforting. "It took a lot of courage to do what you just did. Thank you! Anne and I agree with everything you said, and we will participate in the discernment process. I think it will be an excellent exercise for us." Pausing briefly, David debated whether it was appropriate to question their New Friend. An answer was quickly received.

"Please release the question from your mind. It may be beneficial for all of us."

"Thank you," replied David. "Actually, I would like your permission to share this experience with other folks. People will benefit from hearing about our encounter with you, and if you concur, I would also like to share your comments regarding the Earth's crisis. This is powerful information that needs to be extended to others. The more folks who explore your call to task the better, and if you agree, perhaps they can pass the story on to others as well.

"You may not realize this, but having a conversation with a deer is a big deal for us! Trust me, people will be interested in this exchange and astounded by your plea for help." The New Friend remained still, gazing off into the distance, as he contemplated David's request. His behavior was remarkably similar to that of most humans when they pause to ponder a topic of interest. It makes one wonder about other similarities that the species might share. In due course, the Great Buck returned his focus back to Anne and David.

"Your suggestion surpasses our hopes and expectations. We of the animal kingdom are delighted that you will share this event with others. Our only concern is that you include in your discussions that your kind must be respectful of our kind. Not all members of our species are ready for interaction with your species. They have disturbing memories from previous encounters and are not yet healed from those experiences.

Our interaction today unfolded nicely, because I had prepared for this occasion. As said earlier, I have been observing you for some time and discerned that you were people with whom a new beginning could be set in action. We have achieved that! I am very grateful for your open-heartedness and your acceptance of my invitation." With that said an image of the three new friends standing together and looking off into the distance appeared in the couple's minds. David and Anne immediately took their positions: Dave on the buck's right side and Anne on the left, each with a hand resting gently upon the deer's back. About forty feet away in the tall brush and grasses, the Madisons could see the buck's companions. He was not alone.

"My Friends have been observing our interaction. They are very pleased with the progress that has been made. I hope that we will meet again soon. This has been a most comforting experience." Anne reassured their New Friend that they too desired more connection, and she restated their commitment to do the necessary inner work so that change could be accomplished. With that said, the buck stepped off the path and moved in the direction of his friends. After a few steps were taken, he turned around and faced the Madisons once again. Perhaps it was just a trick of the eye, but Anne and David both thought the gracious animal had slightly bowed his head to them. Trick or not, it was a tender moment for the three New Friends. The couple remained perfectly still until the buck rejoined his friends. Greetings were exchanged among his peers before the small group disappeared into the heavy thicket. At that point, Anne and David finally relaxed.

Time passed without their awareness as they continued to gaze in the direction of their last sighting of the buck and his friends. It was difficult to just walk away; each was longing for one more glance of the gentle creature. Lost in the reverie of their interaction with the stellar buck, the couple eventually continued their walk without even knowing that they had done so. It wasn't until they reached a juncture in the trail that they were forced to awaken from their enduring stupor.

"Goodness," declared Annie. "How on Earth did we get here? I don't even remember leaving our New Friend." The two dear friends giggled about their loss of time, and then giggled some more when they simultaneously recalled a much repeated comment that they both enjoyed accessing. *We know this trail so well that we could walk it blindfolded.*

"I think we just did it!" The couple stated in unison, which brought about another round of giggles.

"It really is amazing that one's body continues to function as needed, while the mind wanders off in another direction. I don't remember our walk either," admitted David, "and yet, here we are!" He pointed to the juncture ahead and asked which path she preferred. It was no surprise that the path with seascape views was chosen. As they moved forward, his lovely wife posed a question.

"Where has your mind been, Dear?" Anne's question was multifaceted. She truly wanted to know what her husband was thinking about, and she also wanted some clues about where her mind had been. She too found it fascinating that the mind seemed to be capable of functioning on autopilot. Anne often wondered how she managed to safely get from one location to another in her car when she had absolutely no memory of the drive.

The question gave Anne's husband pause. He struggled to find an answer, but wasn't successful in his attempts. "I'm not really sure, Annie. My best guess is that my mind was in many different places at the same time. I know that doesn't make much sense, if any at all, but let me see if I can bring a wee bit of clarity to what I'm attempting to say. I have vague memories of reliving the time we spent with our New Friend. I remember the strength that I felt pulsating from him…he was magnificent…a truly powerful life being that bravely crossed the boundary separating humans from other animals. I also recall being in awe of his courage and wondering if I could ever muster the strength that he demonstrated and commanded. Annie, he was a remarkable being, and I felt as if he was communicating with us at several different levels. Of course, he was telepathically speaking to us, but he also was infusing us with a reminder that we are here for a reason. He was inciting a memory to take action on Earth's behalf. I know this must sound odd, but I feel as if our experience with him was much more than a simple encounter. Obviously, we were both enamored with the opportunity to meet and communicate with another species. As you said, it was a dream come true, but this was more.

"Maybe I'm wrong. Maybe, this encounter was how all encounters with other life beings will be. I just know that our experience was much more than I ever imagined it could be. I'm amazed by the interaction, by the stately air of the animal himself, and by the possibilities that await us. I now realize that my thoughts, my ideas, about what an encounter with another species would be like were entirely too limited. This experience was incredible! I am so grateful to have had the privilege to be in his presence." David paused, but his intuitive spouse knew he wasn't finished.

"And there's another aspect to our dream-like walk," he continued. "I remember being enveloped by a deep sense of enduring peace. It was as if someone was watching over us and that we were being held in safety and protection as we walked in what seemed to be an unconscious state. In truth, I think our consciousness was at a heightened state, but we just didn't realize it in the moment. It was a moment that was a lifetime."

Anne had great respect for her husband. Even when he was at a loss for words, he managed to express himself in the most delightful manner. She had known about this characteristic long before they actually decided to get married. They joked about themselves with others, admitting that they enjoyed each other's company so much that they just forgot to do the wedding scene. In their hearts they had been married since the first day that they met each other. In their present situation, Anne found herself falling in love with him all over again.

"I just love the way you articulate yourself, David. Your tenderness and sincerity always touch me very deeply. And as always, you help me understand more about my own feelings. I too was incredibly impressed with the essence of our New Friend. It felt as if we were in the presence of a learned wisdom teacher."

"Yes," agreed her husband. "He did have a sagacious mystique, didn't he? He was a Messenger of Truth!"

The last comment, which felt as if it escaped from David's mouth, summarized the interaction perfectly. Anne looped her arm around his as they embraced the moment of clarity. "Well said!" she whispered. Arm-in-arm, the couple walked for another half mile in silence, or so it appeared, until they reached the point where the panoramic ocean view unveiled itself to them. It was a spectacular overlook that stopped passersby in their tracks. It was one of those precious, treasured spaces on Mother Earth where one is instantaneously propelled into the present moment, as one recognizes the Divine's magnificent creativity. It is a place when appropriate oohs and aahs are offered in homage of that which is indescribably beautiful. No one is able to slip by this special setting without coming to an abrupt halt.

"Oh my goodness! It happened again!" exclaimed Anne as she gasped for air. "This view captures my heart every time we pass this way. It feeds my soul in ways that I am yet to understand." His wife's reaction did not surprise David. She had a special affinity with this location, which never waned. Each encounter brought her to tears. He wondered when she would discover the true connection that existed between the two of them.

"Can you help me understand what this intense sense of connection is about, David?" Once again, Anne had intuited her husband's thoughts, which was simply the norm for these two old friends. Even though they were still delightfully surprised by these moments of unspoken connection, they no longer regarded them as lucky coincidences. For whatever reason, the ability to communicate telepathically had revitalized itself within them. Although they certainly were not as fluent in this form of communication as they desired to be, Anne and David were very pleased with their progress. That being said, each would admit that practice and trust definitely enhance the process.

Her husband didn't respond to her question immediately. Anne had learned years ago that he was one who required time to carefully deliberate upon a question. Because she knew this was his modus operandi, she found it easy to maintain a sense of patience with this particular habit of his...usually.

"I don't mean to be testing your patience, Dear, but your question is..." David paused for deep breath and seemed to be searching for a precise word that was successfully escaping him. "Well," he said in exasperation, "Anne, your question is far more expansive than you presently know. And I think the reaction that you continue to have to this location is a message. There is something here that you need to pursue. I know you already give a lot of your time and energy pondering about this place and the impact it has upon you every time we take this path, but I think you need to do more. Something important happened here, Annie, and whatever it was is reaching out to you...calling you to pay attention. I suspect the tears that well up in your eyes every time we reach this point are a direct response to the plea that is being made to you. You are being 'called' to this setting because there is something here that is unfinished. It, whatever it is, reaches out every time and touches your heart, begging you to pause, to listen, and to remember whatever it is that you are intended to address." David turned to his love and put his hands on her shoulders. "Sweetie, we don't believe in coincidences! We both know something important is happening here; it's time that you give this matter the attention that it deserves. If there's anything I can do to assist you, please let me know. I'm as curious about this as you are, and I want to get to the bottom of this mystery. Whatever it is has a hold upon you, Annie. There's something here that needs your attention. Actually, I didn't state that correctly. There is something that is demanding your attention and it is desperately trying to help you to remember what it is that you are suppose to do."

"Goodness, David! What you're describing sounds like some type of sacred agreement."

"Yes, that is exactly what I'm trying to articulate. Thank you, for finding the right descriptor." The couple adjusted their positions and stood hand-in-hand staring out over the craggy rocks with the never-ending frothy waves surging over them. One could lose time when viewing such grandeur.

"Mother Earth is remarkably beautiful," Anne stated quietly. "And she holds many secrets, but this one is getting ready to reveal itself. I'm very excited, David! Thank you for sharing your thoughts with me. You've opened my heart to exploring this opportunity." Her husband blushed. He was not one who accepted compliments easily. "Oh, don't brush my gratitude aside. I'm serious, David, you always have a way of getting me on the right track. I'm really excited and when we get home I will have an encounter with my journal. Me thinks it is time to develop a plan for approaching this sacred agreement."

Anne's excitement delighted her husband. He too wanted answers to the mysterious plea that was reaching out to his beloved. "Our walk has been most satisfying today," he announced. "First we encountered the grand buck and now we are given an opportunity to solve a mystery. This is developing into a very fine day." With that said, the two hastened the pace back to the trailhead, each wondering what might unfold next.

Three

Far away in a distant star system, a species of ancient explorers established a remote observation station for the purpose of monitoring the development of a new species that recently relocated from a planet whose health had been so severely compromised that they had no other option but to seek refuge in another setting. The news of their tragic situation did not reach other members of the Universal Family in time for an intervention to be made. However, because of the unforeseen development that evolved upon the declining planet, it was discerned that observation of this burgeoning species was warranted.

Those who originally seeded the species had great hope in their evolutional potential. They carefully searched for and chose a home for these seedlings that was environmentally suitable for their future needs. The planet selected, now impaired and falling into dormancy, was then a beautiful haven, abundant with natural resources that would allow for growth and expansion for ages to come. The Seeders were dismayed by what had transpired in their absence. Their hearts were broken. Never did they imagine that such a tragic event could happen. They mourned the loss of all those who deserved so much more.

Prior to their awareness of this unthinkable tragedy, devastating environmental changes transpired across the entire planet. Although signs of her failing healthy had been obvious, the newcomers on the planet ignored the warning signs as if they were irrelevant. This irresponsible reaction did not serve them well. Soon, but not soon enough, the new species realized it was impossible to survive the onslaught of repeated catastrophic events.

Because of the planet's instability, an unfathomable decision became inevitable. Unless action was taken, extinction would be the fate of the new species. It was an agonizing decision. Those who volunteered to participate in the Mission of Hope realized the consequences of their departure, as did those who volunteered to remain behind. Neither option was satisfying.

What awaited this burgeoning species was unknown. No one ever imagined that such an unbearable possibility might be in the future. Extensive discussions were had; ideas were shared followed by more information gathering and more conversations. With each round of discussion, greater understanding of their precarious situation was acquired. Eventually their reality could no longer be denied, and plans were implemented to save their species.

With their newly developed plans came a flurry of action and resurgence of optimism. There was hope that a new location would quickly be discovered allowing for return trips to rescue those who had bravely remained behind. This wishful thought unfortunately would not come to pass. The search for a new setting to inhabit was long, and as time passed, the travelers knew their loved ones would never be seen again. Stricken by grief, their hearts were heavy. Thoughts of all who were left behind resulted in many regrets about the past and doubts about the future. Hope waned as their travels moved deeper and deeper into unknown territory. The morale of the homeless travelers was at its lowest when a distant object captured their attention. Curiosity propelled them to realign their trajectory in the direction of the unknown object. Once again the embers of hope were ignited among the travelers who had come so far. As they neared the object, it became evident that it was a planet that held great potential as a possible relocation site. Not only was the planet indescribably beautiful, but it also offered abundant resources and opportunities. It appeared to be an ideal setting for their species to thrive.

A decision was made to pursue an audience with the planet. They hoped She would be amenable to their request. Her response was immediate. She invited the travelers to land upon her surface, where introductions were made, and heartfelt conversations were shared. The Host Life Being carefully listened to their harrowing stories. Stricken with compassion for their desperate circumstances, the remarkable Life Being graciously agreed to give their request careful consideration.

Her primary concern in her deliberation process was the safety and security of her current inhabitants. These long-term residents cooperatively coexisted with one another. Mutual respect and concern for all involved resulted in a flourishing planetary health system and a peaceful and harmonious lifestyle. This tranquil way of being was the preferred way of being and the planetary Life Being specifically addressed this priority with the new species seeking refuge upon her. She adamantly proclaimed her desire that the present way of being would be the expected way of being in the future, and she suggested that the travelers ponder this planetary preference before they made their decision to establish a home upon her.

The new species enthusiastically agreed to the Life Being's offer of peaceful coexistence.

Observations of the peaceful negotiations between the planetary Life Being and the new species were reassuring to the universal explorers. The new species had demonstrated promising potential when they entered into existence; however, their development on the previous planet had created great concern. For the sake of the new species and those they encountered, the universal explorers decided that continued monitoring of their behavioral development was in order.

Four

"**J**onathan, where are you?" The question entered into existence with hopeful anticipation of a response, but none was forthcoming. "Yoo-hoo! Jonathan! Where are you?" Again there was no response to the question, which did not sit well with the author of this inquiry.

Geraldine looked in every room on every floor in search of her misplaced husband. *Clearly he does not know that I am in need of his assistance.* The testy tone of her thought was a way of hiding the concern that was rising within her. "Now where on Earth is he?" The question was not intended for anyone but herself, but then she directed another question to her empty house. "Do you know where he is?" she asked. Geraldine paused and listened with the ears of her heart. Convinced that their home had a soul, she waited for a response. When nothing was heard, her frustrations were released. "For goodness sake, tell me where he is! I know that you know what he is up to, so speak up!" When silence prevailed, Geraldine threw up her hands and headed towards the backdoor. "Some day," she announced as she marched through the kitchen, "you are going to talk with me. I know it and you know it, but in the meantime, I'm going to keep talking to you because I know you are listening."

As Geraldine exited the backdoor she refrained from saying goodbye to the house, which was her way of expressing her disappointment about her inability to make connection with the house. What she didn't know was that the house was equally desirous of connecting with her.

The view from the deck allowed her to see the inner circle of their backyard. Jonathan was nowhere to be seen, so she decided to check out the so-called garage. While descending the deck stairs, an image of her husband sitting on his favorite bench in the most distant part of their property came to mind. She took this as a sign. Geraldine trusted her intuition, so she confidently walked in the direction that had just flashed through her mind.

The bench was one of her husband's favorite places in the world. When he spoke of his fondness for the location, tears would always appear. The sentimental connection he felt for this tiny space was inexplicable. He only knew that being there centered him and allowed him to feel a sense of peaceful knowing that he rarely was able to reach anywhere else.

Geraldine entered the outer circle of their property by way of a secret passageway. They playfully referred to it as such because they loved the idea of having a secret entryway into the wonderland beyond the carefully groomed backyard garden. When they first viewed this property many years before, they were intrigued by its possibilities. It wasn't a huge piece of land, but it was a large oversized lot in an area of the community that was particularly attractive to them. It satisfied their needs. The house was sweet and accommodating and there was an area in the backyard that begged for a beautifully landscaped flower garden. That garden became the priority when they moved onto the property. It was very important to both of them that they had a lovely view from their back windows. With hard work and long hours, they quickly established the inner circle, as they described it. It was a garden that claimed the status of being in perpetual transition…a blank canvas that came to be a lush home for many varieties of colorful perennials, hostas, and ferns that continued to be added to and improved upon on a regular basis. Such is the fate of well-loved garden!

Once the inner circle reached that certain point of satisfaction when gardeners realize they can focus 'some' of their attention on another project, the outer circle became the center of attention. This was the magical area: heavily wooded and abundant with potential. The work began with two folding chairs, imagination, and consultation. Hours were spent exploring the overgrown area. With special care for the native plants, the Gardners, whose surname accentuated their love for gardening, would meander from one spot to another trying to learn the lay of the land. In each new location, Jonathan and Geraldine would carefully situate their folding chairs so that they could spend quality time with the setting. Through this process of sitting, being, and engaging with the land and its inhabitants, a plan surfaced. In truth, some of the plans were visualized with help from the more mature plant life. Pathways of pine needle mulch were seen linking special sites together, which required very little relocation of the existing plants while creating order and a greater sense of space. All involved in the consultation process agreed that the landscape needed sprucing up and could be done without causing harm to the native vegetation.

Walking along the shortest path to her husband's presumed destination, Geraldine recalled numerous experiences shared with the outer circle's plant life. It was a very special time of connection and collaboration with nature that they would never forget. Every step she took triggered another fond memory. Each curve in the path reminded her of the efforts that were lovingly taken to honor the space of every plant...and it was worth it! The winding, seemingly undirected path, made the property appear to be much larger that it really was. She was so grateful for the assistance that the plant life had offered, including the design for the pine needle path, which came to the Gardners simultaneously from an image that was telepathically projected from one of the residents. The transformation of the outer garden was a remarkable story of cooperation with Mother Earth that needed to be shared with everyone, which reminded her that the children's book she was working on required her attention. And that memory reminded her that she was strolling along on the soft bed of pine needles for a reason.

"Goodness! It feels as if I've been walking for hours. Am I lost on the trail?" she thought to herself.

"You are not! The beloved is but a breath away!" The response was so softly heard that Geraldine didn't know if it was spoken voice or an inner voice. She quickly turned around to see if anyone was following her, but she appeared to be alone. The experience was confusing, but she was not alarmed. Geraldine was accustomed to receiving inner communications.

"Is there more you want to share?" she politely asked. Another response was quickly received in the same manner reminding her that the children's book truly did need her attention.

"Yes, I know," she acknowledged. "I will address the situation this afternoon. That's a promise." The unusual exchange may have seemed strange to an onlooker, but it was normal for Geraldine. One of her many gifts included the ability to hear a wonderful voice from within that provided her with the text for the children's books that she then prepared for publication. This process had been going on for over two decades and continues to this day. Although some folks refer to Geraldine as a channel or a medium, she just rolls her eyes at the notion and replies, "I'm just a secretary. I take dictation from a voice within. Then I arrange the material in manuscript form and make it ready for submission. That's all I do." Few people are satisfied by this response, including her husband, but currently, this is the only explanation that Geraldine is able to offer.

Returning her mind to the task before her, Geraldine hastened her pace. She was almost certain that the next big curve in the path would lead her directly to her husband's favorite bench. And she was right!

As she rounded the curve, she could see Jonathan sitting in the sacred space that they had made for the bench, which he had inherited from his Grandfather. The sitting area was just off the path and partially hidden by a cluster of sumac trees and a very large colony of bright green ostrich ferns. The ferns were so lush and thick that they appeared to be guarding the sacred space, keeping it safe for any passerby who needed a special place to rest. Jonathan seemed deeply engaged with his journal. Geraldine paused, reluctant to interrupt this intimate moment, but then her husband looked up and invited her to join him on the bench. She immediately accepted the invitation.

"Have I arrived at an inconvenient time, Jon?" she asked.

"No, not at all. I was just winding down. Your timing is perfect and I am delighted you are here. What's on your mind this morning? Your energy indicates an adventure is in the making." Jonathan's welcoming manner enveloped Geri. The sense of urgency that she experienced while searching for him was instantly abated and replaced by the warmth of his peaceful, loving nature.

She took a deep breath, placed her hand on top of his, and sighed. "You are such a marvel. I've been in a tizzy, making a big deal out of searching for you, and now that I've found you, my mood has completely shifted. I suspect," she said with a twinkle in her eyes, "my change of mood is a sign. And I think the sign is telling me to be silent as you tell me what is going on with you this morning. So tell me, dear, what's up in your world?"

Jonathan recognized the gift of his sweet wife's invitation. He knew how intuitive Geri was. She was the marvel in the family! And as was often the case, she knew that he needed a sounding board to process his early morning experiences, and because of her generous nature, she was willing to delay her own need to discuss whatever was going on with her. It was not a surprise when she wrapped her arm around his and softly urged him to go first.

"Not to worry, Jon, there is ample time for both of us to share our stories this morning. I'm in a good place, completely at ease, and I'm eager to hear about your experience."

"Thanks, Geri! I really do want to process my thoughts." So Jon took another deep breath while he attempted to gather his thoughts about the sequencing of events that he had experienced in the last couple of hours. He checked his watch and shook his head.

"Geez! Is it really only seven o'clock? I feel like a lifetime has been lived since I awoke, and it's only been two hours. That's amazing!" He paused and took a moment to scan the outer garden that surrounded them. "I'm so grateful for this place, Geri. It truly is a sacred space and it supports and nourishes the inner work that we both seek and participate in. Every plant, every tree, and all the little critters that live here are all fundamentally related and supportive of one another. Including us!" he quickly added. "While I sat here in the wee hours this morning, three rabbits watched over me. I'm not kidding, Geri! They settled nearby and pretended to be feeding, but their presence was more than just having breakfast. They were here for a reason. I know this is going to sound crazy, but I felt as if they were holding the space for me to do my deep soul-searching." His beloved's reassuring smile and nod of agreement reminded Jonathan that he did not have to monitor his commentary with her. Geri thoroughly believed that all of Mother Nature's life beings, including humans, were in alignment with one another. The idea that the rabbits would be assisting Jonathan's work was totally plausible to her. The couple snuggled closer. It was such an amazing gift to have a loving partner with whom you could share those events that some people would perceive as unusual.

"What time did you wake up this morning?" asked Geri, knowing full well that his experience began before he actually awakened.

"It was shortly after four o'clock," he responded. "One minute I was asleep or at least I thought I was, and the next minute my eyes were wide open as if I had been awake all night. Sometimes, I wonder if that isn't the case. We've talked about this before, and once again, I find myself wondering if more is going on during our periods of sleep than we remember. I awoke feeling as if I was in the middle of an unfinished experience. Does that make sense, Geri?" Bypassing the direct answer, his wise spouse cleverly urged him to speak more about the situation.

"Well, it's different than waking up from a dream that you actually remember having before you abruptly exited from it. In those experiences, you are consciously aware of the dream activity. Even if you quickly forgot the exiting experience, you were aware of it in the moment. I believe most folks have those kinds of experiences, but what happened this morning was different. My eyes popped open and I felt incomplete, as if I had been in the middle of something somewhere else, and then suddenly, I found myself back in bed. Again, this is going to sound crazy, but my immediate thought was that I was back from another dimension. And whatever was going on in that other dimension wasn't completed. The experience left me with many questions and a sense that I had not fulfilled a commitment that was made in the other setting. My heart was heavy with feelings of guilt and shame. I wasn't able to gain any clarity about those feelings, which of course raises many questions and concerns. Part of me is very worried that I have betrayed or abandoned someone or others that are still remaining in that other dimension. I don't even know if dimension is the appropriate word to use in this situation." Jonathan's mood shifted into frustration and disappointment with himself. He indicated that he had remained in bed for a while trying to sort through his feelings, but realized he was going to lose everything if he didn't get up and start taking notes.

"Whew! You've had quite a morning," Geri reassured Jon that she believed everything he shared with her and supported his need to process what was happening. She noted their previous conversations about multi-dimensionality and reiterated her own ongoing curiosity about the topic. "Just because we don't fully understand what is going on here doesn't mean it isn't happening. Something important is going on, Jon, and we just need to keep our minds and hearts open to it, whatever it is."

Geri's reassurance was comforting, but Jon was in one of those moments when he really wanted more specifics. "I appreciate your confidence in this mystery, dear, but why can't we make any headway with this? We need more clarity, Geri. How can we advance forward if we don't receive more information?" Geraldine appreciated her husband's frustration; many a time did she fall into a similar place of doubts, impatience, and skepticism.

"Jon, we've both been in this uncomfortable place before, and we always survive it. And we usually have some type of exciting breakthrough that inspires us to new levels of knowing and acceptance. This is the 'in-between' time, dear. The time that is necessary for assimilation of what was most recently learned with all that is already known. It is an essential part of our developmental process. We both know this. We just don't like these periods because they seem dull and boring when compared to the growth spurts that are so exciting and exhilarating. You are not in a lull, Jon. You are in the pause before the next period of advancement." Geri sat quietly as her husband cogitated.

"Well, that was nicely stated and, of course, right on the mark. Actually, you nailed it, Geri. I am in that phase of processing things, and as it slows down, I'm already getting pumped for the next adventure." His wife patted him on the knee and softly giggled.

"Yep! That's exactly what you're doing! You can be very pleased with yourself, dear. You're extremely open to and accomplished at delving into the adventure phase and you're exceptionally dedicated to participating in the assimilation phase. It's just the in-between phase that is a stumbling block. Your impatience overwhelms the importance of this stage. Even though it doesn't seem like it, the in-between phase is as important as the other two. This is the period when one needs to rest and recover from the energy expended in the other two phases. Essentially, it is a time for rejuvenation, which is critical preparation for the next adventure that awaits you." Geraldine turned to face her husband. "You need to give yourself a break, Love! Whether you want to accept this truth or not, rest is a necessary part of the ongoing, never-ending developmental process."

Although this was a difficult lesson for Jonathan to accept, he knew Geri's words were of wisdom. He wrapped his arm around her and she nestled her head on his shoulder. They sat quietly for what seemed like a long time, but time has a way of fooling even the wisest. After only a few minutes had passed Geraldine regained her sense of urgency. She sat up erectly and then apologized for her behavior. "Dear me, I've lost track of the time, Jon. I'm so sorry for interrupting this peaceful moment. It was lovely to just relax together. I thoroughly enjoyed resting with you." Jonathan looked at his watch and grinned. Moving his arm closer to her range of vision, Jon nodded towards the watch. When Geri saw the time, they both started giggling. "We've only been sitting for a few minutes," she said in disbelief.

"Six to be precise!" her snuggle mate replied.

"How can that be? I experienced several lengthy recollections while we rested together. There simply is no way that only six minutes passed. It's impossible."

"And yet it is!" said Jon as he repositioned himself on the bench. "It's still early, Geri, and you haven't told me why you were looking for me. What is going on with you?" His question brought back the antsy feelings that she woke up with in the wee hours of the morning. She wondered why her vulnerability was so much more intense in the early hours. Geraldine didn't regard herself as a fearful person, but there were times when she became consumed by doubts and fears, and usually those times were in the early morning hours. She resented these encounters. They were frustrating, demeaning, and made her feel like a victim of her own emotions. Geri did not like this image of herself and strongly wanted to release this proclivity towards self-doubt.

"The truth is, Jon, I'm okay. When I woke up this morning, I was feeling anxious, insecure, and filled with doubts about this latest project, and all I wanted was to be near you. Now that we are sitting here, the sense of urgency is gone. Look at this place, Jon. We're in a haven. There is no need for concern." As his beloved unwittingly diminished her earlier vulnerable state, Jonathan speculated that she needed time to process whatever had triggered the event.

"These bouts with doubts happen for a reason, Geri. I'm glad you're feeling safe now, but that's no reason to disregard what happened. Let's take a look at it together and maybe some of its power can be diminished and released." She squeezed his hand in gratitude and admitted that he was right.

"I am so thankful that you are my Love. If you weren't here now nudging me to do my inner work, I would probably be racing off to attend some falsely proclaimed 'important' distraction that would enable me to avoid what is truly important. Jon, I just don't understand why I still have doubts about receiving these books. This process has been going on for years, how can I possibly doubt what is happening?"

"Do you have doubts about receiving the books, Geri? Is that what's really going on? Or is it something else?" Jon's questions gave her pause, which was followed by many more questions racing through her mind. She wondered if she was misinterpreting her feelings.

"Excuse me, Jon, but I need to talk my way through this. Bear with me, please?" Geraldine had taught him years before that women needed to talk to process their feelings, so her request was easily accepted. He indicated that he was happy to do so. "Your questions make me wonder, Jon. Do I doubt my abilities to receive these books? In retrospect I don't believe that I do, so what is it that I am experiencing? What am I feeling? I thought the sense of urgency was related to doubts, but now I'm not sure. Perhaps I was totally wrong about this.

"Or perhaps, you are partially right. Maybe, there is more to this issue than you think." Geri nodded in reaction to her husband's suggestion. She took a long deep breath in hopes that she might be able to open herself up to the truth of her discomfort.

"Beloved Friends, please help me to understand this moment of confusion. I seem to be stuck; please nudge me in the right direction."

Jon tightly squeezed her hand hoping that the gesture would provide her support. "Indeed it does!" she said acknowledging his intentions.

"Let's go into silence, Geri. I will hold the space for your inner work, the same way the rabbits did for me earlier." The idea was most appealing. Geri immediately repositioned herself on the bench. Jon made similar adjustments, and without any verbal coordination, the couple simultaneously took deep breaths. In good time, each sank into the silent space they were seeking. Without the couple's awareness, their friends in the outer garden also chose to participate in the meditation. The three rabbits that assisted Jon earlier returned to their previous stations and protectively watched over the couple as they tended their inward journeys. Likewise, all the foliage immediately surrounding the bench seemed to bow their upper stems and fronds in homage of their human friends. Similar gestures of respect were made by nearby greenery as well, and the feathered friends, whose songs were usually robust and abundant, appeared to acknowledge the event by remaining still and quiet. It was a sweet moment of connection among many different species working together for the good of all involved.

Time stood still in the outer garden. While the rest of the world continued its busy pace, the energy within the garden shifted. Existence still continued, but it existed differently. Each individual inhabitant still continued, but the energetic rhythm within each inhabitant existed differently. This condition that was brought about by intention is available to everyone in existence, but unfortunately, not everyone in the Gardner's realm of existence is aware of the possibility.

Deep sighs were eventually heard from the direction of Geri and Jon. This simultaneous reaction was not uncommon for them, but it was enjoyed nonetheless. Each time one of these so-called coincidences happened, it brought about giggles and smiles. Their smiles became much larger when they looked towards the garden. The rabbits vigilantly maintained their positions. Chickadees, finches, yellow warblers, cardinals, and more, all remained poised on their preferred branches, while the beautiful green foliage all around them graciously returned to their erect positions. It was literally a sight to behold!

"Oh my goodness!" whispered Geri as tears streamed down her face. "Look at our friends, Jon! They participated in our meditation."

"Actually, Geri, I think they assisted our meditation. Now, I understand why it seemed as if we were being held in the arms of grace. This is the perfect example of what it means to hold the space for another. My goodness, they did this for us, dear. This is truly a humbling experience." Jon could not restrain his tears, and didn't want to anyway. They were tears of joy.

"Dear Friends," sighed Geri, "we are so grateful for your generous act of kindness. You have deeply touched our hearts, and I so hope that you can fully experience the appreciation that we both feel. Thank you, Dear Ones! Thank you so much for joining us and for assisting our inward journey. We are so grateful that you are present in our lives." With that said, their friends became very active again. Birdsongs echoed throughout the canopy of trees as the various guests flitted about, and with no fanfare whatsoever, the three rabbits quietly and discreetly departed the scene.

"This is incredible!" declared Jon. "I wish we had a film of this experience, so that we could share it with others. Why are we so lucky, Geri? I feel so grateful. It was a privilege to witness this connection."

"Yes, it was! Jonathan, can you say more about how you felt as if we were being held in the arms of grace? That is such a beautiful image. I would like to hear more about it." Jon sat with the question briefly trying to remember exactly how he felt in the moment. This experience was slightly different for him. Although he previously had experiences of being held during a meditation, this one had a new component to it. As he tried to gain clarity, a flash of the contemplative scene came to mind.

"Ah, this makes sense to me." His words were so softly spoken that Geri didn't hear them, but it didn't matter because he was just validating his own supposition. "I think the reason this meditation was so powerful for me was because of the company. The idea of holding the space for you while you did your inner work really appealed to me. It made me feel as if I was finally having a chance to do something for you." Geri attempted to interrupt him, but Jon stopped her. "You rarely ask for my help, dear, even though you are always helping me with some chore or project. I know you don't agree with me about this, but the point I'm trying to make is that I really wanted to do this for you. So, the first feeling that I experienced was joy. It was absolutely delightful to sit side by side here in our sacred space, and particularly for me to have an opportunity to assist you while you were pursuing greater awareness." With tears streaming down his face and his voice breaking, Jonathan expressed how much he loved sharing the experience with his beloved friend and wife.

"In addition to the sheer beauty of experiencing this moment with you, I also was aware that we were embraced by love. Even though I've had similar experiences in the past, this one was different, and now I know why. Not only was I with the most important person in my life, but we were also in the company of Mother Nature's finest. How blessed we were to be ministered to by the flora and fauna with whom we share space! We were shown how much they appreciate us. Dear Heart, I think that was a message, an amazing gift, that we must hold on to. We must continue our efforts to live in mutual co-existence with all our many neighbors." Reaching over to hug his beloved, Jonathan added one more thought.

"So, this morning, I felt joy, love, gratitude, and hopefulness for the future."

Their hug extended until a banditry of bold chickadees landed in the sumac nearby. Their close proximity seemed to acknowledge Jonathan's assumption that the local inhabitants appreciated them.

"What about you, dear? How did your meditation go?"

Geri leaned back into the bench, closed her eyes, and sighed. Her beloved looked on as she quietly repeated several deep breaths. When she finally opened her eyes, she found her husband lovingly looking over at her. Smiles were exchanged, but no words were spoken. They simply embraced the moment of connection and nothing more was required. Time passed. Eventually, a song sparrow, utilizing the echo chamber of nature's canopy, blessed the outer garden with a magnificent aria. The performance was stellar and deserved a standing ovation, which was provided by the Gardners and all the other residents of the garden. The song sparrow graciously accepted the applause and offered a brief encore before exiting the scene.

"What a lovely voice!" declared Geri, as she repositioned herself on the bench.

"Indeed!" replied Jonathan. "Perhaps the song sparrow was setting the stage for you to continue your work. After all, our garden friends assisted us with our meditation; maybe they want to be present while you process what happened during your time in the silence."

"That's a lovely thought, Jon. The idea that our friends want to be part of our discussion pleases me. We've wanted to connect with these beings for so long, and it seems as if our dream is finally coming true." She looked about the garden and recognized this was a moment that needed to be noticed and honored.

"Dear Friends, thank you so much for being here in our garden, or perhaps, I should say thank you for allowing us to be here in your garden. We hope this sacred space that we have attempted to create benefits everyone involved. The time we've shared together today has been very satisfying for us and we hope there can be many more opportunities for this type of connection with all of you. We are very grateful for your assistance with our meditation this morning. Your presence was extremely helpful." Geri took a deep breath before addressing the issue of her inner work. She wanted to share what happened without minimizing the experience. In essence, she wanted to be respectful and truthful. Part of her was nervous about being so transparent, but she knew that she was in good company and that this opportunity was happening for a reason.

"Jon, you are the love of my life!" Her eyes sparkled when expressing this truth about their relationship. "I cannot tell you how much your support means to me. I am the luckiest person in the world, and I am absolutely certain that we are intended to be together. Thank you for encouraging me to go into the silence; it was exactly what was needed. Perfect timing! Perfect setting! Perfect company!" The expression of gratitude was followed by a wonderful hug and kiss. Jon enjoyed his beloved's remarks and had several comments he wanted to make, but wisely decided against it. He had a strong sense that it was important to help her stay focused and he did so by urging her to carry on with her story.

"Well," she continued, "it didn't take long for me to arrive at my destination. For whatever reason, there were no annoying distractions complicating my path into the silence. I suspect the good company that I was keeping played a significant role in my easy travels. As you stated earlier, Jon, it truly felt as if we were being held in the arms of grace. I've never experienced that level of peace before. It was wonderful… and indescribable." She paused for a moment in hopes of finding words that would appropriately honor the situation, but she was unsuccessful. "I'm sorry, dear, but no words can adequately express the beauty of that moment. However, what I can say is this. I want more. I want it for me. I want it for us. I want it for everyone." Geri paused again, desperately wanting to convey what she had experienced. "Jon, it was serenity in its purest form. There were no doubts, no fears, and no stressful anticipations! This probably sounds crazy, but I think I was given a glimpse of how life is supposed to be."

She pointed to the garden in another attempt to articulate what had happened during her inward journey. "What we experienced here this morning was peaceful co-existence with our neighbors here in the garden. Imagine what the world would look like, Jon, if peaceful co-existence spread across the entire planet. What I experienced was bliss!" She turned to her beloved and placed her right hand on his heart and asked him to do the same with her, which he immediately did.

"Jon, remember our conversations about out-of-body experiences? Well, I either just had one or somehow I witnessed what would be felt if one were really having such an experience. My travels during our meditation took me far. I found myself in one location after another, all across the planet, witnessing peaceful interactions among all species. Humans were walking along with animals that we typically fear. And animals, which rightfully fear humans, were actually interacting with us. It was incredible, Jon! And it seemed so natural! This wasn't a movie or a fantasy. It was real! I believe every continent was visited. That may be an exaggeration. Admittedly, some of the locations were unknown to me, but in each one, I had a sense of what country was being viewed. Except one!" Geri abruptly stopped after that remark and seemed to go away. Jonathan presumed that she was searching for a memory so he remained quiet. His patience was wearing thin when she returned with a curious look upon her face.

"Jon, something very unusual happened during my travels. Of course, some people might think this entire conversation is unusual, but as I said, everything seemed peaceful and natural to me...until the last location was visited. I have no idea where we were at that point. I could be wrong, probably am, but the point is...nothing was recognizable. What I saw was beautiful! But it was not familiar. I don't know what else to say about it."

"Do you remember what you were feeling when you viewed that last setting?" inquired Jon.

"Well, I wasn't afraid, but it was discombobulating. I was curious about the setting and why it was being visited. I assumed there was a reason for it; but at that point, I felt like my travels had taken me a very long way from home and I just wanted to come back to you and the garden." Her husband gently kissed her hand.

"Welcome back! I'm glad you're home!" He wrapped his arm around Geri again, which was a favorite position for both of them.

His thoughts were racing, but as curious as he was, Jon didn't want to bombard his wife with dozens of questions.

"It's okay, dear! I can handle your questions. Not saying I will have any answers, but I'm willing to listen with an attentive ear." Once again, his beloved had responded to his unspoken thoughts.

"Your telepathic skills are increasing all the time. It's really amazing." Geri just smiled and rolled her eyes. "I know," he responded. "It's normal for you, but it still takes me by surprise. And frankly, each time you react to my thoughts, you inspire me to practice. As have our garden Friends! If we are going to communicate with our lovely, new neighbors, we will really need to expand our skills. But that's another conversation for another day. Back to your travels today! When you were talking about the last location, you said...*I have no idea where we were at that point.* That was the first time you indicated that you were accompanied. Can you say more about that?" Jon's question took Geri by surprise.

"That's interesting! I didn't mention that before. I wonder why," she mused. "Well, the truth is, I don't have an answer. My heart is telling me that I was aware during the entire experience that I was accompanied, but I didn't question it. I was perfectly comfortable with the situation, so I didn't feel a need to pursue more information. Now, I wonder what happened to my curiosity. You know me! I normally want to know every last detail, but I didn't react the way I usually docs. Hmm!" she got lost in her thoughts for a moment and then added. "Jon, a hypothesis has come to mind. I will continue to reflect upon your question, but for now, my theory is this. I felt safe, Jon. I was completely at ease. At some level, I knew everything that was happening was happening for a reason, and I knew that there was nothing to fear." The two old friends rested on the garden bench. Geri's answer was very comforting and gave each of them hope for the future. Time passed, as is its way. Eventually, the couple realized it was time for breakfast. Even though it was difficult to leave the sacred space, morning hunger was directing their thoughts. Jon took another long look about the garden and softly shared his gratitude.

"Thank you, Dear Friends! We are so grateful for the connection that transpired today and we hope that our relationships continue to grow. Have a wonderful day, and if you need anything, please let us know." Geri wrapped her arm in his as they walked back to the house.

Five

On the day of their arrival, a new beginning began. Welcomed and accepted by the host planet and all her inhabitants, the travelers from afar started anew. Their time of mourning for those who were left behind was not over. Memories of loved ones burdened their hearts and images of the past haunted them. The agony of separation lingered within, but all knew the decision made was necessary. For the sake of their species, this band of survivors departed their spaceship and began the task of establishing a new life, a new way of being, on this newly discovered planet far away from the planet of before.

The challenges were great, but they all persevered. It was a time of great unity as they worked together to create a future for those still remaining. Many had sacrificed their lives for the sake of the few that were to continue. Those who were lost would always be remembered. And those who survived were committed to creating a home that would withstand the ages, a home that would last forever for all those who were yet to come.

Their goals were simple. They would live their lives in harmony with those who already resided upon the planet, and they would honor and respect the planet that so generously provided them with a space upon which they could establish a settlement.

It was a time of extreme gratitude and hopeful anticipation.

Six

"Jen, the car is packed and ready to go!" Her words floated through the house, but the intended recipient was nowhere to be found. The best friend of the one who was missing searched the house for her hiking buddy. "Hey You! Where are you?" A faint sound was heard, but Carol couldn't discern if it came from upstairs or down in the basement. Because she had little patience for wasting time, Carol turned towards the cellar door just a few steps away. The muffled noise was heard again as she descended the stairs. "Hey Girl Friend! Are you down here?" Still there was no answer, but a scratching noise from the far side of the basement grabbed her attention. "Jen, are you down here?"

"I'm right here!" came a reply from behind several stacks of boxes. "Give me a second! I'm stuck!" Quickening her pace, Carol found the lost friend jammed against the back wall of the basement. Surrounded by very large boxes in various stages of being unpacked, Jen had literally backed herself into a corner.

"Oh my goodness! What are you searching for, and how did you manage to get yourself into this predicament?"

Jen turned several shades of red as she reviewed the mess that surrounded her. "Well, this is an example of how little time it takes to create utter chaos."

"How can I help?" ask Carol, who was already strategizing a plan of rescue for her friend. While Jen continued to marvel at the silly situation that she had gotten herself into, Carol decided which two boxes would provide the most efficient escape route. With little effort, she slightly shifted each box allowing a small pathway for Jen to squeeze through. "There you are! You're free!"

"Thanks, Carol. Sorry about this nonsense. I came down to look for a guidebook for today's adventure, but as you can see, I managed to get lost before we even left the house."

"Not to worry. We can repair this situation when we get back from our walk. In fact, this is a good reminder that we really need to finish unpacking."

"Ugh!!" They both groaned in sync.

"Let's get out of here before we become obsessed with a sense of responsibility," declared Jen as she raced up the basement stairs. Soon they were in the car headed for a trail that had been on their To Do List since moving to their new location. Much to their delight, there were so many wonderful hiking and walking opportunities nearby that they didn't have to venture far to satisfy their outdoor needs. The scenery en route to the trailhead whetted their appetite for forest therapy.

"We're so fortunate," Carol noted. "Who knew this area would be so appealing and conducive to our way of life?" Jen remained quiet for a moment before expressing the inevitable.

"Obviously, someone did, or we wouldn't be here now." Each fell into silence as memories about the relocation process flooded their respective minds. It was a moment in time that would never be forgotten. The idea of uprooting their lives because of guidance from an unseen source still amazed them. At times they giggled about the unfolding circumstances that motivated them to move across the country, but mostly they simply lived in awe of what transpired back then and what continued to happen to this day.

"Sometimes, I still can't believe that we did this, Carol. We both gave up a lot to come here, but I don't regret it at all. I'm very happy. Do you have any regrets?"

"None," replied Carol. "I still have moments of disbelief about the entire process. It was so unusual, and yet, so profoundly right for us." Pointing to the view that surrounded them, she validated what Jen had already said. "I'm very happy here. I'm grateful for the inexplicable experience that brought us here and I'm grateful that we are together and still continuing to share more experiences. Far as I can tell, it seems to me that we are living a truly remarkable life. And we're doing it in a beautiful location that nourishes our nature-loving needs." The confirmations shared were deeply reassuring. Even though they both trusted their circumstances, every once in a while, they needed to hear the soothing words again. Comforted by their heartfelt connection, they quietly enjoyed the views with few comments, but occasional oohs and ahs. The drive itself was a delightful adventure, but there was much more to come.

The signs to the new trail were easily spotted, leading the newcomers directly to the trailhead destination. Soon the car was parked and the two friends were donned with the appropriate gear. Excitement was escalating. They raced towards the trailhead, each wanting to be the first to reach the path, and as always, they both stopped before entering so that they could make the first step together. "Here we are!" announced Jen with a huge smile on her face. "Dear Friends, please watch over us as we embark upon another adventure. Your company is desired and preferred, if you have the time." With that said, the first step was taken by the twosome and then a high five was exchanged.

The forest was so lush that entering the trailhead from the parking lot was similar to entering a darkened theater. It took them a few minutes to adjust to the dim surroundings. "Geez! This is eerie! Should we grab a flashlight from the car before we go any further?" Jen's question warranted consideration. They waited a few more minutes and their eyes started adapting to the situation; however, Jen decided having a flashlight was good idea. She rushed back to the car, grabbed the torch from the glove compartment and attached it to her belt. When she rejoined Carol, they tested the flashlight to be sure the batteries were still strong.

"Shall we begin?" They asked in unison. With deep breaths and thumbs up, they entered a forest that was so thick that the trees' canopy obstructed the sunrays from reaching the forest floor.

"Carol, have you ever seen anything like this before?" Jen tried to hide her apprehension, but her friend was very perceptive.

"No, I haven't, and quite frankly, I probably wouldn't enter this trail without a companion. Shall we continue on a bit further or do you want to rethink this adventure?" Neither of the intrepid hikers wanted to give up. They agreed to continue for ten more minutes before reassessing the situation. As they moved deeper into the forest, the light coming from the parking area disappeared. The darkness took their breath away.

"Geez!" declared Jen. "I feel like a scared kid."

"Oh good! So do I," responded Carol. They remained still. Once again, their eyes adapted to the limited lighting so they agreed to continue, but just for good measure, Jen detached the flashlight from her belt and focused it down the path. It was working fine and illuminated the area nicely.

"Whew! That's a relief, but I don't want to wear the batteries out, so let's proceed without the flashlight unless it becomes absolutely necessary. Carol, we need to track our time and distance so we don't end up in a precarious situation."

"Agreed! Let's go another ten minutes and then do another assessment." Jen agreed to Carol's suggestion and the two hikers headed deeper into the forest again. Their moods had turned pensive, which was unusual for the beginning of a hike. Each was lost in her individual concerns about this adventure. Jen eventually broke the silence.

"Carol, may I interrupt your thoughts?"

"Please do. I would love to escape the nonsense of my mind. Tell me, Friend, where are your thoughts taking you?"

"Well, truthfully, I've been engaging with fears and doubts, some of which deserve consideration, while most do not. I find it very curious that we are both questioning why we are continuing to walk deeper into the darkness. Although I keep telling myself that the tree canopy will open up soon and we will be able to see the trail and surrounding area clearly, we've now been walking approximately a mile and that hasn't happened. I wonder many things, Carol, including whether or not we should continue. Perhaps, it would be wiser to return to the car and find out more information about this trail before we actually take it on. I don't want my concerns to spoil our adventure, but this is odd. We've never encountered a trail like this before and I'm antsy. My pride is telling me to go forward, but common sense is telling me not to. I don't want my pride to mislead me...to mislead us. But," she continued, "the fact that I cannot discern what action to take next concerns me. I feel uncertain about what is unfolding here, and I don't like feeling this way." She cleared her throat, took several deep breaths before asking Carol to share her perspective.

Recognizing that Jen was more upset than she wanted to admit, Carol quickly responded.

"My thoughts have been in the same realm as yours. I too am concerned that we are taking a risk by pursuing this path, and still, there is another part of me that wonders if this is happening for a reason. Are we intended to walk this path at this time? I wonder what awaits us. If we continue, what will happen? If we return to the car, what will happen? Are we in the middle of another unusual experience that's going to change our lives again, or are we simply having a knee jerk reaction to being in the dark?" Carol sighed loudly. "Like you, Jen, I am flummoxed about what action to take. This isn't who we are! We are decisive people." The two friends stood quietly in the middle of the trail. The forest was so still that each could hear the other breathing.

Jen finally broke the silence with one of her quirky remarks. "Maybe we should flip a coin! Heads we go forward; tails we return to the car."

"Jen, do we really want a coin to direct our lives?"

"No!" she asserted. "But we don't seem to be capable of making decision at the moment. How do people live with indecisiveness? Yikes! I find this most unpleasant."

"Hmm, that's an interesting thought, Jen. I've been wondering what we were supposed to learn from this situation and you just identified an extremely important lesson for both of us. Our bout with this common human reaction has raised our awareness of the discomfort that many people experience every day because of their fear of making decisions. Unfortunately, because neither of us has experienced indecisiveness before, we never knew what these people were going through. We were clueless. Now that we have personally encountered it, we know first hand how unpleasant it can be. I suspect we will have much greater empathy and compassion for these folks in days ahead now that we understand the impact of their fears. Good for you, Jen! That was a brilliant discovery."

"Actually, Carol, you're the one who brilliantly explained that learning experience. And it was very helpful. And it gives me pause, because the essence of the lesson is infinitely expansive. We all learn at a different pace, so there will always be differences because of our individual developmental process. The task for everyone is to be open and accepting of our differences rather than allowing differences to separate us. It never occurred to me that making a decision could be an extremely upsetting event for some people. Now that I know this, my perception of the world is different. This one insight increases my potential for being a better person. It awakens my consciousness to the differences that exist among us and it inspires me to be more sensitive to other people's circumstances. If I am consciously present in the moment, then I am more in tune with those around me, and this enhances my ability to open my heart to others regardless of our differences."

"Jen, let's practice this concept now!" announced her walking companion. "Let's practice being consciously present now. Rather than allowing our fears and doubts to consume us, let's take a few deep breaths and practice being present in this moment." Carol's suggestion sparked excitement in the twosome. They quickly decided (because they are decisive women) to address this task wholeheartedly. Backpacks were removed and carefully placed on the ground. Positions were adjusted so each was relaxed and comfortable. Then, Carol spread her feet and deliberately planted them firmly to the forest floor. Jen followed her lead, and then they both initiated their deep breathing.

As their breaths slowed and each settled down into the present moment, the concerns that Jen and Carol previously experienced just faded away. It was refreshing to shed those burdensome thoughts, and once they did, the forest came alive. The melodies of countless species of feathered friends, and others species as well, echoed through nature's concert hall. Sopranos took the lead, which often is the case; but altos, tenors, and even a few baritones from the forest choir and symphony rounded out the extraordinary musical event.

At first, the two hikers just closed their eyes and embraced the moment. It was indeed a joyous moment, so much so that the two friends could not refrain from opening their eyes. And when they did, the activation of their sense of sight expanded their joy exponentially. Each member of the forest that participated in the musical rendition glowed when it was his or her time to perform. It was a visual extravaganza. At times when all members were performing simultaneously, the music hall was filled with light. In those moments, Carol and Jen could actually see the forest that had remained hidden until this point.

"It's an ordinary forest," whispered Jen. She turned to her companion who was slowly turning around in circles taking in as many views of the forest as she could manage. "Did you hear me, Carol?"

"Yes, I did, and you're right. It's an ordinary forest whose beauty is hidden by its own magnificence. No wonder it's dark. The tree canopy that we are currently in is so large that it is nearly impossible for sunlight to sneak through, but look what we're witnessing now. The forest has it's own lighting system. Each life being has its own light essence. Hmm!" she muttered softly. "I wonder what happens when the music ends. Will the lights turn off? Will the forest go dark again, or will we see it differently because we now know one of its secrets. And what about the plant life, Jen? They are life beings as well. I wonder why they aren't glowing." Carol's curiosity was boundless. Her mind attempted to lead her in many different directions, but she was determined to stay in the moment. She didn't want to miss any opportunities that might arise. "You know when we were driving here, I had all sorts of happy thoughts about the new adventure we were embarking upon, but when we entered the trail and the darkness enveloped us, all of those thoughts just went by the wayside. It really takes me aback. One moment we were in such high spirits and then we were not. It's really amazing how quickly our moods changed. And now, we are in high spirits again because of this remarkable audio/visual exhibition that we've been privileged to witness. This is an incredible experience!" Suddenly Carol realized that she was being presumptuous. She simply assumed that she and Jen were having a similar reaction to what was unfolding around them. Before she could check in with her friend, Jen responded to her thoughts.

"Carol, you have not been presumptuous. Even though I am trying very hard to be in the moment, my mind has a mind of its own, and it wants answers. I'm not even sure what the questions are, but this experience has been spectacular and I would love to understand what is really happening here. If we are to presume that what we are seeing is real, then we are witnessing a reality that is beyond my scope of imagination. It certainly feels real to me and the fact that we are both witnessing this event helps me to believe that this really is happening. You do agree with me, don't you? We are not having some weird hallucinatory experience."

"I absolutely agree with you, Jen. This is real!" Carol's voice indicated confidence and certainty, both of which were very reassuring. "Actually, I think this is the adventure that we were hoping to have. We just didn't imagine something this remarkable would unfold for us."

"It certainly goes on my list of The Most Remarkable Things I've Ever Seen," interjected Jen. "Obviously, Carol, this is another lesson that the forest is providing us, but I wonder if we are fully understanding the lesson. And I also wonder about how much more are we intended to learn? When do we know when a lesson is completed? It seems to me that the lessons of this forest are never-ending. Every encounter with nature will present us more information. So, how do we discern when we are done?" As is so often the case, the two friends took deep breaths at the same time. Initially, this behavior brought about many giggles, but after a while, it became so frequent that they simply accepted it was a sign of their heartfelt connection.

"Those are great questions, and I suspect we will revisit them often in the years to come, but in this moment, my gut is telling me that we are not finished yet. Even though it feels like we've been here for a very long time, in truth, we haven't even been here for an hour yet. My preference is to stay a while longer and see what unfolds next. How do you feel about hanging out a while longer?" Jen quickly agreed.

"My gut is in sync with yours. So what's the next step?" Carol's response took longer than usual, and then suddenly, as if a decision had been made, she grabbed Jen's hand.

"Oh goodness! I have a plan! May I take the lead?" The fact that Jen agreed without asking any questions was an indication of the bond that these two friends shared.

"Okay, what do you want me to do?" asked Jen.

Carol repositioned them so that they were standing side-by-side looking towards the trail leading further into the darkness. "Okay, let's plant ourselves firmly into the forest floor again, and this time we are going to face the unknown while we are holding hands. Just be with me, Jen. We can do this."

Holding Jen's hand tightly, Carol did what she always does when she was in need of courage; she took several deep breaths in preparation for the next step. Then she opened her heart to whatever might unfold and readied herself to speak to the forest. "Precious One, we are in awe of your beauty and we are grateful to be in your presence. As you have observed, we fell victim to our own insecurities, which caused us to delay our journey down your pathway. Our fears and doubts stopped us in our tracks, but you came to our aid. As we stood unable to discern our next step, you revealed even more of your magnificence. We were not aware that life beings became luminescent when they sang their melodies. It was a life-altering event for us, and we are deeply grateful for the experience. We know that there is much more to learn from you and we are eager to receive your guidance." Carol bowed her head to acknowledge the forest and Jen did the same. They remained still, hoping some type of response would be heard.

Eventually, a breeze in the upper levels of the trees caught their attention. They peered upward, wondering if this movement in the trees would hold some secret that would reveal more of the mysteries that lived in this incredible forest. As the breeze became more robust, a natural event transpired. The trees began to twist and shift with the winds allowing the sunrays to burst through the forest's canopy. It was an amazing sight! Vegetation that could not be seen in the darkness was abundant everywhere and all the different species were as happy to see the sun as were they. Everyone, including Jen and Carol, reached for the sky trying to take in every spark of sunlight while it was available. And then the moment passed and the breeze stopped and the light grew dim again. Carol thought she heard the forest sigh, and perhaps she did, but only the local inhabitants knew the truth about that.

Jen remained quiet for as long as she could and then the questions began to flow. "Carol, was that sunburst event an answer to your request? Or was it just a coincidence?"

"I have no idea. Obviously, I would like to think that it was a response to my request, but whether it was or not, let's revel in this moment. We just experienced a wonderful event. If it transpired intentionally on our behalf then we are extremely fortunate. On the other hand, if it was just a natural response to ordinary wind patterns, then again, we are very fortunate that we were in the right place at the right time to bear witness to this incredible display of nature's normal way of being. Either way, I think we shared an exceptional moment."

"Yes, we did Carol, and thanks to you, we were prepared for this incident. Your plan to engage with the forest was impressive. You successfully slowed us down so that we were focused on the moment, and when you spoke directly to her, I was brought to tears. The kindness and sincerity that you exhibited could not go unnoticed. It was truly a special moment, and the synchronicity of the wind currents developing so quickly after your initial contact makes me believe that the event was intentional. Admittedly, neither of us believes in coincidences, but I am relatively certain that is not currently influencing my conclusion. Something special just happened here and I suspect more lessons were presented through this lovely phenomenon." The two friends stood quietly together just staring out into dark forest. Interestingly, the anxiety that they both shared before the incident was no longer present. Because of the brief view that they enjoyed in the sunlight, they were now able to identify some of the landmarks that were invisible to them before. Knowing what existed in the darkness released the fear that enveloped them before.

"Jen, what did you learn from this experience?" Typically, for a variety of reasons, Jen would sidestep this frequently-asked question, but today was different. She felt compelled to express her thoughts. "Actually, I think we might want to make a list, Carol, but before we begin, shall we continue our stroll down the path?" The suggestion was a surprise, but the fact that they were both in alignment with this next step was not.

"Let's do it!" replied Carol.

"Well, the first thing that I need to say is this. I am so grateful that we are together, Carol. This experience was absolutely amazing, but sharing it with you made it even more special. I am so glad we moved here and that we are exploring our spiritual journeys together. Thank you for loving me, Carol." The sentimentality of the moment demanded a pause for hugs. The tender exchange pleased the forest onlookers. It was rare for the residents of this dark forest to bear witness to such an event. They found the experience most delightful.

As was Jen's way in intimate moments, she resorted to humor. "We are having a spiritual moment, aren't we?"

"Yes, dear, I think this qualifies as a spiritual experience." The twosome giggled a bit and then continued with their stroll. In an attempt to return to the topic, Carol urged Jen to say more about what she had learned from their recent experience.

"My list is long! I'm still taken aback by the emotional shift that occurred when we entered the trail and at some point we need to discuss that more fully. And I was blown away by the way you boldly approached connecting with the forest. That was brilliant! You just decided you were going to do it and you did. Talk about decisiveness. I was so proud of you, Carol. And your courage resulted in something remarkable, which has numerous aspects to address as well, including the fact that there was communication between you and the forest. That's big! Oh, and let's not forget the spectacle itself. When the breeze came up, it didn't occur to me that the entire forest interior would be flooded with sunlight. My altered mood had me believing that we were going to be in the dark forever. It was truly a sight to behold! But!" she declared excitedly, "We mustn't forget the incredible performance before the forest opened up…remember the choral symphony that took place. Oh my goodness! So much has happened in such a small amount of time, and yet, it seems as if we have been here for hours. This has been an unbelievable experience, and I believe every aspect of it." Jen paused for a second and then remembered another point of significance. "Oh, one more thing," she announced. "Look at us now. We're walking down the path as if the darkness doesn't matter. Our mood has totally shifted again." Carol acknowledged that their moods had definitely shifted, but refrained from making another comment, because she was unclear if Jen was finished with her summary of the events.

"Please go ahead, Carol. I have more to say, but it's your time to take the lead." Giggles erupted again. The fact that Jen was a participant in the giggle attack made it perfectly clear that she was aware that she had once again responded to Carol's thoughts. Applause and praise came from Carol, while Jen just rolled her eyes and suggested they get back on task. In the meantime, the forest onlookers were tracking the progress of the two humans. Messages regarding the hikers' conversation were being sent from one species to another throughout the entire forest. En masse the forest residents discerned that the hikers' presence was most enjoyable.

"Your summary of our experiences was stellar." Internally Carol was wondering if they could actually learn all the lessons that were presented. Reviewing the experiences quickly in her mind, she realized how much information was shared. "We have work ahead of us, Jen. We really are very fortunate." Carol had a very deliberate way of thinking, breathing, speaking, and pausing. She paced herself well, and as a result, those who had the privilege of being in her presence found it very easy to listen and learn from her. Although she did not think of herself as a teacher, in truth, she was an exceptional one.

With the deep breath taken, she declared that the spectacle itself would be her focus. "Isn't it interesting, Jen, how quickly we identified the sunrays penetrating the forest interior as the 'spectacle'? That isn't a word I typically use, and I've never heard you use it before either. But it fits! That scene seemed like it was made specifically for a huge screen theater; i.e., it felt as if it was intentionally staged and presented to an audience of two. No!" she corrected herself. "I was thinking so limitedly. This event was multi-functional. It was created for a very large audience, including thousands of species residing in this forest and also two timid humans who just happened to be passing by. And we were all served." A single tear slipped down Carol's cheek as she remembered the breeze that seemed to initiate the event.

"You know what, Jen? I'm not sure how to identify the source energy that generated this event. Was it the forest, Mother Nature, or someone else? I honestly don't know, but we don't have to have all the answers in this moment. The point is something invited the breeze to come this way at just the right time for us to bear witness to a spectacle that transpires on a regular basis for all the wonderful life beings inhabiting this incredible forest world. I wonder how many people have actually seen this." Carol paused as memory raced through her mind. "Ah! We have witnessed a much smaller version of this spectacle in our backyard. When we're sitting under the trees in the shade and the wind surges, we've seen our small canopy of trees open up and allow the sun to rush through. Hmm!" she muttered. "Another lesson learned, Jen. We've had the privilege of seeing this grand spectacle, but we have a small spectacle in our own backyard that we can witness and enjoy every day. That's nice to know. This grand experience will help us to be more appreciative of what we have in our own setting." Carol went inward for a bit, but Jen knew she still had more to say, so she just kept walking.

"In our yard, we know the setting below our small canopy of trees and we know there is nothing to fear. In this adventure, the forest's yard and the tree canopy are enormous, and because we had no awareness of what awaited us in the darkness, our fears and doubts ignited within us. Our overactive minds led us to places that we didn't need to go. I believe that we were shown this magnificent example of the planet so that we will have greater appreciation and empathy for her. Not only did we witness her beauty, but we also saw how all the inhabitants collaboratively co-exist. We have much to learn from them." Carol's final comment sent Jen's mind back to the music festival that also lit up the darkness. It was a beautiful example of many different species living in peaceful harmony.

"I wonder, Carol, why the human species has such difficulty accepting differences. We don't seem to understand the merit of differences, and I wonder what it will take for us to learn this important aspect of life." Jen's comment segued into another important discussion.

"It's mind-boggling, isn't it, dear? How can a species with such amazing potential be so limited? The creatures in this forest have greater communal skills than we do. They actually mutually co-exist, while our species seems to have little regard for anyone but self. I know my words sound harsh and I acknowledge that there are many exceptions to my statement, but generally speaking, the human species has a very large blind spot when it comes to unconditional acceptance. We need help with this issue, but I wonder if we are willing to change. We have chosen a path that we assume is self-serving, but in truth, this path is leading us to destruction. Goodness!" asserted Carol. "This is depressing. I'm sorry, Jen, for bringing this up."

"You didn't bring this topic up, Carol. I did! And you're right, it definitely is a gloomy subject, but it is one that we need to face.

Change will not happen if we don't address our unpleasant truths. However, let's not go down that path now. We are already pursuing a very remarkable path that truly needs our immediate attention." The couple made a commitment to place the human condition topic on the top of their To Do List, and then, Jen took the lead again.

"Carol, may we discuss your successful attempt at connecting with the forest?" Permission was immediately granted, and without any conscious awareness, the twosome continued to stroll down the path without any qualms. They were perfectly comfortable with their circumstances, and Jen simply continued sharing her thoughts about the experience. "I was blown away by your heartfelt appeal to the essence of the forest. And I believe your openness regarding our fears and insecurities made a huge impression. I think the forest truly wanted to ease our discomfort. Did you sense that as well, or was it just my imagination?" The question stirred Carol's memory of the incident, which now seemed like a long time ago.

"Time is an amazing concept," she mumbled. "Let's put that on the To Do List as well, Jen. So much has happened in such a small amount of time that I am struggling to recall specifics that just transpired within the hour. At the time, I remember being excited about the idea of attempting to reach out to the forest. I was confused about the appropriate way of approaching an unknown entity, so I resorted to a descriptor that resonated within me. Precious One seemed like a means of honoring One and All. I think it worked, but honestly, I was just flying by the seat of my pants. This was an unusual experience for me, Jen. I was just winging it, but I was also sincere in my efforts. I am in awe of this setting. It feels like a universe to me and we were welcomed by the life forms that live within this Life Form." Carol stopped and peered into the darkness. "This Sacred Space is a microcosm of the planet. Being here is a blessing! I am so grateful." With that said, the plant life that surrounded them became luminescent. Wherever Carol and Jen looked the forest lit up as if someone had turned on a light switch.

"Is this really happening?" The question asked simultaneously was immediately answered with more light and another chorus of melodies. All were involved in this interaction. All were reaching out to the two humans. All were opening their hearts to connection.

"The answer to your question is yes. This is really happening!" Jen immediately asked her beloved if she heard the voice and was excited to learn that she had.

"Thank goodness! What do we do now?"

Carol waited to see if the invisible voice would respond to Jen's question, but after a respectable amount of time passed, she initiated more contact. "Thank you for communicating with us!" she expressed. "I don't exactly understand how this is transpiring, but we are very grateful to be in connection with you. And may I ask who you are? My name is Carol and my friend's name is Jen and we are enamored with this incredible Sacred Space." The two visitors to the trail stood perfectly still hoping for another encounter with the mysterious forest.

"We are most pleased to be in connection with both of you. Rarely do we have such an opportunity. Usually those who visit the trail are in such a hurry that they do not really spend much time with us. We are merely perceived as a means of transportation from one setting to another. Because this was your first visit to our Sacred Space, as you so accurately described our Home, you are not aware that our canopy becomes less dense ahead. We apologize that the darkness alarmed you. Our awareness of your discomfort demanded that we reach out to you. Hopefully our efforts to reassure you that we are a most congenial community diminished your anxiety."

"Yes, your kindness was noteworthy," replied Carol. "You successfully quieted our concerns and to be perfectly honest, we are in awe! Your Home is one of the most beautiful places we have ever seen. We are delighted to be here and to spend time with you. And we are so grateful that you reached out to us and allowed us to view your way of being. Your hospitality humbles us."

"We enjoyed sharing our space and our gifts with you. Your enthusiasm gives us hope that others of your kind might become more interested in our kind. We find your kind fascinating, but it saddens us that so few of your kind even notice us. We do not understand your lack of interest in species other than your own. You are a species of significant potential, but your lack of curiosity limits you. Our Home is a dynamic life system accommodating countless species that accept one another unconditionally. We enjoy each other's company and we cooperatively contribute to one another's needs and well being. Our lives may seem simple to an outsider, but in truth, we are an eco-system that strives for the good of all. Your appreciation of our natural abilities pleases us. Although our natural abilities are commonplace to us, they are, in reality, vibrant and robust. We actively engage with one another as you witnessed before, and we enjoy interacting with you now. We desire more connection with your kind. We believe if your kind opened your hearts to our kind, then this

magnificent Life Being that we all coexist upon would not be suffering as she presently is. She is not in good health. Our kind is working on her behalf as best we can, but the issues that must be addressed require the human species' involvement. We have tried for a very long time to counteract the unwise decisions made by your kind, but as your numbers and your presumed needs multiply, our kind can no longer maintain the necessary balance that is required to stabilize the planetary Life Being's health. She needs your assistance. We wish your kind would accept your role in this tragic situation. So little is required to participate in her recovery process. She simply needs her inhabitants to live in peace. Is that too much to ask? What you witnessed earlier that you described as awesome was an example of peaceful coexistence among all the species in this Sacred Space. We live this way because it is most pleasing to all of us. Not only do we enjoy our peaceful coexistence, but we also benefit from this way of being. We recommend this lifestyle to your kind and urge you to consider altering your present way of being. Chaos and conflict serves no one and it destabilizes the environment in which you coexist. We take advantage of this opportunity to express our concerns for your kind. If you do not change your ways, your future will be most unpleasant. This saddens everyone with whom you coexist. You do not have to take this path. There is another way that demands so little of you and which will bring you great joy. Be the one you are called to be. Be the one that you came here to be. Dear New Friends, please be the peaceable beings that you are intended to be. If you and all your kind choose to follow the way of peace, the planet will return to full vibrancy very quickly. That's how important your role is in this tragic equation. We have shared ourselves with you, New Friends. We hope you will share our truths, which are also your truths with others of your kind. We are most grateful for this heartfelt connection."

The forest grew even more still than it was before. Jen and Carol also remained still as they tried to digest the wisdom that was just shared with them. Profoundly moved by the candor of the unified voice, Jen was the first to broach additional conversation. "I don't know if you are still listening, but I hope you are. Your words touch me deeply. Carol and I both know that you are speaking the truth. Even though it isn't pleasant to hear, we appreciate and admire your honesty. It validates what we already believe. We know that our species is the primary cause of the planet's declining health, but you add another dimension to our awareness. Beyond our selfish disregard and maltreatment of the planet, you insinuate that our chaotic and hostile ways are also integrally involved in her decline. Can you say more about this? And please feel free to be blunt with us. We want to hear the truth. The more we learn about the impact we are having on the planet, the better we will be able to correct our wrongdoings." Jen took a deep breath as if she was finished, but then remembered another thought she wished to share. "Excuse me, but there is one more thing I wish to say. When you referred to us as New Friends, I was brought to tears. It pleases me that you think of us in that way. I am very honored to be regarded as your friend."

"Yes," interjected Carol. "I felt the same way. It is a privilege to be called New Friend and we consider you as our New Friends as well. Please tell us everything you believe we need to know. We are eager to hear the truth." The couple, avid nature lovers, desperately wanted to participate in addressing the planet's environmental crisis, but like so many others around the world, they often felt helpless, hopeless, and directionless.

"New Friends, we are also pleased to be regarded as New Friends. We are grateful for the relationship that is developing between us. Your request for more information will, of course, be presented truthfully. We know no other way to be. New Friends, allow us to clarify a misinterpretation that has transpired. We do not insinuate that your chaotic and hostile ways are problematic. We emphatically state that this is the reality of your role in the crisis. Actions that perpetrate ill will towards another are profoundly harmful not only to the victim, but also to the planet upon which we all live. She cannot escape the cruelties of ill will. Wherever these acts are perpetrated, she is there. She feels every insult, every injury, and every harmful act that is executed. Each of these misdeeds creates toxic negative energy, which is the equivalent of injecting her with poison. Ponder this, New Friends. Your kind commits acts of ill will on a regular basis, and your population nears eight billion. Can you imagine how many injections of poison she receives every day. The numbers are staggering. No wonder she is so ill." The voice paused, allowing time for the unthinkable message to be comprehended. The New Friends were stunned but committed to hearing more.

"New Friends, we are sorry to burden the two of you with such grave news, but it must be done. Unless your kind realizes the scope of their situation, they will not understand the need for change. Humankind's negative behavior is so toxic that they are the primary factor in the planet's crisis situation. She cannot continue to absorb this negative energy. It is killing her.

"The solution to this crisis rests in the hearts of the human species. Cure your ill will and the planet will rejuvenate very quickly. She is capable of recovery because she is a very resilient Life Being. Or you can continue your present way of being and your demise will precede hers. We hope your kind will hear the truth and understand

that there is an option that can result in survival. In peace be, New Friends. It is the way to the future."

The forest fell silent again. The breeze stopped blowing, the melodies ended, and the voice that shared the essence of the Sacred Space was no more. The interaction concluded. The two New Friends remained still, ruminating over the information just received. As their New Friends had suggested, there was much to ponder. Eventually, the familiar deep breaths were inhaled indicating that the couple was ready to discern their next step.

"Jen, dear, are you ready to return home?" Carol's thoughts were elsewhere. So much had transpired that she needed quality time with her journal. She suspected Jen was in a similar place, but did not want to rush her if she wanted or needed more time on the trail.

"Not to worry, Carol. Although it is not easy to leave this Sacred Space, I too need time to mull over our adventure. This is one that will never be forgotten. I am ready to leave when you are."

"Dear One, it is so helpful when you respond to my thoughts. It makes communication so much easier. Before we leave shall we say goodbye to our New Friends?" And this they did. Heartfelt gratitude was expressed followed by commitments to visit again soon, and then they waved to their New Friends. Much to the couple's delight the plant life responded to their goodbyes by illuminating the forest once again. The more the nature lovers waved, the more the forest lit up on their behalf. It was another fantastic light show that would never be forgotten. Jen and Carol reluctantly turned away and headed hand-in-hand towards the trailhead entrance. No words were spoken. Each was lost in the vast universe of her mind, and neither had any sense of the time elapsed or the space they had just traversed. All they remembered was waving goodbye to their New Friends, and then arriving at the trail entryway. Before heading to the car, the twosome turned around to take another look into the dark forest. They each remembered their hesitation about entering into the darkness and they would never forget the beauty that was discovered.

Seven

On a planet far, far away from the planet of origin, the descendants of ancient travelers celebrated those from long ago who had remained behind. Years had passed since the separation occurred, but these special ones were still remembered. Hearts ached for the sacrifices that were made and sweet memories were frequently and purposefully shared with those of the day. Those who had traveled far did not want those who remained behind to ever be forgotten. The tradition of celebrating and honoring those who bravely volunteered to stay began immediately upon their arrival to the new location. Their new setting, which was rich and abundant with natural resources, was a haven for the travelers who desperately needed a new home.

With good intentions, the travelers were welcomed to the new planet. A lush, fertile area of land was designated for the newcomers to establish their community. The work was hard but the travelers were determined to create a new viable existence upon the land that was presented to them. Their settlement flourished and their numbers expanded and soon the newcomers required more space for their species. Had they simply asked for more space it would have been gladly provided, but this courtesy was not afforded to the gracious planetary Life Being. Instead, the new species expanded their settlement without following the proper protocols. Permission was not requested. The needs of other species already residing upon the planet were not taken into consideration. It was a lapse of good manners that was noticed with concern.

As time passed and more generations came into being, the memories of those who came before were lost. The celebrations for those who had done so much for those who followed fell by the wayside. Why celebrate those who were no longer significant to those of the present? That which was feared had come to be. The past was no longer relevant, the future was yet to be, and the present was evolving in ways that were reminiscent of times that were lived before.

Those of ancient beginnings observed from afar, and from somewhere in the never-ending universe, a softly spoken acknowledgement was heard. *Not again,* the whisperer said. A plea, a prayer, a command? The unknown speaker offered nothing more, but all who heard the whisper wondered what awaited the species whose progenitors had behaved in similar ways.

Eight

"Janet, dear, where are you? I am in need of your capable hands." Peter Hanson had already checked the usual spots where is beloved wife typically preferred to hang out, but so far, she was not to be found. *Where on Earth is she?* His thoughts revealed his frustration. Peter was a man of extreme focus, and when he was on task, his tolerance for distractions or delays was limited. He called out again hoping that she would answer, but once again he heard nothing but silence. *Oh, dear woman, love of my life, will you please respond to my thoughts!*

"Peter! I'm in the tree house. If you're coming this way will you bring me a cup of tea, please?" Peter poured the tea and was out the back door in a flash. He could see his beloved sitting on the platform that she referred to as the tree house. In truth, it once was a tree house, but it was removed from the tree when it appeared to be causing stress to the aging branches that had held it up for decades. Janet simply couldn't let go of this favorite childhood hideaway, so he created a new stilted foundation for it and placed the new tree house under the beloved tree just below its previous location. Janet was very pleased with the transformation and admitted the new getaway was more suitable for a woman of her age. Peter was relieved that she only had to climb three small steps to the new tree house rather than fifteen, which she had managed for more years than she would tell.

"Hello, dear, I've been looking all over the house for you! Should have known the best way to connect with you was through our inner voices. Thank you for responding so quickly, dear." Peter's frustrations immediately dissipated once he located his best friend and spouse of over sixty years. "Have you been out here since the crack of dawn, dear wife of mine?" She admitted that she had as Peter used the railing to get up the steps to the platform. They shared a good morning kiss, which was a habit of long-standing, before he handed the cup of tea to his beloved. "May I join you, dear?" he asked politely feeling confident that he would be invited.

"Oh, yes!" she answered excitedly. "I would love for you to join me. Tell me, dear, why were you searching for me. Are you in need of my capable hands?"

"Yes, I must admit it's so. You know how these old bear paws are. It never occurred to me that in my elder years buttons would get the best of me. From now on, I'm only buying pullover shirts. These buttons are just a nuisance. It is no way to start the day."

"You're right, Peter, this is a nuisance. But you are looking dapper as usual. You must be having trouble with the cuffs again." He nodded and raised both arms to prove his point. Janet reached over and quickly secured both of the buttons. "I agree with your plan! Pullovers are the way to go! So what's on your agenda today, Peter?" Her husband recognized that tone immediately. She was up to something.

"Nothing in particular, dear. I was just planning to have a relaxing day, but I can tell from the tone of your voice that something is brewing. So tell me. What's going on?' His question was playfully firm. Peter never doubted his wife's creative streak. She was always up to something and regardless of what it was; they always had a great time.

"Well actually my plan is to have a relaxing day as well." The answer surprised her husband, but he knew there was more to her plan. "However," she continued, "I thought we might practice some of our inner work exercises while we enjoy a quiet day."

"Janet, that's a wonderful idea," Peter's reply delighted his wife. He knew that she was trying to expand inner communication skills, and he was equally interested in doing the same. "Can we do our exercises here in the tree house? This is such a wonderful setting and I think it facilitates our abilities. Are you okay with doing our explorations out here in your favorite space?"

Janet was beaming. "We are definitely on the same wavelength this morning. I was hoping that you would be amenable to doing our exercises in this setting. Thank you for being my love."

"Easiest thing I've ever done. Certainly easier than the first time I saw you strolling down the sidewalk. Geez! You were gorgeous. It was love at first sight." The two old friends giggled about that precious moment. What Peter didn't know at the time was that Janet was having the same reaction to him. As teenagers will do, they each pretended not to be interested and walked right by each other without any type of acknowledgement. He wanted to say hello, but the word would not come out of his mouth. And Janet was so shy that she couldn't even imagine speaking to him. Nonetheless, that was the beginning of a relationship that continued to this day. And here they were both in their eighties sitting in a tree house still trying to discover how to better articulate their wishes to each other and to the world at large.

"So, tell me, Janet, what exactly is your plan?" Peter thoughts went to breakfast and his wife immediately confirmed that food was on the top of her To Do List.

"Yes, dear, we absolutely need to treat ourselves first or we will not be able to focus on the tasks at hand. So, I suggest we return to the house and, while I make something fabulous for us, you will have time to gather your journal and other necessary items that you want handy for our exercises. And if you will, please grab the Tibetan bowl from my Sacred Space." With those suggestions made, the couple headed back towards the aged, but well preserved home that Janet had grown up in. Returning to this property was a dream come true for both of them. After her parents passed and the grieving subsided, the couple began refurbishing the place on the weekends. It took a while, but it was a creative project that they both immensely enjoyed. Even though they made a lot of changes to the old place, the love energy that existed within its walls remained. It was still the home of the heart that embraced Janet as a child and continued to do so even now when she was way beyond that phase of life. She and Peter felt very privileged to live in the space that her parents had enjoyed all of their adult lives. It was the gift of memories, comfort, and safety…it was home!

Within minutes, the kitchen was filled with delicious aromas. The scones that were made the day before were warming in the toaster oven, the coffee was brewing, and a bowl of fresh fruit was sliced and ready to be enjoyed. The breakfast smells drifting throughout the house reminded Peter to hasten his pace. Journal and accessories were carefully packed in his favorite cardboard box that his beloved had created for him years ago. It was a very efficient tool adorned with two handles that made it very easy to transport small items from one setting to another, and of course, her creative self demanded that the box be tastefully decorated in a manly sort of way. Best of all, it was a very clever way of reusing something that would typically be tossed aside and end up in a landfill.

As he neared the kitchen, his senses jumped for joy. "Yes! We're having scones!" he declared from the hallway. "And not just any old scones," he continued. "We are having Great-grandmother Harriet's orange-cranberry scones with chopped pecans." This special recipe had been handed down through the family for generations, and her descendants were still singing her praises.

"Oh my goodness, Janet, you've created a feast. Shall we dine in the tree house?" Peter's suggestion was exactly what his wife was thinking.

As she replied with a wink and a grin, she grabbed the designated kitchen cardboard box (appropriately decorated) and started carefully packing their morning food supplies. Once the scones, coffee thermos, water bottles, fruit dish, and necessary kitchenware were packed, she snatched a chocolate bar and a small container of almonds from the pantry. "Just in case!" she announced. "Did you remember the Tibetan bowl, dear?" Reassured by Peter's nod, she took a deep breath, reviewed her mental checklist, and determined that they were properly prepared for the tasks ahead. "I'm ready if you are, dear!" With their cardboard boxes in hand, they returned to the tree house. Once they arrived, Peter quickly grabbed the coffee thermos and reiterated that breakfast must be addressed. Janet plated the scones and fresh fruit while her husband filled their cups and then they relaxed into their chairs.

"Thank you for joining me, Peter. I feel a sense of urgency, dear, but what it means escapes me. I hope you may be able to assist me with that."

"How long have you been experiencing this, Janet?" Her response was a bit worrisome. He was surprised to hear that she had been dealing with this unknown factor for several days.

"Oh, goodness!" he replied. "Of course, I will try to assist you in any way that I can. But I must take issue with you, dear. Remember, we've discussed this before, and we both agreed that if some perplexing or unusual experience surfaced, we would reach out. I'm so sorry that I was not able to pick up on your discomfort, dear. You must remember that my intuitive skills are not comparable to yours."

Janet reached out to her husband and tightly squeezed his hand. "I'm reaching out now, Peter. I haven't been in discomfort, dear, and I promise you that I am still committed to the agreement we made. But I believe whatever is going on is intended to be a learning experience. I'm on the cusp of something, and at times it seems so close, literally within reach, and then, in an instant it eludes me. This sensation that I'm feeling is a message, Peter. I'm convinced that it is. I've really tried to discern what is going on, but I'm getting nowhere. So, maybe together we can figure out what this latest message is about." Janet's spiritual journey remained a mystery to Peter, but he never doubted what she shared with him. He simply trusted her and accepted that her experiences were real. He knew for a fact that her ability to communicate without vocalizing her words was stunning. While his ability bordered on pathetic, he was enjoying small advances that to him were notable. This morning's connection was a good example of that. He simply reached out with his thoughts and she immediately responded to him. Although he had no idea how this actually happens, he found it very curious and he wanted to learn more. And Janet was a very good teacher and role model.

"Okay, dear! I'm definitely up for this task, but can we please have our breakfast first?"

"Absolutely, dear. Where are my manners? So sorry for that distraction! Let's take the first bite together!" The first bite was a central feature in this couple's life. All meals, not just breakfast, included the first bite ceremony. Simple, yet connective, the first bite honored their relationship as well as the meal. "Oh yum!" uttered Janet. "If only Great-grandmother Harriet were here to enjoy this tasty treat!"

Peter followed with his own yummy sounds and mentioned that it must give her great pleasure to see all her relatives still enjoying these delicious scones.

"Do you believe she is still here, Peter?" Janet's question revealed her ever-present curiosity about the crossing-over process. Her husband took another bite of the scone before answering the question. It was one discussed numerous times and he still didn't know the answer.

"As you well know, dear, I don't know the answer to your question, but your interest in this possibility makes me more open to the possibility. We both have heard remarkable stories from friends and associates who claim they have had encounters with loved ones who passed. I admire these people and can see no reason why they would lie about their experiences. In fact, the way each one described his or her scenario was so deeply moving that it seems unkind and disrespectful not to believe them. Why did you ask that question, dear? Does it have something to do with your sense of urgency?" Peter took a bite of fruit as he carefully observed his spouse's behavior. She was pensive, which was common for her, but there was something more that he couldn't identify. She didn't seem to be in her body. As this thought whirled through his mind, Peter was taken aback. The unspoken comment totally surprised him, but it also caught Janet's attention.

"Peter, that was an astute observation! Why didn't I think of that?" she asked curiously. "Maybe, what I am identifying as a sense of urgency is a misinterpretation. Maybe, I'm out of alignment! Oh, Peter, this is a brilliant idea. After we finish breakfast, will you help me realign myself?" Her husband calmly nodded his willingness to do so, even though he had no idea what a re-alignment entailed.

"Now, don't worry about this, dear. It's an easy procedure that you will benefit from as well. It's an important aspect of taking care of oneself, and I completely spaced on it. I don't even remember the last time I adjusted myself. Oh dear, Peter, I hope my mind isn't going by the wayside." This made her husband laugh aloud.

"Janet, you are the last person who needs to worry about losing your mind. You're as sharp now as you were in your teens. Now, tell me exactly what are we going to do, and how am I to assist?"

"Okay," she said excitedly. "First, let's move our breakfast table just a little bit so that it is out of our way during the process. Great! Now, let's shift our chairs so that we both are facing the yard." Janet checked the arrangement and declared it was perfect for the work that needed to be done. "Now, comes the educative part, Peter. What you need to know is that we are comprised of a physical form, which is self-evident, and also an energy form, which is rarely evident to most of us. These two essential elements of our existence are at their best, when they are in alignment with one another. That is to say, we are at our best when our physical and energy forms are in balance. The thought you had earlier about me not being in my body was profoundly significant. What I've noticed over the years is that when I become clumsy, such as bumping into a table or a door jam, or frequently stumbling on a walk, these behaviors are actually a sign that I am out of balance. Before I became aware of this connection, I would just try to blow the incidents off as a symptom of being overly fatigued. And truthfully, sometimes fatigue can cause these symptoms; however, as you well know, I am not someone who tends to be clumsy. Even at this age, I am still steady on my feet." Her husband affirmed that assessment.

"I've always thought of you as someone who is very agile, Janet. This surprises me. Have you noticed any clumsiness the last few days?"

"Well, I didn't think about it at the time, but in retrospect, I remember bumping into the door jam twice because the mishaps left me with a small bruise. And both times the incident occurred on my left side, which means my energy form has shifted to the left and is out of alignment with my physical form. So, that's what we need to work on before we address the urgency issue." Peter was a little apprehensive. Never having done this before, he wasn't exactly sure how he was to help.

"Not to worry, dear, you are not the solo practitioner in this process. We will do this together and all you have to do is follow my lead. We will proceed from a meditative state, which is very familiar to you, and then, we will use guided imagery to tackle the alignment problem. You can do this, Peter, and your presence will be very helpful."

The process began as meditations always do. Deep breaths were inhaled, eyes were closed, and each participant prepared, as they were accustomed to do. Since Janet and Peter were seasoned meditators, it took very little time for them to sink into a peaceful state of being. Leading guided meditations was easy for Janet. She had taught classes for years and came to know when the participants were ready to proceed. Because of her exceptional relationship with her husband, it was easy to assess his state of readiness.

She began with a very soft voice. "Thank you, Peter, for joining me on this never-ending journey. I am so grateful for your companionship. Join me now, please, and take another deep breath before we begin the alignment process." The breaths requested were taken by the beloved couple and also by those who were unseen.

"Be with me, Peter." Pacing her words to a rhythm that both were habituated to, the alignment process began with grace. "And with your mind's eye visualize the two of us sitting here side-by-side. What you visualize is the physical form that you are accustomed to seeing. But now I ask you to see more expansively. In your heart please accept the reality that within us also exists an energy form that is purposefully in alignment with our physical form. This energy form is the essence of who we really are. Please accept this reality, Peter, and allow this reality to help you to assist me. In so doing, you will also be assisted." Janet paused and addressed her own rhythmic pace while allowing Peter to have time to consume the information that was just presented. Time passed, but was not noticed. Janet simply knew when it was time to continue.

"So once again, dear, let us utilize our inner vision to see more expansively. Look closely with the mind's eyes and you will see there is a translucent haze that seems to be embracing our physical forms. Observe your energy form first, Peter. Study how it wraps around your entire physical form. It is barely visible, but it is there. And you can see it with your expansive vision. Now notice if your energy form is in alignment with your physical form or if it is irregular. Is it larger on one side than the other? Is it bulging anywhere? Is there anything about the translucent haze that seems out of place? If there is, then intentionally move that anomaly back into alignment. Now, dear, while you are making your adjustments, I'm going to observe my energy form." Time passed again without the couple's notice, until Janet realized it was time to take the next step. How she knew is a mystery, but after years of experiencing this unusual process, she simply trusted it.

"Peter, are you ready to proceed? Just let me know with your inner voice."

"I'm ready, dear. My energy form was slightly larger on the right side of my physical form and I was able to shift it over so that both sides are in balance. I've also observed your energy form and it is definitely out of balance on the left side. When you are ready to make the adjustment, I will be ready to assist."

"Let's take a few more deep breaths, Peter, before we initiate the alignment." The suggestion was wise. Janet slowed the pace down. "Okay, Peter, please assist me in shifting my energy form to the right." The adjustment was quickly done and Janet was realigned and in balance again. "Thank you, Peter, for assisting me. You made the process so much easier. Take a another deep breath, and when you are ready, return to the tree house."

"Wow! That was incredible!" Peter was in awe. He couldn't believe what just transpired, and yet, he believed everything that happened. "How are you dear? Do you feel any different than before?"

"Perhaps, you would like to answer that question first, Peter?" The nudge worked. Her husband had many things to say and questions to ask, but he wanted to focus upon the alignment exercise first.

"Janet, your guided meditation was exceptional. I had no idea it was such an effective teaching tool. Your suggestion that I could see more expansively was amazing. It really worked! In my mind's eye, I could see the energy form that you described. It was vague, almost invisible, but it was there. And then the need for the energy form and physical form to be in alignment made sense. It's similar to having a tire on the car that is out of balance with the other three tires. The car becomes wonky because of the imbalance. This equates to what you were talking about earlier when you recollected walking into tables and door jams. If one side of you is heavier than the other then you will drift in that direction without even knowing it is happening. I get it!" Peter was very excited about his new discoveries, but he still wanted to now how his dear sweet wife was doing.

"What about you, dear? How are you doing?" Sometimes, Janet deflected questions about herself, but this time he intended to be persistent.

"Not to worry, dear. I'm not going to evade the questions. Truth is, I'm not sure how I am. The exercise revealed what was anticipated. That's good! And it was an extremely important reminder to be vigilant about checking our alignment. It's an easy thing to do. We just witnessed that. So maybe, we should devise a schedule so that we remember to do this on a regular and frequent basis." Janet paused and seemed to go away. When she did this, Peter tended to let her be, but on this occasion, he intervened.

"Thank you for bringing me back to focus, Peter. I was briefly lost in myself, but now, thanks to you, I am back. So, regarding how I am, there are several answers. First, it was exciting to do this work with you. I knew we would discover new horizons and we did. Secondly, I am equally excited about realigning my body. I will be on the lookout for any clumsiness that might transpire. And third," Janet paused and took a deep breath. She attempted to start again, but hesitated. Finally, Peter intervened again and suggested she just bite the bullet and say whatever she needs to say. "You're right, of course. Okay! Peter, did you have a feeling that we were not alone during the meditation?" The question took him by surprise. He didn't know how to respond.

"Dear, perhaps this is one of those times when you should answer the question first." His calm, sweet manner tickled them both and resulted in a wave of giggles. "I'm modeling your behavior!" Peter's faced was adorned with an ear-to-ear grin.

"Well, you certainly are a fast learner," she retorted. "Okay, you're absolutely right. I just need to express my thoughts rather than handing the question over to you. Once again, Peter, I have had the sense that we are not alone when we do our meditations. I don't know why this surprises me because, as you well know, I believe we are always accompanied. But sometimes the energy is different from our usual companions and that is what confuses me. I actually sensed this energy before the meditation began, and that's why I asked if you thought Great-grandmother Harriet was still here. We were praising her scones and I just had a sense that she was with us. So when the meditation began and the sensation continued, I was curious." In an attempt to reassure her husband that she was not alarmed about the experience, she reminded him that she was very open to and accepting of the idea of multi-dimensional connections and interactions. "Perhaps it is wishful thinking that it might be Harriet, but it would be a hoot to connect with her. On the other had, I would be tickled to connect with any of our companions, or others as well. The point being, I believe we are being visited and I would like to be more deliberate in trying to connect with them." Peter immediately responded positively, but admitted this was not an area of expertise.

"It isn't one of my skill sets either, dear," replied his wife. "But we are both open to the possibility, so let's just play with this and see what happens." Peter admired is wife. She was spunky and tenacious. Once she set her mind to something, she was determined to see the idea through to a conclusion. Peter accurately assumed that this was the birthing process of one of those scenarios.

"Well, I'm onboard!" he declared. "Am I correct in assuming that you will guide us both through this adventure just as you did with the alignment procedure?"

"Yes, I will take the lead, but remember, dear, I am a novice at this. In our previous endeavor, I was knowledgeable about the issue. That's not the case in this situation. So I suggest that we both try to be very flexible and ready to make adjustments as needed." Peter agreed with her suggestion and expressed his readiness to begin.

"Wonderful! Then, let's begin!" The couple adjusted their respective chairs and made themselves comfortable again. Deep breaths led the way as Janet and Peter embarked upon another adventure. "Ah! I see we are both in a state of serenity. Thank you all who assisted us in our travels to this place of tranquility. We are most grateful to be here." Once again, the pacing of Janet's voice was sublime. Her spoken voice did not interfere with the journey, but actually enhanced the experience.

"Dear Friends, we come to visit you as you so often visit us. I don't know why this never occurred to me before. I am often aware of your presence, but I have been reluctant to connect. Today I am emboldened to do so. Peter and I desire connection with you. Is that possible? And how do we facilitate such an interaction?" Janet took a deep breath not knowing if her request was heard. Immediately, the wind chimes near the tree house sounded even though there was no breeze to cause that reaction.

"Was that you, Dear Friends? Did you cause the chimes to ring?" Peter was glad she asked about the chimes. He too was curious about the synchronicity of the response.

The chimes rang again, more powerfully this time, while the breeze was as still as before. Something unusual was transpiring. Janet could not control her excitement.

"Oh my goodness! You really are here! I knew it wasn't my imagination!" Peter could tell that Janet's excitement was distracting her so he intervened.

"Perhaps you might ask for an identity from the one you are connecting with, dear." His nudge brought her back to task immediately.

"Oh dear me! I'm so sorry, but this is a riveting experience! Is there someway that you can reveal your identity to us? We would love to know who accompanies us during our meditation." Once again, the chimes resounded and this time they were accompanied by the smell of freshly baked orange cranberry scones. Peter quickly grabbed the plate of scones from the breakfast area to see if that was the origin of the smell, but it definitely was not. The delicious smell wafting through the tree house was far more robust than the scones that were no longer warm.

"Janet, I think your Great-grandmother is here!" With that said, the chimes let lose a melodious tune that carried through the backyard. Tears came to Janet's eyes as her dream was actualized. "Dear One, this is your time to say whatever it is you want to say. And I for one really want to thank you, Harriet, for your recipe. You witnessed this morning how much we enjoy them. And now that we know you are here, we hope you will join us whenever you like. Your company is always welcome." Once again, the chimes resounded in response to Peter's lovely comments.

"I knew you were here, Nana! And having a chance to connect with you is so delightful. Are you well?" The chimes answered the question. "And Mom and Dad, are they okay as well." The chimes loudly rang again. Questions raced through Janet's mind, but she didn't know which ones to ask. They seemed trivial and she didn't want to waste precious time. And then she returned to focus.

"Nana, is there another way to connect with you?" The chimes reacted. "If we use existential communication, will that facilitate conversation with you?" Again the chimes reacted. Janet turned to Peter and informed him that she was going for it. "Hopefully, you will be able to hear what transpires, but if not, just stay with me. Okay?"

"Of course, dear. Just do what you need to do!" The sincerity in his voice urged her to take the next step. The crucial deep breath was taken.

Reaching out to her Great-grandmother through her inner voice, Janet said, *"Nana, can you hear me."*

"Yes, dear, I can hear you loud and clear. I am so glad you finally decided to venture into this arena. You've been ready for a long time, and now at last, you have made connection beyond your own realm of existence. What an achievement this is! I always knew that you could do this. Congratulations, Little One! You were always such a bright star." Janet, beaming like a youngster, turned to Peter to see if he could hear the conversation. He gave her a thumbs up.

"Not to worry, Janet. Peter can hear our conversation as well as you can. He really is a wonderful man. You chose very wisely, dear! Everyone is very proud of your accomplishments, and we are particularly pleased about today's achievement. We have been reaching out to you for some time, and we are very grateful that this connection has finally been secured. Dear Ones, I need both of you to listen up. There are topics that must be discussed today and in the days to come, and we need you to listen carefully because action must be taken. Changes are coming! As you well know, the Earth is not in good health. This reality is evident but for reasons that escape me, there are people who are deliberately giving misinformation about her circumstances. Because of this, she continues to decline. Her ability to continue is decreasing at an alarming rate. Unless she receives immediate attention, she will succumb to the stress that humankind places upon her. Others who are far more learned than I will provide you with more information, but you must understand that the situation is critical. She is on the verge of entering into dormancy, and the catastrophic ramifications of this are unthinkable."

The couple did indeed listen carefully. Although the news about the planet's situation was not new to them, it was more profoundly stated than the Hansons had heard before. Each sat perfectly still trying to assimilate the information. From afar, those who were observing this interaction eagerly awaited a response from Harriet's descendants.

"I'm sorry to speak so bluntly with you, Dear Ones, but the circumstances demand that action be taken. Not only are the people of your generation being impacted by what is transpiring, but so too are the children of the future. What is happening will have lasting consequences. The truth must be spoken so that people fully understand what is at stake here. Unfortunately, few are listening to the limited information that is now being provided, and many who are listening hear what they prefer to hear. Obviously, no one wants to hear the truth because it is too frightening to even imagine such a catastrophe, much less accept that it is a reality rapidly unfolding. Take deep breaths, Dear Ones. I know this is difficult to hear."

Peter was the first to respond. Clearing his throat, he attempted to find words that could accurately articulate his feelings. It was not easy. He instinctively responded orally, "I can't imagine what it was like to deliver that message, Harriet. It took a lot of courage...and a lot of love to do what you just did. Now, I understand why everyone spoke so highly of you. Your contemporaries admired you so much, and as you can see, Janet still does." His beloved with tears trickling down her face reached over and squeezed his hand. It was a lovely gesture that communicated her gratitude, and also gave him time to take another necessary breath. "The news you shared is devastating. It takes one's breath away, but we needed to hear it. There's a part of me that wants to run away from this, Harriet. I'm ashamed to admit it, but this is so enormous that I just want to bury my head in the sand. But I know we can't do that. People have been denying and ignoring the evidence for far too long and now here we are in this planetary crisis. You're right, Harriet. Action must be taken. Thank you for making this huge effort to connect with us. I hope you will continue to be available. I think we will really need your guidance in the days to come." First, the chimes rang and then Harriet replied via her current means of communication.

"Thank you, Peter, for your kind words and also for your honesty. Indeed, these are troubling times, and it is human nature to focus upon positive matters while ignoring negative ones. While it is understandable that people do not want to think about this terrible situation, they must! Everyone must accept responsibility for what is happening. Denying one's culpability for this crisis serves no purpose. It wastes precious time that is rapidly running out. Humankind is responsible for the Earth's crisis. Like it or not, this is our truth and we must face it, accept it, and take action. We are the only ones who can save her. There is much more to be said about this, but I wish to check in with you, Janet. How are you, Dear One?"

"I'm a bit overwhelmed, Nana." Janet, like her husband, also reverted to speaking orally, and didn't even notice that she had done so. "Like Peter, I am deeply grateful for your candor and for your courage. This is a difficult task, Nana, and you did it well." A loud sigh escaped from Janet. "You're living your calling, aren't you Nana?" The question altered the topic but it was one that needed answering.

"Yes, Dear One, I am. One's purpose for being doesn't stop when you cross over. You have presumed that for a long time and now you have confirmation that you were correct. Our reason for being continues until it reaches completion. Our forms may change and our locations, but the work continues. Obviously, my love for the Earth continues to live within me and the commitment I made to her long ago still stands. So, yes, Dear One, my coming here today is multi-purposeful. I come to see my beloved Great-granddaughter and I come on behalf of the Earth's well being.

Multi-tasking runs in our family, as you well know." The last comment made Peter roll his eyes. His beloved was indeed the queen of multi-tasking.

"Thank you, Nana, it feels good to have that idea confirmed. And it also makes me ponder the commitments that were made prior to arriving here. Is it safe to presume that Peter and I made similar commitments when we came into this lifetime?"

"Yes, it is! Sometimes, commitments can be completed in a single lifetime, but often it takes many lifetimes. This is not an indication that one is a slow learner, but instead connotes the complexity of the commitment. Many have made commitments of long-standing to the Life Being who has done so much for so many. She has nurtured our life experiences and we are indebted to her care for us. Thus, we continue working on her behalf from whatever location we currently reside in."

"Nana, I remember when I was very young, people referred to you as a woman of wisdom. At the time my understanding of that statement was limited. Now, the reality of its expansiveness amazes me. I am so grateful that you have come back to us. Thank you." The chimes shared their melodious treasures, as all who were present remained silent. Those from afar were very pleased. The connection of multi-dimensional descendants was successful and opened doors for more communication.

"Harriet may I asked another question?" proposed Peter. The chimes sounded in a timely fashion and Janet nudged him forward. "You indicated that there was much more to discuss and I wonder if we should develop a schedule for this. I assume, perhaps incorrectly, that this means of connecting is very draining for you. And now that I think about it, my fatigue level is high at the moment. Point being, do you want to continue the conversation now or at another time?"

"Your administrative skills remain solid, Peter. Thank you, for proposing the idea of a daily schedule. Does this time of day suit you? I am very flexible." They all agreed that the early hour was a lovely time to meet. Sweet goodbyes and more words of gratitude were expressed before the chimes properly closed the wonderful unusual event.

"Well, dear, the morning has been full," Peter's softly spoken comment set off a round of laughter. It was rejuvenating for both of them. So much had happened in such a short time that it was hard to remember it all. While shifting their chairs to face one another, Peter noticed the scones and realized how hungry he was. His eyes went to his beloved who immediately knew what he was thinking.

"Would you like a scone, dear?" she giggled as she plated the scones for both of them. She then poured two glasses of water to exchange for the cold coffee cups that were never finished. They sighed simultaneously before taking the second first bite of the morning. The first bite was refreshing and energized Peter to pose a question.

"What do you make of all this, Janet? It was a fascinating morning, and I feel supercharged about it, but I'm very curious to hear your take on the subject." The deep breath was heard, as the pensive face appeared.

"How do I begin? What a morning we've had! The alignment session was both educational and beneficial and I am so grateful that we experienced it before the following events transpired. Actually, I think it prepared us for what transpired. And of course, Peter, the communication with Nana was a 'never forget' moment. My goodness, what a treat! The entire experience was fascinating. First the chimes, and then actually being able to hear her voice telepathically...all I can say is thank you, thank you, thank you. It was her, Peter! I don't have any doubts about it. She's still a force of nature. Bold, tenacious, kind, and compassionate. What a blessing that was! And of course, the information she presented to us is another experience in itself. We've known for years that the Earth was in trouble, but like most people we haven't known what to do. I think we're going to get a lot more information about this from Nana and hopefully we will be able to assist in some useful way." Another deep breath was heard, but Peter knew there was more to come.

"Basically, I think this was a wakeup call, dear. And I think we are going to discover that we are being called to fulfill a commitment made long, long ago. I think this is the urgency that I've been feeling and the alignment process readied me for what is coming. How about you, dear? How do you feel about what happened here in the tree house?" Peter wondered if somehow the tree house played a role in connecting Janet with her Great-grandmother. His thoughts were unintentionally picked up by his beloved who immediately intervened.

"That was an incredible idea, Peter. You know the tree house was built when she was a child. This was her tree house, then my mother's, and then mine. Isn't this interesting?" Peter agreed it was very interesting. "Sorry to interrupt you, dear. Please continue."

"Well, as you said, this was a memorable morning, an unforgettable morning. I believe everything that transpired, Janet, and still, it was unbelievable. I feel so grateful to be part of this. Even though we've been having some success with our inner communication, I never thought that it could turn into this. My goodness, dear, we just talked to someone who has been dead for decades. You've been right all along, Janet. Life goes on. Harriet still exists and so do your parents."

"And so we will, Peter. There so much more in existence than we can even imagine, but this morning we got a little glimpse of the more that awaits us."

"Yes, we did, and I believe Harriet implied that we may be hearing from others. In fact, she said 'others who are far wiser than me.' Janet, I'm beside myself." Peter giggled a bit and then asked, "Does this mean I'm out of alignment again?" Another round of laughter overtook the couple.

"Actually, dear, I think it means we've had a full morning." And with that said, the two old friends repacked their respective cardboard boxes and headed for the house that held many memories.

Nine

"Jonathan, have you seen the Hansons lately?" inquired Geri whose face was hiding behind the daily newspaper that she was reading.

Jon replied that he hadn't before lowering his newspaper. "Why do you ask, dear?"

"Oh no reason in particular. I was just thinking about them this morning and was wondering how they are doing. You know we do need to be more attentive to them. Even though they are both healthy and strong, they are aging."

"So are we, Geri, but I see your point. Why don't we see if they are available for dinner sometime this week? We can tell them about our latest adventure, and I'm sure they will have news as well. Those two are always up to something. They're a remarkable couple and wonderful role models. It's always good to be in their company." Geraldine agreed with her husband's suggestion and decided to call them immediately. As always, the cellphone was elsewhere.

"It's in the living room, dear."

"You just replied to my thoughts, Jon." He denied doing so and explained he had merely deduced that the phone had escaped her again, and he remembered seeing it on the coffee table earlier when he walked through the room. She ignored his rationale and went to retrieve the phone.

"Janet, this is Geri! How are you two doing?" Jonathan heard nothing but silence coming from the living room and couldn't help but wonder what was going on. Just as he left the table to check on things, he heard Geri say, "Oh my goodness! Can you come over this evening? We would love to hear about this! No need to bring anything but yourselves. We have everything we need to create something delicious. Six o'clock is perfect! See you then!"

"Well, from the little I heard it sounds like an interesting evening is in the making," Jon was delighted by the prospect of having time with Janet and Peter. They were wonderful folks, who always had the most interesting stories to share.

"It seems that our phone call was serendipitous. They apparently had an unusual experience in the tree house this morning. Jon, do you think we could finish sprucing up the new dining area in the outer garden. It only needs a few finishing touches, and I know our garden companions would love their company. It would be a perfect place to share stories this evening." Her husband agreed and immediately; the duo took on the task.

Jon grabbed the necessary garden tools, while Geri placed the acacia folding chairs on the little red wagon from her childhood. It was the handiest tool of all. Once they reached the work in progress and gave it a fresh look, they realized it was already finished. Jonathan did just a bit of raking and cleaning up while Geri unloaded the chairs and headed back to get the matching acacia table. Within minutes the new dining area was ready for entertaining.

"Geri, this looks wonderful. The acacia furniture is perfect here in our little forest. You were right. Great decision!" The couple stood back and admired the new addition to their outer garden.

Geri, speaking specifically to the garden, expressed her thoughts about the new setting they had just completed. "We hope all of you are pleased with the changes made. Your guidance during the process was invaluable. If there is anything that needs changing just let us know. By the way, we have invited the Hansons over this evening. You've met them before, but they haven't seen the recent changes so we will take them for a stroll before dinner if that's okay with you. I suspect you will enjoy their stories.

Over at the Hansons' house, Janet was busying about the kitchen gathering up the ingredients for an apple pie. Peter, who was in charge of peeling the apples, posed a foolish question. "Tell me again, dear, why are we baking a pie when you were specifically told not to bring anything?"

"Well, Peter, it's just the proper manners. We cannot show up empty handed. And it's such a little thing to do. Look! You already have the apples done, the oven is ready, and I will have this beauty put together in just a few minutes. Kitchen duties are easy, dear." Janet's response did not surprise him. The family motto, 'It's just the proper thing to do,' was engrained in her.

"Their phone call was rather serendipitous, wasn't it, dear?" Peter's spouse assumed the pensive look that she often wears. He wondered where she went when that facial expression washed over her face.

"Oh, dear, Peter! My contemplations must be so annoying for you. I'm such a slow thinker. The truth is my mind seems to prefer assessing every option it can possibly produce. In some instances this is extremely helpful, but in others it's annoying for me as well. In this particular case, several scenarios came to the forefront. First, I wondered if they somehow picked up on our experience this morning. They're very intuitive, as you well know. And then, I suspected that they just wanted to check in on us. We're so much older and there are times when I think they worry about us. Which reminds me that we need to have a conversation with them about that. And then, the third item that came to mind may be wishful thinking. I cannot help but believe that they too have had another unusual experience in the garden. So basically, this is where my busy mind has been, and I imagine that all three options play a role in the phone call this morning."

"You are a wonder, Janet. Your mind is as sharp as it ever was, and by the way, your pensive mind does not annoy me. I'm just curious! When your mind takes you away, I wonder where you're going, and part of me wishes that I could go with you."

"Maybe you can, Peter! We just need to keep practicing our inner communications skills. Let's face it, dear, we have no idea what we're capable of, and maybe, with the assistance of Nana, we may have a growth spurt. Wouldn't that be a hoot?" The idea was extremely exciting and sent the couple's minds on another exploration of possibilities. Once again time passed without their notice until the oven timer alerted them that the pie was ready.

Back at the Gardners' house, the meal for the evening was in process. "Okay," declared Geri. "My award winning chicken salad is chilling in the refrigerator, and all the ingredients for the green salad are diced and sliced and ready to be mixed when our guests arrive. How about you, Jonathan? Is your To Do List coming along?" He lifted the picnic basket holding all the essential items for setting the woodland table and then pointed to another basket ready for the wine and water bottles. "I'm ready!" he replied. "But I am wondering about a dessert. Should we make a fruit salad?"

Geri acknowledged that she was concerned about dessert as well, but was reluctant to make anything because of Janet's proper upbringing. "You know, Jon, I told her to come empty-handed, but she really struggles with that. So I think we should just wait and see. If they surprise us and actually show up without some wonderful treat, then we can do fruit salad or ice cream or both. In the meantime, let's go set up the table. I can't wait to see what our new dining area looks like all decked out." Geri grabbed the linens that Jon had laid out and also the candles that were a necessity for every occasion. He carried the basket filled with kitchen items and another bag that he refused to discuss. He simply said it was a surprise that would be revealed later.

"I love surprises!" admitted Geri as they headed towards the secret passageway. As they entered the outer garden, they both stopped in admiration. It was picture perfect. Sunrays scattered throughout the trees creating a magical moment that could only be described as heavenly.

"Geri, we are so blessed. Just look at this divine beauty. I am so glad that Peter and Janet are joining us. I want to share our Sacred Space with them." With great excitement, he led the way to see the dining area. The outer garden was changing Jonathan. Even though he was an exceptional person before the garden project began, he was expanding into an even more loving and compassionate person. This very good man was deepening every day. Although he did not perceive himself as changing, he was in fact having a transformative experience. When the couple rounded the bend, they found the new dining setting glistening with the sunbeams shining through the trees. It was a breathtaking sight.

Jonathan turned to his beloved with glee. "Look what we've been blessed with, dear." Tears streamed down his cheeks. Geri observing the scene realized that everything was happening for a reason.

"Okay, dear, let's add to the magic!" In minutes, the table was dressed to the nines: white linen tablecloth, teal placemats and napkins, their favorite rectangular dishes, and a small candle centerpiece to add to the atmosphere of the setting. While Geri was creating her magic at the table, Jonathan had disappeared down the trail. Upon his return, he applauded her good work and gave her a big hug.

"It's beautiful, Geri! Peter and Janet are going to love this!" More comments of praise were made before the couple realized they needed to return to the house. Their guests would be arriving soon. As they headed back, Geri failed to notice the small solar lanterns that Jonathan had placed along the trail. Her mind was in the kitchen making sure that everything was ready for their company. He was relieved. The surprise was yet to come. For some time, he had been surfing the Internet for the perfect solar lights that would unobtrusively light the trails at night. For the last three days he had secretly charged the new purchases in an area that his beloved rarely visited. Jonathan hoped the evening display would please her.

⊚

"Welcome, welcome, welcome!" declared Jonathan. "It is so good to see the both of you again!" As the two couples moseyed towards the kitchen, many hugs and greetings were exchanged including recognition and applause for the incredible apple pie that Janet and Peter had prepared.

"You rascals!" teased Geri. "We knew you would show up with some delicious treat, but this is way over the top. I think we should do dessert first!"

"That's always an option," remarked Peter. "However," his eyes turned toward the countertop filled with goodies, "I've noticed that your world famous chicken salad is on the menu, and that makes us very happy." He and Janet giggled as if they had a secret to share. Peter urged his lovely spouse to tell the story.

"This is a little embarrassing, but since your phone call, Geri, we've been focusing our intentions upon your wonderful chicken salad. We were both longing for chicken salad, so this is a dream come true. And maybe it's a sign that our manifestation skills are improving." The foursome giggled about that observation and all agreed that the Hansons should take partial credit for Geri's decision to include her ever-popular chicken salad in the meal. One thing was certain; everyone was hungry.

"Okay, friends," announced Geri, "everyone grab a dish and we will load up the aged little red wagon." The directions were easy to follow; however, the need for the little red wagon was a surprise.

"Hmm!" mused Janet. "Sounds to me as if these two are up to something, dear!" Peter nodded in agreement. The Gardners remained silent, but their smiles indicated that an adventure was in the making. Once the wagon was loaded, the parade began. Jonathan led the way, as Geri instructed everyone to follow. When they entered into the secret passageway, oohs and ahs began.

"Oh, my goodness," Peter exclaimed softly, "you two have been very busy. How on Earth did you accomplish so much so quickly." Before an answer could be spoken, he whispered, "This is like being in a cathedral!"

"Wait until you hear the choir," replied Geri. "This is a magical place." When they reached the last bend before their destination, Geri paused and let Jon go ahead. She turned to her dear friends and said, "Now, I want to ask you to walk the next few feet with your eyes closed. I'll stand in the middle and guide you. The path is flat and solid so you need not worry about your footing." She situated herself in between the curious friends, wrapped her arms in theirs, and urged them to take a deep breath. "Dear Ones, you are our first guests in this new setting. We hope you will enjoy it as much as we do. Okay, let's take the next step." And this they did. Geri guided their friends slowly and safely around the bend and stationed them in just the right place so that the view was best. "Okay, friends, take another deep breath, and then open your eyes."

The Hansons followed instructions well. Each engaged in the deep breath as suggested and then slowly opened their eyes to view the new Sacred Space. Jonathan stood nearby so that the view was not obstructed. Again, their friends spoke in whispers. Praise, compliments, and more were expressed, but the inclination to whisper was the greatest acknowledgement of the setting. It was indeed a Sacred Space.

As they approached, Jonathan welcomed them. "Dear friends, we are so excited to share this space with you. We feel so blessed and we want to share the blessing with those who are dear to us." Everyone was invited to sit down, but their excitement would not allow it. The Hansons and the Gardners were mesmerized by the setting. The location of the table was perfect, the greenery around the table was perfect, and the views were perfect. Every part of the landscape gave one the feeling that all was right with the world. Finally, after viewing the new setting from every direction, the foursome was ready to occupy the table. Janet and Peter had first dibs on chair selection. Once they were seated, the little red wagon was unpacked and the meal was presented. The homemade apple pie was beautifully displayed on a small folding acacia table that Jonathan had cleverly hidden behind a tree. With all hospitality concerns addressed, the couple joined their friends at the table.

"How blessed we are to be here!" Janet's statement was the beginning of a round of prayers that just naturally unfolded. Hands reached out and soon encircled the table in prayerful fashion. Peter, as often was the case, followed his wife's lead. His words were heartfelt.

"We are so grateful to be here with you two as your Sacred Place is inaugurated. You have blessed this land with your tender loving care. And you have blessed us by letting us be a part of this occasion."

"Well, I'll go next," asserted Geri. "This garden that we refer to as the 'outer garden' feels like another world that we've been gifted to expand our perspectives of our world. Every day it provides us with new lessons. I am stunned by the experiences we've already shared, and I'm eager to see what awaits us. Whoever is watching over us, thank you!" Geri squeezed her spouse's hand nudging him to express his innermost feelings. As always, he took the necessary deep breath. His companions joined him in the process. With head bowed and eyes closed, he offered his gratitude.

"Thank you, Janet and Peter, for joining us. After the project was finished today, you were the ones we most wanted to share it with first. As you said, Peter, this has been a labor of tender loving care. And many more than just Geri participated in this process. There are so many to thank. I hope you will all listen with the ears of your heart. Granddad, you are the first who deserves acknowledgement. You loved this small piece of land with all your heart and we are grateful beyond words that you nurtured it so well and that you left it us to enjoy. I hope you are pleased with the work that we are doing here. Geri and I have made every effort we could to take the land and its inhabitants into consideration as we made what we believed to be honorable decisions. And it's been a remarkable experience for both of us! I think it is fair to say that every discernment process made was a collaborative operation with the flora and the fauna. Their guidance made this transition easy. Thank goodness we opened our hearts to their influence and thank you, Granddad, for role modeling that possibility. Words simply cannot express our gratitude to everyone involved. However, I want you to know that we will continue to listen to your concerns and we are eager to continue working with you. Amen." With that said, a chorus of melodies filled the air.

"Oh my! You two have made an incredible connection with this little piece of heaven." Janet was in awe. "I cannot wait to hear the whole story about your experiences. I'm certain they are many and that they are fascinating." Geri nodded and assured her that they were eager to share more about their experiences. Meanwhile, Jonathan was looking up and down the trail as if he was expecting someone, which he was. Sure enough, less than twelve feet away, the three rabbits seen earlier nonchalantly stepped out on the trail. He pointed towards them.

"Those little ones have been on the scene since early this morning. I know they are up to something; they are reaching out to us! If any of you can communicate with them, please do so."

"I think they just want to be part of the celebration, Jon. Maybe you should acknowledge them personally." Geri's suggestion suited Jonathan. For someone who was a man of few words, he was communicating beautifully.

"Okay, here goes. Dear friends, you've been assisting our efforts all day today and probably others as well, but you have been particularly noticeable today. I would like you to meet our dear friends. This is Janet and Peter Hanson. And all of us have come here this evening to express our gratitude to and for this wonderful Sacred Space. I know it is your Home and I hope you are satisfied with the results of our collaboration with your friends and companions here in the garden. We will try to be good neighbors. We are very grateful that you are here and hope to have communication with you soon." The rabbits appeared very attentive during Jon's comments, and then they moved off the trail into the nearby greenery, which allowed them to be near and still have a little privacy.

"Well, dear friends, let's fill these plates and turn the focus towards you. I'm absolutely certain that something marvelous is happening with you two." Geri's suggestion was immediately followed and soon the plates were full and the sumptuous repast begun. Because the two couples were not people who enjoyed small talk, their stories about recent events continued during the meal.

Peter noted his curiosity about the timing of the Gardners' phone call. "It was just so serendipitous. We were blessed with several exceptional experiences this morning, which we most definitely will share with you, and then you called with your wonderful invitation. As you know, we always enjoy connecting with both of you. Having friends with whom you can share and discuss unusual experiences is a tremendous gift. So, I was just wondering why you called when you did." Jonathan and Geri couldn't recall any specifics, but acknowledged the idea to call just seemed to come to them.

Janet quickly intervened. "Friends, none of us believe in coincidences. I think it's appropriate to surmise that we were somehow brought together this evening, which leads me to believe that our experiences are somehow linked. Your experiences are about connection with your Grandfather and nature and honoring this special track of land. Our morning experiences were initially about connection with our energetic bodies, which then led to connection with my Great-grandmother Harriet, who provided us with information regarding the Earth's precarious state of health. And now the four of us are connecting with intentions of sharing our experiences with one another. This is happening for a reason. I'm certain of it!"

"She's right!" asserted Geri. "Okay, you two! Tell us everything and let's see what we can make of this. Obviously, we're supposed to be learning something from each other's experiences."

Peter began by asking Jonathan and Geri if they were aware that our physical bodies needed regular re-alignment to maintain health and good balance. Admitting that they had no knowledge of this, Peter provided an overview of the exercise that aids in the alignment of the physical and energetic forms. He confirmed that it was educative and helpful and recommended that the four of them should learn more about it. "Janet is a great resource for us and an excellent teacher. I was reluctant when Janet brought up the idea, but I'm not anymore. I think it's one of those little known truths in the universe that is essential for wellness. The next experience is best for Janet to share. It was amazing! An unforgettable moment in time."

Janet took the lead acknowledging that she believed the re-alignment exercise prepared them for the next experience. "I shared with Peter this morning that I was feeling a sense of urgency, which I wasn't able to identify, and he agreed to assist me with a deeper self exploration. In the process of going deeper, we actually had an encounter with Nana." Janet shared the wonderful details of the chimes and the delicious aroma of fresh scones so that Geri and Jon had a good sense of the experience. "Eventually, I reached out to her through my inner voice, and she heard me and immediately responded in like manner, and both of us were able to hear her as clearly as you can hear me right now. We actually had a conversation, which was stunning in itself, but the information she shared was truly overwhelming. My friends, it was a wake-up call regarding the Earth's declining health." Peter pitched in to give more of the details that were shared and then Janet took the lead again. "Basically, the information was grim. And she insisted that we, meaning all of us, must change our ways or the Earth will go into dormancy. She asked us to connect with her every morning for practice's sake and also for the distribution of more information. She insinuated that others who were wiser than she would also have information to share. Obviously, we don't know exactly where this is leading, but we are determined to follow through with it. It's too important to back away from. We will share everything we learn with you two and hopefully we will all find a way to help our planet." Needless to say Geri and Jonathan were overwhelmed with the Hansons' experiences, and of course, they believed every word that was shared.

"Wow!" declared Geri. "Thank you! And thank you, Harriet! It must have been wonderful to be in touch with her." Janet acknowledged that it was a very powerful moment that she would always hold dear to her heart.

"Yes, it really was a remarkable experience to hear her voice again," admitted Janet. "She speaks the truth truthfully! You just don't doubt what she says, because she states it with such authority. She will be a great resource for us."

"You know, this is truly amazing, friends." Geri joined hands with everyone again, and continued, "We really do have the opportunity to learn and grow more rapidly because of our relationships. And the information is linked, as you said, Janet. When we were working in the outer garden, the plant life assisted us in developing the area. They sent us visual images of what could be done in each area that we were interested in changing, and they basically guided us on how to create the trails with very little disturbance to the present plants. I know Jon was very concerned about uprooting healthy plants. But very few had to be relocated and he was shown exactly how to safely remove and replant them. All of the plants that were moved are healthy and thriving. Even the pine needle paths were their suggestion. The point is that we collaborated with nature and everyone benefitted. And you are connecting with your Nana, who is providing you with information about helping the Earth. All of this is happening for a reason, including our time together at this moment."

"This has been a very full day and evening," announced Peter. "I think we can all be satisfied with ourselves." At which point, the solar lights lit up the trail and the area around the dining area. It was magical.

"Oh, Jon, this is a wonderful surprise! When did you place those lovely lanterns everywhere and how did they escape my attention?" The two exchanged a sweet kiss and the Hansons followed.

Ten

Once upon a time, a planet of remarkable beauty began to feel the effects of a species that had over-populated its lands. Unlike other species who were considerate about their expansion, this species did not recognize the hazards of their over-breeding. The demands of this species were so great that it eventually upset the balance of the entire planetary eco-system.

Because the planetary Life Being was one of extreme generosity, she tolerated the inconsiderate actions of the overbearing species in hopes that their maturational process would result in more responsible behavior. Unfortunately, this did not come to pass. Instead the species developed an air of ownership and pretense regarding their role on the planet, which led to significant misbehaviors. Their assumed needs led to greater desires that inflamed greediness and solidified a sense of entitlement that put the species in direct opposition with the Life Being upon whom they resided.

Adjustments by other life beings co-existing upon the planet were made on her behalf, but their efforts were in vain. The devastating impact of the invasive species was evident to everyone except to the eyes of the perpetrators. Their careless and reckless actions continued and intensified. Only a few of their kind understood what was transpiring, while others were neither concerned nor interested. Such was the gross foolishness of those who ancestors had made similar errors on another beautiful planetary Life Being so very long ago.

Eleven

"**G**ood morning!" Jen and Carol waved as they approached the Madisons.

"We were just talking about you two," responded Anne, as she and David quickened their pace. Soon big hugs were exchanged. "Oh, it so good to be in your presence," Anne stated with great sincerity. "Where have you two been? It seems like forever since we seen you out here on the trail."

"Well, believe it or not," inserted Carol, "we were just talking about you as well."

"Yes, that's right!" Jen's excitement about seeing these friends was obvious. "We have things to share with you guys. When can we get together?" The Madisons turned to one another, but before they could even review their schedules Carol was inviting them over for breakfast. She looked to Jen for confirmation that her presumptuous behavior was okay and received an immediate happy face.

"Breakfast sounds great!" replied David. "Shall we pick something up from the bakery on our way over?" The ladies looked at each other and both knew it was a no-brainer.

"Well, that doesn't seem fair," Carol said hesitantly, but then quickly accepted the offer. "We haven't had pastries in a while so your offer simply cannot be refused. We'll provide the drinks and fresh fruit." They all agreed that earlier was better than later, and eight o'clock became the target hour. Each couple continued on their route with anticipation of the visit yet to come.

◎

The ladies, as they were often referred to by folks in the neighborhood, were just putting the finishing touches to the patio table when their friends walked through the back gate. "Perfect timing!" they both hailed at the same time.

"You two do that a lot!" noted David as he exchanged hugs with everyone including his beloved spouse. "Now, don't you pretend that all this attention is about me," he laughed while holding up the bakery bag for all to see. "This is all about the pastries!" More laughter filled the air, as the two couples retreated to breakfast table.

"This is lovely! How did you manage to get all this done so quickly?" Anne praised the table and its sweet decorations and the lush flower garden surrounding the patio before directing everyone to sit down. "Okay friends, let's get serious. We have things to talk about."

David just rolled his eyes and giggled quietly. "Best do what she says, friends. Herself has taken the lead!" The foursome bantered about a bit while the coffee was poured and the goodies were plated, and then, they readied themselves for the first bite. Ecstasy delayed their conversation as the first bite led to another and then to another.

"In my next life, I'm going to be very thin so that one of these delicious almond croissants can be eaten every day without any negative impact." Anne's comment jolted everyone back into reality.

"Actually, dear," David calmly stated with a straight face, "these treats are surely a gift from the heavens; therefore, they simply cannot cause us any harm in any lifetime. So, we can enjoy them daily starting today!"

"Well stated, David! I'll commit to that ritual!" Carol and Anne quickly followed Jen's lead and the joyous camaraderie continued.

"On a more serious note," Anne began, "David and I are so grateful for this reunion today. We've missed you! And we're eager to hear what you've been up to. So, which one of you is going to take the lead?" Carol pointed to Jen who pointed back to Carol.

"Well, I'll give you a quick overview, and then we can both bring you up-to-date about an amazing adventure that we just experienced yesterday. So, dear friends, the reason we've been out of touch is because we've been diligently exploring nature trails throughout a fifty-mile radius. It's been very educative. We're learning more about the surrounding area including the nature opportunities, as well as the nearby communities, and we're feeling more centered now that we have a greater appreciation for the lay of the land. We feel very much at home here and are extremely happy about relocating to this area, but now we feel as if our home is expanding. We've actually taken notes about each trail so that they don't all become a big blur."

"Smart idea!" remarked David. "Nature trails do begin to blend together after a while."

"Exactly," replied Carol. "Even though each one has some noteworthy feature, you can easily forget which one is which unless you visit them on a regular basis. So that's what we've been up to, but now, I'll let Jen describe what happened yesterday." All eyes turned in Jen's direction.

She paused for a deep breath then she started to speak, but suddenly stopped and turned toward Carol. "Where do I begin?" she asked. Carol reached over and placed her hand atop Jen's.

"At the entryway, dear. That's where the adventure began." Carol's quiet manner helped Jen to gather herself. This was the first time the story would be told and she wanted to honor the event as deeply as they had been honored by the experience.

"I'm sorry, friends, but this experience was extremely powerful. It started awkwardly, and we initially were challenged by some personal fears and doubts." Jen looked towards Carol for confirmation that she agreed with that statement and immediately received a nod of reassurance. "The forest was so dense and dark that we were reluctant to enter it. Never having been there before we had no idea what to expect. My fear of the darkness forced me to return to the car to fetch a flashlight. It amazes me even now how foreboding I found the darkness to be. I felt paralyzed and simply could not go forward." Carol caressed her beloved's hand again. She was embarrassed that she didn't realize the extent of Jen's fear at the time. "But with Carol by my side and the trusty flashlight in hand, I was able to enter the pitch black forest." She laughed at herself, but emphatically insisted that the darkness warranted caution. Carol confirmed that the dark entryway was ominous.

Anne, shivering in her chair, asked if the story had a happy ending. Carol reassured her that the experience was amazing.

"I'm sorry, Anne, perhaps that part of the story should have been left out, but it was a critical learning experience for both of us."

"Oh, don't worry Jen. I want to hear everything! It was just a moment of the heebie-jeebies. Please continue, dear."

"Okay. Not to worry, the story turns sweet now," Jen assured her friend. "We continued with some hesitancy to follow the trail deeper into the forest. Fortunately, at some moment a breeze stirred in the upper level of the trees that allowed streams of sunlight to shine through, revealing a cavernous landscape abundant with plant life of all sizes, shapes, and forms. It was a spectacle to behold! And if that wasn't enough, then the majestic forest choral symphony performed an amazing concert for us. The event was beyond one's imagination. And even after the performance quieted and the sunlight faded away, we could still see vague images of the landscape all around us. Our joyful gratefulness was boundless and the forest residents were deeply moved by our reactions, and in return, revealed one of their incredible secrets. The plant life is translucent! And wherever we focused our eyes, the plants lit up for us. The forest actually communicated with us and expressed how happy everyone was to be noticed. The heartfelt connection we felt with the forest was amazing and overwhelming. I'm still trying to process the depth of emotion that was felt, both from the forest and from myself. It was a stunning experience." Jen paused and then turned to Carol and invited her to express her impressions of the experience.

"You know, friends, Jen's description tells it all. I've never experienced anything that intense before. It was a privilege to be in the presence of that community. I think there is much more to learn from that forest, and we were invited to return! Isn't that exciting? Maybe you two would like to join us. The community was so excited about connecting with us; I just know they would enjoy your presence."

"That is one of the most powerful stories I've ever heard," Anne acknowledged. "And the answer to your invitation is YES! I would love to join you. How about you, David?"

"Indeed! I'm up for this adventure and would like to pursue it sooner rather than later. Jen, may I ask you a question?" She urged him to do so. "You mentioned that entering the darkness was an important learning experience. Can you elaborate upon that?"

"Yes, David, I am happy to share what has been learned so far, but I suspect that more is yet to come. I was afraid to enter the darkness because my mind had preconceived ideas about what might exist in the darkness. But what I found in the darkness was totally opposite. I found beauty, love, kindness, and compassion. My prejudgment almost kept me from experiencing one of the most powerful events that I've ever had. This event makes me wonder about other aspects of my life. How does my judging nature affect me in ways that I am not even aware of, and how am I affecting others because of preconceived ideas that are founded in misunderstanding and lack of awareness." Jen paused and took a long deep breath. "There is so much more to learn from this adventure. There so much more to learn from the wisdom of nature."

"Sounds to me that you had a life-altering event," affirmed David.

"Yes, we did!" As often is the case, Carol and Jen responded in unison.

"Thank you both for being such wonderful listeners. Having friends that we can share this experience with is essential to our well-being. We are so grateful to have you in our lives. Your support means so much to us." Jen's heartfelt acknowledgement of their friends quickly turned humorous when she mentioned their serendipitous encounter on the trail earlier. "Don't you love how we just happened to bump into each other this morning? One might think that it happened for a reason or we could just dub it as a lucky coincidence." She winked at her friends and then turned the focus towards them.

"We're convinced the two of you have recently had an adventure, as well." Jen's smile was big and inviting. "We're right, aren't we?" The Madisons confirmed their assumption and were indeed ready to share their latest adventure. The couple looked at each other, and without any outward indicators, quickly decided that Anne would facilitate the story.

"Oh, dear friends, please join me in the first of many deep breaths that will accompany our story." And this they did! With eyes still closed, Anne followed with another similar inhalation and then her face brightened with a smile equal to Jen's. "I think the best way to begin this story is to say…once upon a time, a little girl had a dream that she desperately wanted to come true, and even though it took a very long time for the dream to manifest, she never gave up. Her belief in the dream was so intense that she never lost hope. She always knew that some day in some way, the dream would come true. Well, as I'm sure you've already guessed, I was that little girl with the big dream." The gentle smile that crossed Anne's face warmed the hearts of those around her.

"I'm very happy to report that the dream has come true. While you two were exploring the gifts of Mother Nature in her forest concert hall, we were engaging with a magnificent white tail buck. Let me elaborate upon what was just said: we were actually communicating with this incredible creature, who by the way, initiated the encounter. He told us that he had been observing us for some time and that he had discerned that we were people of goodness."

"Actually," David inserted, "he situated himself in the center of the trail when he realized that we were approaching and boldly stood there awaiting our arrival."

"Yes, bold is definitely an accurate description of his presence," continued Anne. "I would also add confident, stately, and commanding.

Obviously, we were very excited about being so close to this incredible creature, but we were also confused about his intentions, even though we were certain that he was the one in charge. He began connecting with us through visual images, which indicated that we were being invited to approach him. It was difficult for me to be calm, because the kid in me wanted to race towards this beautiful specimen and smother him with hugs and kisses."

David jumped in again and reassured Carol and Jen that his beloved managed her inner child very well. "I could tell that Little Annie wanted to act out, but Anne managed to contain her youthful self. She managed the situation with grace and dignity and demonstrated the best of humankind to our new friend." David's praise embarrassed Anne but she continued with the story.

"The deer's ability to communicate with visual images was truly fascinating. Although I do not know how this transmission transpires, we were able to receive the image in our minds; thereby, knowing what the buck wanted us to do. The first image showed David and me standing in front of him stroking his muscular neck. It was amazing to see the image and then to follow through with the action. Need I share how excited my kid was? Over the top!" Anne smiled and giggled at herself, as David lovingly looked on. She turned to him and urged him to continue the story.

"Dear friends, I am reluctant to take over, because Anne is a masterful storyteller."

"She is indeed, David, but so are you, and we are eager to hear your perspective as well." Carol's encouragement supercharged his confidence.

"Thank you, Carol, for that boost. I must admit that the experience was one that will never be forgotten. Although, we have always believed that interspecies communication was possible, this interaction was more than we ever imagined. Eventually, the buck moved beyond visual images and reached out to us through telepathic communication. We don't understand how that process works either, or if we are using the correct descriptor for this type of connection, but the bottom line is this. We could hear this animal's voice within our minds as clearly as we hear your voices, and he understood our oral voices and was able to hear our attempts at telepathic communication. Trying to describe what happens in these interactions is cumbersome, because we really don't know how to articulate the details other than to say that communication successfully took place between two different species. Fortunately, we all know how complicated it is to talk about these interactions. This is another reason why it is so comforting to have you two in our lives."

"You're absolutely right, David! We are very blessed to have one another. The trust level that we share among us allows this conversation to happen." Jen reached out and hands encircled the table. "Thank you so much for having the courage to share your story."

"And you too!" added Anne.

"So what did the buck say to you?" asked Carol. The Madisons turned to each other again and without any oral interaction discerned the next step.

"I'll take this on," responded Anne. "Friends, it was amazing! The wisdom that eloquently flowed from this dignified animal was the equivalent of listening to an ancient master. He revealed that connecting with us was also a dream come true for him and he expressed a desire for more connection. When we asked permission to share our encounter with others, he became protective of his kind. He reminded us that many of them had suffered harm at the hands of our kind and they were not ready for contact. However, he believed with that caveat included, the story of our connection could be beneficial for both species. He indicated that healing was required because of previous unkindness that was perpetrated by our kind, but he also expressed that more conversations were necessary. Before he departed he projected another visual image showing us standing on each side of him and looking out towards the west where several other deer were observing the interaction. We took our places as was indicated in the visual image and stood with our hands on his back. It was a magnificent send off. He slowly departed the trail, then turned around to snatch another sight of us. We both think that he bowed to us, and we did the same to him. And then he gracefully bounded through the grasses to join his companions." Anne released a long sigh.

"We were and still are overwhelmed by the experience. There simply are not enough superlatives to describe this time of emotional exchange. We feel blessed! And we can't wait to meet with him again."

"Geez!" exclaimed Jen. "Look at the similarities. Different settings, different species, but both experiences are about connection and communication with other species. Do we all agree that this is happening for a reason?" The response was immediate and unanimous.

"I wonder what we are supposed to do with this information," mused Carol. "Do we go public? Do we seek other folks who may also be involved in similar experiences? Or do we just keep gathering information, and keep it among ourselves?" The four friends sank into his or her individual cocoon of deep thought. The questions were not new to them. Each couple had already deliberated over the options, but decisions were still elusive.

"It seems to me that all three questions demand attention, but not all at the same time." David's calm voice settled the anxiety that was building within the foursome. "In essence, we've already addressed the last two. We gathered information and we sought trusted friends with whom we could share this information. Those were important first steps that need to be built upon. This is certainly not the only gathering we are going to have about these experiences. I foresee many more of these occasions. And I believe we can find other folks who will also be interested in these experiences and who may have some of their own. A few couples readily come to mind."

"The Gardners and the Hansons are candidates!" announced Anne. David confirmed that he believed they would be very curious about our adventures. He inquired if Carol and Jen had met these folks?

"We've met them on our evening walks and they seem like lovely people, just like you two. If you think it is safe to share these stories with them, then, let's do it." Carol turned to Jen and suggested that they host the gathering and she agreed.

"Actually, I think this is an excellent plan! It's multi-purposeful." Anne's mind was in first gear. "It gives you two an opportunity to learn more about your neighbors. That will be nice, and these folks will be very receptive to our stories. They are curious people who are very open-minded about a variety of topics. I like the rhythm of this. We continue reaching out to our new friends, while we also reach out to established friends who are of similar mind. Then, at some point, I assume we will take into consideration the idea of becoming more public about our experiences. Is this where we are headed, David?"

"Yes," he spoke quietly. "From a practical viewpoint, we need to proceed wisely and cautiously, and as we gather momentum and expand our numbers, the next step will become more obvious. So, I suggest that we wholeheartedly pursue our new relationships and also take steps to organize the next gathering." Everyone agreed that the plan had merit, and each couple accepted tasks for coordinating the gathering.

"Before this wonderful conversation comes to an end, may I ask you a few more questions about your time with the white tail buck?" The Madisons both nodded and encouraged Carol to continue.

"I'm curious about how you described the deer's eloquent manner of speech. That surprised me, which is probably evidence of my preconceived ideas. Can you say more about that?" David pointed to Anne, who was delighted to address the question.

"It surprised me too, Carol. I'm not sure what I was expecting, or maybe it is better said that I don't know what my Little Girl was expecting, but it certainly wasn't what we heard. I'm not kidding you. It felt like a venerable teacher was addressing us. His impressive stance when we initially encountered him was the first surprise. There was no fear or insecurity emanating from him. He was the epitome of strength and courage. Combine this with his powerful and persuasive manner of speech and he was indeed an impressive figure. His words were precise, truthful, and matter of fact. He showed no hostility or disrespect towards our kind; nevertheless, he did not mince words about our irresponsible behavior." Anne directed herself towards Carol and quietly said, "Being in his presence made me feel as if I were in the presence of a divine energy. It was humbling. What I'm realizing is that there are no words that can adequately describe the breadth and depth of that experience. We were in the presence of a beautiful animal, and that animal was so much more than I ever imagined possible. It makes me wonder what other encounters will feel like. I felt very small compared to that amazing Life Being. Not because he made me feel small, but because in that moment I realized he was far more evolved than anyone I had ever encountered before."

"Yes," whispered Carol. "Our experiences may be more similar than we originally thought. While I understand the sense of inadequacy that you revealed, I want you to know, Anne, your words are far more expressive than you realize. Your comments are actually helping me right now in this moment to better define and understand my experiences in the forest. I too felt small during our interaction. Like you, words escape me. The presence that communicated with us was way beyond my scope of understanding. The only thing that I can say with certainty is that I want to spend more time with that presence."

Hands joined again for another expressions of gratitude, and with that done, the day awaited them.

Twelve

"**D**avid, do you think the grand buck will address us today." The drive to their favorite trail, which was only three miles from the house, was intolerably long for Anne this morning. Even though she attempted to manage her excitement, it was noticeable. David's efforts to be calm for both of them were not successful.

"Old Girl, whether we encounter the grand buck or not, we will have a wonderful walk just like we always do." His comforting words were not successful either. In fact, they annoyed Anne.

"Listen up, Old Man! I want to see the deer and I want to see him today." David couldn't help himself. An uncontrollable giggle started and soon they were both having a good laugh. As they turned into the trail parking area, Anne acted out again. "Thank goodness, we finally arrived! That was the longest drive ever!" They giggled a bit longer before leaving the car.

"Okay, David, should we take the same route that we took last time…just for good luck?"

"Anne, dear, I'm as excited about this opportunity as you are, but we both need to get a grip. Our energy is so scattered now that our new friend may not even recognize us." David's perception stilled Anne. "I think we need to settle down and accept what comes. If he wants to approach us, he will! But if he doesn't, we are going to have another lovely walk, as we have had all the years that we've been coming here."

"Agreed!" replied Anne. "You are so wise, David. I apologize for acting like a child, but I feel like one. The kid inside of me is so excited!"

"I know, dear, but let's try to calm ourselves. Maybe, we should do a brief walking meditation until we reach the fork in the path." David's suggestion met with approval and the first step into the path was taken in unison.

When the couple reached the fork, no words were necessary or desired. They just drifted to the left in acceptance of whatever might transpire. Anne contemplated each footstep trying to master the art of being one with the Earth. She loved this simple exercise, because it produced numerous benefits. When done with intention, the process of focusing upon each step results in the blessing of being present, and living in the present inspires Oneness with the Earth and all others that are encountered. And in this particular situation, the carefully placed footsteps quieted the agitated mind, facilitating peace of mind and heart for Anne.

David appreciated Anne's commitment to her practice. He knew once she stepped onto the trail that she would take charge of her rambunctious behavior.

"Thank you, dear, for rapidly directing us to the trail. As said before, you are very wise."

"Shh! Looked straight ahead, dear!" Anne did as instructed and recognized the group of deer that was seen the previous day. She was certain this was the same cast of characters.

"I don't see him, do you?" David immediately responded to Anne's unspoken words, while remaining focused on the herd.

"Let's be patient, dear. We can't expect him to appear the minute we arrive. We may have surprised him!" As they continued watching the deer feeding some forty or more feet away, they failed to notice that another had approached them from the rear. He was observing the new friends as they were observing his old friends.

"Hello, New Friends, it is most pleasing to be in your company again." The familiar voice brought tears to Anne's eyes. She and David whirled around expecting to see the grand buck directly behind them, but instead discovered that he was several yards away.

"Hello again, New Friend! We were hoping you would be available today." Anne's excitement was so intense that she didn't even realize that she had shifted back to her normal way of speaking. "Is this location suitable to you, or would you prefer another setting?" The buck approached without hesitation.

"This setting will do fine, unless others of your kind come this way. They are fascinated by my kind; thus, we must be vigilant for the sake of all involved." The Madisons concurred and suggested that he retreat into the nearby brush if they were interrupted.

"Yes, that is an acceptable strategy. However, for now, I wish to express my gratitude for your return. We have many more topics to address, and we, my friends and I, are most happy for this opportunity."

"We also have good news," declared David. *"We spoke of our previous encounter with two of our dear friends, and they were extremely excited. They too would like to have a conversation with you whenever you are amenable to that."* The buck was very pleased with this news and agreed that the meeting should happen sooner than later. *"So, these friends are amenable to my kind?"*

"*Oh yes!*" exclaimed Anne who had returned to practicing her telepathic abilities. "*In fact,*" she continued, "*they recently had an encounter with a very dense forest and are as excited about their experience as are we about ours. We would love to introduce you to them, or if you prefer to meet them on your own, we can arrange that as well.*" The handsome animal contemplated the options and decided that an introduction was appropriate. They agreed to discuss a suitable time and place at the end of their conversation.

"*New Friend, may I ask you a question?*" As always, David's manner was gentle and soft- spoken.

"*Indeed, you may!*" he responded.

"*I wonder if your friends would like to join us. We would be delighted to meet them.*" The question surprised their New Friend, and once again, he took time to contemplate the situation. Before he answered, the buck walked across the path and stared at his companions. David and Anne assumed he was communicating with them; however, they were not able to hear the conversation. After a few minutes passed, one of the does cautiously approached. She came considerably closer, but gave herself sufficient room for a quick getaway if she needed it. The buck remained near the path but positioned himself in between the doe and his New Friends. He turned towards Anne and David to continue their conversation.

"*My friends are grateful for your gracious invitation, but they are still hesitant to mingle with your kind. This young one is very curious. She may come closer as we continue to converse. I believe there is wisdom in your invitation, New Friend. It is important for my kind to witness goodness in your kind.*"

"I am so sorry for our cruel behavior. Your kind has years of history with humankind. It is understandable why you do not trust us. You are wise to be on guard around us." The herd reacted to Anne's sincerity. David witnessed that each deer looked up and focused upon her. It was evident that they understood what she was saying. "New Friend, it saddens me to say this, but you and your kind must protect yourselves from our kind. While there are many like ourselves who have the utmost respect for you, there are others who do not. I am so sorry to be this blunt with you, but the truth must be spoken." The stately buck and the other five deer stood tall as Anne apologized for the inhumane behavior of humankind. Anne's heartache was palpable. The deer and all the others who were listening shared her pain. All were mourning the tragedy that so many had suffered.

The buck moved closer to Anne and nudged her arm. At the same time an image of them standing head to head appeared in her mind's eye. She accepted the invitation. The tall majestic animal bowed his head to her level and she placed her head against his. It was a moment of sweet beauty. The doe moved several steps forward to bear witness to the event, and the four remaining deer approached as well. David stood still in honor of the heartfelt connection.

"*New Friends*," the grand buck, returning to his stately stature, took command once again. "*You have honored my kind and we are deeply touched by your kindness. Much healing has transpired today and we are all grateful.* As he spoke the other deer continued to move closer. Soon they were all gathered around the buck. "*As you can see, great progress has been made.*" Another image entered the Madisons' scope of attention indicating that the other deer desired physical touch as well. Needless to say, they happily took on the task. Gently and lovingly, Anne and David reached out to stroke each and every one of the herd. The deer seemed to thoroughly enjoy the connection and even wiggled about so that they could receive repeated strokes from both of the Madisons. It goes without saying that the humans were overjoyed with the experience.

"*Dear New Friends, our connection today was more than anticipated. There remains much to discuss; however, this experience demands great contemplation among my friends. Shall we meet again tomorrow? And will you invite your friends to join us. We would be pleased to meet other humans of goodness.*"

With that said, the herd returned to their feeding zone, which was safe and secure from other passersby, but they all continued to watch the two gracious humans who had brought new meaning to their lives. And as the Madisons departed they could not help but turn around to wave goodbye to their New Friends.

Once they were in the car, Anne and David sank into their seats.

"Is it possible to be exhilarated and exhausted at the same time?" inquired Anne. Her husband lost in his mind's meanderings was incapable of answering the question. In fact, in his dazed state, it was unlikely that he even heard the question.

"David, dear, are you okay?" Again, there was no response, so Anne reached over and nudged her husband. Her efforts were in vain. Finally, she grabbed David by the elbow and shook him more roughly than she would normally do. The manipulation jolted him out of his stupor.

"What's wrong, dear?" David's reaction was evidence that he had been completely oblivious to her efforts to connect with him.

"My goodness, David. Where has your mind taken you?"

"Well, I'm not quiet sure, Anne. Were you trying to get my attention?" She described the scene to him and he was amazed at how distant he had been. But he had no answers to explain his behavior. "Let's try this again, dear. So your question was in reference to the aftermath of our experience." She nodded and elaborated upon the contrasting emotions.

"I felt both exhausted and exhilarated at the same time and I was curious about your reaction to the experience as well." David considered his behavior and realized that he had frightened his beloved.

"Anne, I'm so sorry. My odd behavior caused you alarm. I apologize for zoning out like that, and the truth is, I still can't explain it, but it may be related to the question you were asking about. I was so pumped during our exchange with the deer. It was, as you said, exhilarating, but when we got in the car, I just collapsed. It was like all the remaining energy within me just drained out and left me exhausted. I'm not sure where my thoughts were, or if there were any at all. I have no memory of thinking about anything." David was confused and curious. "Tell me more about your reactions to our experience, Anne."

Anne relaxed back into the car seat again and tried to tune into her body. She remembered how supercharged she felt being surrounded by the family of deer. It truly was a dream come true for her inner child, as well as her adult self. She loved animals and often longed to walk among them. That was her idea of heaven. "Hmm," she mused. Several thoughts popped into her mind, which made her rethink the experience. "David, have you been taking in any of my thoughts?" He acknowledged absorbing the heaven scenario and suggested that the event may have been a small glimpse of what heaven is like. Anne agreed.

"Well, I just had another thought or insight about our time with the herd. You know, dear, I was so enamored with their presence that my antennae, which are usually so helpful to me, were simply overridden by the moment. But now as I look back on the occasion, I wonder if those incredible creatures were ministering to us. I was so excited about being with them that I just assumed the exhilaration that was being experienced was due to my own excitement. Now, I'm wondering if they were actually transmitting healing energy to us."

"What an incredible idea, Anne! Do you think that is possible?" David's own energy shifted just thinking about the possibility.

"I'm not certain, dear, but I do wonder. We both know how energized we become when we are around dogs. They bring us great joy and we always feel uplifted after we've had a canine encounter. Dogs are healers. Why not other animals? I was so focused on petting the deer and making a heartfelt connection with them that it didn't occur to me that they were doing the same with us. David, I think the reason we were so drained by the experience is because we literally were supercharged by the healing energy of the herd, and then, we were exhausted by the overload."

"If this is true for us, Anne, then we must find out the impact of our energy on them. We must discuss this with the grand buck tomorrow. What else has that beautiful mind of yours brought to the surface, dear?" She admitted that she was still cogitating on possibilities.

"I suspect that interaction was far more expansive than we realize, David. If my supposition about the energy infusion that we experienced is correct, then we certainly have a greater understanding of the power that exists within those incredible animals. And it makes me wonder what might be accomplished if humankind and the animal kingdom joined forces in helping the Earth. Just think about it, dear! Every day we send energy to the Earth in hopes of revitalizing her. We do this because it is a way that we can be of service. Our efforts are small, but worthwhile. Just imagine how much more effective we could be if more people would get involved in this simple exercise. And then, imagine the added impact of other species." The idea of worldwide participation energized Anne. As she envisioned her dream of assisting the planet, David's thoughts took him elsewhere.

"Anne, I think other species are way ahead of us. They aren't the ones who are destroying the planet. Humans are! They have always coexisted with the Earth; we are the ones who have upset the eco-system. I think what we just witnessed is how one species collaboratively functions with the planet and how they are trying to assist her. The deer are reaching out to us for help. They initiated communication. They stretched beyond their comfort zone to interact with us, and without our awareness, they blessed us with healing energy. I think other species are trying to raise human consciousness. They already understand what is going on with the Earth's declining health and they are trying to awaken us to the severity of the situation. They need us to face the truth. The Earth can no longer tolerate humankind's neglect and abusive behavior."

"David, you truly are a man of wisdom. Everything you just said is absolutely true. Humans are lagging behind while other species are leading the way. We are so fortunate, David, that we were in the right place at the right time. Now, I understand how important it is to share our experiences with others. More people need to be informed about the importance of individual commitments on behalf of the planet. Too many, including ourselves, feel helpless, but we do indeed have something to offer. Each of us in our own small ways can provide the Earth with restorative energy every day, and even several times a day. We, you and I, know this, and we know it is effective. Now, we know that other species are more aware of this than we are. That's inspiring! We are not alone. And now, we need to inspire others to get involved as well. I keep imagining a day when every person on the planet will join forces and send healing energy to her. Just imagine the power of that simple act: over seven and half billion people consistently sending her positive energy. She's a very big Life Being and she needs all the medicinal help she can get. Over seven billion doses of healing energy would make a difference, and if we did it daily, she would heal very rapidly. We can all do our part, David. We can make a difference just by sending her a dose of healing energy." Anne paused but had much more to say.

"We have to step up, David. For the sake of the Earth and for the sake of every species that resides upon her, we must accept responsibility for doing our part. No act is too small. Every thought, word, and deed that is offered on her behalf makes a difference." The couple sat quietly for a few minutes trying to assimilate the morning's happenings. Eventually, they agreed it was time to return home. David accepted the task of calling Carol and Jen to apprise them of the morning activity and also to relay the invitation that was extended by the grand buck. Anne took on the role of arranging the gathering. Calling the Gardners and the Hansons would be her first assignment.

Thirteen

"**W**elcome everyone!" David, living into his role as greeter for the gathering, invited the Hansons and the Gardners into Carol and Jen's backyard, where introductions were made. Anne quickly moved into her role as facilitator for the gathering by bolding pronouncing that it was high time for the four couples to meet one another. "I think we will all find that the eight of us have a lot in common." With that teaser tossed out for people to ponder, Anne then directed everyone to have a seat. Wonderful comments were made about the garden, which naturally led to more conversations about everyone's gardens and their mutual appreciation for Mother Nature.

"So," declared Anne, "as you can see, dear friends, we already have a shared passion. We are all nature lovers."

"Anne, I do believe you are up to something!" Janet teasingly pointed her finger at her dear friend. "And you have already successfully raised my curiosity level. So, out with it, girl. Just tell us what you are up to." The onlookers enjoyed the sweet connection shared between the two women.

Peter then chimed in with his observation. "I don't think that Anne is the only one involved, my Love. It appears to me that all four of them are up to something."

"Oh what fun!" squealed Janet. "But Anne is definitely the ringleader, so fess up girl! Tell us everything!" Jonathan and Geri were not sure what was actually happening, but they enjoyed the playfulness.

Anne put up her hands as if she were ready to confess, but then surprisingly turned the lead over to Carol and Jen. "Dear Ones, you were the ones that volunteered your wonderful space for this occasion, so it seems right that you should have the honor of introducing the reason for our gathering."

At first Carol and Jen looked to each other for support, and then they both realized that Anne was absolutely right. In unison, they spoke the truth. "It is an honor to introduce the reason for this gathering."

David started giggling. "Folks, these two do this all the time. You might as well just get used to it."

Without any apparent discussion, Carol and Jen mutually agreed that Carol would go first. She took the necessary deep breath and then turned to her beloved. "Jen and I are very happy to have all of you here in our backyard. And yes, we both openly admit that we often speak simultaneously. It's been going on for so long now that neither of us remembers when our concurrent speech pattern began."

Jen quickly interjected that they were very thrilled to learn that they were not the only couple participating in this kind of communication. "In fact," she noted, "I believe our frequency level has elevated since we started hanging out with these two." She pointed towards the Madisons, who were very lighthearted about their mannerisms. They enjoyed the banter.

"Well," began Carol "Anne and David have indicated that all of us have some type of affinity with nature. The reason we called this gathering is to meet other people who have similar interests. And particularly, we want to meet people who have had unusual experiences during their endeavors to connect with nature." Carol's emphasis on unusual experiences definitely captured everyone's attention. She looked toward Anne for feedback and noticed a slight nod of approval.

Geri, who is rarely at a loss for words, raised her hand, and Jen who was looking in her direction invited her to speak. "Well, first I want to thank you for inviting Jonathan and me to your lovely backyard. We are really grateful for this opportunity to get know all of you. And I must admit, Carol, that your comments caught my attention. Am I correct in understanding that you and Jen have encountered some surprises on your adventures, and is that also true for you, Anne and David?" Carol looked to Jen and the Madisons, all of whom gave her the nod to respond.

"Yes, Geri, you are correct, and we really want to discuss our experiences with other people. We do not believe that we are the only ones who are having these encounters and we feel it is essential that these stories be told. And we want to hear what other people are experiencing. We've come to believe that there is much more happening on this planet than we ever imagined. And it's so exciting!" Carol's sincerity impressed everyone. Geri's questions led to more questions.

Peter Hanson was intrigued, and after his and Janet's recent experience, he was ready to believe anything. "Friends, can we just cut to the chase here? Is everyone who is present having unusual experiences?" Everyone raised his or her hand.

"Oh my goodness!" exclaimed Anne. "David, you were right. We certainly invited the right people to our gathering."

"Okay folks, I have a suggestion to make," asserted Anne. "I think it's obvious from everyone's reactions that we all have stories to share. Who is willing to go first?" Janet and Peter quickly raised their hands.

Two and a half hours later the last story was told, processed, and applauded.

Jonathan looked around the circle and could not help but notice how it had changed during the storytelling period. "Look at us, friends. We started this gathering with a much larger circle. Our chairs were spaced far apart, as if we were keeping a safe distance from one another. And now look at us. Our circle has become a tightly knit group united by similar interests and stronger relationships. This is a remarkable transformation. I must admit this was one of the most invigorating experiences I've ever had. And I hope we are going to have more gatherings."

"I do, too," chimed in Janet. "I find this fascinating. We are receiving messages from various sources, but all the messages are related to saving the Earth. This is not a coincidence. Nana's message was adamant about the Earth's decline and the reality that we are running out of time. That is such a shocking reality to face, but we have to. And I'm so grateful that the four of you reached out to us, because I don't want to do this alone."

"Me neither!" echoed Carol and Jen.

"I think it is essential that we keep meeting," Jen insisted. "Not only will the gatherings provide support for all of us, but they also will facilitate greater understanding and hopefully faster resolutions to the issues." She paused briefly and seemed to be lost in wonderment. Carol urged her to continue.

"Well," she paused again, reluctant to reveal her feelings, but then she realized they really needed to be shared. "Doesn't all of this seem very odd? Just forty-eight hours ago, we were dealing with our unusual experiences alone, except for the blessings of our partners. Then Carol and I just happened to run into the Madisons on the trail, and the Hansons and Gardners just happened to reconnect, and now, here we are all together. I think this is very fascinating. It almost seems like all of this is being orchestrated."

"That's an interesting thought, Jen." David reflected upon the idea as his mind instantly reviewed the events of the last few days. "Perhaps it really is being orchestrated. Maybe the Earth's declining health is so critical that other inhabitants on the planet are attempting to awaken humankind to the severity of the situation."

"And don't forget our ancestors!" added Peter. "Janet's Great-grandmother is definitely a part of the rescue mission as well. And if she's involved in this, it makes sense that others from her realm of existence are, too."

"Yes, I agree," Janet joined in. "Nana was insistent. I feel confident that she will be providing more information. Actually, now that we are talking about this, I think Jen is right. In some way that we are not privy to at this point, there seems to be a grand effort that is unfolding, which is both comforting and shocking. It's nice to know that others are rallying to help the Earth, and it's frightening to know that we are in this precarious situation. The bottom line is evident. Humankind has to step up. We cannot continue to ignore the obvious. We have to do everything we can to help our planet." Peter smiled as he listened to his dear sweet beloved. She sounded remarkably like her Great-grandmother.

"Well, dear friends, I think we have had a very successful first gathering." As Anne looked about the circle, she witnessed what Jonathan had mentioned earlier. "What a blessing it is to see how close we have become in just a few hours! Let's pray that other gatherings similar to this one are happening all around the world. I am very hopeful, Dear Ones, and very grateful for this new heartfelt connection. Thank you all for coming today, and thank you, Carol and Jen for hosting our first meeting. And thank you, Mother Earth, for all that you do for so many. Please hold on! We hear your pleas and we are aware of your situation. We are here to assist."

And with that said, the four couples quickly agreed to meet the next week at the Hansons' tree house. Goodbyes were said and wonderful hugs were exchanged. Anyone observing the interaction would have assumed that these folks were Friends of Old.

Fourteen

Long ago on a planet of exceptional beauty, a species with great potential experienced an evolutionary mishap that resulted in a profound change in the species' behavioral patterns. At first, the changes were small, but noticeable nonetheless. As time passed, the changes began to negatively impact the development of other species also inhabiting the planet.

Before the species with great potential arrived, the planet and all the resident species mutually coexisted. The needs of everyone existing on the planet were respected. Rules of decency were honored. All who lived upon the gracious Life Being existed harmoniously and none was regarded as more than another. All were equal and all were treated as such.

As the impaired species' behavior began to decline, it caused great hardship to the planet and other species. Because this species had been openly welcomed to the planet, all involved tried to acclimate to the disruption that was being caused. Many hoped that the species would eventually become aware of their ill-fated ways, but that hope did not come to fruition. Instead, their behaviors grew more aggressive and violent. Their actions intruded upon every area of the planet and profoundly disrupted the environmental eco-system.

The species, once believed to have great potential, sickened the entire planet and all its life forms with the toxic energy that each member of the species personally emitted. This tragedy did not have to happen. It was not intended to happen. Those who held such great potential fell into their own selfish and greedy ways. So unfortunate this was.

Only one hope remained. An act of kindness was necessary: so little to ask of those who had taken so much and given so little in return.

Fifteen

Janet and Peter were extremely excited about hosting the second gathering. Even though the idea of meeting in the tree house had been in debate all week, a decision still needed to be made. Concerns about the size and the sturdiness of the tree house were discussed ad nauseam, but the truth was, they both wanted the meeting to be held in that wonderful space. So on the day of the event, the Hansons rose early and brought up six more comfortable folding chairs to see if the space would accommodate the group.

"What do you think, dear?" asked Janet, who was very optimistic about the plausibility of having the meeting in their sacred space.

"Actually, I'm surprised," Peter replied. "I didn't think it would be this spacious. Let's both sit down, dear, so we can view the setup." Janet did as instructed and it became obvious that eight bodies could easily and comfortably be situated in the tree house. "Let's do it!" encouraged Peter. "This is absolutely charming, and there is no need for concern regarding the durability of the tree house. It is solid and stable on its new platform. This is a go, dear!"

With that decision made, the couple agreed to separate and address their respective To Do Lists. Peter returned to his special space in the house, while Janet decided to have her meditation in the tree house. Quiet time was the first item on her list. At first, she was distracted by the extra chairs, but soon was able to detach from their presence. She drifted into the desirable place of solitude. *"Nana, are you here? I would like to chat, if you have some free time."*

"Yes, child, I am available, and I am delighted to be in your presence. Just so you know, I am also currently speaking with Peter in his sacred space. It is one of the many joys of being on this plane of existence. It is so much easier to accomplish tasks when you can multi-locate." Janet had many questions, but decided to add them to the long list she already had for her Great-grandmother. *"Not to worry, Janet. At some point we will have a long sit-down and tackle that list of yours, but not today, dear. We have other matters of more importance that demand our time. But first, let me applaud your decision to use the tree house for today's gathering. A brilliant idea! Secondly,"* she declared with authority, *"I am here to apprise you and Peter that you will not be alone. Please think expansively, dear. Obviously, your human friends will be in attendance, but others will be as well. I know your curiosity is creating more questions; however, their identities are not the*

issue. *What is important is that you and your friends will have contact with others from locations that are not presently known to you. I ask that you listen to them with the ears of your heart. Their messages are essential to the survival of the Earth."*

"And will you be present, Nana? Everyone was so excited to know that you had contacted us. I hope you will help facilitate the meeting."

"Rest assured, Janet! I will be present to assist in any way that is needed. However, you do not require assistance as a facilitator. Your skills are exceptional, and you and Peter work well together. The meeting will unfold as easily as did the first, and you will be most pleased with the interactions that will unfold. Have faith, Dear One. You are exactly where you are intended to be, and all that is unfolding is happening exactly as it is intended. I am most eager to meet your new friends, who are actually very old friends. You will come to understand this reality very soon. Please attend to your To Do List now…and I will attend mine."

"Nana, please don't tell me there are To Do Lists in your realm of existence as well?"

Janet's Great-grandmother Harriet reassured her that she did indeed have To Do Lists.

"And mine are much longer than yours, dear! I'm not complaining. It's just the truth. I will see you later, Dear One! In peace be!"

Meanwhile, in Peter's Sacred Space, he too was addressing the first item on his list. Having slipped easily into the place of silence, he simply rested knowing that whatever was intended to happen would happen of its own accord. This had not been easy for Peter to accept in his early phase of meditating. He was a man of superb organizational skills who was accustomed to orchestrating his own life. It was a surprise to him that meditation did not live by his rules of order. With commitment and persistence, he finally came to have a relationship with the silence.

"Good morning, Peter, may I join you?" Great-grandmother Harriet's voice was pleasantly recognized. His thoughts immediately went to Janet, but Harriet interrupted his ideas of inviting her Great-granddaughter into the interaction.

"Rest easy, Peter! Janet and I are already in conversation in the tree house. You need not worry. She and I are having a wonderful connection at that location, and now, I hope to have the same here in your location. We have much to discuss Peter, but currently I bring you information regarding today's gathering. As I said to Janet, the tree house is a wonderful setting for the gathering. I believe everyone in attendance will find the setting charming and delightful. Peter, I am very grateful for the tender relationship that the two of you enjoy. Janet can be headstrong at times, but the two of you have managed to create a beautiful, lasting relationship. I am very grateful,

Peter. Please continue to stand by each other. Many changes are coming, Dear One, and the changes will be most disconcerting. I am so glad that you have each other." Peter expressed his appreciation for Harriet's kind words and reassured her that his devotion to Janet was everlasting.

Using his inner voice, he continued to communicate with the elder who had passed decades before. *"Let's face it Harriet! Janet and I are growing old together. And if something unthinkable lies ahead, we will face it together. I'm assuming that your comment about the group's attendance is your way of informing us that we will not be alone during this meeting."*

"You are so bright, Peter! Indeed, that is my reason for connecting. All will be well. Do not be concerned for your guests; they are ready for this experience, as are you and Janet. Simply take it in stride."

"And will you be with us as well, Harriet?" Peter inadvertently returned to speaking orally. The habit was not easy to break.

"Not to worry, Peter. I am capable of hearing you either way, and this is true for the Companions who will be joining us. I am happy to say that I will be present as well. Thank you for being available, Peter. In peace be!"

Peter sat quietly taking one deep breath after another. He wondered if Janet was still engaged with her Great-grandmother, when he heard a faint knock at the door.

"Come in, dear! I was just thinking about you." His words preceded his approach to the door. As he reached out to invite his beloved in, Janet was already turning the doorknob. Hugs were exchanged.

"Did you have a visitor, Peter?" He nodded, grinned, and another long hug was enjoyed. The two shared their encounters with one another and then sat down to process their experiences. "Isn't this remarkable, dear? We're actually engaging with Nana as if she never died. It's as if she never left us."

"Yes, it gives one pause," he mused. "I find myself wondering about all the others who have passed. Do we have the option of connecting with them? Or are they off on other adventures that keep them occupied? My questions are endless, and perhaps, they don't need to be answered, but it leaves one to wonder." The couple sat in silence for a moment each lost in the wonderment of their respective minds. So much was happening. There was much to ponder, and still, there was much to do before the gathering that they were hosting. Janet found that her wonderment quickly turned into worriment regarding preparations for the said gathering. She politely interrupted her dear husband and requested that a game plan be made. Within minutes, each volunteered for various assignments and agreed that the tasks would be accomplished by a designated time. Peter and Janet were delightfully independent people who enjoyed addressing tasks in their own preferred ways. Because they trusted each other to follow through with commitments made, this process of working conjointly but independently worked well for the couple. They agreed to reconvene at the tree house twenty minutes before the meeting was to start.

"Everything looks lovely, Peter! The tree house is in her glory!" More praises were made regarding the setting around the beloved tree house, as well as the refreshment table and the backyard in general. In a brief moment of panic, Janet realized that she hadn't even thought about the front yard. "Oh, dear!" she exclaimed and headed in that direction.

"Not to worry, dear," Peter responded to her thoughts. "I did some tidying a bit ago. All is well. The house and yard are in good form and looking very welcoming."

"Oh, we are so blessed, Peter. We have this sweet place to enjoy and wonderful friends with whom we can share these blessings. Thank you so much, dear. You are my greatest blessing." The couple was embraced in a long, emotional hug when the guests began to arrive.

"Welcome, everyone!" exclaimed Janet and Peter simultaneously. More hugs were exchanged as each couple entered the backyard, and of course, comments were abundant regarding the tree house. An onlooker, not knowing any better, would have thought these four couples were friends of old, and of course, they would have been correct, even though the couples themselves were yet to discover this truth about their relationships.

After warm greetings were enjoyed and an appropriate amount of chitchat was done, the guests were welcomed up into the tree house. "Okay, Dear Ones! Let's convene in the tree house!" Janet led the way while inviting everyone to be careful as they came up the steps into the new location of the tree house. "As you can see, Peter, has made the tree house amenable to people of a mature age."

Her dear husband elaborated upon the relocation process, describing how he had taken great care to situate the house directly under its original location. "The tree's health demanded a change, and quite honestly, it is a much better situation for our health as well. Climbing up and down that ladder wasn't really working for us anymore. This arrangement allows us to feel as if we are still in the tree, and I think that actually pleases her. We love her company and I think she enjoys ours as well." One after another the Hansons, the Gardners, the Madisons, and Jen and Carol climbed the steps into the tree house. When everyone was safely seated, a deep breath was shared.

"Oh my goodness!" whispered Anne. "This is incredible!" Similar comments cropped up as the group settled into their new environment.

"This is the most delightful sacred space," stated Jen. "I'm sure the tree is very grateful for your thoughtfulness. It is such a privilege to be here!" Many more observations and expressions of gratitude were made before the gathering was actually convened; however, each comment made warmed the heart of the old tree and of the child, now an elder, who spent so many wonderful times growing up in the tree's presence.

"Dear friends, welcome to our home in the tree and thank you for honoring this special space with your lovely comments. I can feel how much she is enjoying your company." Janet reached out to those sitting next to her and others followed in like manner. Soon all hands were connected and it was time for everyone to unite through the simple process of a deep, elongated breath. "Oh, how sweet it is, dear friends, to be in your presence once again. Let's take advantage of this moment of union to join our energies. With each deep breath that you inhale feel your energy mounting, and then, shift that powerful energy to the person to the left of you." Janet paused allowing for this first step of the exercise to be enacted. "And now, dear friends, allow yourself to receive the energy that is being gifted to you from your right. Send your energy to your left and receive the energy from your right. Just be with that transfer of energy for a moment while we all take a few more deep breaths." Pausing again, Janet waited for the breaths to be taken.

"And now, dear friends, let us focus on this combined energy that is now residing in each of us. Imagine this powerful energy circling about your heart. This energy is our combined energies that we have intentionally shared with each another, and which is now available to be shared with another. Dear Ones, let's invite this wonderful old tree to be a part of our gathering. She stands here beside us now ready and willing to participate in our activity. Let us focus our intentions upon this energy within us and let us infuse this special energy with love and gratitude for everything the Earth has done for us. Let's do this now." A moment of silence was provided, as the act of kindness was prepared. "And then," Janet continued, "let us share this wonderful, healing energy that we have amassed with this blessed tree so that she can pass it along through her deeply embedded roots into the bowels of Mother Earth. We can do this, dear friends. Allow the energy within you to pass from your heart to this magnificent tree. And she will do the rest." Time passed, or stood still, or did whatever it is that time does during moments such as these, and then the chimes boldly announced the completion of the act of kindness. The unknown melody joyously performed brought everyone back to the present. The group was in awe as the tree generated breezes that assisted the concert heralding the collaborative action taken on behalf of the Earth.

"Do you believe this?" mused Geri. "I think the chimes are telling us that the Earth received our healing energy! Can that be possible?" She turned to her companions for feedback, hoping that someone would validate her ideas, and then quickly turned her eyes to her hostess. "Janet, do believe the chimes were communicating with us?"

"Dear Heart, I want to believe this as much as you do. In my heart, I am absolutely certain that the chimes indicate our intentions were successful. But I have no scientific proof of this." Janet suddenly went silent as a thought entered her mind. She rose from her chair and faced the large weathered trunk of the tree. "Old Friend, thank you so much for assisting us today. We desperately want to help the Earth and I know you do as well. Can you tell me, Old Friend, was our energy transfusion successful? Did the Earth receive our good intentions?" With the questions asked, the chimes let loose with another magnum opus courtesy of the rush of breezes streaming from the tree. Peter could not control himself. He jumped up to hug his beloved, and soon everyone was on their feet exchanging hugs, laughter, and gratitude.

"That was spectacular!" Carol's outburst caused another round of high spirits and conversation. Astonishment, amazement, awe, belief, wonderment! You name the emotion and it was activated by the event just witnessed. And then deep breaths were taken in concert and the elevated energy waned back to a state of normalcy.

"How lovely it is to witness the merriment of Dear Old Friends!" The message spoken by Great-grandmother Harriet penetrated the inner pathways of all who were in attendance. Janet and Peter immediately checked in with their guests to be certain that everyone had heard her voice, and all concurred that they had indeed heard the lovely greeting.

"Nana, thank you so much for coming. Did you see what just happened? We sent energy to the Earth with the assistance of this grand old tree?" Janet's excitement was the equivalent of a great-grandchild seeking approval from an elder. Before Harriet could respond, Janet apologized for not introducing her friends.

"Not to worry, dear, I am acutely aware of the identity of these Dear Old Friends. It is so good to see all of you; it has been a very long time. I am most pleased to be in your company, again. I am enamored by your enthusiasm and I wish to confirm that you did indeed accomplish your energy transfusion to the Earth. Your kindness is deeply appreciated and needed. For future reference, Dear Ones, the procedure that you just initiated can and must be repeated frequently. The Earth's needs are great at this time and each energy transfusion that she receives is significant to her recovery process. I urge you to send her energy every day. Several times a day, if possible! Each of you has the ability to actualize this energy transfusion on your own. Whether it is done alone or in the company of others, the act of kindness matters. Please hear this! The act of transferring positive energy to the Life Being Earth is significant to her recovery process."

Listening to Harriet's appeal was also a significant experience to those who had little or no experience communicating with someone who was deceased. The experience was one that could take your breath away, as was the message itself.

"Harriet, can you elaborate upon the importance of these energy transfusions?" inquired Peter. "Obviously, I trust what you are telling us, but I'm confused about the efficacy of this process. More information would be helpful."

"Peter, dear, your question does not surprise me. You are one who prefers details. When I was in human form, I was much like you. I needed to see to believe. I needed to understand to believe. Now, that I am in another form, my requirements are less tedious. I can believe without seeing. I can believe without having full clarity. I invite you, Peter, to expand your awareness. You are more than you appear to be, and you are more capable than you presently can imagine." The concept was mind-boggling, but the eight listeners maintained their attention to Janet's Great-grandmother.

"Dear Ones, these words are true for all of you. You are all more than you remember, but your forgetfulness does not change your reality. You are more than you appear to be. Your true self will become clearer as you focus your intentions upon healing the Earth. She needs your assistance. Without your help, she will not continue. And without her vitality, your kind will not continue."

The force of Harriet's words stunned the group. Each member was reeling from the concepts suggested.

"Dear Ones, please take a deep breath. I apologize for speaking so bluntly, but the truth must be spoken forthrightly and it must be heard regardless of the

unpleasantness of the message. The news of the Earth's condition is startling. I know it is difficult to assimilate such dreadful information. However, Dear Old Friends, do not allow the complexity of this situation to override the other information that was presented. Too often those in human form focus their attention upon the negative aspect of a situation while ignoring the positive details that are also reality. The reality in this situation is that humankind is more than they appear to be. Please ponder this truth for it is the answer to the problem that confronts you. Blessed Friends, remember who you are."

Silence engulfed the group for what seemed a very long time, but according to Peter's watch only a few minutes had passed. He was surprised.

"Dear Old Friends!" Harriet's voice interrupted the machinations of the participant's minds. *"Time marches on in the wonderment of the mind, but in reality, there are matters that must be discussed. So I ask you to return to the present. All of you have recently had experiences that seem to be extraordinary. In truth, your experiences are exquisitely ordinary. Such events happen on a daily basis, but few people are aware of this because they are consumed by distractions that they accept as ordinary. Dear Ones, connection with other species is not only possible, it is desirable. All species have intelligence and all have means of communicating with others. This transpires constantly. Please breathe that in, Dear Friends."* Harriet, realizing that her audience needed time to assimilate her messages, allowed a few moments to pass.

"Please forgive me for sharing so much information with you, but it must be done. Everything that I am sharing, you already know; however, much of what you know has been forgotten. So, in truth, I am not providing new information, I am reminding you of that which you already know. Dear Ones, this may be confusing, but it is your truth nonetheless. I know you have many questions, but there are others far more capable of assisting you with your insatiable curiosity. It is time for you to engage with these individuals. Before I take my leave, I ask a favor of all of you. Please remember that you are more than you appear to be. And please listen with the ears of your heart. You are here in this place at this time for a reason. Be present. Be conscious. And remember you are not alone. I bid you adieu for now, Dear Old Friends. You are always in my heart."

The Circle of Friends fell silent, as did the breeze and the chimes. Silence engulfed the tree house. If the eight friends were able to remember their gift of exceptional sight, they would have seen the invisible shield that encircled the tree and the tree house. The shield, necessary for a variety of reasons, provided complete privacy and protection for all in attendance. As they sat quietly reviewing their experience with Janet's

Great-grandmother, preparations were being secured so that all present would be safely protected within the confines of the setting.

Without reason or any form of apparent communication, all the participants sitting in the tree house inhaled a very deep breath at exactly the same time. This was not one of those occasions when one person just happened to take a deep breath and everyone else joined the process, nor was it the natural reaction of seasoned meditators and breath workers who simply merge with the process when it unfolds before them. This was different and everyone present knew it was different, even though not all who were present were capable of explaining what was different. Among those who were incapable of expressing the differences that they sensed were the eight friends who had gathered in the tree house. Little did they know what was about to unfold.

"Greetings, Dear Friends! We are Friends from afar and we come in peace. We respectfully request a moment of your time." The pronouncement heard from within took the neighborhood friends by surprise. For a brief moment they remained speechless as curious glances darted from one to the other, and then Janet remembered what Nana had told her before.

"Dear New Friends, please excuse my poor manners, but your arrival took me by surprise." Quickly making eye contact with the seated friends in the tree house, she continued, "My Great-grandmother Harriet informed me early this morning that you would be coming, but I misunderstood the timing of your arrival. She also told me that we must all listen to you with the ears of our heart. You are most welcome here, New Friends. How may we be of service to you?" Through Janet's gracious welcoming of the new guests, the current guests gained a little more clarity about what was going on. Curious and excited, they all looked on with anticipation.

"Thank you for accepting our request. We understand that our arrival can be unsettling for some individuals. We hope that we have not caused anyone any harm. Our mission is one of peace. Although we wish that we could arrive without any disturbance, our circumstances are so different from yours that it is not easy for us to make an entrance without creating a stir. Please excuse us for intruding upon your time, but there are issues of the utmost importance that must be discussed. With the assistance of our Dear Friend, your Great-grandmother Harriet, we have been monitoring your encounters with other species and we are most pleased with the interactions that are transpiring. Although you do not presently remember this, your desire for connection and communication with others species is happening for a reason.

At times you feel compelled to reach out to them. This intense desire grows stronger every day. It calls to you. The calling that you feel is directly related to a commitment that you agreed to long ago. It is part of your genetic makeup that has aroused and guided you in this direction since you entered into this lifetime. Dear Friends, you are here for a reason, and we are here to remind you of your commitments that are now actualizing into actions. Within each of you is an ache to assist the planet. You feel it and you want to take action, but you are confused about what actions to take. At times the ache is so present that you feel as if you are about to burst." The words of the invisible speaker touched the hearts of the earthbound friends. Tears could be seen glistening in the eyes of several members, while others sat as if they were in a daze.

"Who are you? How do you know these truths about us?" The questions Anne posed were calmly stated and brought the other group members to full attention. They sat erect, eyes wide opened, but not knowing where to focus.

"Dear Friends, we apologize for not materializing before you. We know you are not accustomed to speaking to an invisible voice, but the materialization process demands a great expenditure of our energy. To participate in that process would diminish the amount of time that we can spend with you, and we believe it is in the best interest of all involved that we optimize our time together. In reference to your questions, we will address the last one first. Dear Friend Anne, we know these truths about you, about all of you, because we were there when the commitments were made. We all made commitments on behalf of the Life Being Earth. She welcomed our kind to her surface at a time when we were desperately in need of a place to create a home. We had been searching for a new place to reside for a very long time. Hope was becoming a distant memory when we noticed a beautiful blue planet in a solar system not explored before. We approached and she graciously received us. Our kind is deeply grateful for all that she has done for us."

While everyone was digesting the information provided, more questions were forming in Anne's mind. They were surfacing rapidly and each one seemed important to articulate, but Anne was not one to rudely interrupt someone. She strived to be patient, but it was not easy. As she repositioned herself in her chair, she feared that her need for answers was going to override good manners. Suddenly, and just in time, her beloved husband, David, reached out and placed his hand atop hers. The gesture quieted her impulsiveness.

"Ah!" came a sigh from nowhere. *"A loving act of kindness. We bear witness to the gentle, sweet exchange between two beloved friends. How effective inner*

communication can be! For those of you who did not notice what just transpired, your companions, Anne and David, successfully connected without speaking aloud."

All eyes turned to the couple and David accepted responsibility for explaining their situation. "My beloved's mind has been very busy formulating questions that she wanted to ask our invisible guests. She was valiantly attempting to manage her impatience, but her self-control was waning. Just as she was about to speak out, I reached over to touch her hand. The heartfelt connection we shared diminished the impulse and she was able to relax. The primary factor of relevance here is that we do practice telepathic communication on a regular basis and it is becoming increasingly more effective. And we believe this has aided out ability to connect with other species."

"Indeed, it has!" confirmed the unseen voice. *"Other species have communicated in this manner since they came into existence. Long ago, the human species did as well, but the ability that lies within you has been forgotten. Nonetheless, it still exists, and it can be activated by practice, patience, and perseverance. The Madisons are examples of this, as are the rest of you. All of you have been dabbling in these experiences and we encourage you to enhance your abilities as quickly as possible. Your skills are needed. The other species of the planet are already actively involved in assisting the Earth. They can provide vitally important information to the human species that will enable you to be better stewards of the planet.*

Dear Friends, you are here for a reason, and we are here to remind you that your reason for being here at this time in this location is because you are intended to create greater stewardship for the Earth among those in this vicinity. Other people of similar interest are also gathering in various places around the planet in order to assist her recovery process. These acts of kindness are of extreme importance. The deed is important and the intention is as well. The deed enacted helps heal the injuries that she has incurred, while the intention soothes her spirits and gives her hope that the relationship between humans and all other species will mend. Acts of kindness come in many different packages. Each is a gift that inspires the Earth to continue.

The eight of you are Friends of Old. Please accept this reality as your truth because it is. Your commitments to the Earth were done hand-in-hand. Hold that image within, Dear Ones, and you will understand that the heartfelt connection among you is of very long-standing. Throughout numerous other lifetimes you have served the Earth just as you will in this life experience. As suggested during your first gathering, your reunion was orchestrated, but what you do not remember is that you are the originators of the orchestration. You requested that you would be brought together during your efforts to assist the Earth, and we abide by your request by facilitating the reunion in each new lifetime. Each of you experiences an intense sense of knowing that you are intended to be together. That knowingness is the result of the memories of old. You are intended to be together because you wanted to be together. This is evidence of the strong bond that exists among you. Old Friends, you are together again, at last." The chimes marked the moment of awareness with a lovely sweet melody.

Carol shared the tissues she had pocketed in her jacket. She remembered grabbing them on the way out of the door thinking that they might come in handy. "This explains so much," she sniffled. "While we were walking here, Jen and I were talking about the intense connection we feel with all of you, and how amazed we were that it happened so quickly. Our biggest concern about relocating was making new friends, but after our first gathering that concern was taken off the list. We both feel so blessed to have met you. And now, we know this all happened for a reason. I'm living in gratitude!" Similar feelings and expressions of gratitude were shared by Jen and mutually felt by their new friends.

Jonathan, sitting quietly with his elbows on his knees, suddenly sat up straight and made eye contact with Carol. "Geri and I had similar reactions to the first gathering. The depth of connection that transpired so quickly during the meeting really surprised us. Although we already felt connected with most of you, there was a deepening that happened when the eight of us came together. We didn't understand it at the time, but we were very pleased. The idea that we are Old Friends gives me pause, and it inspires many more questions, but they can wait for the moment. Even though I'm struggling to wrap my mind around this new information, I must admit that it is very comforting to know that we are Old Friends. It warms my heart."

The tenderness demonstrated by Jonathan inspired his lovely wife, Geri, to add her own perspective to the mix. "The word that comes to mind for me is magical. I believe what is happening here is real and I believe everything that has been shared with us is true, and still, it seems unbelievable." Geri shook her head in disbelief. "The experience that we're sharing reminds me of our outer garden. Everything that is happening in the garden is real, and by the way, it validates what we just heard. I don't have any doubts that what is happening here is real and sometime in the future, we will think that it is ordinary; but in my mind, in this moment, it all seems magical to me. The plants in our garden are showing us how to design the outer garden. It's happening; it's real! The eight of us are sitting here in a tree house and we're listening to an invisible voice that is informing us that we are Dear Old Friends, and it's real! The garden is real, the tree house is real, and the invisible voice is real. It's all real…and it seems absolutely magical!" Geri smiled and giggled and her companions joined in the frivolity. "I'm loving this!" she declared to her Old Friends. The laughter eased the underlying concern that all shared regarding the Earth's health. They all knew more information was coming, but for a brief moment the Old Friends just enjoyed each other's company.

From a faraway place and time, others who also participated in the commitment vows to the Earth watched the reunion. They longed to be side-by-side with their Friends of Old, but that was not to be. Those who returned to assist the planet in distress had their work to do, while those who remained had to help from afar. All were necessary to the strategic plan of saving the Earth.

"Old Friends, how wonderful it is to see you together once again. We desire to continue the discussion if you are available." Janet immediately repositioned herself back into the chair as she watched her friends do the same. She thought it was interesting to see their response to the invisible voice, which reminded her that the identity of the voice was still unknown. She looked towards Anne who was poised to ask the question again. She encouraged her friend to take the lead.

"Hello, this is Anne again. I wonder if you would like to address the question regarding your identity at this time. I don't mean to be pushy, but it seems odd to have these important discussions with someone who is unseen and unnamed." Her manner was gentle, but firm. Janet's Great-grandmother readily introduced herself to the Circle of Eight and Anne wanted the same courtesy from the invisible voice. A moment of silence, which seemed to linger on and on, finally came to an end.

"Yes, Friend Anne, it is time for your question to be answered. Forgive us for avoiding the question, but it is one that is not easily answered. The voice that you hear sounds as if it is the voice of one, and if that were true, the answer would be easy. However, what you hear is not the voice of one, but it is the voice of many, which makes your question difficult to answer. In essence, we are a Collective of Friends from many different places and times. All of us are deeply concerned about the health of the Life Being Earth. She is a cherished member of the Universe. Her presence not only brings great joy to All in Existence, but she is an Essential Being to all other Beings in the Great Existence. Her presence affects all other Essential Beings and her absence is unimaginable.

We come en masse to approach the Children of Earth. We beg you to change your behavior. This is not too much to ask of a species that has been gifted with so many privileges. You were provided with a beautiful residence, abundant resources, diverse interspecies cohabitants, harmonious opportunities, ingenuity, and the gift of time. All that was needed was provided, but unfortunately, poor decisions were made. Now, your species is in grave trouble, and the Life Being Earth suffers the consequences of your ill-fated decision.

No one wishes to endure the loss of an Essential Life Being or the demise of a prominent species; however, time is of the essence. There is still time to save your species. All it takes is a decision founded in kindness. Your species dwells in negativity, which produces toxic energy that sickens the planet and yourselves. You do not need to continue this behavior. You are not intended to live your lives in this manner. Change your ways, please. Live with goodness in your hearts. Treat others with kindness and dignity and you will receive the same. This is not difficult! It is simply a lifestyle to accept and to expand upon. Treat others in the same manner that you desire to be treated. Recognize that all life is essential and that all are equally important to the cycle of life. Accept that no one is more than another. All are equal. These simple rules of decency will change your present course of destruction and it will revitalize the planet. This request is so little to ask of you. Release your negativity; it serves no one. In truth, your negativity is destroying your chance for a future.

We beg you to choose to live life from a place of kindness. Treat others as you desire to be treated and your species will survive and thrive. Continue your present course of negativity and unkindness, and your fate will be most unpleasant.

Old Friends, we are sorry to remind you of the reality of your circumstances. It is most unpleasant. You are here now, because you knew this truth long ago, and you committed yourself to assisting the Earth. The project to save the Earth continues. "The time is now," is a phrase you have heard more times than you can imagine, and yet, it must be repeated again. The Time Is Now. Change your ways now. You cannot delay this decision. You must act now." Silence befell the tree house and all who were seen and unseen. The news was unthinkable, and yet, everyone knew it was accurate. Time slipped by, which was a problem. This was not the time to waste even a moment of time.

"Friend Anne, we still have not answered your question; however, we answer it with a request. Please call us Old Friend, for this is our truth, as it is also yours. Old Friends, we have reminded you of your pasts and your current circumstances. We wish the message was more positive. Please know that we are but a breath away, and you may contact us at any time. Just reach out to us through your inner voice, and we will hear you. We leave you to ponder your next steps. Please know that

you are children of goodness and you are deeply cherished by Those of the Universe. In peace be."

The Circle of Eight, the Dear Old Friends, remained still for what seemed an eternity, but in truth, was only a few minutes. Peter was the first to seek connection. He cleared his throat, hoping to articulate something, anything that might break the silence, but his effort failed. Janet took the lead.

"Well, Dear Old Friends, I believe it is time that we pull ourselves out of this stupor that we are in. It is time that we contemplate our next steps. Will you please join me?" Everyone rallied to Janet's request. "Dear Ones, I am going ask you for a favor. I want to practice being a person of kindness before we end our gathering, and I would like you to practice with me." The group came to attention ready to follow Janet's lead.

"First of all, I wish to express my gratitude to all of you. Your presence today warms my heart, and I want to acknowledge that your attendance and participation in our meeting was an act of kindness. Your presence made me feel more hopeful. Truthfully, I'm not sure how I would have managed today's meeting without you. We received a lot of disturbing information, but we also received some very exciting and uplifting news. We are Old Friends! Imagine that! How grateful I am to be in your presence again...thank goodness we were all here." Janet's acknowledgement brought smiles and similar expressions of gratitude.

"And we had time with my Great-grandmother. Isn't she a hoot?" She got a round of applause for that comment. "I'm so grateful for her presence and her availability. She will be a great resource for us. I'm glad all of you had an opportunity to feel her presence. And let us not forget that we encountered Beings from other places and times who regard us as Old Friends. We are not alone. That's exceptional news as well. We have much to be grateful for including the news that must be addressed with haste. I want to make a commitment to all of you. Dear Old Friends, tomorrow I will rise early and I will walk with my beloved, and as we walk I will happily engage with everyone we encounter. I will be available, I will offer a listening ear, and I will treat everyone in the same manner that I desire to be treated. And then, when we return home, I promise all of you that I will begin making a To Do List specifically focusing upon Daily Acts of Kindness. I have taken to heart this challenge of being a better person. This is my commitment to all of you." Janet's new family of Dear Old Friends listened with the ears of their hearts and they were bowled over by her expressions of commitment.

Her beloved husband watched the reactions of their guests and started to giggle. "Welcome to my world, friends! Janet is a whirlwind of action, and more importantly, she is one who follows through on the commitments she makes. It's clear to me that tomorrow will be a day of self-exploration for the two of us, so I will commit to doing my part. I will review my negative behaviors; even though, part of me doesn't want to do this. I would prefer to remain blissfully ignorant, but that's not an option." Peter released an audible sigh that revealed a truth that he didn't want to admit. "Too many of us have ignored the truth for too long, including me. Well, we can't do that anymore. So tomorrow, I will make a list of the negative behaviors that I recognize within me, and I will also find ways of changing that behavior. This is my commitment to all of you and to Mother Earth."

Jen took to heart the commitments that her friends were professing, and tears welled up and trickled down her cheeks. "I am deeply moved by the bold statements of actions that are being expressed," she said as she received a tissue from Carol's stash. Wiping the tears from her cheeks, she admitted that she was afraid to tackle this task. "My list of negative behaviors will be long. This is so embarrassing to acknowledge, but the truth is truth, whether it is spoken or not. I'm afraid to face these behaviors and I am afraid that I will be unable to change." More tears flowed as Jen's fears flashed through her mind. The group of friends sat quietly as her emotions surfaced. Everyone there understood her fears. Each met with a similar fear when the invisible voice invited them to ponder their next steps.

Anne was rocking back and forth in her chair. The movement was barely noticeable, but it was her way of supporting Jen. Eventually, she was able to put her thoughts into words. "Jen, dear, I don't mean to be competitive, but I suspect my list will be longer than yours. You're not alone with this fear, Jen. I think everyone here is concerned about his or her negative habits. The truth is my biggest fear is about my negative thoughts. Oh goodness! The idea of writing these hidden secrets down on a piece of paper is truly frightening. But just admitting this fear out loud lessens my anxiety. I doubt that I'm the only person who has a mind that dwells on negative topics. In truth, I wonder if people have any idea how many unkind thoughts are generated by our respective minds. This exercise of self-examination is going to be very useful, Jen.

Let's embrace it rather than fearing it. Just imagine how much we are going to learn about ourselves, and in so doing, we will be empowered to make changes." Jen's fearful disposition changed as she listened to Anne.

"Anne, thank you! You totally shifted my mood and I'm already feeling calmer and stronger. Embracing this task is an absolutely brilliant idea." Jen took a long deep breath and her Dear Old Friends joined her, and then she announced her commitment. "I'm on board with this and I will begin this new adventure this evening. I will begin making my list of behaviors that need to be released or improved upon. And I will also create a list of strategies for change and improvement. I will devote two hours to this work before retiring and also create a schedule for subsequent sessions of exploration." Jen's enthusiasm inspired everyone in the tree house, including the observers from afar.

Jonathan and Geri were riveted by the changes that were occurring right before their eyes. Jon looked to his beloved and urged her to go first. She was happy to do so.

"Well, this burst of energy is a marvel to witness," she declared, "and I would be remiss if I didn't acknowledge the acts of kindness that are transpiring here on behalf of the planet. I so hope Mother Earth is absorbing this positive energy. I feel certain that she is." Geri's emotions rose to the surface, and for a brief moment, she was speechless as a wave of gratefulness overwhelmed her. "Excuse me, please, but I just realized how easy it is to help the Earth. Like all of us, she needs to be loved. She needs to feel that she is loved and she needs to be treated respectfully. She's just like us! When we feel loved and respected, we flourish, and when we don't, our energy wanes." Geri leaned forward, placed her hands on her knees, and breathed in the biggest breath she had ever achieved. Then she turned and made eye contact with all her new Old Friends. "I get it!" she announced. "Dear Ones, we need to do some multi-tasking. Every day, we need to rise with love in our hearts and we need to express that love to the Earth and everyone else who is important to us. We need to feel the love within us, and we need to expand it. And then, we need to spread it across the planet. With that single effort, we can change the path ahead of us. With love in our hearts, embracing the tasks of change will be easier. Facing our negative behaviors will be easier. The energy of love and the energy of hopefulness will advance our efforts of change." She paused and made eye contact with her companions again.

"When Janet and Peter braved the trail and made their commitments to the Earth, I was inspired. When Jen shared her fears, I was wading in my own. And when Anne reached out to give Jen a boost, I felt emboldened. It was inspiring to see the positive energy that was produced by these acts of kindness. In truth, it was overwhelming to witness the acts of loving-kindness that were shared during our brief discussion. The change happened so quickly. One moment we were being challenged by an invisible Collective of Old Friends to review our behaviors and to make changes, and in the next moment, action was being taken. Acts of kindness flourished. We weren't just reminded of our past indiscretions; we were also reminded of our relationship with the Earth. That connection lies deeply within us, and as we allow ourselves to remember the heartfelt bond that we have with her, changing on her behalf will be easy. Dear Friends, I'm in! I will let my love for the Earth be my guide, as I discover the negative behaviors that must be addressed. This discussion is my first step in healing the Earth." Once again, the flurry of positive energy was admired from afar. Those referred to as the invisible Collective were most pleased by the reactions of those who were just reminded of their calling to be greater stewards of the Earth.

Jonathan, who was waiting in anticipation to follow his spouse, suddenly changed his mind. Even though he was ready to take the lead, Jonathan knew from within that someone else was in need of expressing his thoughts.

David Madison twisted about in his chair trying to make himself more comfortable, but the truth was, his discomfort had nothing to do with the chair. He cleared his throat, as men often do when they are feeling insecure, and then he turned toward Jonathan. "Thank you, Jon, for letting me take the lead. I hope your act of kindness doesn't alter the rhythmic flow that you and Geri share." David then turned his attention to the group and praised Jon's intuitive skills. "For those of you who didn't notice, Jonathan was waiting to follow in the footsteps of his beloved, but he stopped himself because he sensed that someone else needed to speak. He sensed the urgency that I was feeling and generously allowed me to go first. His intuitive abilities are far more keen that he presently knows." Jonathan blushed but was also deeply grateful for the feedback. His beloved reached over and tightly squeezed his hand.

"I often worry about the Earth," confessed David, "because people just don't seem to grasp the severity of her situation. She's in trouble! I appreciate what has happened here this afternoon. Even though the information that was provided is hard to hear, I prefer to know the truth. I believe the people of this planet can handle the truth. If we know what we're dealing with, we will find solutions. I've always believed this, but so many lies and disinformation have clouded the truth, that I am losing faith in our ability to turn this situation around." Tears welled up and David required a moment to regain his composure.

"I just can't imagine the Earth's pain, not only the physical suffering that she has endured, but also our blatant disregard for her. What is wrong with us? Our behavior has been shameful and it still continues. I am embarrassed to admit this, but I carry a lot of resentment about the Earth's situation. There are times when I just want to lash out at people who don't show her the respect that she deserves. As you can see, my negative energy is large, and part of me worries that I will not be able to manage it." David deliberately quieted himself with several deep breaths before continuing.

"I'm going to need some help, Friends. As you just witnessed, Anne is incredibly supportive, but I can't burden her with all my negativity. I'm going to need a lot of help and I want to put all of you on alert that I'm going to be reaching out to you." Offers rushed forward and David accepted the acts of kindness graciously. "Thank you. I appreciate your responses. It's comforting to know that we now have our own collective to turn to. Excuse me, but there's one more thing I need to say, before closing this down. What's been going on here in this discussion is impressive and it truly gives me hope. The speed with which love and positivity can change the mood of a setting is phenomenal. I hope that my candor hasn't altered the mood in this tree house. Being able to speak my truth has greatly assisted me. I commit to all of you that I am here to save the Earth and I will vigilantly work towards changing my negative energy into healing energy. Thank you for listening and for supporting me." David's acknowledgment of his anger about the Earth's mistreatment triggered similar reactions in other group members. He soon learned that he was not the only one harboring resentments. He thanked everyone for revealing the unspeakable truths and then turned towards Jonathan. Everyone presumed he was going to invite him to take the lead, but they were surprised.

"Jon, are your empathic abilities in overdrive?" Jonathan smiled and nodded. "May I invite Carol to go next?" He nodded again. Carol witnessed the interaction with a bit of embarrassment, but appreciated the courtesy that was gifted to her. She reassured Jonathan that she was okay, but he insisted that she take her turn.

"Thank you, Jon and David. I think the two of you have much to teach us." Carol smiled at the two men who so graciously offered her an act of kindness. Then she closed her eyes and took the necessary deep breath to calm her racing mind. After this act of self-care was taken, she made eye contact with everyone. "Well," she stated softly, "this is certainly a day that will be remembered." Carol raised her hands in prayerful fashion and placed them gently against her lips. Her feelings were running amok and she was struggling to capture a thought to articulate. Jen reached over and placed her hand on her beloved's knee. Carol responded by placing her hand upon Jen's. "Thank goodness, you are here, dear!"

"Wouldn't want to be anywhere else, C. Just take your time. We're all here for you." The tender reassurance touched more than just the recipient.

"Much to my Mother's surprise," Carol began, "I was not the prissy little girl that she had hoped me to be. No dolls ever piqued my curiosity and the puffed sleeves in the precious girly dress that she adored drove me crazy. Unbeknownst to her, my tomboy antics began at a very early age." Carol looked towards Geri and acknowledged a comment she had made earlier. "Geri, when you mentioned that our invisible guests had reminded us of our relationship with the Earth, a memory from childhood surfaced. This is a story I've never shared with anyone, and to this day, I am deeply ashamed of what I did, but it was a touchstone in my development because it was my first awareness of the importance of life." Another restorative breath bolstered Carol's courage.

"I don't know my exact age at the time, but I was not in school yet, so I was less than six years old. My brother who was four years older than me was in school, so it was a perfect moment for me to pursue my hunting skills. So, I sneaked into his bedroom, without Mother's notice, grabbed his Red Ryder BB Gun, and tiptoed out the back door. The adventure began! I made my way through the thick cedar hedge without encountering any big game, but I was not discouraged. Then the brushy area behind the garage was explored. Still, no opportunities ventured into the sights of the BB Gun. The shrubs and flowerbeds surrounding the house became the next hunting area, but this reaped no results either. My hopes were dwindling until I turned the corner around the southeast side of the house. There, in the massive live oak tree at the edge of the lawn, an opportunity opened. A beautiful male cardinal was sitting on a branch responding to the melody of his mate. At last, the prey had been discovered. Because I was so small, I struggled with lifting the BB gun to my shoulder. I had to swing the gun upward from my side and as that transpired, I pulled the trigger at the same time. It was a tragic turn of events. The beautiful cardinal fluttered to the ground. As I watched it fall, I realized that I had done something terrible. I ran to the bird, but it just lay there with its head hidden in the grass. I was heartbroken. It was my first encounter with death.

"As I look back on that event, I have great sadness for that child. She had no idea when she embarked upon her adventure that it would end in such an awful way." Once again, tears visited the gathering. "That little girl," continued Carol, "had no understanding of what happened, but she was so ashamed that she buried the bird in the flowerbed so no one would ever know what she had done, and then she sneaked back into the house and returned the BB Gun to her brother's closet. She never touched a gun again." Sharing her childhood experience depleted Carol. Her heart was filled with sorrow for the child and for the cardinal that changed the life of that little girl.

"Needless to say, that event taught me about the importance of life. Life is a gift and it is fragile, and we must all treat life with the greatest respect. Thanks to that beautiful cardinal, I became aware of that at a very early age. This childhood memory helps me to understand my anger regarding the maltreatment of the Earth. Sometimes, my disappointment in humankind breaks my heart, and other times, my rage frightens me. I don't want to be this way. My little girl was an innocent. She simply didn't know the consequences of her behavior. It was beyond her scope of awareness. As adults, we don't have the privilege of claiming ignorance as an excuse. We are all responsible for the health of this planet." A large sigh of relief escaped from Carol, and suddenly her energy shifted.

"Dear Old Friends, I renew a commitment that was made to the Earth a long time ago. I promise each of you that I will explore my negative behaviors and I will make changes. This beautiful planet will not go the way of that beautiful cardinal. I refuse to be a part of the Earth's decline. I will face my negative ways and I will change them, and every day, I will express my gratitude to the Earth and send her positive, healing energy. This is a promise!"

"Thank you for sharing that story, Carol." Anne's sincerity, accompanied by a few tears, could not be missed. "You must have been a very impressive child!"

"Oh, I'm not sure about that, Anne, but it is a lovely thought. I suspect my Mother would have described me as a handful."

At this point, everyone turned toward Jonathan who had graciously allowed others to precede him. He seemed very happy with the turn of events and easily stepped into the rhythm that his beloved had created earlier. "Well, as you said, Carol, this has been a memorable day. From meeting Janet's Great-grandmother to meeting invisible Beings from afar, to reuniting with Old Friends with whom we have made long-lasting commitments. Wow! It has been a day of great expansion, and even more so because of the discussions and the heartfelt feelings that have been shared with one another. I feel very optimistic. And that feels great because often I have wondered if this beautiful planet was going to survive the abuse that she's been subjected to. Sometimes, I talk with my Grandfather about this. Like your Great-grandmother, he is a person of wisdom as well. His stories about the old days and his descriptions of how the Earth looked back in his time are hard to believe. How can she have changed so much in such a short period of time? I guess the real point of that question is another question. How much will she change in the next twenty-five years if we don't do something to help her now? What I've heard here today inspires me. Like many folks, I wonder what I can actually do to help her. Geri and I aren't rich. We can't go out and buy a new electric car, nor can we afford to turn our old home into a certified green home. We've made a lot of improvements, but there is more that could be done. Our focus has been being good stewards of the property that we have, including making the outer garden, as we refer to it, an ecologically friendly space. We're proud of what we are achieving, but we still want to do more for Mother Earth. I feel that we can now. It is life-changing information to know that we personally produce negative energy and that it is the primary factor of the planet's decline. While I feel impotent in trying to change the ways of industries and governments, that is not the case in managing my own affairs. I can change my ways, and I accept responsibility for doing so. So, let me add my commitment to the rest of our collective's intentions. I commit to tracking my behavior for the next seven days. During that time, I will make a list of every negative action that I make, whether it is a thought, a spoken word, or an act. At the end of each day, I will total my offenses, and I will journal about them and create options for change. At the end of the week, I will total the week's offenses." Jonathan took a deep breath and shivered. "I'm a bit apprehensive about seeing that total, but Geri will help me face the moment. Once the dreadful number is calculated, I commit to lowering my offenses by twenty-five percent the next week. I will continue that process until new habits are made. This may sound like a trivial exercise, but it isn't. Just think about it, folks! If we track our negative behaviors, then we can also track our improvements. If we just talk about changing our ways, but don't actually note our mistakes and improvements, then we really won't have any real evidence that we're changing. I want data. That will keep me focused. That will help me to change. I commit to dedicated introspection and rapid change."

Janet immediately applauded Jonathan's proposed exercise. "Thank you for sharing that simple but profound exercise, Jon. It's going to be incredibly useful!" Similar enthusiastic remarks circled around the group. Little did Jonathan know how significant his exercise would be for the group...and many, many more.

"Dear Ones, is there anything else that needs to be said before we close our meeting?" Accepting silence as the answer to the question, Janet reached out to her nearby friends and all joined in. "Dear Old Friends, both far and near, we are grateful for your loving presence. Please join us again whenever you desire; your assistance is appreciated. And, Dear Mother Earth, we so hope that you are reassured by the efforts that were made on your behalf. Our commitments to you are firm and we will gather others to assist you as well. In peace be, Dear Friend, and know that you are deeply loved and cherished."

As the meeting came to a close and the Dear Old Friends departed the tree house, the chimes rang robustly, as if caught by a large gust of wind. It will come as no surprise to the astute reader to hear that the wind was perfectly still.

Sixteen

"Jonathan, when are you going to start tracking your negative actions?" The couple, strolling hand-in-hand down the sidewalk, continued to reflect upon the happenings just experienced at the Hansons' tree house.

"Immediately, Geri! Our commitments to the Earth have to be a priority. For me, that means taking action right away. In fact, I'm thinking about spending some time in the outer garden when we get home. It's the perfect place for introspective work. Would you like to join me?" The invitation boosted Geri's energy. She loved the idea. Their pace quickened and they arrived at the house faster than expected. There was still ample time for an adventure in the sacred space recently completed. Journals and jackets were gathered and the leftover veggie casserole was popped into the oven on their way through the kitchen. Geri set the temperature on low so that they would have plenty of time to address the work that each wanted to do.

"I just love our secret passageway," whispered Geri as they entered into the outer garden. "This may be the coolest idea you've every had, Jon." Her husband grabbed her hand as they continued their walk towards the area that honored his Grandfather. The special bench, which was cleverly hidden by the colony of ostrich ferns, was the intended destination.

"Ah, here we are," announced Jon. Before they entered into the alcove, the couple just stood quietly admiring the view. Then Jonathan invited his beloved to take a seat at his Grandfather's bench. They made themselves comfortable and became captivated by the view from the inside of the alcove. Geri noted that both the inward view and the outward view were equally beautiful.

"Your Grandfather must be so happy to see what you've done with this property. I suspect he walks these trails on a regular basis."

"That's a lovely thought, dear. I'm going to keep that image in my heart and in my mind, so that I can tap into it at any time. It will always bring a positive energy to the forefront." With that said, Jonathan opened his journal and invited his lovely spouse to do the same. At one point, Geri gently touched Jon's arm. She didn't want to disturb him, but she also didn't want him to miss the company that had just arrived. He looked up to find the familiar three rabbits feeding just across the trail.

"Welcome, Dear Ones!" he gently voiced. "Thank you for joining us again. I'm certain that your presence will enhance our self-explorations."

"Sorry, to interrupt you, dear, but they are so precious. I wonder if they are trying to communicate with you, Jon. They do seem to show up wherever you are in the garden."

"Yes, that's true, but perhaps it's just a coincidence." Geri rolled her eyes. "Okay, I admit that was a ridiculous comment. But let's just return to our work and see what happens." Journals were reopened and pens were poised to do what pens are meant to do when one of the rabbits stood up on its hind legs and stared at them. His two companions continued to munch on the bed of clover that was particularly appealing to their taste buds.

"Jonathan, I believe this visitor is trying to reach out to you. Perhaps, we should be more engaging."

"Do you have any suggestions, dear?" As Geri pondered the question, she noticed that the ferns across the pathway appeared to be different. The fronds were standing more erect and all of them seemed to be facing the humans sitting on the bench. Another quick glance revealed a similar reaction from the plant life that formed the alcove shelter for the special bench. Everyone seemed to be on alert. Without moving her head towards her husband, Geri apprised him of her observations.

"You're right," he whispered. "Something is definitely happening here. I'm going to try communicating telepathically." As Jonathan attempted to quiet his energy, Geri joined in the process. She initiated a deep breath and the ferns swayed so slightly that she thought she had imagined it, but then she took another deep breath, and it happened again.

"I saw that!" asserted Jonathan. *"The outer garden is interacting with us again."* With that statement made, the surrounding plant life shivered as if to say thank you for noticing us. *"Please forgive me, Dear Friends, for not acknowledging you daily. I have been remiss, but I'm working on improving myself."* Placing her hand atop his, Geri also apologized for her poor manners.

"I'm just now recognizing how limited my perspective has been regarding all the other life forms on this planet. I am very sorry for my insensitivity. I too am exploring my disrespectful manners and I promise you that changes are in the making." The Rabbit that remained standing during Jon and Geri's confession,

gracefully lowered himself to the ground and relocated to the entryway into the alcove, which was barely five feet away from the Gardners. He glanced back to his companions who were now settled in the middle of the trail pathway. Their proximity seemed to confirm that an encounter was in the making. Strengthened by his friends' presence, the nearest Rabbit reclaimed his upright position. First, he stared at Jonathan and then did the same with Geri.

"I bring you greetings from all the residents living in this sanctuary. We are very grateful for your respectful care of the garden. Everyone is very excited about the gathering that was held at the nearby tree house. Great progress was made! We have wanted to connect with you for a long time, but our efforts have not been bold enough. However, after witnessing what transpired in the tree house, we decided to invite you to a conversation with us."

The Gardners accepted the invitation immediately. And once again the plant life shivered.

"Because of the way you tenderly care for the garden, the residents have discerned that you are humans who can be trusted. We know of the commitments that were made earlier and we are very grateful for your concern about the Earth. She is a remarkable Life Being and she needs your help. Not many of your kind are interested in other species. They are so self-absorbed and distracted by matters of presumed importance that they do not even notice that other species mutually coexist with them.

"Our numbers are far greater than yours, but you act as if we do not exist. How can your kind be so limited? You are gifted with so many exceptional skills and yet your species has little compassion or concern for others. Perhaps it is our peaceable ways that cause you to be so negligent. We live our lives without infringing upon your space. Is that why we are of so little concern to you? We ponder about these issues.

"Our attempts to connect with your kind are rarely worthwhile. So distracted are your kind that we cannot get your attention. It is very disheartening. Some of us wonder if we must become violent to get your attention. Humans seem to be very attracted to violence. This attitude is beyond our comprehension. Our species are not drawn to that way of being. We are peaceful beings because we choose to be. It is a manner of being that is kind and respectful of everyone. Living peaceably serves everyone."

Jon and Geri sat quietly listening to every word that was communicated. The wisdom flowing through this precious creature spoke volumes and they were both at a loss as to how to respond to the questions being asked.

"We approach you today to ask for your assistance. What must we do to convince your kind that we are beings worthy of your acceptance? We have vital information

that will assist your efforts to help the Earth. If we all work together, we can improve her health significantly and quickly. Can you help us? We cannot save the Earth by ourselves. The human species must accept their role in her decline. If you do not change your ways, the future will be most unpleasant. This is not intended to happen. Please help us to help you so that we can all restore the Earth to her full vibrancy. By working together on this critically important project, perhaps your kind might learn to have respect for all other species that live on this planet with you.

"We are essential to the Earth's future. We offer our services on behalf of Mother Earth."

The Gardners remained silent, waiting to see if the well-versed rabbit had more to say. The Rabbit remained silent as well, waiting for the conversation to commence. And then, the most delightful incident occurred. The Rabbit's companions came forward, and each took the same upright position as the first. The action was clearly an invitation for the couple to speak. *"We sense your apprehension. If my words have offended you, I am very sorry. Perhaps, my manner was too bold. We sincerely desire to make connection with you and are eager to hear your perspective of what is transpiring upon Mother Earth."*

"No!" declared the couple at the same time. Geri urged her husband to take the lead and reminded him to connect telepathically. He nodded and then took a deep breath. The garden shivered at the same time. *"Dear Friends!"* he began. *"I hope it is okay to call you Friends, because we, Geri and I, definitely want to be your Friends. Your words have not offended us in any way. You spoke the truth and we are very grateful for that, but it was difficult to hear nonetheless. We are the ones who owe all of you an apology. We, as a species, have not behaved respectfully. In truth, our behavior has been reckless and we have caused great harm to the planet. Everything you said about us is true. We are very sorry."* Tears filled Jon's eyes and Geri stepped in to express her feelings as well.

"My husband's tears demonstrate the sadness that he feels for the Earth. We are both aware that she is very unwell and we know that it is due to our dreadful mistreatment of her. Although apologies will not change what has happened, we are very sorry. We do want to join with you on her behalf and we definitely want to learn from you. Anything that you can tell us that will give us guidance will be deeply appreciated, and we will share that information with other humans." Geri hoped and wondered if her interspecies communications skills were effective.

The Rabbit quickly replied. *"The garden residents can hear you clearly. Your skills are trustworthy. You do not need to worry about your communication abilities. We hear and feel the sincerity of your intentions, and your apologies do soothe our hearts. There are others who also wish to speak with you. Is this a suitable time for more conversation?"*

"Yes!" the couple responded together again, but Jonathan continued. "We would love to continue our conversation and meet more of the residents from the garden. *Oh my goodness! I slipped into speaking orally. Do I need to repeat what was just said?"*

"No, you do not need to repeat yourself; however, for your edification, your telepathic voice reaches more of the garden residents than your oral voice does. I amplified your oral voice so others were able to hear you, but it is easier for us if you use the inner voice." The information provided by the eloquent rabbit was very helpful. The Gardners actually knew very little about telepathy, but they both believed in the possibility of it. For sometime, they had been practicing between themselves in hopes of enhancing their skills. The Rabbit's feedback was encouraging.

"Our conversation is happening because of the efforts you made. We are most pleased that we can finally connect with you. May I introduce to you another member of the garden who has information to share with you?" Jon and Geri graciously welcomed the opportunity. The three Rabbits moved to the side of the entryway, obviously making way for another guest. From the other side of the trail, movement could be seen through the plant life. As the yet to be seen visitor approached, the couple's excitement mounted. They were very surprised when the resident Woodchuck peeked through the grasses before boldly stepping out on the trail. Geri marveled at the courage it took for this delightful being to cross the path and advance towards two humans.

The lead Rabbit took its upright position again as the Woodchuck approached. Once the new arrival was just a few feet away from the bench, she also assumed an upright position. Jonathan, impressed by the courtesy exhibited by these wonderful garden dwellers, felt awkward about remaining seated. He was concerned that his seated position was not respectful of their guests: however, he did not want to stand up and tower over them. Before a decision was determined, the Rabbit facilitated the introduction.

"Please do not be concerned about your present position, we do not feel disrespected, because we know that you are people of goodness. The concern that you have shown this sanctuary is evidence of your good hearts. Now, I would like you to meet another resident of the garden. She is one of extreme intelligence and profound wisdom."

"We are very pleased to meet you," voiced Geri. "Thank you for taking the time to be part of this conversation. We are eager to hear your perspectives of the Earth's precarious situation." The Woodchuck curiously stared at her audience. She had never been this close to members of the human species before. She found their presence to be very likable and wondered why they were so problematic. Jonathan and Geri definitely felt as if they were being sized up.

"Greetings! It is most pleasant to be in your company. Forgive me for staring, but I have never had the experience of being this close to one of your kind before. I have viewed you from afar, but never dared to approach. Unfortunately, your reputation precedes you." The comment felt like a stab to the heart. Both Geri and Jonathan immediately gasped and wanted to express their sorrow for the outrageous actions of the human species, but the Woodchuck interrupted their thoughts.

"Please do not feel that you must apologize for your kind. We are aware of the nature of your species. Many like you are people with kind hearts and good intentions, but others are not. Your kind was not always like this. When you first came into existence, you were a species of gentle ways. In those times, our kind and your kind enjoyed each other's company. We shared the gifts provided by the Earth and we all showed her the utmost respect, but then circumstances changed, and your kind grew distant from our kind. We attempted to regain relationships with you, but you were not interested. Our presence seemed to annoy you and eventually you reacted harshly to our gestures of friendship. Your behavior became so erratic and so cruel that we could no longer pursue relationships with your kind. For the sake of our kind, we had to separate from you. That was long ago, but the memories of the pain and injuries caused by your kind are still remembered.

"No longer can we continue to live these separate lives. Our kind and your kind must come together again on behalf of the planet. Mother Earth cannot continue to carry the burden of humankind. Your species has lost their way. So focused are you upon your own needs that you have no consideration for the needs of others. Your selfishness causes great hardship to the other species that mutually co-exist upon this planet. The negative energy that your species individually creates is the primary reason for the Earth's serious health issues. So much damage has been done by your species. The acts of cruelty that your kind has perpetrated against her are unthinkable! She suffers because of your kind, and the worst offenses that you create are the individual acts of unkindness that you perpetrate against one another. Your inhumanity towards one another is depriving her of the positive energy that she must have to exist. Your negative energy founded in anger, hatred, violence, greed, entitlement, duplicity, manipulation, exploitation, etc. is so powerful and so toxic that it is overtaking the pure, clean, positive energy that she needs to survive. This cannot continue.

"I speak bluntly with you, because it is necessary. And I share your sorrow for what has been done and for what continues to be done. Your species must change their ways, and they must do so immediately. Please hear our plea. We can help you and if you will join with us, there is still time to heal the Earth." The garden was completely silent as the Woodchuck spoke. She was held in high esteem among the sanctuary residents. All knew that the message presented was not easy to deliver or to hear. The residents of the garden waited for a response. The Rabbit took the lead again and encouraged the Gardners to take a deep breath. The invitation caused an immediate chain reaction led by the couple to others throughout the garden. Everyone, regardless of size, shape, or form responded respectively.

"Thank you!" The expression of sincere gratitude was stated simultaneously by the couple still reeling from the Woodchuck's comments. They agreed that Geri would respond first.

"Your message is difficult to hear, but I am so grateful that you had the courage to approach us today. We need to hear this, and your timing was perfect. As you already know, the gathering held in the tree house has inspired eight of us to change our ways. I know that we need many more to create the changes that are necessary, but it's a start, and now that we know you will also be helping us to move forward, I am feeling optimistic. I know our companions will want to work with you. We are so grateful for the truths that were spoken and for the friendship that has been offered. I am humbled by your kindness." Geri took a deep breath and the residents of the garden joined with her. It was a lovely gesture of connection.

Jonathan slowly and gently reached down and patted the ground. *"I am so grateful that all of you are here enjoying the garden. I know that my Grandfather is very pleased. He's probably observing this event from a distance."* The thought brought a smile to Jon's face.

"This interaction is life-changing. I've always had a strong sense of connection with nature, but this experience has made me consciously aware of your presence. I am so grateful to be with you, to converse with you, and to hear the truths that we have forgotten or never knew. When you spoke about our relationships in the past, it brought me to tears. I want that type of connection with you again, now! I don't know what happened to our species, why we turned from gentle ways, but I'm very sorry for what we did to you and to the Earth. I'm also sorry for us. We failed ourselves, and it is time to create a new path, a new way of being that will foster unity, harmony, and goodwill among all species. I want to be part of the change. I commit to being a change maker." The Rabbit looked on, waiting to see if the Woodchuck had more to say. At first she appeared to be satisfied with the message as it was delivered, but then another thought came to mind.

"Dear New Friends," the revered Woodchuck began, *"we bear witness to your behavior in this garden and we are deeply grateful for the manner in which you address our Home. We are very happy here and we enjoy observing the careful, heartfelt consideration that you give to this sacred space. Your intentions are of goodwill. The residents of the garden are most grateful for the tender way that you approach us. You listen to us and you initiate consultation with us. Just look at the results of our collaborations. We work well together. This reminds us of old times, and we look forward to working with you on more projects in the near future. Thank you for this conversation. It was most healing. In peace be, New Friends."* And with that said, the Woodchuck departed the scene. The Rabbit took one more glance at the couple before joining her companions on the path. They too departed, disappearing into the lush green vegetation.

Jonathan and Geri remained sitting silently on the bench. Each was lost in the cobwebs of their respective minds. They didn't even notice the garden growing darker until the solar lights dimly lit the pathway home. Second thoughts about the solar lights entered the couple's minds at the same time. "I wonder how the residents of the garden feel about the solar lights," stated Geri.

"My thoughts exactly," replied Jon. "It never occurred to me to consult with them before I purchased the lights. I was just thinking how nice it would be to have a walk in the garden with the lights showing us the way. We really do live our lives as if they do not exist. We need feedback about these lights, Geri. I want to know what is best for our friends here in the garden."

Seventeen

Greetings, Old Friend! We are most grateful to be in your presence once again. As you read this sentence, please take a deep breath, and allow yourself to accept the reality that a message is coming forward that is intended especially for you. Please listen with the ears of your heart, as you continue to read these words. You are here for a reason, and this chapter is specifically written for you.

By now, it is obvious that this book was written for a reason and it is here to remind everyone, including you, that the Earth is in very serious trouble. This reality can no longer be denied. The planet is reaching a point of no return. Even though that sounds unimaginable, this unbelievable possibility is rapidly becoming more and more probable than anyone wishes to believe. Essentially, this means that every life being residing upon this planet is in jeopardy. Bluntly stated, we cannot exist without the Earth's vitality, and she cannot recover from her health crisis unless the human species immediately ceases infusing her with their highly toxic negative energy discharge. The previous, profound statement must be read and reread until its full impact is thoroughly digested, assimilated, and accepted. We cannot change what we refuse to believe as our reality, and as long as we deny the outrageous destruction that we have caused the planet, her health will continue to decline at an alarming rate. However, if we accept the reality of what we have done, then we can change the future for the Earth and all her inhabitants. Please reread the previous sentence repeatedly until you grasp the truth of its message.

Dear Reader, you are here for a reason! You have the ability to assist the Earth. Just by agreeing to review your behavior, you have the power to ascertain your negative impact upon the Earth; and with that knowledge, you can alleviate undesirable behavior and replace it with positive energy that will actually heal the Earth. If this sounds too simple to believe, then just take a deep breath and accept that changing one's negative energy into positive energy is a choice, not an arduous task. More information about this process will be provided in the upcoming chapters, but for now, please just accept that you have the ability to shift your focus from negativity. Even though the human species has dwelled in negative energy for a very long time, it is not a choice that benefits humankind or any other kind. The exploration of negative behavior has not positively served anyone. The time for disengaging from negative behavior is long overdue.

You, Dear Friend, are one who is capable of excelling in this situation. You are a person of goodness who desires to assist the Earth. You are one who understands the futility of living from a negative perspective, and you are one who recognizes the benefits of living in a positive environment. You are here for a reason, Old Friend, and you are needed.

Dear Reader, Dear Friend, if you are still reading this chapter, then you are aware that the message is personally reaching out to you, attempting to remind you of a memory of long-standing. Although the specifics may remain unclear, you are indeed one who is here to participate in the changes that are necessary to revitalize the Earth. Breathe this truth in and allow it to rest within you. Do not move from this moment of knowing. Simply be with the truth that you are here to help the Earth and accept the reality that the time for action is upon you. Again, you are encouraged to simply be in this moment of awareness. In recognizing that one has been called to action, the first step is accomplished. The next step demands introspection, courage, and trust. These are qualities that you already possess, so there is no need to worry that you are not enough to meet such a task. You are enough! In truth, you are exactly what is needed for this task to be accomplished. To save the Earth, the people of Earth need to address their negative behavior. Individually, each person is needed to take stock of his or her positive and negative deeds, and collectively, the human species must make a choice. The task is that simple. You must honestly review your tendencies. Do you personally lean towards positive, uplifting behaviors, or do you move in the opposite direction? Positive inclinations accelerate the energy of self and others around you, including the ever-present Earth, while negative inclinations decelerate one's energy, which profoundly diminishes the energy of everyone near you, including the beautiful planet upon which you reside. The truth is your behavior matters. Please read the previous statement over and over again until the simplicity and the profundity of the message is captured. Your behavior matters!

The human species must face the truth of their impact upon the planet Earth and all the countless other species that mutually coexist with her. Although humans are not inclined to accept responsibility for their actions, each individual must assess and accept his or her role in the planet's declining health. Don't waste time blaming others. You cannot justify your own wrongdoings by pointing fingers at others. Accept responsibility for your own misconduct and take the necessary actions that will correct the harm that is presently being done.

Please do not think that your negative actions are trivial and irrelevant. Remember, you are not alone. There are over seven billion people around the globe who are also contributing to the problem. Think of the smallest transgression against the Earth that you can commit and multiply it by seven billion people who are also pretending that their transgressions are trivial. Every misdeed matters! Every act of unkindness towards self or others, regardless of their sizes, shapes, or forms, matters. Until this reality is accepted as truth, the Earth's potential for recovery remains tenuous.

Dear Friend, you know the truth. Now, you must accept that the time for change is upon you. You are here to take the next step on behalf of the Earth. She needs you. She needs your help. Breathe this reality into your innermost being. You are here for a reason, and the time is now!

Eighteen

"Carol, I'm so glad you suggested returning to this trail. Our previous experience continues to fill my mind with many questions and makes me think that we are intended to spend more time in this setting." Jen's demeanor turned pensive as the couple entered the trailhead that led into the dark forest. They were prepared this time, each with a small, but powerful flashlight that was easily accessible if needed. "I feel that something awaits us," she added as they strolled ahead.

"That's interesting," noted Carol. "Earlier this morning, I wrote a similar comment in my journal. In fact, that's when I came searching for you to see if you were up for another trek into this mysterious forest. I too believe that something awaits us." They walked in silence until the darkness engulfed the trail, at which point Jen and Carol both came to an abrupt halt. Standing side-by-side, audible deep breaths were taken. These instantaneous reactions were so common between them that neither even acknowledged the event. It was just one of the many ways in which they were simpatico.

"Well, are we just going to stand here forever, or are we going to take the next step?" asked Jen.

Carol, momentarily lost in her own thoughts, remained silent while her magnificent mind raced through countless possible responses. Eventually she was able to articulate some of her confusion. "I understand why we have a tendency to be leery about entering into a darkened space. The truth is, we're not nocturnal beings. Our safety issues are challenged when we cannot rely upon our sight. Compounding this with the fact that we had never been down this trail before, it all makes sense that we were unnerved when we first encountered this dark scene. But our experience was incredible; one that we will never forget. So why are we standing here, locked in place, as if something foreboding is up ahead?" Carol turned her gaze from the dark trail that quickly disappeared into the trees. Behind them was the trailhead parking lot filled with sunny bright light. Her spirits lifted just by turning her head in that direction, and then, turning back towards the darkened pathway, she felt her energy shift again. "I just don't get this, Jen. What are we afraid of? As we were driving here, I felt such excitement, such hope, that we might have a similar experience as the last one. And now we stand here filled with apprehension. Is that an

145

accurate description of your feelings, Jen, or am I the only one feeling agitated again?"

"Actually, apprehension is a good descriptor, but I do not know why. Like you, I was and still am very excited about this new adventure, but there is a sense of the unknown that is unsettling. I wish it were not so. I don't like the idea that my mind moves in that direction rather than leaning towards joyful, hope-filled possibilities. Why must fear come into play? Carol, I do not want fear to be my guide, but it seems that I need your assistance to take the next step. Dear One, will you fearlessly walk with me into this wonderful forest that holds so many mysteries about our beautiful planet? Something awaits us, Carol, and I am certain that it is founded in goodness. Let's do this together, dear!" A long hug was exchanged before the two brave women faced the dark trail ahead. The first step taken together was the first of many more that were yet to come.

"Oh, my goodness! Look at this! It's more beautiful than I remembered and my memories are spectacular." The forest also had memories and the moment Carol and Jen entered into the darkness, the floral chamber welcomed the two new friends home. Glimmering lights sparkled throughout the bed of the forest and all the way up into the highest levels of the trees. It was a grand welcome that filled everyone's hearts with joy. The shared connection was indescribable, but the wonderment of the occasion would be remembered forever. Wherever the couple looked, the lights brightened as if that grouping of plants were personally greeting their new friends. Carol and Jen waved in response to the efforts being made on their behalf. It was truly a joyous experience.

Eventually, the spectacular light display returned to its normal operations. It reminded Carol of a dimmer switch being turned down to a very soft glow. The plants along the trail still brightened the path, providing a very safe environment for the friends to enjoy. They seemed to be inviting the walkers to continue, which, of course, the couple happily did. When the first juncture in the trail was encountered, the plant life took charge. One path lit up while the other went dark. Carol and Jen saw no reason to question the situation; they simply followed the lead of their new forest friends. The walk was lovely. The connection they felt with the forest was exquisite.

"I am so grateful we came," whispered Jen. "Is this really happening? Are we really walking through a midnight dark forest being guided by a variety of flora life beings along a trail that we've never traveled before?"

"Yes," Carol replied in a soft voice. "This is really happening! I feel like we need to be pinching ourselves, but we're both here and we're both sharing this incredible experience, so I think we should trust what is happening. Jen, remember how we both believed that something awaited us here in the forest? Well, I think we're being led to whatever that something is."

Jen quickly acknowledged that she had been having similar thoughts. The two joined hands as they continued walking down the trail. "Let's remember that there is no need to slip into apprehension of any kind. We will not allow fear to be our guide. How could we?" she asked adamantly. "My goodness, we are surrounded by beloved friends. We are so blest Carol. I am so grateful that we pushed through our uncertainties and entered the forest. We are so fortunate." As if responding to Jen's comments, the forest provided another amazing light show that actually appeared to be a choreographed performance. The intelligence behind this display gave one pause and inspired many more questions. The audience, Jen and Carol, happily offered a standing ovation for the spectacular light show. Soon the lights dimmed again while the trail ahead became brighter. With joyful anticipation, they followed the lead of those who were orchestrating their walk.

"Geez! This is just the coolest experience I've ever had," declared Jen.

"Me too!" replied Carol. "The forest is truly reaching out to us, demonstrating its capabilities and its brilliance. The collaboration of efforts that we just witnessed is indicative of extreme intelligence and connectedness. This is amazing. Jen, I am so grateful to be a part of this."

"We are very fortunate, Carol. I believe this is evidence that the life beings within this magnificent forest actually trust us. It is such a privilege to bear witness to our neighbors' way of living. Can you believe this reality has been going on all of our lives and we have been totally oblivious to it?"

"It makes one wonder how much more we are missing, doesn't it?" Carol's question gave both of them pause. They continued in silence for a while, each engaged with their respective imaginations. Jen wondered if all forests were the same as this one, or did they have different characteristics and behaviors based upon the type of life beings that inhabited them? She wondered if deciduous trees reacted differently than coniferous trees, which led her to wonder about the forest bed itself. So many different plants lived within the forest, and based upon the light performance just witnessed, they seemed to do so in peaceful harmony. Jen was amazed and wondered how they managed it.

Meanwhile Carol's mind was equally engaged with the marvels of the forest. She was dumbfounded by what they were observing. The evidence of extreme intelligence operating among these countless life beings was undeniably blatant. She realized how little the human species knew about the other inhabitants of this planet. Her heart was profoundly saddened by the acts of disrespect and unkindness that she had committed over the years, because of her own personal ignorance, and she was deeply grateful for the education she was receiving on this remarkable walk. She lusted for more truths.

"May I interrupt your thoughts, dear?" whispered Jen.

"Oh, yes! Please do," encouraged her companion.

"Carol, I'm thinking about asking the forest if we might take photos or videos of their incredible abilities. I would never do it without their permission, and I don't really know if our cameras would do them justice, but what we've seen here is beyond belief. People need to see this. They need to know about the reality of this world that we've been privileged to see. Maybe then the human species would realize that we aren't the only intelligent beings on this planet. I'm really overwhelmed by our experience, Carol, and I know there is much more to discover."

"Jen, I share your desire to bring this information forward to the rest of the world, but I also believe we must seek guidance from the forest. We cannot allow our excitement to override the safety of these life beings. They know far better than we how our species have treated them in the past. They are taking an incredible risk now by reaching out to us. We must be respectful of their needs."

"Indeed, I agree with you, Carol. That's why I would like to communicate with them again. We would definitely need to strategize how to pursue this in a way that totally protected the plant life from an onslaught of researchers and visitors. If news of this became public, the forest would be in jeopardy. We both know how many wonderful trails across the planet have been devastated by too much human traffic. We certainly don't want to put this trail in that kind of situation. I suspect our tree house friends would be a good group of folks to consult with about this." The two women agreed that they would proceed with caution for the sake of the forest and all its residents. With the decision made, they noticed a flickering of lights throughout the surrounding area. They both wondered if it was a message of appreciation or if it was just their imaginations working overtime again. Soft giggles surfaced simultaneously, as they continued to progress deeper into the forest.

"I wonder what awaits us?" Carol whispered, as she wrapped her arm around Jen's.

"Oh, let's just enjoy the walk and not worry about what's going to unfold. We've seen so much already. My goodness, how can we be so fortunate! I'm so grateful we are sharing this experience together. I love you, Old Thing!"

"I love you too, Old Thing!" Carol sincerely replied. "And you're right as always. Our good fortune is over the top. We have been graced with great beauty, our awareness of the world has expanded exponentially, and we are blessed with the knowledge that there is more to come. I am filled with joy, Jen. And I am so grateful that we are here together."

As Carol and Jen continued their walk, a passerby would not have known that these two were friends of long-standing. Many lifetimes had they shared together and in each one they chose to be assistants to the other. Both shared a love for the Earth and always wanted to return for another opportunity to help her with the burgeoning human species. None knew that the new species would develop in this most peculiar manner. No one imagined they would become so problematic. "Jen, I'm having one of those unusual experiences that you and I often have. You know," she said assertively, "one of those odd moments when you think and feel as if you've experienced a similar situation in another time and place. Well, I think we've walked another trail similar to this one in another lifetime. No specifics are available to me, but this feels very familiar and I think we're going to run into a Dear Old Friend."

With that said, the breezes in the highest level of the forest canopy shifted unveiling another view of the environment in which they were walking. Rays of scattered sunlight filtered through the trees allowing glimpses of the expansiveness of the forest. "Jeepers!" declared Jen. "It feels as if this forest is a universe within itself. I continue to be overwhelmed by the enormity of this existence within our existence. Carol, this is unbelievable!" Meanwhile, her beloved was equally astounded to the point of being speechless. She responded to Jen by squeezing her hand so firmly that it was surprising. "Carol, are you okay?" whispered Jen.

This time, Carol reacted by coming to a full stop. Her hand continued to clench Jen's while she looked in all directions. "Listen!" she softly spoke. "Something is approaching, but I can't tell from which direction it is coming. Prepare yourself, dear. I think we are about to discover what awaits us."

Jen became vigilantly attentive, searching for signs or sounds that might provide them with a hint of what was transpiring around them. "Should we be afraid, Carol?"

"No!" she replied quietly. "I don't believe we have anything to fear, Jen. Let's open our hearts to this experience. I think it is one that we have both awaited for a very long time."

With that said, Carol and Jen both relaxed the rigid protective stances they had taken earlier. No longer feeling apprehensive, their breathing returned to its normal state and the tightly clenched hands finally slackened as well. And then it happened. The forest canopy opened to the skies above allowing the call of a great bird to be heard as it soared beyond the trees. Once again the expansiveness of their current location stimulated the imagination.

"My goodness!" expressed Jen. "I feel like we're being given a peek into heaven. Can this be true?" The great bird continued to soar above them looking as if she were a universe away, while also looking within reach. "This is amazing," continue Jen. "Part of me thinks that I can actually reach out and touch that Eagle and another part of me sees him beyond the stars. What of Earth is going on, Carol?"

"I'm not sure," she replied. "But whatever is happening is happening for a reason. So let's just accept it as it is, even though we don't fully understand the circumstances." Jen nodded in agreement as they continued to observe the view beyond the trees.

"Jen, let's invite the Eagle to join us." The suggestion was happily received, so Carol took the lead. First, she verbally invited the great bird to join them, and then she urged Jen to join her in attempting to telepathically communicate with the Eagle. And this they did. Each in her own unique way used the inner voice to welcome the bird to come closer. The reaction was immediate. The elevation of the soaring Eagle quickly diminished until it seemed to be directly above the tree line. Separately, but conjointly, they both assumed the Eagle was in a process of discernment, when suddenly a decision became apparent. As the tree canopy broadened its opening, the Eagle swooped through and continued to circle within the chambers of the forest. With each loop made, the magnificence of the great bird became increasingly more apparent. Its wingspan, which spread beyond the shoulders of the two admirers, took their breath away. Neither Jen nor Carol had been so close to an Eagle before; the up-close perspective was indeed awe-inspiring. Overwhelmed with anticipation, the welcoming committee telepathically repeated their desire for connection, at which point, the great bird narrowed his loop and lighted on the lowest branch of a young but sturdy pine tree just a few yards up the trail. The tree immediately surrounded the Eagle with ambient light allowing her to be easily seen by the forest's guests. Once she was comfortably settled on the outreaching tree limb, the two walkers asked permission to approach her. Although Carol and Jen saw no outward signs of approval from the Eagle herself, they did notice that the plant life along the trail leading to the pine tree became brighter and more sparkling. After a quick consultation, they decided to believe that the lighted path was a welcoming gesture collaboratively initiated by the forest's life beings. With respect for all involved, the forest seekers moved slowly towards the point of intention. The Eagle could not have chosen a better location for connection. The low-lying branch placed the large bird at a similar height as the standing humans allowing for a face-to-face conversation.

Jen and Carol remained on the edge of the trail admiring the beauty of this incredible heralded life being. Each species was stunned to be in the presence of the other. As the humans stared at the Eagle, she stared at them. The truth was, this gathering was a first for all involved. The majestic Eagle had never been this close to a human before. Likewise, the two women had only observed eagles from afar. Each was enchanted with the other.

"We would love to speak with you, but we're not exactly sure how to do this," stated Carol. "Perhaps, you might wish to take the lead." The Eagle cocked her head to the right side and then to the left and then stretched forward as if she was trying to see into the innermost being of Carol. The intensity of the Eagle's stare took Carol aback, but she did not fear the situation. She simply wondered what the Eagle was able to see.

"Please pardon my manners," apologized the Bald Eagle. *"I have been told by Friends that my stare can be intimidating. I am most grateful that you were not alarmed by my inquisitive nature. To answer your question, what was seen when I looked within you was the essence of who you really are. You are one who*

cares deeply for the sanctity of all life, not just human life, but all life. You are a person of goodness, and I am most pleased to be in your presence." Before Carol could respond, the Eagle turned to Jen and repeated the same intense observation. Jen's reaction was similar to her beloved's. She opened her heart to the Eagle's scrutiny and was eager to hear the results of her examination.

"Ah! You are beings of like manner. For many lifetimes you have traveled together seeking ways in which you could serve the planet you call Earth. Great kindness lies within you and many have been deeply touched by your gracious ways. I am most delighted to be in your presence as well. This is indeed an experience that brings me great hope. You are needed, Dear Friends! The Earth is in great stress and she needs humans, such as the two of you, to join with the other species of the planet who are desperately trying to revitalize her present decelerated energy level. She is ailing in so many different ways across her vast expanses that she is struggling to maintain her wellness." While listening to the Eagle's perception of them, Carol and Jen returned to their preferred way of being. Without knowing it, they had moved closer to each other and were once again holding hands. This gesture of connection was one of long-standing that had been cultivated over many lifetimes.

"Thank you for your kind words," responded Carol. "Being in your presence is a joy for both of us. And we are eager to hear more. How may we be of service?" The Eagle, staring off into the distance, appeared to be thinking about the question, but neither Jen nor Carol was able to ascertain the innermost thoughts of the incredible bird. They were acutely aware that she was a being of extreme intelligence, but beyond that, she remained a mystery to them.

"I do not mean to be mysterious, Dear Friends. There was a time, long, long ago, when your kind and my kind were very close. We lived as friends and we shared many great adventures with one another. During those times we assisted each other in our efforts to live harmoniously with all other species. We lived as equals, for all beings in the Great Existence are equal. No species is regarded as more than another species. That was a misunderstanding that separated the human species from other species. Because of this misunderstanding your kind forgot that you are one with all others. We are all One, Dear Friends, and as such, we must all treat each other as equals, because we are.

"In essence, your kind lost your senses. You lost your sense of Self, and you lost your sense of Oneness. When one lives in awareness that he or she is One with all others, that individual is aware of the significance of all others in existence, and actions in alignment with that awareness are demonstrated. When one is delusional

about his or her sense of Self, one is in contradiction to the sense of Oneness. If one believes they are more than another, they are in error. If one believes they are less than another, they are in error. For reasons that escape us, your kind began to demonstrate behaviors that were harmful to and disrespectful of other species, and then, hostilities disrupted within your own kind. These actions of ill will are incomprehensible to others in existence. It is because of humankind's disruption to the planetary harmonious nature that the Earth is in her current health crisis.

"All existences throughout all existence are One. This simply is the way of existence. It is most unfortunate that the human species lost their bearings. Those who remember their goodness are deeply saddened by their change of heart." The great bird paused, puffed her feathers, and then resituated herself on the tree branch.

"What I see within each of you reminds me of those long ago. Those from whom you came were also people of goodness. They cared about the Earth and all the other species that reside upon her. They were a dynamic species."

Jen could no longer contain herself. The need for more information about the change that occurred in the human species was pushing her to speak out. She debated internally whether she should communicate telepathically or orally, but before a decision was made, the Eagle encouraged her to use her inner voice.

"I hope you can hear me. I'm not very skilled at this."

The Bald Eagle reassured Jen that her skills were sufficient and would grow stronger with practice. *"The skills that you witness within me also exist within you. The ability to communicate in this manner lies within all life beings. Long ago, your kind was equally skillful in using this form of communication. Unfortunately, this ability went by the wayside when humans separated themselves from the other inhabitants of the planet. It was a great loss for everyone."* The Eagle paused, looked in another direction, and seemed to be lost in thoughts of the past.

Jen waited for an appropriate amount of time before she took advantage of the silence to telepathically express her appreciation for the Eagle's complementary remarks. *"Thank you, for your kind words earlier, and also for providing us with all this information. It is difficult to hear these truths, but it is necessary. We must learn about what happened to us, so that we can correct our behaviors. When you speak of the friendships that your kind once had with humans, it breaks my heart. What happened? How did we go wrong? And will we be able to alter our ways and become in alignment with the Earth again? Can you speak of this?"* Although Jen maintained her composure, tears were streaming down her face. Carol drew closer to her as they both waited for the Eagle to respond.

The Eagle continued to stare off into the distance. Time passed, but it was impossible to assess moments such as these. It may have been a few minutes or an eternity. All were consumed by their own thoughts. At some point, Carol and Jen both sensed that the Eagle was in despair. Jen regretted having asked so many questions and wished she could take them back. Her thoughts caught the attention of the Eagle.

"Please do not worry about me, New Friends. Your questions took me to the days of old. I remember the stories that my ancestors told about their relationships with your kind. They had such fond memories of those times and they always held your kind in the highest regard. Their hearts ached for what was. I remember the sadness they felt when they spoke of your ancestors. Your empathic abilities allowed you to feel their heartache through my thoughts of the past. By feeling the pain of my ancestors due to the loss of their relationships with your ancestors, you are now able to appreciate how deeply they loved your kind." The Eagle's words spoke a truth that Carol and Jen never knew. The interconnectedness shared by all species was an existence unknown to them before.

"Perhaps, this is why we long for connection with plants and animals," Carol spoke aloud. *"Sorry for that lapse into old habits. I am just wondering about all the folks we know who yearn to connect with other species. Maybe, the innate desire to be in Oneness is calling to us, trying to help us to remember who we really are."*

Stretching her head forward as far as she could, the Eagle once again targeted that intense stare in Carol's direction. *"Indeed,"* she agreed. *"The truth always rests within, regardless of how many lifetimes have been experienced. Even though you were raised to live within the parameters of your current human preferences, there is a preference within that is much stronger than the one of the present. You are beings of Oneness and you always will be.*

"A great imbalance occurred when the human species decided to live separately from the other species existing on this planet. Confusion was widespread. Tension among those who were once friends and allies resulted in severe distress, and as you just experienced, great sadness was felt throughout all species across all lands. What prompted this change of course was a mystery. Various species made attempts to regain connection with your kind, but the efforts were not successful. As time passed, hope waned. The relationships, which were once so dear to all, simply were no more.

"Your question regarding what went wrong is one that has been asked countless times before, Dear Friend. Our kind assumed for a very long time that we had done something to offend your kind. This is why so many attempts were made to

make amends. But the truth is, we do not know what went wrong. Your kind seemed adamant about pursuing their own path, and as they did so, they became more and more removed from the reality that many other life beings also inhabit this planet. Their oblivious attitude about this reality caused great harm to those other inhabitants who were and are equally essential to the well being of the Earth. Humans have made many errors during their evolutionary development and still they seem unwilling to honestly review the horrific impact they have caused. Unless your kind accepts responsibility for your misguided actions, it is highly unlikely you will make the changes that are necessary for the Earth to regain her robust state of health.

"It is hard to imagine that anyone still believes that the planet is not in serious trouble. Her health issues are profoundly evident. Why would anyone ignore the reality that the planet upon which they reside is reaching a crisis point of cataclysmic proportions? Such blatant disregard for the Earth's health begs one to wonder why. Why would anyone treat another life being so cruelly? The insanity of such behavior must be questioned." The grand bird fell silent. Her stare was focused elsewhere, but Jen and Carol knew the magnificent bird was still on task. She was on a mission. Although the couple did not know why they were so privileged to be the recipient of the Eagle's wealth of wisdom, they were extremely grateful.

"Thank you for having the courage to speak these truths," Jen used her inner voice to express the gratitude that was welling up within her. *"Your questions are difficult to reckon with; however, it must be done. For the sake of every living being on this planet, humans must face their irrational behaviors. Essentially, we must take the necessary steps to reclaim our humanity. But how are we to do this? The question is so large that I feel paralyzed just thinking about it."* Jen closed her eyes and took several deep breaths. Fears were taking her to places she did not want to visit.

"Please forgive my present emotional state," she apologized, *"but there is a part of me that feels hopeless about the future, and I fear many others have similar feelings. We must, of course, overcome these fatalistic thoughts and push forward. It is not a time to wallow in our fears: we must take the necessary steps to correct the terrible mistakes that we've made. This means we must grapple with our fears so that we can face the truth and alter our ill-fated behavior. No longer can we put our selfish needs above the needs of others. That path has proven to be a disaster. Those who continue to believe that they are superior to all others on the planet will take exception with this notion. That is to be expected. Their thoughtless, self-serving attitudes have misguided the majority for long enough. Those who accept and regret the truth about the human species' negative impact upon the Earth must now step forward. For the sake of the planet, for the sake of all the species who live upon this*

remarkable planet, we must choose a lifestyle that respects and honors all other life beings." As Jen spoke her deepest truth, the Eagle listened and observed her carefully. Meanwhile, Carol was observing both of them. She was in awe of her beloved who spoke so powerfully and earnestly, and she was very curious about the Eagle's impression of Jen's heartfelt thoughts. Her curiosity did not escape the attention of the esteemed bird, which instantly turned in Carol's direction and cocked her head inquisitively.

"You wish to know my thoughts regarding your companion's commentary."

Carol's face turned red with embarrassment. "Oh, my goodness!" She instinctively spoke aloud. "You heard my thoughts!"

"Your curious nature was so energized, I could not help but hear your inner voice. Please excuse my impertinence. As you are inclined to speak orally, I am inclined to hear the unspoken word. In regards to your curiosity, my New Friend, I am most pleased to acknowledge that I am very impressed with your beloved's depth of understanding regarding the serious situation that is currently unfolding upon the Earth. It is a relief to hear one of your kind speak so candidly about humankind's role in this crisis.

"When the Forest Collective contacted me about their previous experience with the two of you, I must admit that I was apprehensive about meeting you, but they spoke so positively about the experience that I agreed to be available if you returned again. I now understand why they were so eager for us to meet. This is an important reminder for me! I erroneously assumed that you would not be willing to listen to our appeal. This was an act of unkindness on my part. I did not honor you with unconditional acceptance, and I am deeply sorry for my poor manners.

"Your willingness to participate in this conversation gives me great hope. We still have faith in humankind and we long for the relationships we once had with you. Together we can make the necessary changes to restore the Earth back to a fully vibrant state of being. She is a very resilient Life Being, and as is true for all life beings, she reacts positively to loving-kindness. That is the primary factor in her recovery process. She needs to know that she is loved." The wise bird paused allowing time for the surprising statement to be contemplated. *"Please do not minimize what was just said, New Friends. I speak with sincerity. Allow yourself to deeply consider the importance of this truth. Presently, the Life Being Earth is in great distress. Examples of her ill health are evident everywhere, while solutions to her health issues seem minimal at best. As you said earlier, Friend Jen, the enormity of the problem is terrifying, resulting in great fear and hopelessness. Although these emotional reactions are justified, they are not helpful. On the contrary, fear and hopelessness exacerbate the problem. The decelerating energy of these two emotional states is profoundly devastating to everyone. It harms those who*

generate the energy and it harms everyone who comes in contact with this negative energy, including the Earth. Imagine how much suffering Mother Earth endures daily just from the emission of negative energy associated with fear and hopelessness. No matter where this pain and suffering is generated, the Earth is always present and the recipient of its aftermath. If just these two types of negative energies were managed and diminished, her well being would significantly improve.

"Obviously, much more assistance will be needed, but a respite from humankind's chaotic moods would provide time to address other vitality important issues. To quickly and efficiently assist the Earth, we must first relieve her of the emotional traumas of the human species. Your kind must awaken to and accept the reality of your erratic behavior. You are the cause of your own suffering. It is in your best interest to alleviate your fears, your anger, and your hostilities. No wonder you feel hopeless. This makes no sense. Your species has such privileges and such great potential. Why do you not appreciate the gifts of this existence? Why do you disregard all that is provided and instead focus upon that which is unnecessary? Your avaricious nature stuns other species. And your ill will is beyond our comprehension.

"Changes must be made and they must be made soon. The repercussion of your behavior has created an imbalance upon and within the planet that will produce extreme consequences for all concerned. Dear Friends, we need your help. You must change your destructive way of being. We cannot do this for you or we would have already taken action. The truth is, your species must become the peaceable beings they are intended to be, or the consequences will be unthinkable. Please help us, Dear Ones. We do not wish to lose our Friends of Old. Nor do we wish to lose our cherished Mother Earth who has provided everything that was needed for millennia.

"In times past, there was mutual cooperation among all species that allowed for a gracious way of living. Our hope is that the human species will choose to return to that manner of being. We so desire to resume the special relationships we once had with your kind. We have missed your camaraderie and your kindness.

"Dear New Friends, please hear our plea. Peace and harmony are possible and it is an admirable way of living. We hope you will seriously consider your present circumstances and choose to live differently. Your future depends upon it, and your decision affects every other life being on the planet, including the Life Being Earth. Please join us, Dear Friends. There was a time when you truly loved and respected us. We are still the same lovable and amenable life beings that you once cherished. We long for your return." With that said, the Eagle ruffled her feathers and peered intensely at Carol and Jen. Her head cocked from one side to the other as if she was waiting for a response. Carol was the first react.

"It is humbling to be in your presence. And I am so grateful that you were willing to meet with us today. This has been an experience that will never be forgotten. I

157

want you to know that I believe everything you have shared. There are no doubts; however, I do have concern about how to bring your message forward. That will require much more thought. Our friends from the tree house will certainly be receptive to your information and we will relay this conversation to them within the week. I am confident that they too will want to be agents of change. Thank you for your courage. I hope our paths will meet again." The Eagle listened carefully to every word. She seemed to be pleased, but it is difficult for a human to surmise the facial expression of this grand bird.

"Dear Friend, I am delighted and encouraged by your comments. And I too hope to be in your presence again. Thank you for listening and for the work that will be achieved in the days to come." The Eagle's attention then turned towards Jen whose emotions were in turmoil.

"I am so grateful to have shared this time with you. It has been exhilarating! Although your messages were difficult to hear, I am so grateful that you had the courage to present them to us. I feel as if my eyes have been opened to a reality not known before. Hearing your perspective of what has been transpiring on the planet is validating. As Carol just said, I believe everything that you told us, and you're absolutely right about our arrogant and selfish behaviors. We've lost our way. And you have reminded us that there is a better way to be. Peaceable! What a concept!

"This is going to be a challenging project, but best as I can tell, we don't have any other options. We need to grow up and behave in an appropriate manner that is suitable for all or we can continue to travel our present course that is leading us into a path of no return. The answer is obvious, but the human species is not inclined to be concerned about the needs of others. The task is large, but I don't feel hopeless anymore. I have the power to change my ways. This is something that I can do, and I am happy to do it for the betterment of all others.

"Thank you so much for bringing the truth forward. I look forward to seeing you again soon. Is there a way that we can reach out to you?" Jen's comments were also happily received and her final question caused the Eagle to stand high on the branch. She peered at Jen in a manner that only an Eagle can do and then flapped her large wings.

"I am always available," replied the grand bird. *"Simply focus your thoughts upon me, briefly speak your intentions, and I will respond. My range is rather expansive, but this forest is my preferred resting place.*

I am but a breath away and I look forward to seeing both of you again in the very near future. This has been a unique pleasure. I wish you peace and harmony." As the Eagle gracefully stepped off the branch, her magnificent wings stretched out over six feet, and with one giant flap of her wings, she lifted upward into the canopy of the trees. She truly was a sight to behold.

Carol and Jen remained steadfast until the roof of the forest opened up allowing the Eagle to reach towards the skies. It was a majestic event: a beautiful closing to a remarkable interspecies connection.

Once the canopy closed again, the forest dimmed except for the path leading back to the trailhead. It was clearly a suggestion for the new friends of the forest to return home. They walked silently back to the parking lot, each lost in her thoughts about the experience just shared.

Nineteen

Old Friend, we bid you peaceful tidings. Once again, we come forward to remind you that you are here for a reason. Perhaps you have forgotten the previous reminder...the one that was presented a few chapters ago. Indeed, it is true that one is inclined to forget reminders regarding obligations and responsibilities. Do not fret, Dear Reader, we are here to remind you again.

The truth regarding the Earth's declining state of health still remains an issue of extreme importance. Because this truth is so difficult to accept, we understand that the human mind prefers to ignore the topic. Therefore, we are committed to assisting you and your fellow humans.

Our intentions are to be persistent in our endeavors to awaken you to the truth of the Earth's condition. Therefore, we will continue to remind you of the serious situation that awaits you. Hopefully, you will become so annoyed by our reminders that you may actually feel compelled to take action. Dear Friend, Dear Reader, we do not wish to hound you, nor do we wish to bombard you with dreadful information about your current and future circumstances. However, the truth must be told. More importantly, the unfortunate truth must be accepted.

We find it difficult to understand why anyone on this planet would choose to put the planet at risk, and still, there are those who continue to use, misuse, and abuse this incredible Life Being for the sake of personal gain. Those who think they can escape the cataclysmic turmoil that is unfolding are living a delusion. Everyone will feel the effects of the Earth's tragedy. No more will be said of this unpleasantness, for there is another course of action that can and must be taken.

Simply stated, the human species must change their ways. Your lack of compassion must be replaced by loving-kindness and genuine concern for all species, including your own. Your sense of superiority must be laid aside. There is no room for such ideology in any civilization. All who came into existence are equal. This is the way of existence and it is the way of existence on the Life Being Earth. Destructive systems that serve a small few while harming the masses have obstructed the balance of nature. Those who came to believe that they were more than another were and are in error. This misunderstanding has destabilized the health of the planet.

Dear Friends, you are people of goodness. You know the difference between right and wrong and it is time for you to review your behavior. You must ask yourself if you are treating others with the kindness and respect that you desire and deserve. Will you do this, Dear Friend?

Will you ask the necessary questions to discern whether your personal behaviors towards others are in alignment with the way you prefer to be treated? As you review your behaviors, please think expansively. You live in a community that is far greater than the human population. Do you treat all members of your Earth community as you wish to be treated?

Please give this exercise the time and consideration that it deserves, for what you discover may change the course of the future. Remember, you are here for a reason. Perhaps your participation in this behavioral review is one of the reasons that you are here.

Twenty

Janet and Peter sat quietly enjoying the early morning hour in the beloved tree house. Numerous discussions were already behind them, allowing for this brief moment of serenity and sweet connection. Their chairs, sitting side by side, made it easy for them to enjoy one of their favorite activities. You see, Dear Reader, the Hansons were exceptionally adept at holding hands. It was a tender gesture of reassurance and connection that still brought them great joy.

"It's interesting, Peter, that after all these years, holding hands remains one of the most important interactions of our relationship. I'm so grateful that this loving gesture is mutually enjoyed."

Peter nodded as his wife spoke. He remembered the first time that he reached out to hold her hand. The memory brought a smile to his face. To be perfectly honest, it wasn't Peter's finest moment. He was very shy and so nervous that his attempt at grabbing her hand was rather clumsy, but Janet saved the day.

"We really were a silly pair, weren't we, dear?" Janet remarked, intuiting that he was reflecting upon that past event of long ago.

"Well, one of us certainly was," laughed her husband. "I was pathetically awkward and you were grace personified. I remember how surprised I was that you didn't make fun of my klutziness. You were wonderful, dear, and you won my heart in that moment of kindness. And you still possess it."

Janet acknowledged Peter's comment by squeezing his hand more tightly, before posing a question. "We've had a very good life, haven't we, dear?"

"Oh, yes! I think it's fair to say that we've had an exceptional life, and recently, it's become even more exciting. If you recall just a few weeks ago, we were wondering if we were wearing out, and now look at us! We're as active as we ever were, maybe even more so, and we are having the most incredible experiences. We're meeting new people with similar interests, communicating with other species, and enjoying the company of your Great-grandmother Harriet. My goodness! I think we're having a great life!"

Her husband's exuberance brought a big smile to Janet's face. "And just look at the new role the tree house has taken on. She's become a gathering place! Our friends, new and old, are truly enjoying meeting here in the tree house. I just know Nana is very pleased about this. It's such a lovely setting to share with others. We are indeed fortunate."

"Yes, you are!" Harriet's voice was recognized immediately.

"I knew you were near," declared the great-granddaughter of the unseen voice. "What are you up to today, Nana? Is this a fly-by or are you stopping in for a reason?"

"Both!" she replied. *"Of course, I always enjoy your company, but today is a busy day, so let me get to the point. It's time, Dear Ones, to initiate another meeting. You both already know this, so consider my fly-by a confirmation of your intentions. Much is going on among your friends; it is time for another gathering. Please make haste. Extend your invitations this morning if possible.*

"I'm sorry there isn't time for a visit today, but know that I love you, and I am so proud of you both. The work you are doing on behalf of the Earth is very important. Thank you so much for your efforts. Extend my gratitude to your friends as well. In peace be, Dear Ones."

Janet and Peter both expressed goodbyes and appreciation, even though they had no way of knowing if their words were heard. They sat quietly for a few minutes just taking in the moment. After all, communicating with a deceased family member does give one pause. And then, life just moves onward.

"It was nice of Nana to stop by and validate our thoughts about having another meeting. We both sensed it was time, but it was good to hear her perspective. My curiosity is piqued. I look forward to hearing about everyone's adventures. What's your preference, dear?" Janet inquired. A plan was quickly made, and within the hour, invitations were extended and accepted. The next meeting was scheduled for the following evening.

✆

"Welcome, Dear Ones! So good to see you again!" greeted Peter. The guests, having all arrived at the same time, entered the back gate in single file. It was interesting to observe everyone's preferences. Some focused on the treats that were displayed on a small table situated on the way to the tree house, while others were immediately captured by the garden. Both groups were only briefly distracted and then quickly turned to business. It was obvious that they were ready to start the meeting. Although Janet encouraged everyone to take goodies up into the tree house, none did. The group was ready to be fully engaged.

After the friends were seated, Janet took a deep breath, and everyone followed her lead. "My goodness!" she noted. "The group's energy is intense this evening." She made eye contact with each person and then sighed. "Well, I think Great-grandmother Harriet was correct. We needed to come together again." Just mentioning her ancestor's name created a stir resulting in numerous questions. Janet told them about Nana's brief visit and conveyed her message of gratitude. "She insinuated that a lot is going on among our group members, so as you might imagine, Peter and I are very excited to hear your stories. However, I wonder if we should begin with a bit of silence." The suggestion met with approval. Janet took the lead and invited everyone to take a long, deep breath. This act of self-care served its purpose. Each individual escaped into his or her inward journey, and as if directed, the chimes began to accompany the journeys. As often happens during these sweet moments, the traveler loses track of time. For some the adventure may seem like a lifetime, while others have no awareness of time whatsoever. Janet's experience took her to places she had never been before or so she thought. Fortunately, at the allotted time, another took the lead of the process and invited everyone to return to the present. The voice, both unfamiliar and familiar at the same time, welcomed the travelers back home.

When all eyes were opened again, there was a sense of confusion. Janet felt responsible for this and decided it was best to speak her truth. "Dear Ones, I must apologize for my indulgence during our meditation. I truly got lost in my adventure and was taken by surprise when someone else so graciously brought the session to a close. Thank you, for taking the lead." Janet's comments did not resolve the confusion as she had intended. "May I ask who did close the session? Your voice was so soft and peaceful that I could not discern who was speaking?" Heads turned from one to the other and it became clear that no one in the group had ended the meditation.

Janet's mind was racing and then a smile crossed her face. Peter recognized that smile. He knew that she had finally gathered what had happened. "Well," she continued, "perhaps we should think more expansively. To whoever so graciously stepped up and assisted our group, I am very grateful. Please accept my appreciation for your services. Although your identity escapes me, I would like to properly welcome you to our group. We are very happy that you have joined us. Shall we all introduce ourselves to you?"

"That will not be necessary," the soft-spoken person responded. *"I have had the privilege of knowing each of you at another time and place. Suffice it to say, our relationships are of long-standing. Being in your presence once again has brought to mind many memories of times gone past. Dear Ones, it is most agreeable to be with you. Even though you are in different forms, I recognize each of you. My heart is full and my emotions abound. Thank you! Being here amongst you brings me great delight. It is a privilege to join with you in this most cherished and sacred space."* Although the guest failed to introduce herself to the Circle of Friends, each member immediately felt a connection with the unseen visitor. Janet reassured the newcomer that she was welcome, and requested guidance on how to facilitate her visit.

"Although my suggestion may seem absurd, I wonder if it would be helpful to bring another chair up into the tree house for you to occupy. That will provide a focus for the rest of us who are not gifted with existential sight." The visitor agreed with the suggestion and cordially thanked Janet for her hospitality. Jonathan, sitting near the steps, quickly retrieved a chair and positioned it in the tree house. Although no movement could be heard around the chair, everyone assumed that the visitor had relocated herself.

"Yes, Dear Friends, I am now within the Circle. I apologize for the inconvenience of my present form. Unfortunately, my travels were extensive, leaving me with little energy for materialization. Perhaps another time will allow for that opportunity, but for now, I must simply acknowledge my limitations. It seems unfair that I have the pleasure of seeing you, while you must endure my invisibility. My Friends, I reassure you that we have enjoyed many, many times together and there are many more adventures that await us. Please be patient. Our true selves will soon see the true selves of each other."

Many questions raced through the minds of those who were listening to the invisible voice. The comment regarding extensive travel created great curiosity, as did the reassurance that the relationships shared with this visitor were of long-standing. And of course, the suggestions that many more adventures were yet to come sparked the imaginations of each member of the group.

Jen's curiosity simply could not be quieted. She had attempted to squelch her questions from the moment the guest arrived, but the need to know more overwhelmed the desire to be polite. "Excuse me," Jen was surprised that she managed to speak gently. "I must admit that my mind is cluttered with questions, and I don't know what is appropriate at this point. Can we ask you questions?"

"I am not opposed to questions; however, my time here is limited. Perhaps by addressing the task for which I have come, many of your questions will be answered. May we proceed in that manner, and then if time allows, specific questions will be attended."

"Yes, that seems like a wise and efficient use of your time," reacted Jen. "And we are certainly eager to hear more about you and your reason for visiting with us this evening. Please do continue with your task." Janet nodded appreciatively towards Jen for her skillful facilitation of the situation. She also appreciated Jen's list of questions and suspected that hers was equally long.

"My Dear Old Friends, please breathe with me." The Circle of Friends responded immediately. *"Let us join in this unique and ageless action of self-care so that we can quickly reclaim the Oneness that exists among us. With this simple act of breathing in unison, recognition of our wholeheartedness becomes apparent. We are One. So deeply grateful am I to share this moment in time with you. It is a joy to be in your presence once again."* The words spoken in gentle loving-kindness blending with the breaths of all present created an atmosphere of sacred togetherness. Breathing in and breathing out, uniting through the breath and the heart, Those of Old merged with Those of Recent Times and also with Those of the Moment, and All were One. Each different in his or her unique way, yet as One, they would always be.

"Dear Ones, I come with news that will not be new to you, but it is news that must be repeated nonetheless. Because this news is so shocking, it is difficult for the receivers of this news to fully comprehend the magnitude of the crisis. As such, fear and terror overwhelms the receivers of the news, diminishing their ability to remember that preventive action must be taken. I share this information with you so that you can review your own reactions to the information that is forthcoming. And then Dear Friends, you must recognize how much more frightening this information is for those who have not yet developed the skills to receive this tragic information from friendly sources. The crisis situation is tragic enough without it being presented in reckless, inhumane ways. Those who present misinformation for their own gains must be held accountable for these actions. The truth about the Earth's situation is known and it is available; but unfortunately, those who foolishly think they can profit from this crisis are confusing the masses with their lies.

"It is critical that the peoples of the planet know the truth, because they are the solution to the crisis. When the truth is provided and the masses accept their role in the solution, they will understand how quickly changes can be effected.

"The peoples of Earth are founded in goodness. The outrageous behavior that is currently being acted out across the globe at this time is evidence that something is

seriously wrong. Although the human species has been an aggressive species for a very long time, it has fallen to new lows in terms of its lack of compassion and concern for anyone else, including its own kind. Please forgive me for speaking so bluntly, but the reality of what is transpiring cannot be ignored. The manners of the human species have been in the process of devolution for some time now, and the consequences of this degeneration are quantifiable. For a species that professes great knowledge and superiority, it is amazing that humans can remain blind to the ruthless impact they have upon the Earth and all her resident life beings. Their acts of cruelty are incomprehensible." The invisible companion, deeply concerned about the impact of the message she was delivering, paused so that the listeners could catch their breaths. She cared about these good people and did not want to overwhelm them with the truth about their circumstances. Anne Madison sensed the emotional shift in their guest.

"Dear Friend, thank you for trying to take care of us," Anne's voice was as soft-spoken as the visitor's. "Delivering unpleasant news is a very difficult task. I don't envy your position, but I am very grateful for your gentleness. You treated us so kindly and lovingly that it has made it easier to hear the dreadful news regarding our own behaviors. Thank you, for being the bearer of bad news! I'm sure it was difficult for you to do this, but we need to know the truth. The eight of us are strong and we are a good support system for each other, so please trust that we will take care of one another. I hope you have a similar network of support. We are ready to hear more, when you are ready to continue." The other members of the group were impressed by Anne's sensitivity to the situation and grateful for her gracious response. Similar expressions of support were offered to the invisible companion.

"I am deeply moved by your support, Dear Friends. Your actions remind me of times past. I am grateful we have been brought together once again. I believe at this point we are all in consensus that we are here for a reason. So let us move forward on behalf of the Earth." The statement of unity emboldened the circle of friends. Rather than dreading the news yet to come, they were ready to take action.

"Let us continue, Dear Friends, with another truth. There is reason for hope! Please hear these words and breathe them into your innermost being. Let the reality of this truth fill you with hope, courage, and resolve that the Earth will continue forevermore." The instructions were immediately followed. *"As you participate in accepting this reality of the future, please remember that you are not alone. Many others who observe this gathering also stand ready to assist the Earth.*

"Dear Ones, let me speak another truth, as simply as it can be said. The negative energy generated by humankind's ill will is the primary factor in the Earth's instability. Although few humans are aware that they personally produce negative energy, it is a reality that must be faced. For decades, warning signs indicating that the Earth was struggling have been recognized. Information regarding the misuse and abuse of the planet has made headlines, but minimal efforts have been made on her behalf. During this time, the primary focus has been towards industries, governments, corporations, reckless mismanagement of vital resources, and the pursuit of prosperity versus the health of the planet. In essence, the focus has been on conglomerates rather than the individual. While that phase of discovery and understanding was meritorious and absolutely essential, the efforts made were not enough to correct the damage already done to the planet. Much more preventive restructuring is necessary from these multinational companies in the immediate future.

"In the meantime, the focus must now change to include the devastating effects that individual human beings have upon the Earth. Changes must be made, and these changes can transpire quickly once the people of Earth understand the impact that your ill will has upon self and others. We believe in the goodness of humankind, and we believe that you are unaware of your toxic energy. It is incomprehensible to other members of the Universe that humans would purposefully behave so irresponsibly. We have faith in humanity and we believe that once you understand the ramifications of your ill will you will be eager to address the issue.

"It makes no sense that anyone in existence would willfully choose to harm another, yet members of the human species do this on a daily basis. Actions of unkindness are pervasive and increasing. Intentional brutality is so frequent that it is no longer shocking. And mass killings are commonplace. Dear Friends, these atrocities are not normal. They are an indication that the human species is seriously unwell." The speaker wisely invited her listeners to take several deep breaths. She, too, took a reprieve from the unthinkable truths by joining in the breathing exercise. Eventually a long sigh was heard signaling that the discussion was about to continue.

"My Friends, there is much more about the human condition that humans must come to understand, and you must do so quickly. Unbeknownst to most humans, you live much of your life from a negative inclination. You are so accustomed to this behavior that you no longer even recognize that you are participating in negativity. When this began remains a mystery and it is unnecessary to have these details at this time; however, what is necessary is that the human species accept responsibility for your negative ways.

"This will require personal examinations and honest reviews of your discoveries. The truth lies within each member of your species and verification of what is

proposed can be gained quickly. Once the truth is discovered for yourself, the people of Earth will realize that you must change for the sake of the Earth and for the sake of your own survival. Your present way of being is leading you down a path of no return. Negative life styles serve no one. You are a species of great potential. Never were you intended to live life in this way." Once again a deep breath was taken simultaneously by all involved. The silence that followed was welcomed, a brief respite from the intensity of the moment.

"Dear Old Friends, excuse me for interrupting your thoughts. My time here is coming to an end, and I wish to express my appreciation for your tender care of me during this visit. I know this news is disheartening and complex, but please remember there is reason for hope. Your gathering is one of the reasons we are hopeful. Your willingness to connect with, and seek guidance from nature, gives us hope. Your excitement and acceptance of visitors from the past, such as Great-grandmother Harriet gives us hope. And your willingness to welcome others who remain unknown to you also gives us hope. Many are reaching out to the peoples of Earth trying desperately to get your attention because they are also committed to assisting the Earth through this crisis period. Resources of all kinds are available to you. The knowledge of the ages is available to you.

"Dear Ones, I know you have many questions, but please let me address the one that is in the forefront of your minds. You wish to know if there is still time to save the Earth, and the answer is yes. She is a resilient Life Being capable of rapid recovery when the surrounding conditions are conducive for healing. What she is most in need of at this time is a peaceful environment. It's that simple. If people across the planet would just live peaceably, the Earth's rapid recovery would astound your scientists.

"As you can see, Dear Friends, the human species is the primary factor in the Earth's crisis and they are also the solution to the problem. The truth is Earth will survive the abuses of humankind; however, it is doubtful that the human species will survive its own toxic mannerisms. If humankind is to continue, they must change their ways. The path of ill will is not a viable option. A peaceful mind, a compassionate heart, and concern for all other beings are options that lead to a peaceable state of being. The choice is obvious.

"Dear Friends, many in the Universe stand ready to assist you in your endeavors to alter your present life styles. The path to peace is so much easier than the path to ill will. You have lived in chaos and heartache for long enough. Please decide to live in peace instead. My Dear Old Friends, I must bid you adieu. It was most delightful to be in your presence again. Please remember, I am but a breath away and available at your request."

With that said, the tree house residents knew the communication was over. Silence prevailed briefly and then the chatter began. Tension demanded that they move about for a while, so the decision to exit the tree house was made.

In the garden, light conversation circled among the friends, but the conversation everyone really desired to have was appropriately on hold, waiting for their return to sacred space in the tree house. The wait was brief.

"Dear Ones, I sense we are ready to make our way back to our lofty space. Please help yourselves to more refreshments, and bring them with you if you like." Janet's invitation was well received. The group was as eager to return to the tree house now as they were to leave it just a while before. "I think it is fair to say that we are a bundle of emotions," observed Janet. "Let's make ourselves comfortable again and see where the conversation leads us."

Anne, sitting perfectly still in her chair, quietly spoke. "Well, I must admit that I am intrigued by the encounters we are having with these invisible folks. The information that they are providing us is exceptional and breathtaking, and I am deeply grateful for their assistance. But I am still taken aback by their presence. Who are they? Our visitor this evening was so kind and sincere in her desire to assist us, and it was a privilege to be in her presence, but the question remains. Who are these beings? Who was she?" Her eyes reached out to her visible companions. "Am I the only one wondering about this?"

Geri, experiencing similar feelings to Anne, quickly responded to her appeal. "Oh, Anne, you are not alone in this conundrum. While I was listening to the soft, gentle voice of our guest, it seemed like a normal conversation, until I wanted to respond to something that was said. Then the reality of the situation registered and I realized that this conversation was anything but normal. Like you, Anne, I feel so fortunate to be part of the experience, and still, this is very unusual."

"Yes, it is!" agreed Carol. "I was wondering about this unusual interaction while we were trying to relax down in the garden, and I think we are being prepared for a new normal." Carol's comment caught everyone's attention. "Please bear with me; I'm still trying to work my way through this, but it seems of late that we all have had unusual encounters. Various members of the wild kingdom have purposefully reached out to us and given us important information and guidance regarding the Earth's crisis situation. Janet's Great-grandmother has reengaged with her and is also providing valuable information.

And now, we are aware that others from unknown locations are also attempting to get our attention.

"We definitely are discovering that there are many others who are far more aware of the Earth's condition than we are and that they desire our assistance. This is comforting, reassuring, and mind-blowing. I think we are being introduced to the reality that already exists around us. Until very recently, we were oblivious to this reality. We lived our lives unaware of all these other life beings. It seems to me that they are intentionally making their presence known now. Our disregard of these wonderful beings has caused them great harm and our ignorance has resulted in a global crisis. What seems like a new norm for us is actually an old norm of which we were totally oblivious. Friends, I think we have a whole lot of catching up to do. We are way behind our fellow species."

"Oh my, Carol! Your comments bring to mind a remarkable encounter Geri and I recently had with three Rabbits in our outer garden." Jonathan briefly shared the story so that their friends could appreciate the interaction. "These little creatures are intelligent and their sophisticated observations of humankind's lack of regard for other species was stunning. This was also true of the highly regarded elder that we were privileged to meet. Listening to the wisdom that was provided by the revered Woodchuck felt like a spiritual experience." Geri affirmed her husband's comment with a quick nod and smile. She was pleased that Jonathan mentioned the spiritual connection they had experienced.

"I think," continued Jonathan, "it is fair to say that we humans are naïve. It's time we started paying attention to these life beings that we've ignored. They know a lot more about the Earth than we do. And what's truly amazing to me is that these animals still care about us. Even after we have treated them so unkindly, they still have compassion for the human species. That, in itself, is a testament to their humanity. We have a lot to learn from these benevolent creatures." The Gardeners' experience inspired the Madisons to share their encounter with the Great Buck, and then, Carol and Jen relayed their interaction with the Eagle in the dark forest. Each story excited the circle of friends.

"Hmm!" mumbled David. "Is it my imagination or does it seem like a movement is underway?" Peter immediately agreed with David, acknowledging that he had never heard of so many encounters with animals and plants as were happening among the eight of them.

"This cannot be a coincidence," Peter asserted. "They are reaching out to us for help, which is an incredible feat of courage... and desperation. So, what are we going to do? How are we going to respond to this plea for help? What is our next step?" The wind chimes, without the assistance of any noticeable breezes, seemed to respond to Peter's request. Unfortunately, while the rendition was beautiful, no one understood the meaning of the melodic message. Glances were exchanged while everyone waited in anticipation.

"Hello, Dear Ones! It is wonderful to see you gathered in the tree house." The reassuring voice of Great-grandmother Harriet was immediately recognized. *"Thank you all for quickly responding to Janet and Peter's request for another meeting. I know these gatherings must seem rather odd, but Dear Ones, you are needed. Please hold on to that truth, and rest assured that you will be receiving more information that will answer many of your questions. It appears that the agenda for your meeting is full today, so I will turn this over to Those who are much more knowledgeable about the Earth's condition than I. Thank you again for coming!"*

"Thank you, Nana! Next time, please come and stay a while!" The brevity of Harriet's visit saddened Janet. She longed for the times when they would sit and chat for hours. She hoped that might happen again. But Janet understood the circumstances and recognized that another unusual experience was in the making. Her focus returned to the present just in time for the next event to unfold.

"Greetings, Dear Friends! Our numbers are too many to join you in the sacred tree house; however, please know that you are surrounded by Those who love and cherish you. For your convenience, One of us will occupy the available chair in the sacred space. Although the spokesperson will be the focal point, please understand that this One represents all who desire to be in your presence.

"Will we be allowed to ask questions?" Jen, feeling both bold and desperate, focused her question in the direction of the seemingly empty chair. "Please excuse my impertinence, but we really need guidance. The information that we've received from various sources is compelling. We believe what we've been told and we definitely want to be of assistance in creating changes that will facilitate the Earth's recovery. But the truth is, we really don't know how to move forward." Before an answer was given, David, Carol, and Geri added comments that complemented Jen's remarks. The silence that followed felt like an eternity. In truth, it was mere seconds, but during that time Janet recalled the adventure she had experienced during the brief meditation at the beginning of the meeting. The flash of memory surprised her as much the second time around as it had when first experienced. A deep breath was automatically triggered. Peter noticed that something was happening, but was unable to connect with his beloved telepathically.

"Your requests are heard and appreciated, Dear Friends; however, at this moment, one of you is in discomfort. May we be of assistance, Friend Janet?" All attention turned in Janet's direction. Peter's hand was already resting upon hers as he watched her take several more elongated breaths.

"Dear Friends," he said quietly, "I think it would be very helpful if we all joined Janet in her deep breathing exercise." Everyone in attendance immediately provided support.

"Thank you everyone. I'm okay now. Please relax, I'm really okay."

"What happened Janet?" her husband asked. "I tried to reach out to you dear, but wasn't successful. I'm sorry I couldn't break through to help you."

"Actually, you did connect, Peter, but I just wasn't able to reply. I heard you loud and clear, which was very comforting. Your telepathic skills are developing nicely, dear."

"Well, that's good to hear, but we still don't know what happened. It seemed like you were lost in another world, dear. Is this connected to your disorientation at the end of our meditation?" Peter had no idea how accurate his description actually was. Janet paused for a moment and then smiled at her friends.

"Dear Ones, I am really fine. Please don't worry about me. It seems," she paused again. "Well, this is going to sound weird, but I think I had an out-of-body experience during our meditation. Peter you were right. I felt like I was lost in another world.

"It was very strange! The experience itself seemed eternal, and when the meditation ended, it was quite a jolt to return to this world. There were times during the journey, and that was exactly what it felt like. It was a journey. Some of the time, I felt completely at home and was able to recognize various landscapes, even though I don't remember ever seeing those landscapes. And then other times, I truly felt like I was in another world, viewing it from various perspectives. Sometimes the views were galactic, while other times, the focus was upon a particular planet. And this observation of one scene after another seemed to go on for ages. It was an incredible experience, but the memory of it was lost as soon as our visitor arrived. And then it returned again, when our new group of visitors joined us. I'm sorry that my description of what transpired is so scattered, but words fail me." Janet lovingly touched her husband's face and reassured him that his attempt to assist her was indeed successful.

"Thank you, Janet." Anne's tone indicated her concern for her dear friend. She was relieved to hear that Janet was truly okay and she was also intrigued by the experience that she shared. "It really was a remarkable journey, Janet, and I hope you will keep us posted as more memories surface. By the way, Janet, perhaps it would be interesting to hear what our guests know about your experience." The suggestion piqued everyone's curiosity and all eyes looked towards the empty chair.

"Welcome, Dear Visitors!" exclaimed Janet. "I'm afraid you haven't been appropriately welcomed to our little space of heaven. I'm sorry that my uneasiness took us off in another direction. Thank you for bringing attention to my moment of discomfort. As you can see, we are a wonderful support group for each other.

"We are very glad you are here, and we are eager to hear what you have to say. And as you just witnessed, we are curious to know if you have any insights regarding my unusual experience; however, we do not need to focus upon that now. Please take the lead, Dear New Friends. What do you wish to share with us?"

"Your gracious hospitality is deeply appreciated. We trust that you are indeed feeling grounded and in alignment once again?" Janet nodded and reassured their guests that she was fine.

"Our preference is to elaborate upon your experience first, if you will allow that. It will give us great pleasure to do so."

"Yes, please do so!" exclaimed Peter. "I think this is a good way for our conversation to begin. We would appreciate any information that you can share about Janet's experience." Peter forthright manner was impressive. He was definitely feeling protective of his spouse and wanted as much information as possible.

"We agree, Dear Ones! Friend Janet, your description of your experience was more accurate than you realize. For a very brief moment in time you were elsewhere in the Greater Universe. While in that expansive setting, you experienced time differently than it is experienced on this planet. You spent time in a time that you define as the past, the present, and the future; thus, your journey was extensive and experienced as an expenditure of a great amount of time. While this transpired for you, only a few minutes in your linear time frame actually passed.

"The settings that you visited were places where life experiences have occurred or will occur at some point yet to come. More memories may surface as you mull over your travels; however, the purpose of such travels is to remind the traveler that they

are more than they appear to be. You have lived a very full and expansive life, Dear Friend, and it is not over. Your life will continue forevermore.

"Dear Friends, what your friend and companion has experienced, so too have you in your own unique ways. Each of you has lived many lifetimes within your life experience and each of you has endless more lifetimes to experience. This is the reality of all in existence. Suffice it to say, the journey is long and never-ending.

"In this particular life experience, all of you have come together for a reason. Even those of you who have just recently met sense from within that you have known each other for a very long time. Your intuition, your sense of knowing, is correct. You are Old Friends found anew. It is not a coincidence that all of you are having unusual encounters with other life forms on this planet. When missions of great importance are embarked upon, it is essential that those who are long-bonded join together. As was stated earlier, you are a good support system for one another. Collaboration and camaraderie typically result in faster and more efficient results. By sharing your experiences, your knowledge base grows more rapidly, empowering you to facilitate changes. Dear Ones, you are here to create change!

"As you well know, this remarkable planet is under tremendous stress. You knew this before your recent encounters with the beloved inhabitants of the Earth, but they validated what you already knew. Just as you are here to assist the planet, so too are they; however, they have been working collaboratively with her since they came into existence here. Their knowledge of the workings of this environmental system far surpasses that of the human species. They understand how precarious the Earth's situation is. This is why these wonderful creatures are reaching out to you. Much can be learned from them, if only the human species will give them credence.

"Dear Friends, each of you felt deeply privileged to be part of these incidents of connection, and indeed you were. These experiences were not mere happenstance. You were observed, studied, and determined to be of good will before the connections were made. You were purposefully selected.

"Unfortunately, history has educated these life beings to the behaviors of humankind. They were well aware that precautions needed to be taken before they approached you. They were wise in their preventive measures, and they were wise in their discernment of reaching out to the eight of you. They chose wisely.

"We are sincerely grateful for your positive reactions and wholehearted acceptance of their efforts." The compliment was joined by another lovely rendition from the chimes. *"Ah,"* whispered the spokesperson. *"The gentle breezes carry the energy of gratitude from the flora and fauna who are observing our conversation. These wonderful life beings are hopeful because of their positive exchanges with each of you.*

"Dear Ones, these connections are gateways for more connections. You need not wait for them to contact you. You can also reach out to them. It is not a time for shyness; it is a time for advancement, accompanied by patience and gracious manners. This approach was used when reaching out to you; hopefully, you will offer them the same courtesy."

"You're right," interjected Anne. "Our connection with the Great Buck was masterful. He was both gentle and a pillar of strength at the same time. He literally guided us through the encounter in such a way that we enjoyed a remarkably positive interaction while also having an inspiring experience. His manners were gracious and impeccable." A smile crossed her faced as she added, "I can't wait to visit with him again." David remained quiet, but his facial expression affirmed Anne's description of the event. He added a nod and the thumbs up gesture for good measure.

"Dear Ones, your desire for guidance is appreciated and understood. There is no singular course for confronting a planetary crisis, so we encourage you to think expansively while maintaining a willingness to be flexible. Obviously, the eight of you are eager to assist the Earth, and within this group are different kinds of talents and preferences. The beauty of this combination is that you are suited to being singularly creative while at the same time having opportunities to assist one another in various projects.

"What are your gifts? How can they be used to directly assist the Earth? How can you use your gifts to inform and educate others about the Earth's crisis? How can you inspire your fellow humans to open their hearts to the truth about Earth's declining health? How can you welcome others to participate in healing the Earth? How can you demonstrate to others that every action of kindness has a positive reaction upon the Earth's strained health? How can you share your thoughts with others regarding the impact of negative thoughts, words, and actions on self, others, and the Earth? How can you invite conversations about the effects of humankind's ill will without instigating more ill will? How can you maintain courage and optimism when approaching others to address these complicated topics?

"As you see, Dear Friends, the path to resolving the Earth's health issues demands kindness, patience, and perseverance. Begin with kindness! Treat everyone as you desire to be treated, and remember to think expansively when referring to EVERYONE. Everyone is not limited to a select few; everyone means everyone. Also remember that being genuinely kind to everyone means being kind all the time: not just once a day or once every other day, but all the time. Give this careful consideration, Dear Friends, because the human species seems to have a difficult time monitoring their moods.

177

"Accepting responsibility for being a person of kindness demands one to examine his or her behaviors carefully and honestly. We encourage you to review your behavior before you embark upon this new lifestyle of consistently living your life as a person of kindness. You may be surprised by what you discover. Then after you make the decision to practice being kind to everyone you encounter throughout the day, you may find it beneficial to examine your behavioral patterns at the end of each day. Again, you may be surprised by what you discover. The point of this exercise, Dear Ones, is to discern whether you really are a kind person or if that is merely a false perception of self. Please do not be alarmed by this challenging remark! Whatever you discover can be improved upon, and the choice to become a kinder person is so much easier than living one's life in the burdensome state of unkindness. Kindness begets kindness, while unkindness leads to separation, loneliness, and despair. The choice seems obvious, doesn't it? Being a person of kindness benefits one's self and everyone encountered, including the Earth whose ever-present presence flourishes from your positive energy.

"Dear Ones, open your hearts to greater understanding of patience. With kindness comes patience. They are inseparable. If you find yourself feeling impatient with another, then your kindness is waning and it is in need of adjustment. Again, we advise you not to be alarmed by this challenging comment. Recognizing that one is slipping in a particular area facilitates the opportunity for a quick recovery from the downward motion. When one is openhearted about his or her imperfections, the ability to change is easy and without restrictions. Wisdom comes to those who are willing to observe their flaws with grace.

"Unfortunately for some individuals, the idea of change of any kind is indeed challenging. Rather than viewing change as a positive opportunity, they perceive it as something that must be avoided. Choosing to live one's life from a perspective of kindness requires that an individual be openhearted to the reality that change is a factor of life. One cannot run and hide every time change is encountered. Simply stated: change is the way of existence. Appreciate change for the gift that it is or face hardships and unpleasantness in days to come. In actuality, change is merely an opportunity for flexibility while discovering and honing new skills for the many changes that await us. And this is where perseverance comes into play. To meet the many changes that lie ahead demands perseverance. Please do not fear this statement. It is not meant to frighten you, but it is intended to prepare you for the challenges that are coming. Dear Friends, you are more than you appear to be, and you are capable of meeting the challenge of assisting the Earth in her healing process. It will demand daily commitments to be of service, but this is not beyond your capabilities. You already have the skills of managing daily responsibilities. Each day, you do this. You rise, you attend to your personal obligations, as best as you are able, and then

you rest. Every day, you persevere! This is not a new skill set for you. Perseverance is a skill that you have already mastered, which means you are sufficiently prepared to assist the Earth.

"In essence, Dear Friends, all the relevant components that are needed to assist the Earth exist within you. Kindness, patience, and perseverance are the significant factors that can heal the Earth and also alter the course of humankind." Once again the chimes managed to release another round of pleasant melodic sounds without any breezes assisting its efforts. The harmonic tunes seemed to applaud the messages brought forward by the visitors while also providing time for the profound messages to be digested. Anticipation seemed to be in the air. The visitors waited for reactions regarding the messages that were delivered, while the Circle of Friends waited to see what was going to happen next. Peter, unable to endure the uncertainty of the moment, broke the silence.

"Excuse me," he stated gently. "Is this an appropriate time to discuss your comments regarding the difficulty we humans have in facing changes?"

"Indeed!" answered the invisible visitor. "We are eager to hear your thoughts."

"Wonderful!" replied Peter. "However, first I would like to thank you for joining us today and for sharing your wealth of knowledge with us. I am somewhat overwhelmed, but I'm deeply grateful for the efforts that you are making on the Earth's behalf. Your concern for her is obvious, as is your loyalty." Janet was very pleased with her husband's expression of gratitude. She too felt a strong sense of appreciation for the visitor's commitment to the Earth. She was reassured by their presence even though she was not able see them.

"Now," Peter continued, "regarding the issue of our resistance to change. I understand and concur that we are a complicated species and that we can be very strong-willed and stubborn. It is obvious that you are acutely aware of our limitations; however, am I correct in sensing that you remain optimistic about our ability to change?"

"Yes, Friend Peter. We are indeed aware of the obstinate traits of your kind, and still, we have faith in the human species. You are capable of great change. If you will allow yourselves to face the fears and misunderstandings that restrict you and mislead you, then you will find the truth of who you really are and the power with which you are all endowed. You do not need assistance from others to correct the damage that you have perpetrated against others while living upon this planet. You have the power and the ability to heal yourselves and the planet. This is another truth of your existence. You are powerful healers and you can heal the Earth. If only

you would seek within and discover who you really are. Rather that lashing out at others, you would be wise to seek within for resolution of your issues."

Peter's reaction to the profound message was mixed. His mind was in a whirl when Janet inserted herself into the conversation. "Dear Ones, your message is one that deserves serious contemplation; its wisdom does not escape us. We are all advocates of this method of self-discovery; however, we feel a sense of urgency. Some of us have been seeking within for a very long time and still feel that we are novices. We need help in moving forward at a more rapid pace. We desire to assist the Earth and we feel we are being called to help, but we're uncertain about the next steps to take. And I think all of us are afraid that your suggestion to seek within will delay our efforts rather than move us forward.

"Please understand that I hold your suggestion in the highest regard, but I wonder if you might also provide more concrete guidance for us to pursue." Janet immediately regretted being so outspoken, but before she could apologize, the chimes filled the air. She wondered if the chimes were validating her efforts or chastising her for speaking so forthrightly.

"Please do not scold yourself, Dear Friend. We are pleased by your request. As you well know, the process of seeking within is ongoing, never-ending. Each of you has pursued the inward journey in various ways during this and other lifetimes, and always, the goal was the same. The desire to know more about self and all that is propels us forward in our everlasting evolutionary experience.

"Even now when your planet is in great crisis, the journey within continues. It is through this process that one discovers the true self, thereby developing into that truth while also continuing to expand to the next truth about oneself. Pursuing the inward journey does not mean that you neglect the life experience that is before you. It is a process of mutual co-existence. One journey exists within the other. While you grow from your inner exploration you become more equipped to deal with the challenges of your current experience.

"What we see as a necessary step for humankind's evolutionary development is a combined effort that promotes daily introspection of one's personal impact upon the planet, as well as all those around you, while also making the essential changes that will bring you into harmonic resonance with the Earth and all her inhabitants. The human species is presently out of alignment with the other life beings that are mutually co-existing with the planet. While these other species are on a path of everlasting coexistence with the planet Earth, the human species is on a path towards extinction.

"*Dear Ones, this is not the way of existence. Your attitudes of superiority have led you astray. You are not more than any others. The guidance to seek within illuminates your misperceptions of self, while instigating kindness, patience, and perseverance mobilizes the changes that must be made. This gathering is an example of the efforts you are already making. By sharing your stories, your connections have grown stronger and your growth has been more rapid because of the communal environment you created. As you discuss your thoughts and concerns, you are observed by the surrounding species and they have shared your intentions with others. The connections that have emerged because of the gatherings held in this sacred tree house demonstrate how rapidly goodness and kindness can spread when hearts and ears are open to all the existences around them. Without even knowing it, the eight of you have been actively creating trust among other species. They listen to your heartfelt conversations about the environment and they are comforted by your intentions. You give them hope and because of this, they have become more intentional about reaching out to you. They enjoy your company and desire more time with you. These wonderful life beings are optimistic about the future because of the interactions that have transpired. We encourage you to be equally optimistic.*

"*As we have stated before, your species is in crisis; however, we remain optimistic that you will regain your humanity. You have everything that is needed to rise to the occasion. You are founded in goodness, and because of that truth, you are capable of achieving the tasks that await you. Dear Ones, within all members of your species is a tender heart whose primary function is to embrace and accept all others.*

"*Perhaps, this statement gives you pause. It would be understandable if it did. Unfortunately, your species was misled by fears and misunderstandings, which resulted in prejudices and judgments that have worsened throughout your history. Instead of becoming a united species, you have been torn apart by differences that were not regarded as the gifts that they were. Diversity is one of the greatest gifts of existence, but your species rejected this reality. Such heartache has been caused by your disdain of differences. What was meant to stimulate curiosity instead resulted in fear and outrageous misunderstandings. These misunderstandings can be corrected. With kindness, patience, and openheartedness, the human species can choose to view their surroundings from a different perspective. Great beauty is everywhere in this remarkable world of diversity. If only your species would embrace and accept this truth.*" A great silence engulfed the tree house and the backyard. Even the chimes remained silent. The enormity of the crisis became vividly clear.

"Your confidence in humankind is admirable," Jen's comment was barely heard. She unsuccessfully attempted a deep breath that resulted in a series of coughs. "Excuse me. I think I choked on my own fear and dismay." An audible sigh was heard before Jen was able to continue. "Humans have been at odds with one another for a very long time. It amazes me that you still have faith in our ability to change. I don't mean to be pessimistic, but our track record for being kind and patient is not exactly stellar.

"The fact that your messages consistently express hopefulness in our ability to change gives me hope, but the task is so large. Please excuse my mood, but in this particular moment, I'm having a hard time imagining us coming together on any project, much less one of this magnitude. Not only are we resistant to change, but we also are not inclined to agree with one another. We are obstinate people who expect others to acquiesce to our whims and preferences." Jen shook her head in disbelief at her behavior. "I'm so sorry for my outburst of doubts. Ordinarily, I'm not this pessimistic, but fears have overcome me. Not to worry," she stated reassuringly to her companions. "This will pass, but there will be similar reactions by others when this news reaches the masses. As you said earlier, we are a people who struggle with our moods. Well, this project will certainly challenge our stability.

"We will need to strategize ways to help folks with these emotional hurdles. I realize now how important it will be to prepare people for these jolts of fears. Essentially, we will need to normalize fear-based reactions. We can lessen their impact by educating the public. If folks are aware that these types of reactions are likely to happen, that alone will significantly reduce their influence."

"Goodness, Jen. You just demonstrated how to assist folks with this issue. You experienced your own fears and doubts and you noted your changing mood. And then, you changed again as you became engaged with finding a solution to the impact of these fearful moments. Obviously, we are going to have those moments of despair. But you pulled yourself out of it within minutes, and witnessing your remarkable resilience gives me hope." Anne's comments validated and applauded Jen's experience. "Once you focused upon helping others, you regained your stability quickly. It was masterful, Jen."

"Exactly!" declared the invisible voice. *"You have rediscovered the missing element that is essential to humanity's state of well being. Generosity!*

"For the sake of humankind, you must regain your generous nature. Once you were a people who lovingly cared for one another. You were openhearted to and accepting of all kind and you were noted for your generosity. You misplaced the most important aspect of your true self because of misunderstandings that led you astray.

But your generosity is not lost forever. Your tenderheartedness still lies within you, and it awaits reactivation. Oh, Dear Friends, ponder this please. Earlier, you expressed the desire to advance forward more rapidly, and now, you can bear witness to the gigantic step just made.

"Generosity is the key to revitalizing the human species. When combined with kindness, patience, and perseverance, humankind's generous inclinations will culminate in the healing of the Earth and all the other life beings that share this beautiful planet.

"Dear Ones, your growth has been exceptional. We are most impressed and grateful. You have much to contemplate. We will give you to time to consider all that has been learned today, and if we may, we would appreciate spending more time with you in the near future." The request was met with applause and openhearted acceptance, and of course, was accompanied by another series of lovely melodious tunes. The musical performance eventually ended, leaving the tree dwellers sitting quietly in their circle.

"Have our guests departed?" Jonathan's softly spoken question set off a round of giggles and humorous comments.

"It's difficult to know, isn't it?" replied Anne. "Perhaps we should just check in with them and see if they are still hanging about." Her suggestion brought about more giggles, but Janet was inspired. Accepting the role as hostess of the gathering, she took charge.

"Hello there!" she said spiritedly. "Are you still near? We're not in need of assistance at this time other than to know if you have moved on or if you are still here. Don't mean to bother you. We are just curious." The giggles came to a halt when Janet posed her question. Sitting still and quietly, the circle of eight friends waited for a response. Only a very faint sounding of the chimes was heard.

"Well, this has been another remarkable gathering. I wonder if we could tape these sessions," mused Carol. "So much information is shared. I feel a strong need to curl up with my journal, while everything is still fresh in my mind."

"That's a great idea," Geri concurred. "I also want to allot some time for reviewing my behavior so that I have a better sense about my true self. I like to perceive myself as a kind and generous person, but am I really? I want to challenge that perception of self and face the truth. I'm going to make a list of positive and negative findings, and then create an improvement chart. And," she said tentatively, "I'm going to report my discoveries to all of you." She shivered at the thought. "Yikes! The idea of facing the truth is both challenging and inspiring. I think this exercise can help me target my flaws, and by sharing by findings with all of you, it will force me to be accountable to you and myself. Yikes!" she repeated.

"We can change!" she added. "And I'm ready to do whatever is necessary!" Her companions applauded!

"Great pep talk!" stated Anne. "You've inspired me!"

"She's inspired us all!" declared several of the friends at the same time.

"Thank you, Geri. That was a wonderful way to close the evening. May I suggest we gather again? Sooner rather than later!" The suggestion was well accepted and another meeting was scheduled for the same time, same place in forty-eight hours. Many hugs and expressions of appreciation were shared as they separated for the evening.

Twenty-One

"**G**reetings, Dear Friends! We are most grateful that you are home safely. It is good to be in your presence once again. We trust that your time on the planet Earth was fruitful."

"Indeed, Dear Ones, our travels were most productive. We are grateful to be home and eager to share our good news with all of you. We believe you will be equally optimistic regarding our encounters. As you know, our mission was to engage with the family and friends of our Dear Companion Harriet. Her Great-granddaughter along with her husband and three other couples are keenly aware of the circumstances unfolding on the planet and each one is actively seeking and pursuing ways in which he or she can assist the Earth. All of these fine individuals have recently experienced profound interspecies connections. These exchanges have heightened their curiosity about these other beings and they are excited about learning more. Their enthusiasm gives us great hope. They listen with the ears of their hearts, and when they hear the unpleasant truths about their roles in the Earth's declining health, they do not become defensive or self-justifying. They simply listen. And then they seek information about how to assist her. These humans are compassionate and truly care about the Earth. Unlike so many of their species, who are unwilling to accept the truth, these eight friends concur with our messages and are willing to take action on her behalf. We are extremely hopeful and wish to attend their next gathering, which will be in forty-eight hours, according to their linear time. We hope you will agree with our desire to reunite with them again."

"Dear Friends, your intentions are wise and we support your decision. Your successful mission does indeed bring great joy and optimism to our hearts. We have hoped for this type of connection for a very long time. We are very grateful to hear this promising news. Is there anything else you wish to report?"

"Yes, Dear Ones, there is another astounding factor of optimism that we wish to share with you. We know this news will fill your hearts with joy. Dear Ones, the other species that engaged with these individuals are very hopeful about their encounters and they are sharing their stories with others. The humans are also sharing their positive encounters with others as well. Change is happening, Dear Ones."

Twenty-Two

Peter and Janet sat on the middle step going up into the tree house overlooking the backyard. It was the most comfortable step to sit upon. The bottom one was too low to the ground for folks of their age, while the top one was simply a step too many after a very long day. Yes, the middle step was definitely the best. Sitting there allowed you to rest your back against the top riser while you took in the lovely view of the dimly lit yard.

"That was an incredible meeting, wasn't it, dear?" Peter reassured Janet that it was. His own mind was reeling from the event and he wondered if Janet's was as well. She responded telepathically.

"Of course it is, Peter. My goodness, we've just enjoyed the company of unseen visitors and we have six other witnesses that can vouch for our sanity." The couple giggled about her comment and both made a few wisecracks about the aging process before continuing their conversation.

"Tell me more about your perceptions of the encounter, Janet. And please continue to use your inner voice so I can practice using my inner ear.

"Good idea! We must practice more often so that our skills will be more in sync with our fellow life beings."

"Those were my thoughts too, dear." Realizing that he had successfully responded with his inner voice brought a smile to Peter's face.

"Well done, Peter! You're really very good at this, but you just don't trust it yet. That will come, as we practice more diligently and frequently." Her husband nodded in agreement and urged her to share her thoughts about the recent encounter.

"I'm struck by the wisdom and level of compassion that we are engaging with— it's really exceptional. Of course, I am very curious about the origins of these beings, but it really doesn't matter. One can tell when another is being totally honest with you, and these beings are definitely speaking the truth.

"Now that I said that, I find myself doubting what was just stated. How can one really know if someone is truly being honest with you? I guess the answer is ever changing. You don't really know, but a discernment process is activated within, and then you either choose to trust the other or you don't. I choose to trust these visitors. And I choose to trust my inner knowing. I believe these life beings are sincere in their efforts to assist the Earth and I admire their courage to approach us on her behalf.

"I'm afraid I'm rambling about. Does any of this make sense to you?" Peter didn't hesitate. His response was quick and firm.

"Janet, everything you said makes sense, and I agree with you. The notion of trust is complicated and it varies from one circumstance to another. Needless to say this particular situation is unusual in that we cannot see our visitors, nor do we know anything about them other than what they are presenting to us. And yet, like you, I trust them. Without any proof whatsoever, I totally trust them.

"The second component about trust that you brought up was brilliant, Janet. The idea of trusting oneself is a completely different aspect of awareness that seems extraordinarily relevant to me. Trusting oneself when making decisions about trusting another entails a much deeper level of self-understanding."

"That's true," interjected his beloved friend of many years. *"I think of it as an issue of self-confidence. Trusting oneself means that we are capable of, and willing to, accept responsibility for our decisions. In essence, we believe that we can manage and cope with whatever happens regarding a decision that we make, including the disappointment of being wrong. When I apply this to our current situation, I feel confident about trusting our invisible visitors. Thus far, everything that they have shared with us has moved us in a direction of goodness. All their suggestions have been about improving the human species, which includes altering our treatment of the Earth. Not once have they advocated that we should do harm to another. On the contrary, they have warned us about our past and present unacceptable behaviors. I just don't see any reason not to trust these life beings. And if my present regard for them were to change in the future, then I trust myself to do the right thing."* As always, Peter was amazed by his wonderful spouse. He had the utmost respect for her, and he absolutely trusted her goodness and her intuition. Janet, listening to his unspoken compliments, patted him on the knee.

"Oh my, if you keep thinking those wonderful thoughts, I may become a bighead. I appreciate your compliments, dear; but the truth is, you bring out the best of me. I am so grateful we are together. Life has been wonderful, and now, it's becoming even more interesting." Janet paused, took a deep breath, and then encouraged her husband to share his thoughts about the gathering.

The truth is, these two lovely friends brought out the best in each other. Janet's comment embarrassed Peter, but she spoke the truth. His love for her and his trust in her many talents bolstered her confidence. Likewise, Janet's awareness of Peter's remarkable gifts helped him to understand aspects of himself that he was not aware of before they met. They had different skill sets that complemented one another, making them a very dynamic twosome.

"Well, thank you for those kind words, dear. I too am very grateful for the life we've shared. We've truly been blessed and the blessings seem to be never-ending. Thank you for addressing the issue of trusting our new companions. That topic was on my mind as well, but your thoughts helped clarify my own concerns. I too believe these folks are sincere in their efforts to assist the Earth, and for reasons that still escape me, they seem committed to aiding us as well. Needless to say, our species needs all the help we can get.

"I wonder what happened to us, Janet. Why have we become such an aggressive species? There must be something in our evolutionary process that caused us to move in this direction. I would love to know the answer to this question, but I'm not sure if having the information would make a difference. We are who we are." Peter, realizing how complex the situation was, took a deep breath. *How does one talk about the unimaginable?* His unspoken thought was heard, but Janet didn't respond. She knew he was simply processing his own thoughts.

"The problem is so expansive!" he continued. *"As I sit here wondering about all 'those' people around the world who are acting in inappropriate ways, those very same people are wondering the same about the rest of humanity. We all believe that someone else is the problem and that they are the ones who need to change. When in truth, we all need to honestly review our behaviors, just as our visitors suggested. We have to accept responsibility for our own misbehaviors and make the necessary changes to better ourselves. That is a monumental task compounded by the reality that each one of us has his or her individual viewpoint about what improving ourselves means.*

"I believe that we are basically good people, Janet; however, based upon the facts, including our violent aggressive behaviors towards one another and our mistreatment of the Earth, we have to acknowledge that our behaviors are not in alignment with who we think we are. We cannot continue blaming others for their irresponsible behavior; instead, we need to accept responsibility for improving our own behavior. Regardless of where we fall on the continuum of 'good vs. bad behavior' we can all use some fine-tuning. I'm afraid we've grown accustomed to placing culpability on others while ignoring our own wrongdoings, and as a result, we are truly out of touch with our own blameworthiness and stagnation.

"I really need to take an honest look at myself, dear. I'm one of those people who has become complacent with myself. It's time for me to face the truth. I want to know the truth and I want to take the necessary steps to be a better person." Janet was so impressed with her husband's sincere desire to improve himself. From her point of view, Peter was an excellent example of most of the human species—a very good person who was in need of refinement.

"Dear, dear friend of mine, I want to join you on this journey of self-discovery. Let's grow together!" And with that said, the two dear friends strolled back towards the house.

⊚

Over at the Gardner's outer garden, Geri and Jonathan were doing their version of processing their thoughts and experiences regarding the latest gathering.

"Jonathan, I found the entire experience spellbinding. We're engaging with other life beings! We can't see them. We don't know where they are from and we don't know anything about these beings. And yet, I am absolutely certain that this is one of the most important experiences of our lives. Is this really happening?"

"Yes, dear, it really is happening and I share your enthusiasm. The positive energy that these beings exude makes me trust them. And the information they shared is in alignment with our way of thinking, but in a much more expansive manner. Of course, my mind races with many questions, but the bottom line is this: I trust what is happening and I trust these beings." Other residents of the outer garden were keenly aware of the excitement being generated by the couple. Observations were discreetly underway.

"Geri, there's another aspect of the interaction this afternoon that really fascinates me. Did you notice how similar the conversation with these beings was to our conversations with the Rabbits and the Woodchuck in our garden?" Geri responded immediately.

"Yes!" she declared. "The wisdom shared was breathtaking, which is exactly what we thought about our encounters here with our lovely new friends. What happened to us, Jonathan? How and why did the human species lose touch with nature and with our fellow beings? It's heartbreaking to hear how we once were." Tears streamed down Geri's cheeks. Jonathan wrapped his arms around her as they both grieved a time gone past. Eventually the tears stopped and the couple turned their gaze to the outer garden. Much to their surprise, the three Rabbits were sitting at their feet.

"Oh my goodness! It is lovely to see you again." Geri's voice was filled with gratitude. The Rabbits responded by taking their upright position.

"We came to reassure you that we have great hope for you and your kind. We believe that you will come to the Earth's aid, and we hope there will be friendly

relationships among us in the near future. We are very grateful for your contributions to our Home. What you have achieved here in the outer garden can be done all around the planet. Every contribution made is significant.

"*Please understand that we still love your kind. Perhaps we spoke too forthrightly in our initial meeting. We were desperate to get your attention, and our manners may have been off-putting. We apologize if we offended you. That was not our intention. We are very grateful for your presence and for your care of the garden.*" The kindness offered by these delightful little beings overwhelmed the couple. For a brief moment, neither could speak a word. Jonathan finally took a deep breath.

"Your kindness touches us deeply. We are so grateful to be in your presence again. We admire your courage and your willingness to speak the truth to us. We needed to hear every word that you said; we are still learning from our first encounter. No apology is necessary. Please continue to connect with us any time you wish to; we are eager to receive more feedback from you. And dear new friends, thank you for your support today."

Carol and Jen held hands as they watched the sun go down from their car. After the gathering came to a close, they decided to drive to a nearby overlook to catch a glimpse of the end of the day. The view was one of their favorite places. It provided beauty beyond imagination and the right atmosphere for great discussions.

"Well, we've just had another amazing experience," Jen chuckled quietly as she made the pronouncement. "Do you believe this, Carol? Is this really real?" They both laughed aloud and agreed that their experiences of late were absolutely real.

"We are so blessed, Jen. And I am grateful, but everyone on the planet needs to have these experiences for themselves. They are life changing. When you've had a heart to heart conversation with an Eagle, your attitude about the Earth changes. All of a sudden you're aware that there are other intelligent beings on the planet that are much more conscious of and caring about her needs. They truly co-exist with the Earth, Jen, while we act as if she is here to fulfill our needs.

"I'm embarrassed by my negligence. I'm one of 'those' people who have lived my life without conscious awareness of her presence. Truthfully, I haven't paid attention to her. I've just taken her for granted." Carol shook her head in disgust. "How can I have been so dismissive of this huge, ever-present, beautiful Life Being? Geez! It's time for me to make amends. I want to become actively involved in assisting her. NOW! The problem is that I don't really know what to do." Carol hoped for answers from Jen, who unfortunately was feeling equally inept about being an Earth activist.

"I'm at a loss as well, Carol, but let's not give up on ourselves. We've just received another huge dose of information about the Earth's state of health and about our role in her decline. Let's be honest about this. The information is overwhelming and we need time to recover from the trauma of hearing this most unpleasant news. However, we cannot allow ourselves to get lost in our fears. So let's make a commitment that we will be kind to ourselves in the moment, and that we will persevere in our desires to find ways of serving the Earth.

"Carol, we're already contributing in some ways." Jen paused briefly and then explained that she had not meant her statement to sound defensive. "The truth is we are participating, in some small ways, but it isn't enough. We both know that. So let's begin by reviewing what we are currently doing. Let's face the truth by creating a list of the ways we are participating and then let's discuss how we want to expand our efforts. Our new goals will call for another list that will hopefully keep us on track. No, let's call it a chart! Our chart will include short-term and long-term goals with anticipated dates of completion. I think having this information posted in a frequently trafficked area, such as the refrigerator, will challenge us and keep us accountable.

"We're both sincere about this, but we must also be diligent in our efforts. Fortunately, we have each other to keep us on point. Carol, I'm excited about doing this work together. We can help the Earth! We can make a difference." Jen's confidence and optimism pulled Carol out of her downward spiral.

"Oh, thank you, Jen! Your ideas are inspiring. As you know, I am a big fan of lists. They keep me focused and on task. And the chart will keep us motivated." Carol took a deep breath and Jen joined her. "You're right, dear, we are very fortunate to have each other. These are important times, and I am very grateful that our paths crossed. And let's not forget the incredible support system that has come our way. Goodness, who would have ever imagined where that first gathering would take us! Thank you! Thank you! Thank you for the blessings of dear friends."

"Amen!" added Jen. And with that said they headed home.

◎

The Madisons, still highly energized from the gathering, decided a stroll through the neighborhood would be the perfect way to wind down. They opted for light exercise rather than rushing home to sit on the front porch, which was one of their favorite places for heartfelt conversation. Both agreed that they were tired of sitting. Walking and talking was also a favorite activity of theirs, so the idea of processing the events of the evening in that matter was much to their liking.

"David, dear, will you share your thoughts first, if you have the energy to do so? I must admit I'm in the mood for listening to you rather than myself." Her husband was obliging, but needed to collect his thoughts for a moment. They strolled in silence while he determined what he wanted to share.

"Well, there are many things that deserve our attention, Anne, but the first thing I would like to say is that you were wonderful throughout the meeting. I'm so proud of you." His beloved blushed from the compliment and poked him in the ribs. "I mean it, Anne. Your manner calms people, and that alone is significant. People become more relaxed when you speak, which enables them to speak more candidly. Your presence facilitates heartfelt conversations and connection. It's just who you are, dear." Anne wrapped her arm around David's and thanked him for the kind words. And then as was her way, she redirected the conversation back to the meeting.

"What did you think about the visitors, dear?" David knew what she was doing. He just smiled and followed her lead.

"I was and remain stunned by the presence of these other life beings. It's exciting. It's puzzling! And the bottom line is we know nothing about these beings other than the fact that they are intelligent, thoughtful, compassionate, and devoted to the planet Earth. That actually speaks well of them, doesn't it? But one cannot help but be curious. Who are they? From where do they come? Why are they so involved with the Earth? Are they our ancestors or are they beings from another planet or another dimension? The questions can go on and on, but at this point, we only know what we've been told, and that seems to be more than we can bear. I don't doubt what they are telling us about the Earth. It's difficult to hear, but their perspective is in alignment with ours. Actually they validate everything the Great

Buck shared with us. Best as I can tell, all eight of us seem to trust what is transpiring. So to me, it seems more important that we accept the information that they have shared with us rather than wasting time being concerned about how little we know about them.

"We're very intuitive people. I think we would know if something was amiss, don't you, Anne?" David was surprised at first that his beloved's response wasn't immediate. But then he realized that his impatience was a sign of his insecurity.

"Not to worry, David, I do agree with you, and I also recognize the tenacity of insecurity. We are a people who typically demand proof before we accept anything, and in recent times, even absolute proof has not convinced those who prefer to disbelieve the reality of factual information.

"Our conversation has become very complicated, dear. There are more layers to it than I originally thought. I definitely agree that the circle of eight have accepted our invisible guests as life beings of good intention. We have come to trust them. However, I'm not certain how other people in our community and around the globe might react to this situation. Our differences have separated us from one another and created great distrust among us. So, I am afraid that difficulties may await us." The couple simultaneously took a deep breath.

"Well, David, life is complex. So, we must place our energy towards positive outcomes rather than negative ones. Obviously, the Earth is the priority, and we will focus our efforts upon healing her."

"Nicely stated, Anne. Shall we head towards home?" And this they did.

Twenty-Three

"**W**elcome Everyone! So good to see you again." Peter was a lovely greeter, cordial and polite. "Janet is still in the kitchen grabbing a few trays, but will be here shortly." Carol and Jen, who had just walked through the gate, immediately headed for the back door.

"Janet, may we be of help?" they called out together.

"Oh, yes! Please come in. If each of you could grab a tray, that would be very helpful. I seem to be running a bit late," admitted Janet.

"Actually," inserted Jen, "I think your guests are the ones who are a bit early. We can hardly wait to see what unfolds this afternoon. Any idea what's on the agenda?" The three women giggled about the question.

"Who knows!" declared the hostess of the gathering. "Your guess is as good as mine. Peter and I are clueless about these adventures."

"Ah! That's the perfect descriptor for these meetings. They really are adventures. Janet, Jen and I are so grateful to be part of this incredible journey. Thank you for including us."

"Well, we are delighted that you joined us, but truthfully, I'm beginning to believe that we weren't in control of the guest list. I think we were all purposefully brought together." Janet winked at them and then pointed to the door. "Let's get these treats out before everyone gathers in the tree house. Thank you for helping, friends."

The goodies and the delivery staff were applauded as they exited the back door.

"Okay, everyone! Fill up your plates and make haste to the tree house!" Peter's commanding voice brought about peals of laughter, but nevertheless, his orders were heeded. Within minutes, plates were filled, and everyone was seated in his or her preferred chair.

Janet, comfortable with her role as hostess and facilitator, snatched one of her favorite treats, lifted it into the air, and joyfully announced, "Cheers, everyone!" Her gesture was happily imitated and the festivities began. After numerous yummy sounds were made, the group settled down and just enjoyed the gift of togetherness.

"We're very fortunate people," stated Anne in her usual soft-spoken manner. Before continuing she turned to Janet. "Dear heart, do you mind if I take the lead?" Her friend and neighbor of many years happily urged her to do so. "Thank you, Janet. Dear Ones, I've been giving a great deal of thought and consideration to our recent experiences. I'm sure that doesn't surprise any of you, because I'm certain that you've been doing the same. Well, as a result of my deliberations, I've come to the conclusion that something very special is happening here in this sacred space, and I believe it is important that we all recognize and accept that we are being called to action.

"I keep asking myself, why me? Why us? And then, lightning finally struck. Why not me?

Why not us? We are residents of this planet. The Earth has graciously provided for us since our beginnings. Why shouldn't we be called upon to help her? We are indebted to her. Although we will never be able to repay her for all that she has done for us, we owe her! This is no time for us to bury our heads in the sand. This is no time for us to succumb to our fears. We can help the Earth and it is our responsibility to find crucial ways in which we can be of service. We're here for a reason and the eight of us have been brought together for a reason, so let's make the best of our combined talents and energy.

"Dear Friends, it's time for us to make a plan." As David listened to his wife's inspiring message, he wondered how their friends would respond to her challenge. He was not surprised when they all cheered and applauded her rousing insights.

"Thank you for that inspiring message, Anne. What a wonderful way to begin our meeting!" As Janet looked about the circle, a memory of old flashed through her mind. The download of information took her aback, and the expression that crossed her face alerted her friends. Although the particulars of the memory remained vague, the heart of the matter was received. A reflexive action resulted in a deep breath followed by the closing of her eyes. Janet's friends, feeling somewhat apprehensive, remained quiet while holding the space for her to process whatever had just transpired. They were all relieved when she opened her eyes again. Her face was radiant. "Dear Ones, thank you for your patience. I've had the most interesting confirmation regarding our relationships. When I looked about our circle just a moment ago, a view of a past experience rushed through my mind. I saw us all together much as we are now, but in another time and place. We were huddled around a fire pit desperately trying to stay warm as we made plans for a mission that was about to be undertaken. We were all there, working together, for a cause of great importance." A gentle smile, indicating a sense of knowingness, crossed Janet face.

"We've been friends for a very, very long time. I think we've all sensed that, but my flashback confirms it. No wonder our coming together has gone so smoothly. We're having a reunion!" Her manner was comforting and familiar. The information that she brought forward did indeed verify what everyone else had been feeling as well. A sigh of contentment echoed around the circle of friends.

"This is fascinating!" Geri's expression inspired nods and similar statements from other members of the group. "Not only did your flashback confirm our relationships, but it also confirms Anne's announcement. We're here for a reason and it's time for us to make a plan."

"Greetings, Dear Friends! May we join your reunion?" Cheerful responses welcomed the unseen visitors.

"Thank you for coming!" Peter, taking on the role of official greeter, reassured the guests that they were most welcome. "We were all secretly hoping that you would join us today. As you can see, our meeting has begun in the most delightful and inspiring manner."

"Indeed, it has! You have taken a monumental step, Dear Friends! You remembered that you are Friends of Old and you remembered that you are here on a mission of extreme importance. That hurdle is now behind you and the time for action is the next challenge to address. In truth, Dear Friends, you are already on the path of preparation, which will lead you to the point of implementation.

"We previously discussed the need for humanity to reclaim their good will. For this to unfold, the populace must come to understand the consequences of their behaviors. This means they must first accept the reality that their behavior does have consequences. It was suggested that each individual review his or her individual behavioral characteristics and note the times when he or she personally participates in negative actions through thoughts, words, and deeds. This exercise increases the participant's conscious awareness of his or her role in these negative behaviors. It is believed that once humankind truly understands the negative influence they have on others that they will be inspired to alter their ways. This will not be an easy task, but it is critically important for the future of the human species. Their manner of being at this time is destructive. They harm themselves and others they encounter. We speak bluntly, because it is necessary. Please understand that we are acutely aware of the goodness that still exists within the human species. We are aware of it and we are also deeply concerned. The ill will that presently stretches across the globe is expanding at a frightening rate. Good will must make a fast and powerful comeback, and it must be done immediately.

197

"Dear Friends, please take a deep breath and try to regain your composure. Manage your minds' meandering ways, for it takes you down paths that do not need to be visited at this time. We are talking about the needs of the present; do not allow the mind to take you into unknown places." The visitor's guidance was timely and noteworthy, for the human mind is a remarkable distraction. The request to return to the present successfully brought everyone back to the present moment.

"Whew!" declared David. "Thank you for that rescue. My mind was on an adventure of its own making. Goodness! What a trip! Talk about negativity! I don't know about the rest of you, but my mind just demonstrated the fear it can create in an instant. My mind definitely has a mind of its own and what you just said is absolutely true. The mind can be a remarkable distraction."

"Unfortunately, the human mind can lose itself to negativity. One must always remember the gifts of the beautiful mind, but at the same time, one must be cognizant of the mind that prefers chaos. Not everyone is aware of this, and this is the reason so many people go astray. But do not fear, Dear Friends. You are in charge of your mind. Do not forget this truth. You are in charge of its manners and its direction. Reclaim control over your unruly mind by frequent meditation and also by consciously listening to the antics of the mind that erroneously believes it is in command. Reclaim your beautiful mind, for it is the one that assists you and accompanies you through your purposeful life, while the mind that has a mind of its own complicates and disrupts your positive intentions.

"We speak of this, Dear Friends, so that you will pay attention to the workings of your mind. The more you know about the cogitations of the mind, the more powerful you will be because you will be in charge of your mind and your future. The beautiful mind will always collaborate with you. The unruly mind will always attempt to overrule your will. Learn everything you can about your mind's functioning style, and you will truly be in charge of your mind. This is what is intended, Dear Friends.

"The reason we speak of this is to remind you of your responsibilities. As the leader of your future, it is your responsibility to understand how your mind works. It is after all one of your greatest assets, and it is in your best interest to care for it properly. With your guidance, it will become your greatest assistant. If on the other hand you choose to ignore it, your mind may usurp your preferences. This statement may give you pause. We hope it does. The truth is you will never really know if you are in command of your mind unless you pay attention to it. Dear Friends, for the sake of your personal wellness and for the sake of your species, we urge you to take charge of your mind. It is paramount that you do so.

"As you learn more about the workings of your mind, you will also gain important information about the influence it has upon your own behavior. By carefully listening to the mind at work, you will learn whether your mind assists or impedes you in living life from a positive perspective. Essentially, by studying your mind's operational style, you will have a much greater awareness about who you really are. And with this knowledge, you can refine yourself to be the person you truly wish to be.

"We have faith in humankind, and we believe that you will want to change behaviors that do not serve you or those around you. Dear Friend, this process of self-study will awaken you to mannerisms that you were not aware of, but do not fear. You will not be alone. Everyone must review his or her behaviors on a regular basis. For evolution to transpire, self-examination is necessary. As the human species recognizes that self- improvement is necessary, then hopefully, they will realize that their collective behaviors and attitudes toward other species also demand improvement. Recognition and acceptance that all species are equal and One is an essential element of the evolutionary process. The human species has reached a pivotal moment in their development process. They must embrace treating others as they desire to be treated. All species within existence enjoy this privilege. So too should the Earth. So too should all her inhabitants. Existence does not exist for the few. She exists for All."
As the simple, but powerful words saturated the tree house dwellers, a marvelous event was underway. Just a few feet away from the tree house steps, another gathering had come together. The three endearing Rabbits, the Woodchuck, a Chipmunk, a lovely Cardinal couple, and one large Crow observed the gathering above.

"Oh my!" Jonathan whispered. "Look everyone! We are not alone! Another circle of eight has joined us." All eyes moved towards the action in the back yard.

"Greetings, Dear Friends! Thank you for joining us." Noiseless applause and whispers of welcome came from the tree house group. The appearance of the neighborhood guests lifted the spirits of everyone.

"Goodness, Dear Friends, this arrangement simply won't do. I suggest we join our dear friends on the lawn. Is that agreeable for everyone?" Janet didn't wait for anyone's approval. She knew they were in agreement. Moving towards the steps, she sought permission from their new guests. "Dear Ones, may we come join you? It will be so much cozier if we are all on the same level." The late arrivals moved further out on the lawn allowing space for the transition from the tree house to the garden area. Chairs were carefully spaced so that ample room was available for everyone. Janet continued her role as hostess and facilitator as she invited everyone to select a spot that was suitable to them. Much to everyone's surprise, the Chipmunk rushed over to David, ran up his leg, and fearlessly sat on his knee. Needless to say, the little fellow charmed everyone.

"Looks to me like you two have a relationship," chuckled Peter. David blushed slightly as he admitted his uncertainty.

"Judging from his behavior, I think you're correct Peter, but these guys don't wear name tags and they really are difficult to distinguish one from another. Oh!" a big grin crossed David's face. "You see that spot on the left side of his cheek." Everyone looked closer trying to see the tiny spot on the tiny critter. "Yes, this is Cooper! And we definitely have a relationship. I'm the 'hand' with the peanuts and he's the 'keeper' of a secret, secured storage unit. It's interesting to see Cooper here in the Hansons' yard. Makes you realize how large their territory is. It's also heartwarming to see that he recognizes me." Cooper turned around to face David.

"I'm very pleased that you recognized me as well." He stated very politely. *I was very happy to be invited to this gathering today because I wanted to express my appreciation to you. You are a very generous friend. The nuts that you provide will sustain me through the winter. Mother Earth provides many options, of course, but you have made the harvesting season much easier for me. I am grateful for your kindness, but even more, I enjoy your company."*

As attention was being paid to the endearing Chipmunk, each of the remaining seven newcomers situated themselves in front of the other seated friends: A circle of eight within a circle of eight. The attention to detail did not go unnoticed. Carol's thought went to the unseen guests. She wondered if there were eight of them as well.

"Ah! Now our gathering is complete. Dear Ones, we are honored to be in your presence. Today is a day of reunions! The day when Old Friends come together as they once did very long ago. Let us begin with an expression of gratitude.

"To all who are here, and to all who are in distant places, we thank you for the efforts made to bring this group of Old Friends together. We are most grateful! Please remain with us if you are able and bear witness to this special occasion. Today is a day of new beginnings…a day long awaited. As One we entered into existence, as One we remain in existence, and as One we will always be in existence. Our hearts are full and our gratitude abounds. Peace to All!"

Janet's excitement was difficult for her to manage. She needed to express her gratitude, but was uncertain of the agenda. Before a decision was made, she was invited to take the lead.

"Friend Janet, your energy exudes joy and gratefulness. Would you like to share your thoughts with us?"

"Yes, I would," she replied using her inner voice. "Before I continue, let me check to be sure that everyone heard my unspoken response." The responses from her human friends were easy to understand, but she was concerned about her new guests. She looked towards them and reverted back to telepathy. *"Dear new friends, I am still new at interspecies communication. I hope you are able to hear me."* The Spokesrabbit from the Gardner's outer garden took the upright position that drew everyone's attention.

"Your communications skills are excellent. We are all able to understand you. If however, this manner of communication is a burden, we understand the human voice as well. Please use whatever means is most comfortable for you. Our Friends who remain unseen to you will also facilitate our communications if it is necessary. Thank you for welcoming us into your garden. We are most pleased to be part of this gathering."

Janet's heart was pounding. She prayed that Great-grandmother Harriet was nearby. Having these delightful creatures in their backyard was a stellar moment in her life. She had to restrain herself from sitting on the ground and stroking each one of them. A vision of a time many, many years ago raced through her mind. She, at age eight or so, and Nana were doing exactly what she was dreaming about doing now. They were rolling on the grass in this same garden with the large white ducks that ruled the backyard. It was a memorable moment that tempted her to do the same now.

Much to Janet's surprise, her guests were privy to her flashback and they all drew nearer to her. Each one was happy to be touched. From a few gentle pats that honored the Redbirds to several long strokes that were enjoyed by the Woodchuck, each new friend enjoyed the tender connection that was offered. *"Oh my goodness! This is a glorious reunion! Thank you so much for joining us this evening. And I also want to express my gratitude to all those who made this possible. My heart is so full, it's about to burst. Our unseen Friends referred to us as Old Friends coming together again. That description of our relationship rings true for me. I cannot imagine why the human species separated from you. We belong together! Whatever caused us to behave in such a disrespectful manner? I am so sorry for our behavior. I am so sorry for the way we have treated you."* Tears streamed down Janet's face. She was not alone. Many tears were shed during this precious moment. For a brief moment, time stood still. During this time without time, the human friends grieved mistakes made. The fauna friends appreciated the heartfelt apology. And the unseen friends observed with hopeful optimism.

"Dear Old Friends, what was desired and hoped for is transpiring. Healing is occurring. This is the beginning. Although more healing is still needed, this interaction of tenderness and loving-kindness gives everyone hope. Our hearts are filled with gratitude." The joyful moment brought happiness to everyone involved, including those who were observing the event from afar. The reunion, unfolding in the most desirable manner, was a reminder of a long ago past. It was a time when all species on the Earth embraced one another as friends.

The Madisons were thrilled. Even though they sat quietly, their combined energies were noticeably engaged with the reunion. The large Crow was particularly interested in their presence. Moving in their direction, he made the Crow caw as only a Crow can do. His unusual call grabbed everyone's attention. Standing in front of the Madisons, he stared first at Anne and then tilted his head in the other direction and stared at David. He cawed again. *"I recognize you!* He announced with his telepathic thoughts. *"You often walk the trail along the ocean."* The Madisons nodded and acknowledged that the ocean trail was one of their favorite places to walk. *"Yes, I often see you there. It is my favorite area as well. I was there when you encountered the Great Buck. That too was a wonderful reunion. The Buck is aware of this gathering and wanted to attend, but as you can appreciate, it would be very difficult for him to make his way through the traffic to visit your home. Needless to say, he would attract a great deal of attention. He sends his best wishes to you and looks forward to another meeting with you soon."* Then the Crow moved towards Carol and Jen and stared at them in the same manner as he had stared at the Madisons.

"The Grand Bird also sends greetings to you. She too wanted to attend this meeting, but her situation is similar to the Great Buck's. Because she is so large and well known, she creates a stir wherever she goes. She hopes that you and your friends will join her in the forest some day soon." The invitation was well received. Carol thanked the Crow for his presence and for delivering the invitation.

"Jen and I are so happy to be part of this reunion. This is a life-changing experience and we are grateful to be here. Thank you all for coming. It is a privilege to be with you." The Crow ruffled his feathers, mumbled a caw, and then returned to his original position. Once he was situated, the lovely Cardinal couple fluttered into the air, circled the group several

times, and then landed on the knees of Geri Gardner. She was ecstatic! Everyone's attention turned towards the beautiful Redbirds. The female's behavior was similar to Janet's. She made eye contact with everyone before she began to speak.

"As many of you have already said, we too are very grateful to participate in this remarkable gathering. Stories that were passed down from our ancestors speak of these types of gatherings. We cannot imagine what happened to cause this rift among those who were once like family. Those of us today wonder what happened long ago. Whatever it was, it is long past, and we see no purpose in continuing this antagonistic relationship. We maintain a separation that began so long ago that none of us can even remember the cause. What is the point of denying each other's existence? We are One. We come from the same essence that is within all existences within existence. So why do we not honor this sacred truth? We are One. We are Family. And we are not intended to live in this shameful segregated way.

"Dear Friends, we must change. We must come together as Family again. For the sake of ourselves and for the sake of the planet, we must learn to mutually coexist. Our kind is eager to participate in this transformational process. We desire friendships with the human population again.

"Thank you for your gracious hospitality. It is a pleasure to engage with all of you."

Janet, instinctively accepting her role as hostess, thanked the Cardinals for their presence and their perspective. Once again, the depth of wisdom shared took one's breath away. As the latest comments were being cogitated, the senior member of the outer garden patiently waited for her opportunity to address the human group. After a few minutes passed, the stately Woodchuck made her way to the center of the gathering. She stood there for a moment but found it unacceptable. Realizing that position would not honor all the guests she moved to another location just slightly in front of Geri and Jonathan. Since the three of them had previously enjoyed an intimate conversation in the outer garden, she assumed the Gardners would not be offended if she stood in front of them. Her assumption was correct. From the new position everyone else could easily see her. Standing upright, the Woodchuck greeted everyone.

"I come in peace, Dear Friends. That was the way our relationships began and it is the way that our relationships are intended to be. Although none of today remembers those times of old, the stories from that time still hold the memories of our loving and tender relationships. We were friends and we regarded each other as

Family." The Woodchuck, an eloquent speaker, captured the attention of her audience with the very first sentence spoken.

"*I come today to speak a truth that will be difficult to hear. But for the sake of the planet, the truth must be spoken. Dear Friends, I ask you to listen with the ears of your heart. There was a time when you were guided by the goodness within your heart. Your kind entered into existence as compassionate, loving beings. Your way of being was gentle, gracious, and generous. Your peaceable ways melded well with the society of other peaceful life beings already inhabiting the Earth. Those were good times, precious times, when diversity was cherished for the gift that it was, is, and will always be.*

"*Diversity is a gift of divine grace. It is the epitome of never-ending surprises that delight one's curious nature while stimulating the senses to crave greater understanding about everything in existence. Ponder this, Dear Friends, and allow yourself in the upcoming days to imagine what life would be like on this planet without diversity.*

"*But for now, observe our small gathering, please! Look at the differences that exist within our small group. There is so much to learn from one another. So much to share; so much to absorb!*" The wise Woodchuck paused, providing a brief, but necessary moment for reflection.

"*Now, if you will, observe this lovely garden and enjoy the magnificent display of diversity. We are surrounded by many different varieties of flowers and plants all happily coexisting. This space is literally a sight to behold.*" The Hansons, pleased to have their garden highlighted, enjoyed the lovely comments from their friends.

"*And then, Dear Ones, expand your wonderment to the neighborhood and beyond. Our planet thrives upon differences. The reason this planet is so remarkable is because of her diversity. Never was the gift of diversity intended to be anything but a gift. For eons, the gift brought immeasurable happiness to the Earth and all her many inhabitants. Life on Earth was blissful.*

"*When the travelers from afar approached the Earth and requested a home for their seedlings, the Earth consulted with her inhabitants and all agreed, the new species would be a wonderful addition to the planet. They were graciously welcomed and accepted into the planetary community and they lived harmoniously with the other species for a very long time. Unfortunately over time, the new species evolved in ways that were surprising. Their preferences changed. They were no longer interested in relationships with the other species and they distanced themselves from those who had welcomed them to the planet. The separation caused great sadness and created many misunderstandings, and soon, the memories of sweet connections were forgotten. The new species, no longer in alignment with the harmonious nature of the planetary system, evolved into a species whose priority was self-focused.*

"*Our kind never understood what happened. Our ancestors made attempts to reestablish relationships but your kind was not interested. Eventually, the need for self-protection from your species became evident. Since that time so very long ago, we have adjusted to your need to live separately. Our ancient stories remind us of the relationships of old, and we still grieve the loss of connection, but survival is instinctual, and it was necessary for all of us to go on with our lives.*

"*Many changes have occurred since the original break in our relationships. Your kind overpopulated the Earth at the expense of the rest of Earth's population. Once you separated from us, you became oblivious to the life beings around you. Your obsession with expansion ignored the needs of others. You proceeded selfishly and thoughtlessly, monopolizing the Earth's natural resources as if it were your privilege to do so. Few of you considered the impact that your actions had upon the rest of us, and those few were treated as poorly as were we. Only recently have some of your kind noticed that the Earth was suffering because of your maltreatment of her.*

"*The human species' disregard for other kinds is staggering. You do not comprehend that the Earth is a cherished Life Being in the universe. She is Home to billions of life beings who are deeply grateful for the privilege of living with her. She is a Sanctuary.*

"*My Dear Friends, your kind is in great misunderstanding. The Earth that you take for granted is not a possession. You do not own her, even though you treat her as if you do. We do not understand how your kind came to this most unfortunate conclusion, but the fact is, you are in error. No one has dominion over another life being. This concept seems to challenge the human mind, but it is truth nonetheless. We are all equal; we are all One. And no one has power over another.*" The Woodchuck paused, wondering if there was more to be said. Sadness overcame her. She did not like being the bearer of difficult news.

"*My Dear Friends, my heart is heavy. The truth is painful. Even though these terrible acts of unkindness began long before you came into existence, you are still responsible for changing the future. Your assistance is needed. The acts of brutality and meanness cannot continue. Those of you who know better must stand up to those who still believe that they have the right to harm others. The outrageous behaviors must stop. This is not how life is intended to be. The madness must end.*" Time passed as the Woodchuck stood with her paws in prayerful position.

Janet, sitting directly across from their guest, placed her hands in similar fashion and bowed to the sagacious orator. "*You have blessed us with your presence. Your message was powerful and it was important for us to hear it. Speaking the truth can be a very difficult thing to do. Thank you, Dear Friend, for your courage, and for your devotion to the Earth and also to us. After all the destruction we have done to this planet, I am stunned that you still have compassion for us. The fact that you call us Dear Friends touches me deeply. Please know that you are always welcome here."*

The Woodchuck returned Janet's bow and expressed her appreciation for the gracious response. *"Thank you for your kind words and your recognition of our concern for humankind. We still regard you as friends and wish the relationships of old could be reestablished. Having this conversation gives us hope that some day we might again consider each other as Family.*

"Dear Ones, you have treated me and my Friends with the utmost respect. We are all grateful. Unless there is more to be said, I will turn this over to those from distant places." As the Woodchuck descended from her upright position, the circle of humans began to applaud. Although it is difficult to read the facial expressions of another species, she seemed to be touched by the gesture. While the revered member of the outer garden returned to her original position in the circle, the applause continued, accompanied by many expressions of gratitude.

"Well, Dear Friends, we have had another incredible experience!" Without even noticing it, Janet had returned to speaking orally. "And I think there is more to come. So, Dear Unseen Visitors, we patiently await your return."

Little patience was needed. The unseen voice immediately accepted the role of facilitator. *"Indeed, this has been a most pleasant reunion...a dream come to true! Our hearts are full; no words can adequately express our appreciation."* A pause that was difficult to decipher without visual cues was simply accepted by everyone present. No explanation was demanded or needed. After a deep breath was heard, the visitor continued. *"It is time, Dear Friends, for us to focus our intentions upon the plan that is already underway. Although you may not realize it, you have taken another large leap in your evolutionary development today. This reunion has reunited the human species with the Friends of Old and the connection made was very powerful.*

"What transpired here has the potential of changing the future, and yet, it was such a small feat. Think about it, please! The fear of coming together has been conquered. This reunion exemplifies the obvious. The human species and the species of old can reunite. Old relationships can be born again. And this process of reaching out to those with whom one has been distant can unfold as easily as did our reunion today.

"My Friends, let us begin the next step with a long deep breath. In union, we are! And with this deep breath, we join as One, as we always were, even though this truth was forgotten by some members of our universal Family. So good it is to be in awareness once again.

"Dear Ones, your assistance is needed. As you have learned in recent weeks there are many around the planet who have been actively involved in living harmoniously with the Earth since they came into existence. Unlike the human species, these gracious inhabitants recognized that the health of the planet demanded global cooperation among all species. In order to maintain and sustain an ecological balance, all inhabitants must realize and accept that the needs of all species are equally important.

"Fortunately, the human species is finally awakening to this vitally significant reality. However, the masses of humankind are still uncomfortable with the concept that they are equal to the other species on the planet. For so long did you believe that you were more than others that the idea of equality challenges your sense of self. This misunderstanding created great hardship for many other species including the planet herself.

"In order for mutual co-existence to be actualized on the Earth, the truth about equality must be addressed. This will not be an easy task, for there remain many humans who refuse to accept the idea of equality because they regard it as a diminishment of a life status to which they are rigidly attached. These individuals are intolerant of any ideas or suggestions that seem to threaten his or her sense of privilege and entitlement. What is unknown to those who cling to these most unfortunate misunderstandings is the truth that equality brings more abundance than their misguided ideologies ever will. If only their hearts would open to this simple truth, then the fears that possess them would be released.

"The beauty of a healthy planetary ecological system is that everyone benefits equally from the abundance provided. When one group over-consumes available resources, then the operational system is thrown out of balance, resulting in complications that impact everyone, even those who think they are impervious to the changes that they deny exist.

"Dear Ones, you are aware of the changes that are transpiring upon this beautiful planet; and because of individuals like you, there is hope that the Earth will recover from her present circumstances. However, the reality of her illness must be faced and addressed now. The fate of this planet depends upon the people of Earth. That reality must be accepted. You are the primary factor in her declining health, and if you do not change your ways, she will become so unstable that your species will not survive. We do not wish to bring this horrific news to you, but it must be done. You ignore the evidence that grows more and more profound every day, and you squabble over the truth of this evidence, as if it is not the proof needed before action can be taken. The proof lies before you, and your selfish manipulations of this proof are incomprehensible.

"Unfortunately, Dear Ones, there is another truth that must be stated. We are reluctant to speak so bluntly, but we must. There are those on the planet who are invested in maintaining their ill-fated behaviors. These individuals are unwilling to make changes because they are convinced that their investments are more important than the needs of others. These people are putting billions of people in jeopardy. They foolishly think that they can survive any cataclysmic events that may occur. They are in error! The Earth will survive the health problems that she now experiences, but her recovery process will be unlike anything this civilization has experienced. The transformation that she will go through will cause great destruction and alteration to the current topography across the planet.

"Fortunately, there is a movement of people rising from various areas of the planet who recognize this reality as a strong possibility. These people are taking action and they are making changes that will actually assist the Earth. As their movement grows, and it will continue to do so, those who refuse to make changes will find themselves in an increasingly difficult situation. Their reluctance to assist the Earth is not in their best interest. If people from all lands cooperate on behalf of the planet, and make the necessary changes that are needed, the Earth's recovery will be less chaotic and disruptive. We remind you that your planet is already in great disruption. Your forests are ablaze, your weather is unpredictable and frightening, and your sea levels are rising at alarming rates. The catastrophic events are already in progress, and these events will become much, much worse, if the truth continues to be ignored." A deep breath was heard, which inspired the visible participants to do the same. Time passed as everyone mulled over the information presented. Eventually, the speaker continued.

"Dear Friends, we know this news is difficult to hear. Our hearts are broken. Speaking of these most unpleasant truths causes us great sadness. We wish we could tell you that there is nothing to fear, but that would be a lie! Regrettably, there are too many lies being spread about the Earth's condition already. We will not participate in such foolishness. The people of Earth need to know the truth. You can deal with the truth! You are bright and resourceful people who are capable of healing the planet. The truth enables you to make the necessary changes that will turn this catastrophe around. Please hear this message clearly. The intentional misinformation that deceives and misguides you must be recognized for what it is. Anyone who denies the truth that the Earth is in jeopardy is not a friend of the Earth and her inhabitants. The Friends of the Earth must unite on her behalf. In so doing, the catastrophic changes that are currently unfolding will calm, diminishing the probability of a period of dormancy.

"Dear Friends of the Earth, please make haste. Every citizen of the planet must participate. Each of you has a role in her recovery process. You cannot delegate

another to do the work that you must individually do. As you now well know, the negative energy that humankind produces is the primary factor in her decline. You are a part of that factor. You produce negative energy, as does every other human being. Accept the truth of this reality! Of course, it is difficult to accept this truth; no one wishes to think poorly of him or her self. But take comfort in knowing that you are not alone. Now is the time to face your flaws and take the necessary steps to diminish your negative ways. Dear Friends, this is not the time for an encounter with righteous indignation. The Earth doesn't have time for the human ego to create another distraction from the work that must be done. Denial is not an option. It is time for the human species to face the truth. You are more than you presently appear to be, and it is time to become the good people you are intended to be.

"Changing your negative ways is not as difficult as one may think. In truth, it is much more difficult to live with your negativity than it is to give it up. You will benefit from the decision and so will those around you, including the Earth herself. Letting go of your negative mannerisms is in your best interest. Life will be easier, more comfortable, and more loving when the negativity is released. Throughout this text, you have learned that humankind's negative energy is so toxic that it is actually sickening the planet Earth. If this is true, which it is, then imagine the impact your negative energy is having upon your own body. Once again, we remind you that releasing your negative energy is in your best interest.

"Dear Friends of the Earth, Dear Old Friends, please cleanse yourselves of this toxic energy. Release the anger, hatred, and violence that sicken self and all others. You are not intended to live this way. You came into existence as peaceable beings. This is who you really are. Please reclaim your humanity, your peaceable ways, and in so doing, restore the Earth to full vibrancy as she was before you came into existence." Silence came over the gathering. Each human, each animal, each feathered friend waited in anticipation. Stunned by the appeal, all wondered what would happen next.

"Dear Ones, what needed to be said was said, and now 'The Plan' must be presented in a format for all the peoples of Earth to access. The plan is simple. The commitment is large. The benefits are monumental. Everyone can manage the requests made in this plan to restore peace on Earth. No one is too young to participate. No one is too old to participate. No one is too busy, too important, too rich, too poor, too wise, or too dull...everyone can and must participate! For those who are impaired or in need in any manner, another must offer assistance. Such kindness is worldwide and those who rise up to help others will find their own negativity diminishing more rapidly. As each human regains the goodness existing within him or her, the Earth will also regain her state of well being. She is a resilient Life Being capable of a rapid recovery. If the daily infusions of negative energy are profoundly reduced, her health

will improve, and the more rapidly the negative energy diminishes, the more rapidly a complete recovery can be expected. Succinctly stated: there is hope for the future of humankind and for the remarkable planet Earth.

"*Dear Friends, our time together has been most productive. Perhaps, it is wise to rest now. May we request another gathering at the same time tomorrow? Then we can finalize The Plan.*" The suggestion was well received. Everyone agreed that rest was needed. Janet was also glad that the meeting was coming to an end, but desired a brief moment to acknowledge the significance of the gathering.

"Dear Ones, we are so grateful for the old relationships that were renewed during our time together today. This has been an extraordinary experience. Our hearts are full. And we are eager to meet with all of you again tomorrow. Isn't it wonderful that we can end this meeting in awareness that there is reason for hope? Peace and blessings to you all, Dear Friends!"

And so, the meeting ended with some friends taking flight, while others exited in ways that were unseen. Gracious exchanges were conveyed among the four footed friends and the two-footed taller friends. It was a most congenial separation. All returned to their respective dwellings, sighed in fatigue, and wondered what the next meeting would bring.

Twenty-Four

"**W**elcome, Everyone! Please come in and make yourselves comfortable. We've created the same seating arrangement as before." Peter enjoyed the role of greeter. It provided him with an opportunity to practice being an extrovert, which was a skillset that continued to escape him. After years of reassurance from Janet regarding his communication skills, Peter still distrusted himself. He was very surprised when the last two human guests commented that he was an exceptional host.

"You are so gracious, Peter! How do you manage to make each and everyone of us feel at home?" Carol's comment was affirmed when Jen acknowledged that the role of host and greeter was the most important part of a gathering.

"The minute we see your smiling face and hear your lovely voice, we are completely relaxed and ready to proceed with the meeting. Thank you, Peter!" declared Jen. "It's always a pleasure to be here." Peter accepted their comments graciously and admitted that he was particularly excited about the upcoming gathering.

Once the neighborhood folks seated themselves, the other neighborhood guests entered the backyard. These Dear Ones decided to change their seating arrangement, which was a brilliant idea. Their various entrances were a delight. The Cardinal couple helicoptered into the center of the group before gently landing on the shoulders of the Hansons. Then came the three Rabbits through a small opening in the back fence. They positioned themselves in front of the Madisons and were followed by the Crow swooping overhead before landing in the center of the circle. From there, he hopped towards the Gardners and settled himself before them. Even though David was disappointed not to have Cooper sitting on his knee again, he was delighted to see the playful fellow jumping back and forth from Carol to Jen. They were, of course, enchanted by his presence. Everyone was enjoying the reunion with the Dear Friends when Janet, always vigilant, realized that one guest was missing. She turned around just in time to see the revered Woodchuck making her way through the bed of hostas. It seemed appropriate that she would be the last to arrive. She entered the circle and bowed to everyone.

"It is most pleasant to be in your presence again, Dear Friends! Thank you for your hospitality. This is such a lovely setting for us to accomplish the work that must

be done. We are most grateful to be a part of this gathering. I feel certain that our Friends from afar are eager to proceed with the meeting, so without further ado, I invite them to take the lead." With that said, the Woodchuck situated herself in front of Janet and Peter. She looked towards the heart of the group, as did everyone else and wondered what next would unfold. From a distance, the gathering was a sight to behold, a microcosm of the Earth at large; a view of what once was and what was intended to be.

"Oh, Dear Friends, what sweet beauty you are. All different, yet One! It brings us great joy to witness this reunion of Old Friends found anew. May we join you, Old Friends? We have much to do this day of new beginnings." The reaction was unanimous. This too brought great pleasure to the unseen Friends.

"Dear Ones, let us begin our journey with peace in our hearts. Please take a deep breath, as each of you is wont to do. As we join in unity, we are One, as we were in the beginning and as we will be for all times to come. In Oneness, all things are possible, Beloved Friends. On this day of new beginnings, we embark upon an adventure that demands acceptance of and openheartedness towards all others.

"Breathe in this reality for it will stir the truth that already exists within. All in existence are One. This is and always has been the truth by which all live. Dear Ones, we are One, and we are here to awaken others to the reality of their existence.

"Enjoy another deep breath, Dear Friends, and feel the connection that exists among all of us. We are One. Let us begin this meeting with this truth as our guide." The message of Oneness repeatedly stated facilitated the necessary first step towards transition. For those who lived their lives as beings of Oneness, the transition was already completed; however, for those who pursued life from a different perspective, the concept of Oneness was more difficult to navigate. With each deep breath quietly taken and accompanied by the repeated statement of Oneness, hearts opened and acceptance emerged more tangibly as the awareness of old surfaced from the past. The concept of Oneness actualized into the reality of Oneness.

"Dear Old Friends, we are united again, and for this, we are most grateful. Please feel our gratitude and know that you are all loved and cherished by more than you can imagine." Another instantaneous deep breath was consumed as the precious message registered in the hearts and minds of those in attendance.

"We are pleased by your reaction to the message of sweet beauty. Your lists of relationships are very long, Dear Ones. Many friends from many different life experiences remember you well, and even though your memories escape you, these Old Friends hold the memories for you as you engage in your present experiences. Suffice

it to say, you are never alone. And never is there a moment when you are not held in the highest regard. Please remember this! It is most unfortunate that this truth of existence is frequently forgotten during periods of new experiences. This is a precious reality that one must attempt to hold in his or her heart. So very comforting it is to know that you are loved and cherished. Just as each of you needs to know this truth, so too does the planet Earth.

"This remarkable Life Being, who has provided so much to so many, also needs to know that she is loved and cherished. And this is why we are here. Dear Friends, the Earth has been poorly treated for so long that her awareness of her significance is waning. Such a tragedy this is! It is an unbearable thought that she suffers in this way. This abuse can no longer continue. Action must be taken!" The heartache experienced by the planet Earth penetrated the circle of friends. Their lives would never be the same again.

"Oh my goodness! What have we done?" Tears streamed down Anne's cheeks as the magnitude of the Earth's crisis overwhelmed her. Similar reactions came from other members of the human crowd, as they finally comprehended the truth of Earth's condition. The reality was so much worse than any of them had imagined before.

"Dear Ones, we are so sorry for your pain," announced the revered Woodchuck. *"The tragedy that you just witnessed in your minds and hearts is indeed unbelievable, and it is unfortunately true. What you briefly experienced, the Earth feels every minute of every day. Imagine her suffering! But do not dwell in this pain. Dear Ones, we must lift ourselves above the pain so that we can assist her. Feeling sorry for her is not enough. We must take action. As you can see, Dear Friends, the human species must become involved in this healing process. Human behavior, as you now know, is the primary cause of her declining health, and it must stop. She can no longer withstand the violent, reckless acts that humans perpetrate against one another. Not only do you harm each other, but you also behave outrageously towards other species, including the Earth herself. How can humans be so cruel? How can you be so foolish?*

"Dear Friends, you are here because you accept the truth about your species, and you are willing to change. We believe the human species is capable of changing. Once they understand the truth regarding their actions, we believe that humans will be willing to change. We pray this is true.

"We are so sorry that your hearts are heavy, but the truth is now known. It was necessary for you to face the consequences of your ill will so that you would understand what is at stake. The human species must accept responsibility for the chaos that is transpiring on the planet and they must change their ways. There is no other viable path. If your species is to continue, you must examine your present behaviors. You

are not the dominant species on the planet. This is a misunderstanding. Although you are definitely domineering, you are not the dominant species. All are One here on this planet, and elsewhere. And all, wherever they may exist, are equal. This is the challenge that humankind must face, and it must be done immediately.

"We believe in you, Dear Friends, and we are eager to work side-by-side with you in the days ahead. I am certain that our unseen Friends have much more to reveal about this topic, so I will end with a statement that is hopefully reassuring.

"We will stand by you, Dear Ones." With that said, the sagacious matriarch once again settled comfortably in front of the Hansons.

"Thank you, Old Friend. Your words of wisdom inspire us. As our Dear Friend just stated, change is necessary. Indeed, this is a reality that cannot be ignored or denied. There is no longer time for such nonsense. Although there will be those who continue to play foolish games, we believe the vast majority of the human species will see the merit of change once they understand the factors underlying their questionable actions. The human species is innately founded in goodness. With self-examination, we believe they will remember this truth, and hopefully, they will choose to revitalize this precious strength within them. Likewise, because humans are not innately foolish, we believe once they realize the imprudence of their behaviors, they will prefer to release that which does not serve them.

"We wish to be of assistance, Dear Friends. As the honorable Woodchuck earlier expressed a desire to be of assistance, so too, do we. We do not presume to dictate the path for another; however, we feel compelled to inform the peoples of Earth that the future is in danger. To continue the present course of misguidedness is unwise for everyone involved…and everyone is involved. The Earth, and all her inhabitants, will be profoundly impacted by continued misadventures. Change is inevitable; however, one can choose a type of change that benefits everyone, including oneself, or one can continue the present course and cause great harm to this beautiful planet and all who occupy her.

"To those who have a heart, the answer is simple. We appeal to those who have a heart…to those who care about the Earth. Your assistance is absolutely necessary. With your help, we can heal the Earth, heal each other, and still have a place to reside. As said before, the answer is simple. Change is inevitable! Everyone changes every day. Whether you are aware of this or not, it is a truth throughout all existence. So, if change is inevitable, why not choose to be an active participant in the process? You can sit back and allow others to make choices for you, or you can choose to take a positive first step by announcing that you are going to be actively involved in improving your personal well being. In so doing, you will also improve the health of the Earth. Because you are integrally linked with all others, your improved state of being will facilitate wellness in all those around you. Just imagine your efforts positively

affecting others on a daily basis. And then expand your imagination. Imagine all the other beings on the planet who have a heart similar to yours and who also heard the appeal to assist the Earth. Just imagine all of you working together for the benefit of the planet and all her inhabitants. Just imagine!

"*Dear Friends, change is inevitable. We must make the most of it!*" For a moment, it seemed like a pause was in the making. Eyes glanced from person to person, from animal to animal, from person to animal, all waiting to see what was going to happen next.

Eventually Peter spoke. Unable to bear the anticipation a second longer, he posed the question that everyone was waiting to hear. "I believe we are all in agreement regarding the need for change, and we also understand from a previous gathering that an examination of our personal behaviors is an essential part of the process. But if memory serves me, we also discussed the need for a plan and I'm in a place where I'm ready to take action. A plan would be very helpful. So, tell me. Is there a plan that can guide us through the process?" Peter felt reassured when he heard several sighs of relief from his friends. "I don't mean to be pushy," he added, "but I really do want to move forward. I think we all do, but I would like to proceed in a logical and methodical manner. And I suspect you have a plan that will help us to advance efficiently and rapidly." Suddenly, Peter realized he had returned to verbalizing his thoughts. He quickly apologized to their guests, but none was the least bit concerned.

Before the unseen guests could respond, David also expressed his concern about moving forward. "I'm less afraid of this task than I was when it was first suggested. I agree that the self-examination process is an excellent means for change, but I want to be certain that I'm doing it correctly. I don't want to waste precious time. Like Peter, I'm ready to move forward."

"Yes, I too feel as if time's a-wastin'. Do you remember that old saying?" Carol looked about the circle and observed the smiles and nods affirming her use of the old adage. "We've already reached an awareness that change is inevitable, so we need to proceed in the most efficient manner possible. Obviously, everything we learn from our personal self-examination will move us forward, and we will grow even more rapidly by sharing our experiences with one another. This will certainly help us when assisting others. However, we need a means of spreading this information across the planet as quickly as we can. While one-on-one is effective and preferable, it is a slow process.

People need to know the truth now and they need to know how to take action immediately. That requires a plan that is succinct, easily understood, and inspirational. I don't mean to be pushy, but we really need your help. We need a plan, and we need it now!" Carol took a deep breath, leaned back into her chair, and immediately started doubting her insistent manner. Jen sensed what was happening and quickly offered reassurance by placing her hand upon Carol's. Then Cooper, the endearing Chipmunk, rushed over from Jen's knee and positioned himself upon both of their hands. The gesture of support did not go unnoticed.

"Dear Ones, we are most grateful for your concern and your enthusiasm. Our primary reason for today's gathering is to bring forward a concise plan that will create great change within and among the people of Earth. As you well know, the negative energy that brews within humankind is extremely harmful. Your ill will sickens your own kind and it also sickens the Earth. Few of your kind are aware of this truth, and as those who live in ignorance of their impact upon others, the negativity within continues to become more damaging. This cannot continue. The truth must be faced and action must be taken.

"We agree with your comments that the message of change must rapidly span the planet. Our preference is that the information is made available to everyone at the same time. We will discuss that aspect of our project later. Now, let us focus upon The Plan.

"Dear Old Friends, the planet Earth is in need of your assistance. Whether you are one who believes that the Earth is in transition or not is not the issue. As a resident living upon this host planet, you have a responsibility to treat her with respect and loving-kindness. When you were first welcomed to the Earth, you contributed to her well being and you lived harmoniously with the other inhabitants that were already residing upon the planet. Your entry into the environmental system enhanced life on the Earth. Those times of mutual coexistence were most pleasant. Everyone enjoyed each other's company and everyone equally participated in caring for the planet and each other.

"Unfortunately, those good times did not last. A change in attitude caused a disruption that separated the human species from the other species upon the plant. At first, the Earth was able to compensate for the humans' behavioral changes, but over time, the changes became increasingly problematic. As the human population began to expand, they became territorial, selfishly assuming that the Earth's abundant resources were theirs to possess. How this misunderstanding came about remains a mystery, but the misunderstanding led to profound consequences. As the behaviors of the human species became more oppositional and violent, the landscapes of the

planet changed, and as their destructive behaviors escalated so too did the damage to the Earth's environmental system. The relationship between the Earth's health crisis and humankind's aggressive nature are directly correlated.

"The planet can no longer tolerate the abusive behaviors of the human species. This species, which had such amazing potential, turned into an invasive species that is threatening the future of the Earth and all her inhabitants. Never did anyone imagine that the term 'invasive species' would be applied to humankind. Acknowledging this unbelievable reality is most difficult, but the truth is the truth, and action must be taken to rectify the situation.

"In order to assist the Earth, behavioral changes must be made by the human species. Many may find this difficult to accept since they truly are unaware of the consequences of their negative energy. Fortunately, this is a misunderstanding that can easily be corrected. All that is required is presence of mind and a commitment of time. We sincerely hope that each of you will care enough about yourself and the planet that you will participate in an exercise of self-examination. Through this project of self-care, you will discover whether or not the supposition about humankind's negative energy applies to you. For your sake, we hope that you find that you are consistently a positive person who exudes loving-kindness to all whom you encounter. There are humans who actually practice this way of being every day. They do not allow themselves to be distracted by the nonsense of the negative world. They intentionally maintain a lifestyle that promotes wellness and happiness. This was once the way of all humans, and it is the life pattern that must be reclaimed.

"The exercise that is requested of you is simple. We ask that you commit to a period of time when you will deliberately and intentionally track your thoughts, words, and deeds. Obviously, the more time you commit to this effort, the more you will learn and the more quickly you will be able to make changes.

"To assist you in this process, we encourage you to keep a pen and paper close by so that every time you notice a negative or unkind thought, word, or deed, you can make a hash mark on the paper denoting the negative event. This exercise may surprise you. We hope you are pleasantly surprised; however, if you find yourself accumulating many hash marks, do not despair. Instead, be grateful for what you are learning. The point of this project is to increase your awareness of the negativity that exists within you, the negativity that you are so accustomed to that you do not even notice it anymore. Once you realize where you stand in this process, you are more than capable of making the necessary changes to improve your manner.

"Living in negativity is burdensome. You will understand this when you gain awareness of your negative habits. Do not chastise yourself! That is not the point of this exercise. Every time you notice a negative action occurring or recurring, express gratitude for recognizing what happened. Each time you take notice of

another negative incident, applaud yourself! You are becoming aware of the negative energy that your negativity creates. The more astute you become about the effects of your negative energy, the more you will realize how important it is to monitor this behavior. With awareness comes recognition of the need for change, and you will be able to make the necessary changes to live a life from a positive perspective. Life will be so much easier for you and for those around you.

"Have faith in your kind. You are so much more than you appear to be, and you have the potential for discovering the real you through your participation in this self-examination process. Hopefully, you will see the merit in continuing this exercise until you feel you have successfully corrected undesirable behavior. A suggestion that may assist you in advancing your progress is offered. At the end of each day total up your hash marks and do some self-reflection regarding what you witnessed. Again, please do not shame yourself! Discover who you are through these eventful observations. And then at the end of the week, total up the hash marks again, so that you can establish a goal for the following week. Perhaps, you may wish to diminish your weekly hash marks by twenty percent or more. The decision is yours. However, think expansively! The sooner you make the necessary changes, the healthier your life will be. The changes are worth the effort. And also be compassionate with yourself. Some days will be harder than others—such is life! Reflect upon the situation, strategize how you can make improvements, and remember tomorrow is another day! Growth happens more rapidly when tender loving care is present. And growth diminishes when punitive, unkind remarks are encountered. Treat yourself to the love and respect that all life beings need to flourish.

"The goal of this self-examination experience is to enlighten the human species to their frailties. Each of you has unlimited potential, but it is your responsibility to manage your development. For some time, you have strayed from the state of goodness that you were birthed to, but that misstep is easily corrected. This small, but dynamic exercise can assist you in reclaiming the state of being that is yours to enjoy.

"You deserve to live in peace with self and all others. This exercise will help you discover the peaceful path that lies within you. And because we are all One, you will never be alone during your self-examination process, nor will you be alone as you blaze your new path into the future. The breadth of this exercise is life altering, and as you delve within, you will find many other seekers who also are reclaiming their state of goodness. As you share your experience with others, not only will you enjoy their company, but also you will see more rapid advancement.

"Sharing your experiences with others will also bring up the issue of common decency. As you have learned, all are equal in existence, and all deserve and are intended to be treated with respect and kindness. As one desires this for self, others deserve the same. On your journey to reclaim your goodness, do not forget to share your

bounty with others. Attend all others and remind them that they too are loved and cherished by all others in the universe. This state of being is the same for all beings. The blessings for one are the same for all. When one accepts this reality, existence is a most delightful place to be.

"Functioning from a place of appreciation for all others reminds one of the importance of caring and supporting one another whenever one is in need. At this time, the Life Being Earth is desperately in need. She needs assistance from everyone who resides upon her. Please help her by releasing your negative energy so that she is no longer impacted by it. Your wellness will help her recover from her ill health. Treat her with the love and respect that she deserves. Positive actions taken on her behalf will rectify the errors of the past. She is a resilient Life Being who can recover from her present state, if the bombardment of negative energy from the human species stops. It's just that simple. If humankind reclaims its humanity, the positive energy that the people of Earth exude will rapidly assist the planet in regaining her health.

"Dear Old Friends, this is The Plan that we wish to introduce to the peoples of Earth. All people of all nations must have equal access to this self-examination process and every individual must be encouraged to participate. Every person who participates wholeheartedly and fully will alter the energy of the Earth. The participants in this project will essentially be medicating the planet with the positive energy that they produce, while also decreasing the toxicity caused by the negative energy that was previously exerted. The combination of these life changes will greatly assist the Earth in her recovery process.

"There is still time, Dear Friends, for the people of Earth to change their ways." With that said silence engulfed the backyard. Not only were the backyard guests still and quiet, but so too was the entire neighborhood. Not a sound was heard, until a shift in the backyard energy occurred. Nothing was visible, but the change was palpable.

"Dear Friends, there is reason for hope!" The voice, clearly heard, was unknown to the eight human friends, but definitely recognized by the other guests. Everyone came to attention in response to the inspirational declaration. *"Our Dear Friends from afar have provided a simple, yet concise plan and they have offered us reassurance that there remains time for the curative changes to transpire. That is very good news! And our New Friends who have graciously welcomed us into their space have shown us that they are sincere in their desires to be of assistance. Great change has transpired in this backyard and many more changes are coming.*

"I am grateful for the efforts being made on my behalf. Even more, it is most gratifying to see the connections being made among all species. This is a sight to behold! How long have we yearned for the camaraderie of our beloved human friends?

My heart is filled with optimism. Just witnessing today's gathering has lifted my spirits and increased my vitality. My Dear Friends, I am most grateful for each contribution that is sustaining me through this meeting. Your efforts are successful. Please know that your commitments to assist me are already providing benefits to my well being. Your kindness matters to me. I am deeply touched by your concern and your willingness to work on my behalf. Please let others whom you encounter know about the immediate positive effects of their contributions. I need your help, and those of you who choose to do so need to know how powerful your contributions are. Please do not diminish your healing effortss. Each particle of positive energy that you send my way is immediately effective. You are powerful beings and I am most grateful for your assistance. Please be in peace, Dear Friends. If all my beloved children would simply live in peace, my healing would be instantaneous. Thank you again for your loving assistance. You are always in my heart." The moving message from the Life Being Earth brought tears to everyone present, even those who were unseen. Much was learned from the message heard. There truly was reason for hope.

Twenty-Five

Dear Reader, your participation in reading this book has already benefitted the Earth. We are most grateful for the time you committed to this process. As the Earth just indicated, your kindness matters. Hopefully, you have already noted the changes that have occurred within you as you participated in this reading experience, and now perhaps you will commit to the next step. The Plan that you just read about will be formatted in the next chapter and it will also be available as a free download on The Center for Peaceful Transitions website. As you participate in the self-examination process, please share your experiences with others and encourage them to download The Plan for their own personal use.

Of course, we would like everyone to read **What Awaits Us...** for a variety of reasons. Obviously the book expands one's knowledge of the Earth's crisis situation, but it also provides a viable means for assisting the planet, which is critically important to everyone's future. The Plan begins as an individual experience, but easily and intentionally flows into an opportunity for shared experiences with others. The potential for using this exercise is unlimited. We hope it will span the globe and assist people in becoming the peaceable beings that they are intended to be. We invite schools to use this tool in the classroom, churches to circulate it among their parishioners, organizations of all kinds to introduce it to their members, and friends to share with other friends and neighbors. We imagine neighborhood study groups coming together to expand their awareness about their impact on the planet. These are just a few examples for spreading the news of this healing exercise. The point is: it is available for free to everyone. Please access this self-examination exercise and share it with others. Just spreading the information about The Plan is an act of kindness that will assist the Earth. And each one of you who actually participates in the process will truly make a difference. Your life will noticeably change, and the changes will immediately have a positive effect upon the Earth.

Who knew that assisting the Earth could be done so easily? Obviously, the inner work will be challenging, but it is in your best interest to pursue this task. No longer will you feel helpless and hopeless about the Earth's declining health. With this exercise, you actually can contribute to the Earth's recovery process by being personally involved in changing your own well being. You benefit from the process and so does she.

Dear Reader, you have already participated in an act of generosity and kindness by reading this book. Please continue to help by actively participating in improving your positive way of being. Everyone will benefit from your efforts, and as more and more people also choose to follow your lead, we may have the opportunity to experience peace on Earth.

In peace be, Dear Reader!

THE PLAN
Twenty-Six

<u>Introduction</u>

The purpose of The Plan is to help each participant recognize the nature of his or her behavior. For those of you who do not feel the necessity for such an exercise, please continue to read further. It is in your best interest to do so. Why should you do this, you may ask, and your question deserves an answer.

The Plan proposes an additional perspective to the environmental crisis that our planet is now experiencing. What is proposed does not discount or diminish any of the efforts that are currently underway. Thank goodness for these undertakings. They are necessary and the individuals driving these endeavors should be applauded. They are taking the crisis seriously, and so too should everyone else.

The Plan is presented as a complement to the good works that are already in motion. Founded in the belief that the Earth is suffering from the negative energy produced by the human species, an approach has been developed that can address this issue. The concept infers that the negative energy generated by anger, hatred, and violence is so toxic that it is actually sickening the planet. Recognizing the damaging effects that these extreme acts of ill will have upon the human population, it seems obvious that the negative effect of human misbehavior also has a powerful detrimental impact upon the Earth herself. For those who find this assumption incredulous, you are invited to do your own research.

Even before you make the decision to participate in this experiment, you can at least ponder the idea that negative behavior has impact. Watch the news that reports outrageous events daily or read the atrocities cited in your newspapers. The evidence of the effects of trauma is abundant. Open your eyes to the countless acts of cruelty and unkindness that unfold everyday and you will begin to understand that there are ramifications from these inappropriate behaviors. Families are devastated by acts of violence. Pain and suffering from the losses of loved ones runs rampant across all nations. The reality of human's disregard for other humans is frightening, and the fear that is created by these actions is yet another destructive emotion that sickens the human body.

Throughout all these horrific elements of unkindness, who is always present bearing witness to and experiencing every outrageous act of inhumanity? The Earth is the Life Being that is present for every inhumane action that transpires upon her body. She is present for every act of negative energy perpetrated by the human species. Doesn't it make sense that she would absorb the negative energies associated with these acts of unkindness? And doesn't it make sense that these continuous infusions of human toxic energy would eventually take a toll on the health of this incredible Life Being?

The Plan is proposed so that every person residing on the Earth can have an opportunity to learn about the effects of one's negative energy upon his or her daily life. It is hoped that you are one who will find that you are free of negative energy. It is hoped that millions of the human species will find that they do not participate in producing negative energy. Wouldn't that be comforting and reassuring for all of humankind? But, for the sake of humankind and the sake of the planet Earth is it not important that the truth is discovered? Is it disconcerting to believe that this supposition may indeed be true? Is it frightening to believe that we, each one of us, may actually be poisoning the Earth with our own negativity? Of course it is! No one wants to believe that he or she is harming the planet. No one wants to believe that they have negative tendencies. It is difficult to think about these possibilities. And yet, we must do so. Don't allow fears to misguide you. You are capable of managing everything that unfolds during this self-discovery process. If you find that you have negative inclinations, take comfort in knowing that you will definitely not be alone in that disappointing discovery. Rather than feeling bad about your new awareness, applaud yourself for having the courage to engage in this important inner work.

The goal of The Plan is to enable individuals to discover the truths about their personal behaviors. Unfortunately, most people are so busy living life that they are not aware of all the aspects of their personal behaviors. They are too distracted by life to realize that some adjustments may need to be made. Please do not be limited by your fears.

The Plan is an easy tool to use. By accessing this simple approach, you can expand your awareness of self, and with this new information you can discern what adjustments are needed. At all times, you are in control of your research project. You decide when you to begin the process, when you take breaks, and when you refine your present way of being based upon what is discovered in your self-examination process.

As said earlier, it is in your best interest to participate in this project. You will either gain validation that you are a most fortunate person who emits no negative energy or you may find that you are a person gifted with many opportunities for self-improvement. Either way you will be learning more about yourself. As a person who produces no negative energy, you will learn ways to assist the Earth with your positive energy. As a person who needs to reduce your negative energy, you will delight in the new opportunities that await you.

Because of the Earth's serious health issues, everyone on the planet needs to contribute to her recovery process. By participating in this self-examination exercise, you will have the opportunity to be a vital part of her healing process.

The Exercise

For those of you who sometimes feel helpless and hopeless about assisting the Earth's current crisis, please choose to participate in this self-examination exercise. All that is required is your presence of mind, patience, and perseverance. Those are the character traits that will help you stay on track as you pursue more information about your behavioral patterns. As said earlier, many of us are distracted by life to the point that we truly do not have full awareness of who we are, how we behave, or how we impact those around us. Through this exercise you have the opportunity to gain information about your behavioral patterns and also to discern how you wish to interact with the world around you.

You are not limited to your current way of being. You have unlimited options that include making decisions about how you want to be from this point forward. Imagine that! You have the privilege to make changes. If you discover that you really like your present way of being, then ponder how you want to improve upon your currently perfect self. We are beings who are in constant motion, changing from one moment to the next. Pay attention and evaluate your changes and be sure you are evolving in a way that is congruent with whom you truly wish to be.

If however, you are one of the many who discovers mannerisms that are not to your liking, take a deep breath, and praise yourself for having the courage to face these issues. Most individuals have awareness of some concerns that they may or may not be facing in the moment. These concerns will most likely come to the surface as a result of participating in this exercise. If that is the case, simply know that you are now ready to face the issue and make the necessary changes that will open new opportunities to your present way of being.

It is also highly possible that many more individuals will discover that they have certain behavioral issues that were unknown to them. If you find yourself in this situation, please take a deep breath or several deep breaths, and have compassion for yourself. You are not alone. One of the purposes of this exercise is to awaken us to our unknown truths. Once these truths come to the surface, we have the ability to facilitate change. Just because an unpleasant truth comes out does not mean we have to bear that burden forever. The burden remains when the truth stays hidden. The burden is released when the truth is acknowledged and forgiven.

For those of you who may feel antsy about continuing, please don't turn your back on this opportunity. Your participation matters! You are on the brink of a life-altering experience. Make the most of it!

Phase One

At this point in the self-examination exercise, you will need a means of recording your inward journey. Whether you prefer a technological device or a tablet or journal, along with a writing instrument of your choice, is for you to discern. This is also a good time for you to consider how much time you are willing to give to this project. Think positively about this and develop a schedule that will brighten your day rather than having you running in the opposite direction. Remember, you are in charge of this activity and you can make changes whenever it is necessary. Once again, the privilege of change exposes the benefits of being openhearted to change.

Your first task, Dear Participant, is a delightful one. You are invited to create a To Do List. Now, before you start balking at this idea, please continue reading. The focus of your To Do List is on Daily Acts of Kindness. You may remember that the character named Janet Hanson in *What Awaits Us...* boldly announced that she was going to commit to this To Do List because she wanted to be a better person. Janet's choice of action was founded in wisdom. We learn from others. When we observe acts of kindness initiated by others, we are inspired to act similarly. And when we participate in acts of kindness, we are blessed by the benefits of our actions. Whenever we witness or personally engage in an act of kindness, our spirits are lifted. We experience the goodness that exists in the world and we are positively affected by the sweet moment in time. We feel better because our energy has been positively influenced by the incident. Remember this please, because it is an important fact of the impact of energy. Positive actions create positive energy while positive energy enriches everyone who is within the impact range. So, when you are fortunate enough to witness an act of kindness and you feel the wave of positive energy surging through you, just remember that everyone in the area, including the Earth, is also enjoying this uplifting experience.

With this opportunity in mind, please address your To Do List at your earliest convenience. Make it a point, on a daily basis, to be involved in acts of kindness, and be sure to record them on your list, so you can refer to them at another time when you need an energy boost. Practice this, please. Just review your list at some point in the upcoming days and witness the positive influence it will have on your mood and your energy level. And as you refresh your memory of these incidents, remember that the Earth will also be enjoying another boost of positive energy.

There is a reason that the To Do List is the first task initiated in The Plan. Addressing positive energy is so much easier and more pleasant than addressing the issues of negative energy. It is purposeful for you to be reminded of the powerful influence of positive energy and since our project is intended to reacquaint the human species with this commendable energy, it is introduced to you through this simple, yet heart-opening endeavor.

Another benefit of addressing positive energy first is that it demonstrates how quickly one's spirits can be lifted and activated to participate in acts of kindness. Additionally, one bears witness to how quickly positive energy is generated and how rapidly it can spread. One small act of kindness has unlimited potential. For example, if a young student walking to school sees a blind person attempting to cross an intersection and chooses to lend a helping hand to that individual, everyone at the intersection will bear witness to the act of kindness. And that incident will be shared with others throughout the day. However, if one of the observers happens to film the touching interaction and sends that video to the local news station or posts it on social media, then many more people will witness the act of kindness and be equally touched and inspired. Just imagine how much positive energy would be generated from that young student's generosity. Keep this story or another of similar nature in mind as you approach the next phase of your evolving nature.

Phase Two

Now, Dear Participant, it is time to take several long deep breaths. Remember this natural instinct towards self-care produces a soothing energy that can be accessed whenever it is needed. It is always available to you. Throughout this phase of the exercise, pay attention to your needs and treat yourself to refreshing deep breaths whenever necessary.

It is time for us to explore the elements of negative energy. If the idea of delving into one's personal negativity does not excite you, just remember you are not alone. Obviously, this phase of the self-examination process can be assisted with an act of kindness. As you approach this task, be kind to you. This is not a time for any negative attitudes or comments to be directed at yourself. It takes courage to look at one's behaviors. Most likely, many of you will find some dissatisfaction and disappointment as you review your patterns. Fortunately, this task is a private matter. It's between you and you. At some point in the days ahead, you may feel a desire to share your discoveries with others, but that is yours to discern. When you are ready to reveal your experience, another will be ready to do the same, and each of you will grow more rapidly as a result of what was learned from this private conversation. Just remember you are in charge of your pace.

For this task you will need an open heart and pen and paper that will be at your disposal throughout the day. It will be in your best interest to commit to one week of self-examination so that you can clearly discern the behavioral patterns that drive you. Of course, the most important aspect of self-care is that you monitor your progress, and if at any time you need a break, please take one. Examining one's negative behavior can be a roller coaster type of experience. Fortunately, since you are in charge, you have the privilege of stopping the roller coaster at any time. It will not impede your discovery process; it will simply be more information for you to decipher at a later time when you are ready to do so.

We begin this task with a premise that most of humankind is truly unaware of the negative energy that they create, and it is also believed that most are not aware of the impact of their negativity. Obviously, there are exceptions to this hypothesis. There are those who are not at all naïve about the power of negative energy and they actively and intentionally misuse and abuse this power source at the expense of others.

In this exercise it is hoped that you will discover the power of energy, both positive and negative energy, and that you will learn how to maximize your positive energy while minimizing your negative energy. As you know, positive energy can revitalize the Earth and her inhabitants, including the human species. This positive energy source, which is generated so easily and quickly without cost or harm to anyone, can actually change the precarious course that many are now pursuing. Positive energy creates positive results for everyone, while negative energy serves only a few while harming unlimitedly.

Dear Participant, the time is now! You are invited to read the proposal that follows and then we encourage you to develop a schedule that best suits your current situation. The goal is for you to discover more about negative inclinations that you may or may not know about. This is an exercise that demands your attention. Once you devise your schedule, you will begin every day with a commitment to track your thoughts, words, and deeds. This may sound cumbersome, but you will quickly develop a method that is agreeable to you, and you will continue to finesse it as you become more engaged in the process.

Essentially, your task is to observe your negative inclinations and to record each event by denoting it on your piece of paper with a hash mark or tally mark. This can be done easily, with little interference to your daily routines, while also allowing you to quickly observe how you are progressing.

A negative inclination includes a thought or numerous thoughts about a situation that is bothering you. It also includes words or actions that are expressed either publicly or privately. Each time you participate in some type of experience that is founded in negativity, you score another hash mark. This exercise will make you more aware of what is going on in your mind, while you are multitasking throughout the day. And it will educate you to the level of severity of these incidents of disruption. Are you experiencing a small moment of discord or are you having an outburst of negativity?

Committing to this self-examination process will be extremely informative. You will learn how prevalent your negative behaviors are. You will learn how these moments impact you. You will discover what your trigger points are and what your focus is. You will gain clarity about the source of your disgruntlement and you will learn more about how you manage your fears, vulnerabilities, frustrations, and anger.

As you continue to pursue this quest for greater understanding about your negative inclinations, you may also be confronted with truths that you would rather not acknowledge, but remember, this is a private matter. You can face the truths that are difficult to address and you can improve yourself. Learn about your anger! Learn about its strength and the power that it asserts on you and others. Observe when your anger becomes rage and bear witness to the damage it does. Acknowledge to yourself if the rage becomes more violent. View its power and its consequences. And breathe! Breathe your way through this moment of heartache. Shed your tears! And make a commitment to yourself to be the person you so want to be.

Dear Participant, take another deep breath. Some of you may be angry about the proposal just read. You may think that you are not in need of such an exercise. You may feel that your negativity is not powerful enough to warrant such an exercise. But please continue! You haven't actually participated in the exercise yet. You're just reading about the possibilities that may be encountered. Think of this exercise as a tool that serves everyone, regardless of where one lies on the continuum of negative inclinations.

Facing one's negativity can be personally challenging, but it's worth it! Negative energy has negative impact even to those who do not believe that they experience it. So learning more about this energy is beneficial.

You may be thinking that you do not want to continue with this exercise, because fears are rising up within you. Again, you are urged to take a deep breath. Remember, please, that you are stronger than your fears. As information unfolds regarding your unpleasant behaviors, simply accept it. Be with the reality of your negative patterns. How are these patterns assisting you and how are they harming you and others? Are you being the person you want to be? If not, what do you want to do about it? You are in charge. Open your heart to the changes that you feel are necessary to make and devise a plan that introduces the changes in a way that is workable for you. Change is rarely instantaneous.

Patience and determination are key attributes that will assist your ability to change as well as the growth spurt that you incur.

Dear Participant, if you are having doubts about pursuing such an extensive self-examination process, just take a deep breath. You can do this! All of you can take the necessary steps to become the person you truly want to be. Behavior that is founded in negative energy can be altered. View this behavior as a habit that has been accepted for so long that you no longer recognize the behavior is an issue. Once one recognizes the truth about his or her negative habits, change is possible. Please hold on to this truth and let it be your guide as you continue with The Plan.

The time is upon you. Take that first step and begin tracking your negative activities. As the hash marks tally up, do not diminish yourself with critical judgment. That's just another example of negative behavior, which needs to be released. View the hash marks from another perspective, from a positive perspective. Each time you make another notation on your scorecard, applaud yourself, because you just noticed and acknowledged a behavior that was negative. Good for you! This is a success story! Every time you notice the moment of discord, you are increasing your awareness about the issue, which enhances your ability to change the situation.

As you welcome the incidents in, you gain more power over them. You realize where you are placing your attention. You understand that the negative reaction is not serving you or the other person or persons involved. And you recognize that it is in your best interest to change the behavior because it is interfering in your life.

Once you comprehend that your negative energy is not improving your life, you must acknowledge that you are responsible for changing your behavior to live the life that you desire to live. Another character from **What Awaits Us...** who openly admitted he was apprehensive about addressing his negative tendencies provided us with a beautiful example of how we can take charge of our behavior. He boldly declared that he would track his behaviors for seven days by noting every negative thought, word, and action with a hash mark. Jonathan promised that every evening he would tally the day's results and journal about his experiences. Then at the end of the week he committed to review his weekly offenses, and because Jonathan was a man who needed to see results, he announced that he would attempt to reduce his offenses by twenty-five percent in the following week. And he vowed to continue this process until he could see that his old habits were diminishing while new positive habits were developing. Jonathan's idea is one of merit and is a wonderful example that may help the Reader to develop his or her own self-examination process. And now there is another component of The Plan that must be discussed. As you work to improve your personal way of being, you must also take others into consideration. In the introduction of The Plan, it was noted that everyone was impacted by the energy created by the human species. Everyone includes all people of all nations, all species existing everywhere upon the planet, and the planet Earth herself. Everyone is involved in the ongoing, never-ending process of life. We are blessed with an abundance of diversity that enriches the lives of all of us. And yet, that which was intended to create curiosity and constant forward expansion upon this beautiful planet instead resulted in a division within the human species and towards other species. This was never intended to happen.

Before the human species was invited to this colony in the sky, there was peace on Earth. All species cooperated with one another; they mutually coexisted. If one was in need, another assisted. There were no squabbles or dissension. Harmony existed among all the species and the host planet.

Unfortunately, the blessings of diversity were not embraced by all of the human species. Fear and distrust developed, which resulted in a change of energy within the species. Attitudes changed. Eventually the human species lost interest in the needs of others and they pursued endeavors that satisfied their personal preferences. This estrangement was extremely painful for those who had regarded the human species as friends. As time passed, connection between the human species and other species upon the planet became more complex and limited, and the relationships that once existed were forgotten. The dismissive attitude of the human species then turned upon itself. Small bands of people with similar interests spread to other locations creating colonies that united together. The expansion continued until the human species populated the entire planet. All came from the same species yet their misunderstanding of differences separated them from one another.

Efforts were made throughout the ages to unite the species, sometimes with limited success; however, the misunderstandings regarding their fellow humans remained a problem. For some, the misunderstandings grew to be an intolerance that continues to sicken the species and the planet to this day. The negative energy associated with this disrespectful and unkind attitude is so powerful that the Earth's health is declining because of it. Unless the human species awakens to this reality, they will suffer the consequences.

All in the universe are One. All on the planet Earth are One. Every life being throughout the universe is equal to all other life beings. No life being is better than or less than another. This is a truth that is not debatable. Although there are those who will deny this statement, it remains a truth nonetheless.

All life beings regardless of their size, shape, or form are equal, and as such every life being deserves to be treated with the same respect and dignity as every other life being. No one has dominion over any other life being. The thought that any life being could believe such an incomprehensible idea stuns the inhabitants of the universe.

Every life being is loved and cherished equally. Those who honor this way of existence live most graciously and joyously. Acceptance of all others opens oneself to infinity and beyond, while those who define themselves as more than another live a very limited life.

Dear Participant, your participation in The Plan is more important than you know. By examining your present behavior, you have the opportunity to become the person you are intended to be, which includes being a loving, kind human being whose cares about others. By participating in this project you will be helping the Earth's healing process while healing yourself and others of the human species. This may sound like a grandiose statement, but it is not. What you do matters!

By changing your negative energy into positive energy, everyone you encounter will benefit from your efforts, including the Earth. You can do this!

Thank you, Dear Participant, for your contributions to healing the Earth.

In peace be.

Dear Reader, a simple, yet efficient worksheet is provided for your convenience, until you have the time to design one especially for YOU.

Be gentle and kind to yourself as you become the person you truly want to be. Thank you, for helping Mother Earth.

THE PLAN
(Examine Self, Discover, Change)

Acts of Kindness
(Witness/Initiate/Receive)

Record of Negative Acts
(Thoughts/Words/Deeds)

_____   _____
_____   _____
_____   _____
_____   _____
_____   _____
_____   _____
_____   _____
_____   _____

JOURNAL - TIME TO PONDER

_____
_____
_____
_____
_____
_____
_____
_____
_____
_____

Heal The Earth by Healing Yourself
Your Participation Matters!

Printed in the United States
by Baker & Taylor Publisher Services